MW01687738

Balance of Evil

Kim Rozdeba

Rozdeba Brand & Co.

Balance of Evil by Kim D. Rozdeba

Published by Rozdeba Brand & Co.

Calgary, Alberta, Canada

rozdeba.com

Cover Image by PeskyMonkey/Canva
Editing by Tanis Nessler www.revisionediting.ca
Proofreading by Jennifer McIntyre www.jenmceditor.com

ISBN: 978-1-7780090-8-2 (Softcover)
978-1-7780090-9-9 (Audiobook)
978-1-0696341-0-8 (Ebook)

First Edition: March 2026

To Brenda, Paige, Justin, Mareika, Grace, Ryan, Rosalyn,
Clive, Ayla, and Frankie (the Frenchie).

1

Cabo San Lucas

The salty tang of the ocean hung in the cool morning air, mingling with the rhythmic sound of waves kissing the shore. My gritty footprints broke the perfect edge of the tide's last reach—a fleeting imprint before the next wave claimed it. The sand ripple mark—wet and firm—guided my path like a road holding together the future of my new existence.

It wasn't merely a morning walk—it was part of a desperate act of reinvention. At sixty-one, I was still grappling with the aftershocks of a heart attack that had blindsided me a year earlier. From the outside, I looked like the picture of health: trim, upright, and blessed with a still-full head of silver-gray hair that often earned me comparisons to JFK. But under the surface, I was a man stitched together by prescriptions and haunted by a doctor's words: acute myocardial infarction. A year ago, I didn't even know what that meant; now, it ran my life.

I had survived that ordeal—barely. Six days in the hospital, a laundry list of lifestyle changes. And then came the second blow: the board of Aurora EarthEx, the company I had built from the ground up over three decades, unceremoniously handed me my walking papers. Retired against my will. One year, two broken hearts; one literal, the other existential.

Since then, I'd been trying to piece myself back together, or at least find some semblance of purpose. Mornings like this had become my ritual war against the boredom and restlessness that gnawed at every waking hour. The locals in this sleepy Mexican beach town might envy my idyllic existence: waking with the dawn, meditating to the ocean's eternal ebb and flow, and counting my steps under the relentless sun. But to me, it was colorless, a slow erosion of my soul.

Then—when I thought I'd resigned myself to monotony—it happened.

It began with a glint in the sand. A flicker of light caught in the corner of my eye, nearly lost amid the seaweed and tiny shells. I crouched, ignoring the protest from my knees, and brushed aside the wet debris to uncover a cylindrical object no bigger than my thumb, smooth as glass and silver-bright—a relic in an otherwise barren landscape. My heart leaped, not from medical distress this time but from a flicker of curiosity, a spark I hadn't felt in ages.

I turned it over in my hands, instantly recognizing the metal. Pure titanium. Lightweight, untarnished by saltwater, and strong enough to withstand forces that destroy weaker materials. A faint seam ran through its center, almost imperceptible, like a magician's trick hiding the true nature of an illusion. This wasn't only a practical object. This was extraordinary.

With a twist, the cylinder came apart so effortlessly it might as well have been waiting to whisper a secret to me. Inside was a USB flash drive, a hyperminimalist one devoid of logos, scratches, or fingerprints—flawless. I wasn't holding a cheap tourist trinket mistaken for flotsam. This was intentional. Purposeful. Something of value.

As I shoved the titanium device into my gym shorts and continued my walk, my mind began spinning. What could be on it? My steady rhythm on the wet sand quickened as my mind unraveled scenario after scenario. Corporate secrets? Financial data? Government files? Perhaps it held something nefarious—a crypto key of a cartel kingpin? I couldn't help smirking at my own wild imagination. But the smirk vanished, replaced with a sense of unease I couldn't quite articulate. The thing in my pocket wasn't some piece of junk—it meant something. It belonged . . . to someone.

The sun's rays touched my skin as it climbed higher, but I disregarded the heat. I realized amid thoughts of tech mysteries and drug lords that an insignificant scrap of titanium had cracked open my repetitive life.

I didn't yet know it, but that enigmatic sleek cylinder was about to rewrite everything I thought I knew.

And my life? It would not change—it would ignite.

***

After stepping out of the shower and throwing on a pair of tan pants and a white T-shirt, I made my wife's coffee—black with a dash of Ceylon cinnamon and 1% milk. With the curtains and blinds closed while the sun was moving quickly into the sky, the bedroom was pitch black. As I brought the coffee in, I pressed the button to open the blinds slowly. This was a daily ritual. Over the next hour or so, Colleen would slowly come to life after another night of heavy drinking.

"Good morning, my dear. Another stunning day!"

Her reply was always a telltale sign of whether the morning would be pleasant.

A hoarse, dry "Thank you" came from the twisted white sheets.

It was going to be a good day.

I dashed to the study with my newfound toy. I flipped open my laptop and started it up. As the screen flashed through its startup routine, I cautiously opened the mysterious titanium cylinder. Again, looking for any clues. There were none.

I plugged the USB into one of the computer ports and watched. An antivirus message popped up requesting a scan of the USB. I hesitated but declined the request. For a split second,

I felt like I was trespassing, snooping into someone's private belongings. *Because I was.* Then excitement surged. The USB's name appeared: CS-24-PW-34.

To hell with viruses, I told myself as I clicked to open the file.

The screen flashed bright red with the bold words *TOP SECRET*, then transformed into a sign-in page. At the top of the screen, in a dark-blue banner, was the following message:

> *WARNING: All individuals handling this information require security clearance (TS+SCI) GRANTED BY THE POTUS and are required to protect it from unauthorized disclosure in the interest of INTERNATIONAL security of the UNITED STATES OF AMERICA and its Interests. Access is highly restricted by law (Order 13526), and any violation can incur criminal penalties and death.*

Death.

On a white background, under the banner, was a watermark featuring a crest with the letters *POTUS*. In the center of the screen, floating on a white background, were boxes for entering a security code. I counted thirty-four boxes.

Who has a passcode thirty-four digits long?

I rushed to pull the USB drive out of my computer, but I froze. The USB was flashing. What did that mean? I got up to refill my coffee mug, dropping a coffee pod into the coffeemaker and pressing the START button. As it did its thing, I paced back and forth, looking at my computer and the flashing light. What if it was communicating to its source—to its owner? Alerting them to a trespasser.

"Honey, what's for breakfast?" asked Colleen, appearing from the bedroom in only her housecoat.

I looked at my watch. "You mean brunch?"

"Whatever, Scott. I'm starved." She noticed the laptop with the sign-in screen, but she didn't have her glasses on.

"Well, we can go to Sombra Grill," I said as I casually walked in front of the laptop, then closed it and pulled out the USB. "They should still be open for brunch." I felt guilty, like a child who had done something awful and hadn't been caught. At least not yet.

She turned around and headed back into the bedroom with a matter-of-fact "Sounds good."

What had I done? Or, more importantly, what had I gotten us into? If this USB had communicated with someone or somewhere, would they come looking for it? Were we talking minutes, hours, or days? My heart pounded. *Breathe,* I told myself. The word *death* still echoed in my mind.

I needed to think fast and make a plan. This was where Colleen shone. She always prepared for every situation. She could get us out of any boring dinner party without the host suspecting any wrongdoing. She was ready for any weather event with a massive emergency kit that included water, non-perishable food, a flashlight, and a first aid kit. She had prepared for us to evacuate in the event of a hurricane, earthquake, or tsunami: in the bedroom closet was a backpack containing protein bars, a change of clothes for both of us, extra socks and underwear, a pre-charged power bank, passports, cash, prepaid MasterCard and Visa cards, an Android cell phone, and duct tape. While many women cherished their Louis Vuitton handbags, Colleen was obsessed with her black Herschel backpack.

Overreacting wasn't my nature, but I would rather be safe than sorry.

Colleen came out of the bedroom, ready to seize the day. She had her dyed-blonde hair in a neat ponytail, her burgundy lipstick contrasted nicely with her dark tan, and she wore diamond earrings along with oversized designer sunglasses to conceal her puffy eyelids. Her slim, curvy figure was now a distant memory. To cover this, she wore an oversized off-white kaftan. To conclude her statement, she wore a large straw sun hat to exude a sense of privacy. She stood there waiting for some acknowledgment.

"Are you ready to go?" I asked.

"I need my smoke first." She dug into her Italian leather purse, which matched her shoes.

"Okay, you go ahead, and I'll catch up."

She glanced at me with a quick, forced smile and walked out the door with a cigarette in her hand.

I scanned the villa to see what we needed to take with us in case we never returned. Was this crazy? *Better safe than sorry*, I told myself again. Going to the bedroom, I dug the emergency backpack out of the closet. I added my laptop, wallet, and cell phone, then grabbed a sports coat for myself and a jacket for Colleen. I looked at our stunning waterfront view and closed the door.

Outside, Colleen was standing in the shade outside the Sombra Grill, reapplying her lipstick after finishing her cigarette. I climbed the several sets of stairs that led to the Grill, then stopped to catch my breath. The restaurant was on higher ground, overlooking the villas and the beach. From there, you got a greater sense of the vastness of the beach and waterfront. I could also monitor our villa to notice any intruders.

I concealed the backpack behind Colleen's jacket as I signaled her to enter the restaurant. The hostess, Victoria, greeted us as we walked in.

"How are you today, Mrs. and Mr. Barton?" She grabbed two menus and started walking us to a table.

"Great," I replied.

Given it was such a gorgeous day, I suggested sitting on the deck by the palm trees, the best spot in the restaurant to watch our place. Seated, I mumbled to Colleen that I'd brought her coat in case of a cool breeze. She looked puzzled but said nothing as she opened the menu. I did the same, although I had no appetite.

"I think I'll have the fruit and granola."

"You mean the parfait," she corrected me.

Victoria returned with a fresh pot of strong Mexican coffee and filled Colleen's cup. I received a pot of green tea, a healthier choice. The same routine for the last thirty days. "Do you have any exciting plans for today?"

But Colleen dismissed the small talk. "I'm famished!" she declared, handing her menu to Victoria. "Can I get two poached eggs with the chilaquiles verde and some bacon on the side?"

"Of course. And what will you have, Mr. Barton?"

"I'll have the parfait, please."

Victoria took my menu and assured us our meals would arrive soon. She had made it two steps away when Colleen turned in her chair to look in Victoria's direction, reminding her to bring some cinnamon and milk for her coffee. This seemed to be an ongoing ritual between them.

While Colleen scrolled through her social media and emails, I watched with great interest as the gardener pushed a wheelbarrow toward our villa. He looked as if he were checking to see if anyone noticed him there. Looked into our bedroom window.

"So, my dear, what would you like to do today?" Colleen asked as she continued scrolling on her phone.

The gardener took a couple of puffs of his lit cigarette and then continued toward a group of palm trees with several dead leaves scattered below them.

"How about we go into town and catch the art show?" she said.

Convinced the gardener wasn't a spy or law enforcement but merely a secret smoker, I returned to Colleen's questions.

"Really? Mexican art?"

"You never know. There might be some surprises."

For our sake, I hope there aren't any surprises today.

Victoria arrived with our meals, and Colleen reminded her again to bring her "goddamn milk." I played with my parfait as Colleen continued to debate the merits of checking out the art show.

An hour later, Victoria had cleared our plates and picked up the signed bill, refreshed our drinks, and topped up the pitcher of milk for Colleen's coffee. I started feeling better. Then came a powerful rumbling sound, followed by the appearance of an ominous black helicopter that hurried along the beach.

Sudden fear surged through me. As the aircraft hovered near our villa and whipped up a sand cloud, my heart rate increased and I began sweating. Four people jumped out as the helicopter dropped, then it shot up into the sky and out over the sea. I watched with horror as the four figures in black military fatigues ran toward our villa. My heart was racing and my breathing was shallow. Was I having a heart attack?

Colleen cried out, “Scott, are you okay?”

Her scream brought me back to the table. I jumped up and took a deep breath to calm my nerves. “Colleen, we need to go. Now.”

Instinctively, she jumped up, and we walked swiftly to the resort’s main lobby to grab a cab.

We jumped into the closest one and I authoritatively shouted, “Aeropuerto!” and “Mucho rápido!”

Colleen looked at me, totally confused. “We need to take you to a hospital. Don’t we?”

My wife thought I was having another heart attack, but I was too focused on my phone, looking for a way to get us out of there, to answer her question.

We needed a flight to anywhere outside Mexico and the United States—now!

***

I had much to explain, but I needed a potent drink to calm my nerves before I told Colleen why we were on an Air Canada flight to Toronto. The airline attendant welcomed us on board and placed two small bowls of warm dry-roasted almonds on the drink table between our business-class seats, the last seats on the plane. We each ordered scotch on the rocks—doubles. Two hours earlier, we had been racing through customs and security.

No one seemed to care that we only had one carry-on between us. Thank heavens we still had our Canadian passports. In my haste, I had almost made a fatal error while going through security with the titanium USB in my pocket. When the alarm went off, I'd spun around and showed my watch, which I removed and set on the tray with the USB.

I glanced at my watch: 3:15 p.m. We would return to the ground in four hours at 9:30 p.m. Eastern Standard Time. After a couple gulps of scotch, I felt the whiskey's warm effect on my empty stomach. This was my first drink in ten months since the heart attack.

I leaned closer to Colleen and confessed why we were on the run for our lives, minus a few details about the login page. Surprisingly, she accepted my convoluted story with indifference and seemed excited to surprise her mother, who lived in the small city of St. Catharines in the Niagara Region. After having a couple more scotches and a glass of red wine to wash down the airplane food, Colleen was fast asleep and snoring. I lived it up with soda water and a twist of lemon.

Looking at Colleen curled up in her seat, I was reminded of the carefree days we'd had when we were first married. We'd loved traveling without suitcases or an agenda. *How times have changed.* How had our lives become so complicated and stressful? Colleen's career had taken a confident, bright woman and transformed her into a fearful, bitter person who found solace in a bottle. Right now she slept like a baby.

Away from Mexico and in the safety of an airplane, I now wondered if I had overreacted. I had broken no laws, as far as I knew. But who had sent the chopper and the SWAT team? What was so important about the USB?

On takeoff, the flight service manager had apologized for the Wi-Fi not working because of a technical issue. I'd actually been relieved by that; it meant there was no chance that the titanium USB could alert anyone or signal its whereabouts as we flew thirty-four thousand feet over the United States of America.

We sat in the last row of business class. The privacy partition between us and the cheap seats prevented anyone behind us from watching my screen. Across the aisle was a young couple, maybe newlyweds, with sunburned arms and faces. They were wearing earphones and engrossed in a movie playing on the seatback TVs, too self-absorbed to pose a threat.

I fired up the laptop and inserted the USB drive into one of the ports. I stared at the login page. Breaking security codes was something I knew nothing about. I struggled to remember my own eight- or ten-digit passcodes. How in the hell was I going to guess a thirty-four-digit one? The best course of action, I decided, was to visit the US Consulate in Toronto and hand it over. But my curiosity got the better of me now. If I had a code that long, what would I use? My parents' birth dates, as well as mine and my wife's. That was only thirty-two digits.

What was the chance of cracking the code with Latin letters and numerical digits? It was almost impossible with thirty-six possibilities raised to the power of thirty-four—and that total didn't even include uppercase letters. *Think*, I told myself. *Think strategically*. Why thirty-four digits? Was there any significance to the number?

The first answer that came to mind was the periodic table of elements. Being in the rare earth mining business, I was familiar with all the atomic numbers and chemical properties. Thirty-four on the table was selenium, a reactive nonmetal. No obvious password came to me.

I reread the warning screen to see if there were any clues. I stared at the POTUS seal. What did the President of the United States have to do with this?

"Excuse me. Would you like a drink?"

With my attention broken, I looked up at the airline attendant, who was pushing a trolley of drinks.

"Sure. I'll have green tea if you have it. Black."

Who was the thirty-fourth president? Being a history buff, I was ready with the answer: Ike Eisenhower, or Dwight Eisenhower, which had sixteen letters; if I added his middle initial, *D*, it was seventeen letters—half of thirty-four. Okay, this was going in the right direction. Who else had a seventeen-letter name at the time? John F. Kennedy and Richard Nixon had only twelve letters, Winston S. Churchill and Nikita S. Khrushchev had seventeen. My money was on the Cold War: DWIGHTDEISENHOWERNIKITASKHRUSHCHEV. I typed it in and took a deep breath.

An error message flashed in red on the screen. I tried with and without capitals as well as alternate orders to no avail.

I took a sip of my tea and sat back. Did I seriously think I could break this code?

My mind wandered into the realm of sports. Baseball was the game of numbers. What famous players wore the number thirty-four? Hall of Famers Rollie Fingers and Kirby Puckett came to mind, but nothing added up to thirty-four. What about basketball? I sat up in my chair. The two legends, Shaquille O'Neal and Giannis Antetokounmpo, popped into my head. I typed SHAQUILLEONEALGIANNISANTETOKOUN-MPO into the boxes. I tried with and without capitals and alternate orders. Nothing.

As time passed, I tried every conceivable combination of letters and numbers based on numerology and mathematics to solve this puzzle. I attempted to use the Fibonacci sequence, which includes the number thirty-four. I even tried the 4x4 magic squares, where the numbers one to sixteen add up to thirty-four in all directions. Frustration set in as nothing worked. I checked my watch: one hour until we landed.

Sitting there, racking my brain for an answer, I noticed a crossword puzzle magazine in the seat pouch in front of Colleen. Solving this was like a giant crossword puzzle, and Colleen and I loved to play the *New York Star* Super Mega Crossword. A crossword fifty squares wide by fifty squares tall. Every Christmas, we completed it together; once, there had been a thirty-four-letter word. I remembered Colleen reading out the clue: "Song name from a 1964 Disney musical." Then she cheered, "I got it—*Mary Poppins*! That would be the perfect password."

It also became our family safe word with our daughter, Leah.

I couldn't get the song out of my head. Even though I had lost hope, I had nothing to lose. I typed SUPERCALIFRAG-ILISTICEXPIALIDOCIOUS into the thirty-four boxes and pressed ENTER with my eyes closed.

The computer went black for a split second, and then a directory appeared. *No way!* I planned to buy a lottery ticket as soon as I landed. While the probability of breaking the code had been astronomical, the truth was I was now a felon. Wanted dead or, hopefully, alive.

The directory listed the following folders:

1953–1960

1961–1962

1963–1968

1969–1974

1974–1976

1977–1980

1981–1988

1989–1992

1993–2000

2001–2008

2009–2016

2017–2021

Each folder, I realized, corresponded to a US president's term in office. I scanned the twelve folders. I paused at the second folder, which contained only one deadly document from the two years the president was alive. I could not resist. I opened and read with dread. Hooked, I came back to the first folder, covering 1953 to 1960—a pivotal era in modern history. This period marked six years after World War II and the dawn of the Cold War, a time of escalating tension between the United States, which was championing capitalist democracy, and the Soviet Union, advocating Communism. The rivalry took shape through proxy wars, espionage, propaganda, and a relentless race for dominance—both in nuclear weaponry and the exploration of outer space.

Inside the folder, I found several PDF documents and a single audio file labeled *FIST*, which piqued my interest.

2

US Airspace

When I clicked the Play button, I could tell a reel-to-reel tape recorder had produced the recording because I could hear a faint, consistent background hiss from the old magnetic tapes they used. The voice was weary, uneven, as though its owner was unsure whether recording this was an act of self-preservation or if he was signing his own death warrant.

"My name . . . My name is Viktor Pavlenko. I am the translator. I do not like speaking into this machine. But tonight, I have no choice. If you are hearing this, it means I have realized my worst fears. That I am dead. It will not look suspicious: a car off the road, a dangerous step somewhere in the forest—something easy to explain. But understand this: my knowledge and what I heard tonight will shatter the very foundation of every government. I swear it."

He took a breath, his nervousness palpable. The sound of something metallic scraping across wood punctuated his words—perhaps in his stress he was holding a lighter or tapping a pen against the recorder.

"It is September 26, 1959, at Camp David. I was here not to serve as anyone's confidante, but merely their voice—an interpreter. An observer. Invisible, insignificant. Yet I was neither. The President of the United States. The Premier of the Soviet Union. Two of the most powerful men, two enemies, seated alone in the same room, and there was no one else but me. Do you understand the absurdity of this? A son of Moscow, trusted to interpret history itself from the two most powerful men in the world?"

A frustrated chuckle escaped him, bitter and breathless. He cleared his throat before continuing. I visualized this guy, Viktor, in a cloud of smoke as he tried to calm his nerves.

"Forgive me. I am rambling. But it matters little. What matters is what I heard, what I learned.

"The evening began as any formal state affair might. Scotch for the president, vodka for the premier. They ate like kings, although I imagine neither tasted much—diplomacy is a bitter thing to swallow. Their words started simply enough. Polite. Measured. But as the night wore on, the liquor loosened their tongues. They spoke of things not meant for my ears, nor anyone's.

"The American introduced the idea, all smooth words and grandfatherly wisdom. He named it Balanced . . . Balance of Power. Balance of the stars themselves. 'If we militarize space,' he warned the premier, 'we doom the heavens to the same divisions as Earth.' At first, I thought it was another American plea for diplomacy, but as he spoke . . . it became clear. This was no ordinary discussion about easing tensions or ending nuclear opposition.

"This was something entirely different."

I could now hear his fear.

"The American wasn't asking for peace in the traditional sense. He wanted . . . He wanted a new kind of war."

There was a sharp intake of breath, followed by the sound of him shifting uncomfortably in the chair, the recorder creaking as it was bumped slightly.

"They called it cooperation disguised as competition—or maybe competition disguised as cooperation. I'm not sure which is correct. Their brilliance still scares me, even now that I remember it. The president painted a vision of a world where even rivalry serves a purpose—to stabilize the chaos. Think of that: two nations, bitterly opposed in politics, beliefs, and vision for humanity—working together not to destroy one another but to prevent the collapse of something greater.

"They would not end their conflict. They would orchestrate it. Shape it. Wars, crises, coups, assassinations, foreign interventions—all of it would continue, but controlled. They would write the playbook together and have the world act out every conflict, every settlement. Every victory the premier claimed would strengthen Moscow; every advance the Americans made would embolden Washington. Their power would grow—separately but equally—all for 'balance.'

"And where would this start? Not on Earth. Oh no. Not here, where alliances are too fragile today. No, they spoke of the stars. Later, Earth would follow to contain the third force, the growing power of the Eastern dragon."

There was a pause as the audio hissed, then Viktor's voice came back. It was lower and his breath caught audibly; it sounded like he was afraid to speak the following words.

"They didn't say the name directly, but the president hinted at it: the project. And the premier understood immediately, as if he saw the blueprints in his mind. The militarization of space was inevitable, the American said—it was necessary. Necessary to control the heights. Control perspective. I . . . I know what their words mean. They spoke of ensuring their dominance of the world and securing it beyond Earth. Satellites that could monitor everyone, weapons hidden in orbit, systems so advanced that if either dared defy their 'balance,' they would both fail."

Another pause. Viktor's voice grew quieter as though he realized how easily someone could hear him, even in isolation.

"They signed no papers. They agreed to no treaty. But they reached an understanding there, in that room, with no witnesses except . . . me. The president envisioned a camouflaged détente, but the premier—clever and ruthless—would not agree to anything unless he saw how it benefited him. He called it something else by the night's end: FIST. Force for International Supremacy Taskforce. It would be their secret alliance. Not official. Never acknowledged. Passed only between the two superpower leaders and buried under layers of corruption and patriotism."

There was a long pause in the recording.

"*Brother*, the premier called him. 'Brothers,' they said as they raised their glasses one last time in that suffocating library.

"And as for me? Even now, I still cannot tell if their drunken idea terrifies or amazes me. But what scares me more is what will happen if someone learns that I know. If someone learns what they agreed to on this night."

He strained to clear his throat. The sound was scratchy, as though he was shaking off whatever fear lingered in his words.

"Tonight, the Cold War turned cold not by chance but by design. It became a balancing act, and we . . . we are all walking on its razor's edge above a chasm no man could ever crawl out of. If I—"

I heard a *click* and the audio snapped off.

Before I knew it, our airplane's captain was on the intercom announcing that we would land in the next fifteen minutes. In the dead of winter, Toronto was brisk and clear, 6 degrees Celsius or 43 degrees Fahrenheit. I could already feel the the blood in my veins turning ice cold, and not just from the weather report.

If what I'd heard was true, I was worth more dead than alive.

3

Toronto

While all the other passengers had changed out of their sunny-weather wardrobes sometime between takeoff and landing, we remained in our summer wear. It wouldn't be long before we were on the streets, freezing. Canadian customs was a breeze with our Canadian passports; the officer simply took our printed kiosk receipts and welcomed us home. We jumped into a cab and went to the nearest recognizable airport hotel that accepted cash, having decided to stay away from any high-end chains for fear of being recognized.

We hurried into bed to warm up. Colleen included two mini bottles of scotch from the bar fridge as a remedy.

What's the plan? I asked myself. I knew Colleen was forming the exact words on her lips, but I supposed exhaustion prevented her from speaking up about the problem. We turned the lights out, rolled over to opposite sides of the bed, and stared into the pitch black until we fell asleep.

***

Even after adjusting to the one-hour difference in the new time zone, the morning still seemed to come too early. Opening the curtains to let the sun in, I could now see the coffee machine, which would enable me to make Colleen's coffee instead of calling out for room service. Without fresh milk, she would have to settle for a creamer. I was delighted to find a decent selection of teas.

Colleen had buried her head deep in the sheets and pillows. She wasn't ready to face the day. I brewed the coffee and placed it on the nightstand beside her head. Eventually, the coffee's aroma would force her up.

I was about to turn on my cell phone to check in on the outside world when I recalled that in Mexico we had both shut down our electronics to prevent anyone from tracking us. For a split second, I felt vulnerable without it. Then I remembered Colleen's emergency kit had a generic cell phone minus a SIM card—another thing to add to our shopping list.

"Okay, Scott, what's the plan to get us out of this?" Colleen asked as she sat up against the headboard, her hair flowing across her face. She brushed a strand of it behind her ear and grabbed the coffee.

That's a legitimate question. "Well, dear, that's an excellent question." I grinned. "I've been making a list of things we need to buy."

"Are you avoiding the question?" She smiled with the coffee cup below her bottom lip.

"To be safe, we should hide in this room for a couple of days. That will give us time to develop a master plan."

"Are you suggesting that we relive our honeymoon?" she teased. "Minus the tacky room," she added, laughing.

I was twenty-seven at the time, and she was twenty-five. I'd finished my ten months of articling and had been called to the bar to take my oath to practice law at a small law firm called Smith & Smith. We had a simple, small wedding at her parents' place in St. Catharines. Colleen was still going to university, and we had more debt than savings, so our honeymoon was in Niagara Falls—complete with a mirrored ceiling over the bed.

I chuckled, then jumped onto the bed and wrapped my arms around her. "We can certainly give it a shot. We have three days right here!"

It had been a long time since we'd embraced and felt each other's body heat. We made love as if we were back in Niagara Falls thirty-four years earlier.

Over the next three days, we made love more than we had in the previous three years. During those days, we found the fountain of youth. The time flew by as we ordered in and binged on old movies, including soft porn.

I chose to conceal what I'd discovered on the USB drive from Colleen. Recognizing the seriousness of the matter, I knew that sharing top-secret classified information could put her life at risk, like mine. Based on how I was handling the situation, as though we were fugitives, she seemed to grasp the gravity of it all.

While building my global mining company and navigating the challenges of working with questionable partners and governments, I had developed a healthy paranoia about safeguarding my documents and data. With cyber espionage always a looming threat, I had been fortunate to have hired one of the leading security officers in Canada.

To maintain security, I now activated my untraceable VPN on my laptop and accessed my encrypted cloud storage, which housed all my sensitive data. The first task was to upload the contents from my computer; during the flight, I'd transferred the contents stored on the mysterious titanium USB drive to my hard drive. Before landing, I'd carefully disposed of the USB drive by hiding it in an empty potato chip bag and tossing it into the airline attendant's trash collection during the final cleanup. Its final destination would be an unnamed landfill outside Toronto—a suitable end for something so potentially dangerous.

If anyone was looking for us, one obvious spot was Colleen's mother's house, so we decided against returning to St. Catharines and Niagara Falls anytime soon.

It was Colleen's bright idea that I should contact Senator Alan Goldman to see if he could help. Senator Goldman had served on Aurora EarthEx's board of directors during the early years. He had helped establish global contacts and worldwide exploration deals. I scanned his biography on the Senate of Canada website.

What I found was impressive. Senator Goldman, a brilliant man with degrees from Oxford, Carleton, and York University, had built a storied career as a foreign service officer and diplomat, serving as Canada's ambassador to both Israel and Germany and holding assignments in Washington, Poland, and Ukraine. He had coordinated major summits, including the G8, G7, and North American Leaders' Summit. He had played a prominent role in advancing peace in the Middle East, a contribution recognized with honors such as the Order of Canada. In recent years, Goldman had taken on the role of chair of the Senate Standing Committee on Foreign Affairs and International Trade. The more I read, the clearer it became that his global expertise and diplomatic experience made him an ideal candidate to help us with our current situation.

Of all the people I had collaborated with over the years, Alan held a special place in Colleen's affections. She looked forward to having him over for dinner with an almost contagious enthusiasm. Her fascination with his intellect was evident in the hours they spent engrossed in spirited conversations about global political dynamics, the latest coups, or the newest regime shifts. Those evenings had become a ritual as Colleen animatedly discussed geopolitics with him. I inevitably conversed with his wife, an elegant and charming presence in her own right.

I emailed Alan to inform him I would be in Ottawa, Canada's capital, the following week and hoped he might have time to meet, whether for coffee, lunch, dinner, or even a drink. I tried to keep the tone casual, but it was hard not to let a sense of urgency slip through.

Now, I just had to wait.

Meanwhile, Colleen contacted a couple of former colleagues from her not-for-profit days, sending similar emails to schedule meetings to keep herself occupied while in Ottawa.

***

I glanced at my watch and calculated that our train would arrive in Ottawa in another two hours. We relaxed in business class, dressed in our newly purchased winter attire.

Colleen looked elegant in a cream turtleneck sweater, black trousers, and leather boots. She'd been adamant that her new ensemble required a new pair of diamond stud earrings from Tiffany & Co. She'd completed her outfit with a costly Italian coat, scarf, gloves, and a new handbag. Altogether, her outfit, mine, and the clothes in the new suitcase were worth an impressive $47,639. A figure I knew since we'd bought everything the day before with cash. I was fortunate to still have an active bank account in Canada, with several RRSPs, stocks, and cash accounts to draw from, which had allowed us to indulge in a full day of shopping.

We would arrive around 3:00 p.m., which was enough time to check into our hotel room and freshen up. Colleen had a date with an old colleague from the nonprofit at the hotel's bar, and I was off to Alan Goldman's home for dinner at 6:30 p.m. Alan had first suggested we meet at The Rideau Club, but I convinced him that a more private location was preferable.

I prayed he would find a solution to our predicament.

4

Ottawa

As I walked out of the regal Château Laurier hotel, the cold weather accosted me like a merciless sentry, biting through the fabric of my coat. The sharp air left a sting in my nostrils as I exhaled clouds of frosted breath into the night. I studied my Apple watch—plenty of time to reclaim my much-neglected daily steps recorded. A brisk walk would provide the clarity I craved.

As I turned westward toward the Parliament buildings along Wellington Street, the world around me felt stark, etched in contrasts to Mexico—sand to snow, warmth to chill, sunlight to the dim gray haze of a frozen Ottawa dusk. My lungs protested the sudden invasion of icy air, but I pressed on, steady, navigating the snow-covered sidewalk bordered by uneven snow piles pushed high by plows. Boots crunched into powder, leaving temporary marks that would soon vanish with the wind.

Ahead, the Ottawa skyline stood still yet imposing, cloaked in shades of white and gray. It didn't take long to reach the Centennial Flame monument. Flames leaped and danced amid the icy terrain, their vibrant yellow-red flicker unable to pierce the chill, not so much a beacon of warmth but a defiant expression of light against the dark grip of winter.

Straight ahead rose the Peace Tower, tall and proud against the twilight sky, its stone facade illuminated by subtle spotlights that cast soft shadows across the adjacent buildings. The clock's face glowed faintly, its hands marking the time at a quarter past six. A quick mental calculation told me that lingering too long wasn't an option; the quiet beauty of Parliament Hill was no excuse to be late.

***

Sitting in the cab, I estimated it would be a ten-minute drive to Alan's home in Rockcliffe Park, an exclusive neighborhood where Canada's prime minister and several dignitaries lived. As we entered the area at twilight, the mature Georgian-style mansions loomed among towering bare trees, casting an almost ominous tone. Before I realized it, we were pulling into the circular driveway of Alan's massive brick estate. I handed the taxi driver cash, told him to keep the change, and stepped out.

Standing before the large oak door, I took a deep breath and rang the bell, hoping this was the right decision. After what felt like minutes, the door opened, and there he was—Alan Goldman. It had been years since I last saw him in person, and time hadn't been kind. Now in his late seventies, he had lost his physical presence, but his eyes remained as sharp as ever.

His face lit up with a welcoming smile as he extended a firm, hearty handshake. "Good to see you, Scott. Please come in."

"Thank you so much for meeting me, Senator, on such short notice."

"Scott, please—call me Alan. Let me take your coat. Come on, let's sit in my study." He motioned toward the left, past a grand and tastefully decorated living room. "Can I get you a drink? I'm having a rye."

"Just water is fine, thank you."

"All right, then. Make yourself comfortable," he said, shuffling off to fetch the drinks.

His study was a testament to his remarkable career and intellectual pursuits: refined and inviting. A large polished mahogany desk, its surface organized, dominated the space. But the true showpiece was the bay window that offered a breathtaking view of McKay Lake, framed by the last glow of twilight and the imposing ancient trees surrounding the property. In front of the desk was a cozy seating area, flanked by towering floor-to-ceiling bookcases filled with an impressive collection of books on history, international affairs, diplomacy, literature, and politics. Personal touches, such as framed photographs from Alan's time as an ambassador and the many awards he had received, gave the room both character and gravitas.

Alan returned moments later with a glass of water in one hand and his drink in the other. He handed me my water, turned on a couple of lamps, and closed the study door behind him. "Please sit."

"This is an incredible room," I said, glancing at the closed door. "Is Ruth home?"

"No, old boy. You're dining only with me tonight." He grinned slightly as he eased himself into a vintage oxblood leather Chesterfield chair across from mine, mirroring my posture as I placed my glass on a marble side table. He seemed slightly winded as he continued, "Ruth's in Montreal, helping her sister recover from surgery."

"Oh dear. I hope she's all right."

"She's fine, thank you. This room, though—it's my favorite part of this drafty old house. It's also the safest: soundproof, bulletproof, and under constant monitoring for listening or recording devices."

Good to know, I thought, filing that information away.

Alan leaned forward with a curious smile. "Now, tell me about you. You look fit, healthy—and tanned."

"Thanks. We spent the past month in Los Cabos."

"How's your lovely wife?"

"She's good," I replied. "She's visiting a former colleague from GRF right now."

Alan's bushy white brows furrowed slightly as he searched for clarity.

I quickly explained, "Global Relief Foundation, where she was head counselor for ten years."

"Of course. And your daughter . . . Leah, right?"

"Excellent memory," I said with a nod. "She's fine, I think. She's at UCLA. We picked Los Cabos to make it easier for her to visit, but she couldn't make the time."

"Eventually, they grow up and return home," he reassured me, clearly sensing my frustration. He sat back in his chair and sipped his drink.

"You look like you haven't aged a day," I said, stretching the truth a little too far. Clearing my throat, I shifted the conversation. "Alan, thank you again for meeting me. I'm here because I need your help with a delicate matter—on behalf of a . . . friend."

He scrutinized me, leaning forward. "I see."

"This friend," I began cautiously, "has come into possession of classified government information—a pact between two nations—with massive implications for global affairs. At least one, if not both, of the governments is aware, and now he fears for his life."

Alan raised his eyebrows and chuckled. "And here I thought this was a casual visit to discuss retirement advice." He offered a smile to break the strange tension that had descended on the room. "Are you at liberty to name these two nations?" His glass was now empty, the ice clinking in his tremoring hand. He placed the glass on the table.

"The US and Russia," I said, my voice steady.

Alan's expression turned grave and the room fell silent, save for the faint ticking of the desk clock. He stared down at his hands, lost in thought, as the weight of the revelation settled over him. I could almost see the gears turning in his mind.

The first words that came out of his mouth were "My God."

***

It was late when I heard Colleen unlock the hotel room door. She stumbled as she came in, her eyes glassy, clear signs she'd had too much to drink.

"How'd it go?" she slurred, her voice laced with excessive enthusiasm.

I set down the book I'd picked up from the lobby library and replied that it had gone better than expected and promised to explain things in the morning, after we'd both gotten some much-needed sleep. She made it to the bathroom and closed the door behind her. I turned off the bedroom lights, leaving only her nightstand lamp on, and went to sleep.

The next morning, I got up early, ran four miles, hit the gym, and completed an upper-body workout—all before 8:00 a.m. Nearby, I stopped at Starbucks to get Colleen a coffee and egg wrap and myself a tea and egg bites. I finished my breakfast on the way back to the hotel, where the room was still dark. I opened the curtains and placed Colleen's breakfast on her nightstand, hoping she'd be awake by the time I showered and shaved.

My phone buzzed. It was a text from Alan.

He is ready to meet you. Safe travels, my friend.

When I came back from the bathroom, Colleen was sitting up, flipping through the book I had been reading. In an abundance of caution, I had taken her e-reader, worried it might somehow signal our location.

"Where'd you get this book? It's garbage," she said, tossing it to my side of the bed without waiting for an answer. Still groggy, she began gobbling the egg wrap. "Mmm, this is good," she muttered between bites. Her mood brightened after finishing her food. "Thank you; that really hit the spot."

"You're welcome. How was your evening?" I asked, trying to gauge how much she remembered.

"I had a lot of fun catching up with Susan. She hasn't changed—still crazy and fun as ever. More importantly, how was your evening with Alan? How's the old man doing?"

"He's aged quite a bit since I last saw him. Not as much energy, but still sharp as ever. He missed seeing you," I said, stretching out on the bed.

"And?" she pressed, her patience wearing thin.

"Well, he agreed this is a serious matter and suggested we consult with one of his colleagues in Tel Aviv who works for Israel Defense Forces, specifically the Mossad."

"The IDF? Why them?" she asked as she headed to the bathroom. With the door open, she raised her voice and called out, "That seems like quite a long way to go for help, doesn't it?"

I hadn't told her anything about the pact between the US and Russia, so I could see why Israel seemed like an odd choice. I, too, was skeptical.

"Well," I began, "I believe the people after me are American or Russian. Israel is both a friend and a foe to both countries. After the CIA, they also have the second-largest spy network in the Western world. If anyone understands my situation and can help, it's them. At least, that's what Alan believes."

Colleen emerged from the bathroom, ready to start the day. Since I'd booked a late-afternoon train back to Toronto to blend in with business commuters, we had a few hours to kill. I suggested skating along the Rideau Canal. She embraced the idea.

The canal was steps from our hotel, so we left our bags with the bellhop and traded our boots for rented skates. I helped Colleen lace hers up, then, holding onto each other for balance, we reacquainted ourselves with the ice. Before long, we were racing along the canal, confidence growing with every stride. The exercise and crisp air gave us a sense of peace for a few blissful moments. But it didn't last.

I've always been hyper-alert and couldn't stop scanning the crowd for anything unusual. I watched people as they skated by, looking for anyone who avoided my gaze or moved out of step with the rhythm of the crowd. Out of nowhere, I heard a buzzing sound. My eyes caught sight of a drone flying along the canal. We were nearing a wide bend heading west when I spotted it. I gestured for Colleen to turn back, but her confidence on the ice had grown and she sped up, planted her toe pick, spun with her arms extended, then snapped them in for a tight pirouette. She beamed with a huge smile.

"Let's race!" I called out, digging in my blades.

She took off again, and we both pushed ourselves hard. I eyed the drone—it trailed us. My legs were burning by the time we reached the green arched bridge near Confederation Park, and Colleen was gaining on me. When she caught up to me, I grabbed her arm, forcing both of us to halt.

"Hey! That's not fair! I was beating you!" She laughed, catching her breath.

But I held her close, my voice serious. "I think there's a drone following us," I said flatly.

We ducked into the shadow of the bridge and huddled together, staying perfectly still. I guessed it had been at least forty minutes since we hit the ice, and drones typically can't stay in flight longer than an hour. We stayed hidden for ten minutes before cautiously emerging to look for any sign of it. It was gone.

As we unlaced our skates, Colleen asked, "What's stopping us from going to Tel Aviv tonight?"

I didn't have an answer.

***

Back at the hotel's business center, I booked two business-class tickets from Ottawa to Tel Aviv via Zürich. We grabbed our luggage and then a cab to the airport with plenty of time to spare. While waiting, we picked up clothing suitable for Israel's weather and loaded two generic credit cards. We were rapidly spending money, yet no other choice existed. *Note to self: Thank my financial advisor for the forethought of placing funds around the world in various bank accounts.* It made globe-trotting around the planet easier.

Our flight departed at 7:00 p.m., and we'd arrive in Tel Aviv the following evening. I only hoped that whoever had been flying that drone wouldn't be on the same plane. We were in deep trouble, but we were moving forward for now.

5

Tel Aviv

The sun dipped below the horizon, casting the last rays of warm gold across Ben Gurion Airport. A subtle chill hung in the evening air as we stepped outside, catching our breath and hailing a cab. Amid my excitement, I had made a glaring oversight—I had forgotten to book a hotel.

We had only generic cell phones lacking SIM cards, so we had no internet access. A sense of unease crept in, but I dismissed it.

"Do you speak English?" I asked the taxi driver, and my voice was steadier than I felt.

A smile and a nod. "Yes. Where to?"

"A nice upscale hotel on the beach," I replied, a note of blind optimism in my voice.

He didn't hesitate. "The Kempinski Hotel. It is very new and beautiful. First time in Tel Aviv?"

"Yes," I admitted. "First time in Israel."

He chuckled, glancing at us in the rearview mirror. "This time of year, between winter and spring, it is often cool, breezy, and wet. But you are lucky—it is supposed to be sunny and warm this week."

"What's considered warm?" I asked, shifting closer to Colleen for heat as the evening chill seeped in.

"Twenty Celsius."

I reassured Colleen by translating the temperature into something familiar. "That's about seventy Fahrenheit."

She smiled, missing Mexico.

The traffic dragged on, inching us through Tel Aviv's waning rush hour. An hour later, we reached the Kempinski Hotel, a sleek tower of glass and steel gleaming against the night. I drew doubtful glances from the reception desk with my hurried explanation about cruise delays, the questionable accommodations provided by the cruise line, and a glowing recommendation from the taxi driver. The staff eyed us like unexpected visitors from another planet.

Only suites with executive lounge access, expansive views, a living room, and even a dining area were available. The price? A casual $3,000 per night. I suppressed a grimace. After a tense moment of scrutinizing my Canadian passport and processing my prepaid credit card, they finally handed us the keys.

Colleen didn't care about anything beyond the stocked complimentary minibar. I stood on the room's private terrace and stared out at the dark Mediterranean, watching the faint outlines of waves, waiting for the tension in my chest to subside.

***

By 9:00 a.m., I was reluctantly awake and up fiddling with the room's iPad-like control panel, opening the blinds and giving us our first clear view of Tel Aviv—its glowing skyline framed by the endless blue of the sea. Colleen wasn't happy to be awake, either, cocooning herself with pillows.

I ventured out to grab prepaid SIM cards for our phones, weaving through Tel Aviv's Bauhaus-style white buildings, which gleamed against the backdrop of vibrant murals decorating busy narrow streets and winding alleys. It was a place steeped in history that stood on foundations thousands of years old, yet Tel Aviv had a youthful vibe, with street vendors lining the roads and a constant hum of traffic, bikers, and chatter in Hebrew, Arabic, English, and French. Cafés spilled out onto the sidewalks, inviting passersby to linger.

On my way back, I had the unsettling feeling of being watched—though I shook it off as irrational. By 10:38 a.m., I was back in the suite with a bold coffee for Colleen and a variety of baked goods. I fumbled with a piece of paper I had stuffed into my wallet days before. It displayed the name *Daniel* and the number *03-6845335*. Hesitating only a moment, I dialed.

"Hello, is this Daniel?" My voice cracked.

"Yes," came the reply, in Hebrew-accented English. "Is this Scott?"

"Yes," I said, gripping the phone tighter. The sea view out our twenty-fifth-floor windows failed to calm my nerves.

"I've been expecting your call. Welcome to Tel Aviv."

We arranged the meeting without pomp, but with enough cryptic intent to leave my mind racing. Midday at the Ilana Goor Museum in Port Jaffa, by the rooftop fountain.

"Leave your wife on the lower floor. I will wear a New York baseball cap," Daniel added, casual as ever, before hanging up.

We were en route with my laptop in a cab by noon, following Tel Aviv's south coastline. The sun was warm enough to remind us of Mexico, but the city's character was distinctively its own—vibrant and alive. As we entered Jaffa's narrow streets, the driver chattered and pointed out landmarks, including the ancient Clock Tower, and spoke of the four-thousand-year history of the port. Yet my mind was entirely elsewhere, lost in a haze of speculation.

The Ilana Goor Museum was large, three-story limestone structure atop a hill, framed by olive trees and bathed in golden sunlight.

The staff greeted us as we purchased entry tickets. Inside, the atmosphere was transformative. Every inch of space was filled with sculptures, paintings, and an eclectic narrative of Israel's cultural landscape. As I navigated the bright and chaotic exhibits, I was almost distracted enough to forget why I was there.

I kissed Colleen's cheek and said "Wish me luck" as I dashed to find the stairs to the rooftop.

The rooftop was quiet except for the trickling of the fountain. Finding it behind a series of statues and plants took me a moment. At first it seemed whimsical, looking like six innocent girls in bathing suits playing in a kiddie pool with an oversized athletic man. As I approached it, what I saw stopped me in my tracks. The man was naked, his face contorted with anguish and helplessness, and standing on his back was a defiant young girl stabbing him with a pitchfork.

"It's surprisingly grotesque, isn't it?"

I whirled around at the sound of the voice. Daniel was half-hidden in the shadow of another sculpture and his face was obscured by an NY baseball cap and aviator sunglasses, but his demeanor radiated precision. Without raising a hand or uttering a greeting, he waited for me to close the distance.

"I must say, this museum is . . . overwhelming." I extended a hand, which was met with a firm fist bump.

"Welcome to Tel Aviv. I thought this would be a fitting meeting place—a crossroads of history and modern art." His casual tone belied an edge I couldn't ignore.

As the conversation unfolded, I revealed my secret: a decades-old pact between Cold War leaders, signed under the codename FIST: Force for International Supremacy Taskforce.

Daniel admitted there had been many rumors of such a pact, but there had been no evidence to substantiate it—until now. Over the next ten minutes, I explained I had acquired a USB drive containing over three hundred and eighty files that proved FIST had existed since 1959. To authenticate my story, I pulled out my laptop and opened the folder marked "1961–1962" and opened the document that still haunted me.

His sharp demeanor shifted at the mention of the assassination of the American president, which was a direct result of violating the FIST pact. Speculation gave way to dread as I turned my laptop toward him, presenting the evidence: a handwritten private note in Russian from the First Secretary of the Communist Party of the Soviet Union to the President of the United States, accompanied by an authentic English translation. In my mind's eye, I could still see the black-and-white TV footage of the funeral procession—a horse-drawn caisson carrying the president's flag-draped casket along White House Drive. The rhythmic clacking of the horses' hooves echoed a haunting reminder of a moment in history the world would never forget.

Under his breath in Hebrew, I heard Daniel say, "God help us all." He leaned in closer. "If you can provide us with all the documentation you have on this FIST pact from the various presidents and chairmen, we can safeguard you in our witness protection program in several parts of the world."

We glanced up at the sound of voices as people appeared on the rooftop.

When he spoke again, his voice was lower and full of urgency. "You are not safe here. If this pact exists, the implications are devastating. Israel is crawling with US and Russian operatives—you need to leave." His instructions burst forth, each word calculated. "Contact me in a week. You have my number. Do *not* draw attention to yourself. There is no telling who might already be after you."

The Mossad spy was gone before I could process his warning. With tourists taking over the rooftop, the museum's charm faded into the background. The sprawling displays and eclectic beauty now felt oppressive—like artifacts of a world too dangerous to have been unearthed.

I found Colleen downstairs, and we made our way to the street, my mind racing and my heart pounding.

Before returning to the hotel, we knew we had to eat. All we'd had that day were the pastries I grabbed for breakfast. Earlier in the morning, I'd passed a restaurant with something about hummus in its name. I remembered reading that Tel Aviv was a mecca for hummus lovers and thought, *When in Rome...*

The restaurant was bustling, which I took as a good sign. A host guided us toward the back, where Colleen excused herself to the toilet. I ordered two mint teas, letting my eyes wander across the crowded tables. The atmosphere was lively, full of chatter and laughter, but my gut tightened as I heard Daniel's voice in my mind: *You are not safe here.*

Colleen returned and sat beside me, eager to hear about what had happened on the museum rooftop, a place she'd never reached. I started recounting Daniel's warning about our safety and the plans for next week when she leaped to her feet.

Her voice was low, calm, and urgent, but her face betrayed pure panic. "We need to get out of here . . . *Now!* This way."

There was no time for questions. Grabbing our backpack, I ran after her toward the restrooms, where an emergency exit door marked our escape route. Colleen, with what looked like every ounce of her strength, pushed it open.

My last memory was stepping out into the alley, then a piercing boom splitting the air, plunging me against the brick wall of the adjacent building. The flash and a pressure wave, like an earthquake, rattled through me, leaving me disoriented and crushed within the chaos. A war zone enveloped the alley; smoke and dust filled the air, choking my lungs and irritating my eyes. The putrid smells of burned plastic, wood, and flesh overwhelmed every sense. My ears throbbed, drowning out the disjointed sounds of screaming and destruction.

Through the confusion, a shadowy figure grabbed me and pulled me from the ground, shoving me to move. My legs felt like lead.

***

The next thing I knew, a soft sea breeze was brushing against my face. My eyes struggled to focus through the sting of lingering chemical smoke. Every muscle in my body screamed in protest, and my head throbbed.

A warm hand rested over mine. It was Colleen's. She brushed her lips against my face and whispered, "You're going to be okay."

I wanted to speak, but the effort was too much, and I drifted back to sleep.

When I woke again, I was lying on a bed. The room was dark, save for the dim stream of light from an adjoining bathroom. The surroundings felt small and unfamiliar, but two small round windows gave it away. *Am I on a boat?*

Rolling over, I reached for Colleen, who was sleeping beside me.

My movement woke her, and she sat up to check on me. "How are you feeling?" she asked, stroking my forehead. "Do you need more painkillers? Can you hear me okay?"

I nodded, although my throat felt parched. "I need water," I rasped.

She helped me sit up, then held a glass to my lips. The cold water was a relief, soothing the raw dryness in my throat.

"Where are we?" I asked hoarsely.

A sly smile flickered across her face. "We're on a three-day cruise," she said with a small laugh. "I got the idea from you."

"You . . . what?" I stared at her in disbelief.

"You passed out after we got to the cab. The driver took us to the cruise ship dock at Haifa Port. He helped me get you into a wheelchair. Luckily, this cruise ship had wheelchairs available in abundance. For seniors like you. Oh, and I've been telling people you have dementia!" She burst into laughter at the absurdity of it all.

And for the first time in what felt like an eternity, I laughed. Gathering her close, I whispered, "Thank you for saving my life." Resting my head against hers, I added, "Start from the beginning. What happened?"

Colleen's tone grew serious as she explained. "Remember, you were telling me about Daniel's warning? While you were talking, a scruffy young guy came in. He sat at a table in the front, tucking a shopping bag under it. He glanced at the menu, then looked around. Something about him seemed off. Eventually, he got up and walked to the door—but he left the bag behind. Then he ran."

Her voice trembled. "I panicked. I knew something wasn't right. We got out just seconds before the explosion."

I sat in silence, trying to process her words. My mind felt sluggish and disoriented, and every detail she shared seemed to hit me with the weight of someone else's story. The memory of the blast was hazy, but fragments were falling into place: the deafening boom, the pressure wave that threw me into a wall, the smoke, the chaos. It was not accidental. Someone wanted us dead.

Colleen placed her hand on mine. "It's a lot to take in. Maybe you should rest a bit more."

Exhaustion still clung to me, but I needed to focus. "What's next?" I asked. "What's the plan?"

"Sleep," she said firmly.

***

By morning, my head felt clearer, the pounding had eased, and, thankfully, the ringing in my ears was gone. But my body still ached as if I'd run a marathon, beaten and bruised. Colleen ordered a full breakfast to be delivered to our room, and the smell of eggs, beef sausages, hash browns, and toast made my stomach growl loud enough to make her laugh.

As I devoured my food, Colleen launched into the plan. "The Tel Aviv airport isn't safe. If someone's after us, checking in there would put us in their crosshairs. Trains and buses? Forget it. They don't go anywhere safe." She paused, letting me catch up mid-bite. "So, I thought, Where would they least expect to find us? A cruise ship. This one goes to Limassol, Mykonos, and Athens." She leaned forward, her eyes narrowing. "When we dock in Limassol in three hours, we should get off and find a flight back to Toronto. What do you think?"

I looked at her, stunned by her clarity of thought and determination. Her calm, methodical planning was one of the reasons I'd married her. For the first time in years, I was seeing that brilliance shine. Choking back a lump in my throat, I whispered, "Who *is* this woman? Have I forgotten how amazing you are?"

Colleen laughed as I slowly stood up with egg on my face—literally—and pulled her into a tight embrace. Tears welled in my eyes from a mix of gratitude and relief.

6

Mediterranean Sea

As I continued to recover en route to the island of Cyprus, I reread the translated letter I had shown Daniel as proof that FIST existed.

May 29, 1963
Kremlin, Moscow
Dear Mr. President,
On behalf of the Soviet Union and myself, I extend my warm wishes to you on your 46th birthday. Such milestones are a time for reflection, not just in the years behind us but also in what lies ahead, especially in these precarious times. As I have often acknowledged, you are a man of unique charm and intellect, standing at the helm of a great nation during an era that requires both resolve and prudence. Such weight rests on your shoulders as it

does on mine.

However, I must take this moment of goodwill to remind you of the agreement forged before your time, an understanding central to the fragile equilibrium of our world. The FIST pact was not born out of camaraderie nor a gesture to inspire romantic notions of peace. It was a necessity that your predecessor and I recognized, albeit reluctantly. It was a pact meant to maintain a balance, an enforcement against spinning this world into destruction. Your actions, however, test the limits of this balance, and I must confess, Mr. President, they have not gone unnoticed. Regarding your decisions in Cuba, I see a troubling disregard for the spirit of our agreement. I urge you not to forget the weight of what lies in the palms of our hands. Should this balance falter, it will be not only you or I who suffer. It will be the children we both desire to watch grow—those who deserve a future, free from the shadows of the decisions we must now contemplate. You and I, Mr. President, are not afforded ordinary lives. Our days are counted not by the birthdays we celebrate but by the steps we take to prevent the next catastrophic misstep. If you wish to see your 47th birthday—and if you wish to stand by as your children grow to see their own—heed this message.

Our mutual preservation depends on recognizing a hard truth: neither of us is exempt from the cause-and-effect chain of history. The FIST pact was and remains a reflection of how close to the precipice we stand. Ignore it, and you ensure that no man—not even one as young and ambitious as yourself—can escape its consequences.

Let me be clear, Mr. President: speeches and ideals will not stave off the realities we face. While your rhetoric resonates with hope, hope is a far cry from action and preparation. Look beyond your defiance and see the immense responsibility we share before the world burns because of our arrogance. If this facade of peace cracks, you know who will bear that weight as well as I do. And it will not be you or me alone.

On this, your day of birth, I remind you, both adversary and strange ally, that though we travel on different paths, we are bound by a common fate. Do not let this moment slip through your grasp.

Warm regards,

N.K.

Almost six months later, the President of the United States was murdered in broad daylight in front of six hundred witnesses, with at least thirty-two people filming and taking still photographs of the gruesome event; yet, the reason for the shooting remains unclear, fueling countless conspiracies.

7

Limassol, Cyprus

Just before noon, we disembarked from the cruise ship into Limassol, bathed in the golden warmth of the Mediterranean sun. Colleen pushed me in a wheelchair—not out of necessity but because deep down she enjoyed babying me. Our backpack, stuffed with essentials and, most importantly, my laptop, clung to her shoulder. If anyone was searching for us, they wouldn't suspect a couple with the wife pushing her husband in a wheelchair.

Outside the port terminal, Colleen hailed a cab. I climbed into the backseat with care as the driver loaded the wheelchair into the trunk. For the brief ride into town, the tension that had loomed over us for the past twenty-four hours seemed to fade. Limassol shocked me with its striking mix of modern high-rises beside charming older buildings. Spring flowers exploded in vivid colors along boulevards and in lush parks, a sharp contrast to the chaos we had just escaped.

Colleen's eyes lit up as she spotted a quaint café with outdoor seating shaded by vibrant umbrellas. It offered the perfect spot to set the wheelchair and watch the world pass by. After we settled in, she began strategizing, drinking a coffee with milk while I had mint tea.

"I've been thinking," she started, brow furrowed, "I don't think Canada is our destination right now. Flying out of here might not be smart. As soon as we check in, our passports will trigger flags. Whoever's after us—they'll know."

I nodded, processing her words. "So, what's Plan B?"

She sighed, pushing her coffee aside. "We can travel across Europe by car with less risk. There's a ferry from here to Piraeus, Greece, every Monday, Wednesday, and Friday. It's a thirty-hour trip, but it's discreet. Since we've missed today's departure, we have time to buy a car and sort out the details. We can leave on Friday." She beamed, clearly feeling pleased with her logic.

Who is this woman? "What if we buy the car in Greece and walk onto the ferry here as passengers?" I suggested.

Colleen smirked. She'd expected this. "Good question," she said. "But here in Cyprus, all you need to buy a car is a valid driver's license and money. In Greece—or anywhere else in the European Union—you'd need a residency permit."

I leaned back, impressed by her thoroughness. "You've got this all figured out, don't you? So, what kind of car should we buy?"

Without missing a beat, Colleen chuckled. "Something inconspicuous, dependable, and untraceable. Maybe a red Porsche!"

Colleen knew my soft spot for fast and luxurious cars, as evidenced by the collection I had in storage back in New York. That storage facility near Yonkers Raceway housed seven marvels of engineering.

My breathtaking Bugatti Chiron Super Sport 300+ was there, with its quad-turbocharged W16 engine roaring at over 1,577 horsepower. The futuristic racer's design featured a black carbon-fiber body accented with bright-orange stripes. Mine was the fifteenth vehicle to roll off the production line in 2019.

My 2016 Rosso Corsa Ferrari LaFerrari Aperta, a stunning car, celebrated Ferrari's seventieth anniversary and aligned with Aurora EarthEx's billion-dollar IPO triumph.

Following that gem was my customized metallic silver Pagani Huayra BC, the first of its kind cleared for North American roads. It had taken five years on a waiting list to buy it and was worth every second.

But my most sentimental was an ivory-white 1950 Aston Martin Two-Litre Sports Drophead Coupé (DB1). One of only fifteen in existence, I'd nabbed mine at a Toronto auction to celebrate my first million-dollar paycheck while working at Burnett & Graystone, a niche legal firm specializing in Canada's mining industry.

Every vehicle had a story, representing chapters of my life. The collection included the iconic 1988 Porsche 959, the ruthless 2009 Mercedes-Benz SLR McLaren Stirling Moss, and the 1971 Lamborghini Miura SV masterpiece.

After the near-death experience in Tel Aviv, however, my perspective had shifted. Despite this dream collection's $25 million insurance valuation, it now felt more like an albatross than a passion. Once symbolic of speed, freedom, and achievement, these vehicles suddenly seemed like a statement of my materialistic greed. Sitting idle in storage, they deserved better than a life in the shadows. They needed to be admired by others, to dazzle and inspire. Life was too fleeting to cling to such possessions. *Note to self: Find a museum to donate this collection to.*

But before that, we still needed one more car—something "dependable, inconspicuous, and untraceable." And time was precious.

***

Colleen found a charming neoclassical bed-and-breakfast in the heart of Limassol's old town. Surrounded by lemon and olive trees, it had a beautiful patio and was a short stroll from the beach. But our packed schedule prevented us from visiting the shoreline. We split responsibilities to maximize time and planned to regroup at the B&B by 6:00 p.m.

My first task was to buy a burner phone with a Euro SIM card. Once connected, I called my Swiss bank. My numbered account added critical privacy, which I now needed more than ever. After providing my credentials, I directed my bank manager to wire 100,000 euros to a local bank. She assured me the funds would be ready for pickup at the Eurobank by the following morning.

Next, I turned my focus to cars. A quick search revealed that Omonoias Avenue, a ten-minute cab ride from the B&B, featured over fifteen used car dealers along a two-kilometer stretch. Just before 3:00 p.m., when the dealerships reopened post-siesta, I refueled with a quick souvlaki before heading out.

After I'd visited five dealerships, the sixth, Lavar Motors, showcased a nautical blue Mercedes-Benz S-Class, practically gleaming. Dmitri, a stout salesman too big for his cheap suit and with a bushy salt-and-pepper mustache and a heavy Russian accent, wasted no time launching into its highlights: a hybrid engine, minimal mileage, scratch-free interior, and a long list of features. We had noticed many Russians working in Cyprus, and a used car dealership seemed to be a perfect fit.

After a test drive that showcased the car's smooth handling and power, I interrupted Dmitri's non-stop sales pitch. "I'll buy it. On two conditions: I pay in cash and I need it registered with new plates and ready to drive by tomorrow."

Dmitri's grin widened. "No problem," he assured me, clearly accustomed to cash payments and sidestepping bureaucracy.

On the cab ride back, I called my New York insurance broker with the details and instructions. By midafternoon the next day, we would have our own wheels.

I returned to the B&B, and the day's adrenaline faded and the aches and pains along my left side settled in.

Colleen greeted me on the sunny patio with a hug and a kiss, looking radiant in a new outfit. She had been productive, judging by the bags scattered across the room.

"How'd you do?" she asked, pouring a glass of soda water for me and a glass of rosé wine for herself.

"We've got money, insurance, and a car," I declared with a touch of pride.

"I found everything on my list, too," she said, beaming. "So? What kind of car did you get?"

I smiled, then recited her mantra: "Inconspicuous, dependable, untraceable—a secondhand Mercedes-Benz S-Class hybrid."

"Wow, you really restrained yourself!" she teased, raising her glass.

Our last evening in Limassol was a perfect reason to celebrate. In a cab, we drove along the east coast to the beach of Aphrodite, where I had scoped out a restaurant on the Mediterranean Sea called The Grille. Fresh white linens adorned the tables, and we could hear the gentle sound of waves lapping against the shore as we sat beneath the stars. A comfortable breeze carried the scent of grilled seafood and herbs, which overwhelmed my senses as I felt an appetite grow.

Dinner began with a plate of mezze, a tantalizing array of small dishes that showcased the flavors of Cyprus. The main course was sea bream, grilled to perfection and served with a side of lemon potatoes and charred vegetables. The fish was tender and succulent. I smiled at Colleen as she consumed her meal.

Tomorrow would be a big day as we departed Limassol, and all the pieces had to fall perfectly into place. No room for error. While Europe awaited, the journey ahead promised anything but tranquility.

8

Greece to Austria

Everything meshed into place. By morning, I had a bulging stack of crisp €500 bills tucked into my pocket, and by siesta time, we had our new car. We spent the rest of the afternoon savoring the last moments of our stay in Limassol, a city that now felt like a fleeting haven.

Early Friday morning, we boarded the ferry bound for Greece. As the massive vessel left the harbor, the thought lingered—were we in the safest place possible, or sitting ducks for the next thirty hours? The answer, thankfully, was reassuring. The journey proved long, tedious, and devoid of surprises. By evening the following day, the rhythmic hum of the ferry gave way to the smooth purr of a Mercedes engine. The sun dipped low as we sped off, eager to reclaim the freedom of the open road. We drove until around ten o'clock, stopping in Larissa for the night, about four hours north of Athens. Unsurprisingly, the motel had no problem accepting cash.

The following day began with the rich aromas of hot coffee and tea, along with an array of baked goods. We hit the road before sunrise, the first light teasing the horizon as Colleen settled into her copilot role. Armed with a large paper map—our most valuable tool since I'd disabled the car's navigation system—she plotted our day's route across Greece, North Macedonia, and Serbia, with our sights set on Budapest, a twelve-hour drive. Lunch, she decided, would be in Belgrade.

Over the past few days, I had noticed a renewed energy in Colleen as she thrived in her element, outsmarting and evading the bad guys with relative ease.

After a satisfying meal of traditional Serbian dishes, the road stretched before us like an unwritten chapter, leading us north toward Hungary. The sky darkened, a deep black-gray cloud bank stretching across the horizon. The fertile, flat plains of Serbia's Vojvodina region were still in their off-season slumber. Fields lay untouched, dotted with occasional sprouts of green. Budding trees, their leaves just beginning to unfurl, promised life soon to come.

Raindrops began pattering against the windshield, and the car's wipers came alive, swiping them away with mechanical precision. The storm greeted us head-on, its downpour intensifying as the road shimmered slick and treacherous under our wheels.

Colleen's gaze darted into her side mirror. "Have you noticed anyone following us?" she asked suddenly, breaking the heavy silence.

The question caught me off guard. "Honestly? No, I haven't been looking. Have you?" I glanced in the rearview mirror, scanning for any sign of unwanted company.

She shook her head. "No, but I can't shake this feeling . . . about Leah. If something happens to us—"

That was all she needed to say. I cut her off, my voice calm but firm. "I've been watching. Everything seems normal to me. But you're right about Leah. She doesn't even know we're here. If something went wrong . . ."

The car plunged into the darkness of a train tunnel, the storm's pounding softened by layers of concrete.

Colleen sighed. "I know. I'm not even sure what we could tell her without alarming her . . . or putting her in danger. She seems too busy even to want to talk these days," she added, her frustration mirroring my own.

Leah had deflected every invitation to spend time with us in Los Cabos, whether for a week or even a brief weekend, using one excuse after another. "Too busy," "campus life," and "deadlines" were her favorite shields. After bending backward to be present for Leah, her aloofness had sunk into me like a thorn that never came out.

A single tear marked Colleen's frustration. "We need to talk about her, Scott. Really talk."

The storm picked up, the rain sheeting against the windshield as we emerged from the tunnel. A truck roared past, blinding us with a rush of water. The wipers worked overtime to clear it away.

"What's there to talk about?" I muttered, gripping the wheel tighter. "She's in LA, finishing her master's degree—what more is there to say?"

Colleen turned to me, her voice edged with emotion. "That. That's exactly the problem. You talk about Leah like you're balancing an investment portfolio. Tuition, bills . . . none of those things were what she really needed from you."

The dark sky brightened with a crack of lightning, its thunder shaking the car moments later. The tension inside the car, however, was heavier than the storm outside.

I kept my eyes on the soaked road, my frustration resurfacing like a wound ripped open. "I've done everything I can for her, Colleen. Rehab centers, tuition, plane tickets, even bailing her out in the middle of the night. What else am I supposed to do?"

Her voice sharpened. "She needs more than your money, Scott! She needs you. When she was spiraling, feeling unloved, and needed someone to believe in her, all you gave her was a bank transfer."

"That's not fair!" My voice had risen uncharacteristically. "Every time I tried to talk to her, to dig deeper, she slammed the door on me. What was I supposed to do? Chase after her while she accused me of being overbearing? Come on."

Colleen reached over, placing her hand on my arm, her touch soft yet grounding. "You can't give up on her. She has walls, yes, but those walls are there because she needed you to break through them—to prove you care. She's worth the fight."

I sighed in the silence that followed. I was confused. Was she talking about Leah, herself or both? I loosened my fingers on the wheel. "I don't even know where to begin . . ."

She whispered, "We start small. First, we must let her know we're in Europe."

"It's not safe to call, text, or email. I'm sure they're watching her to find us."

"Then we need to find someone to send her a message from us. Someone we can trust."

As I looked out at the endless stretch of road ahead, a patch of blue sky peeked through the storm clouds. The air smelled fresh, as if the earth itself had taken a deep breath. Yet when I looked in the rearview mirror, I had the uncomfortable feeling that a car was following us.

As we crossed into Hungary, vineyards and pastures dotted the flat terrain. The late-afternoon sun dipped lower, painting the horizon with gold and pink hues. A couple of roadside inns, their signs reading CSÁRDA, caught Colleen's attention.

"Let's find a csárda for the night," she suggested, map still in hand.

As we merged onto the Budapest freeway, rush-hour chaos surrounded us, cars clogging the lanes in all directions.

Colleen's voice was steady but decisive. "If we stay on this road, we'll cross the Danube in about fifteen kilometers. We can bypass downtown Budapest entirely if we're careful."

A short time later, the bypass steered us into gridlocked traffic, and my chest tightened with frustration. With the navigation system offline, we were at the mercy of road signs and paper maps. I slammed my hand against the console and swerved toward the next exit. Wet pavement shimmered under the streetlights, slick and unforgiving. The secondary road stretched ahead, narrow and dark, like a coiled snake waiting to strike. As my adrenaline surged, so did my suspicion. Were we being followed? There was only one way to find out.

I gripped the steering wheel, knuckles whitening, and crushed my foot on the accelerator. The V8 roared with a deep, guttural growl and surged forward with electrifying speed. Rain streaked across the windshield, the wipers fighting to keep up as the Mercedes ate the twisting road.

Colleen gasped, her hands darting to the "oh shit" handle above the door.

"What . . . What are you doing?" Her voice shook with what sounded like a mix of panic and disbelief.

"Figuring out what this car's made of," I muttered under my breath. But beneath the bravado, my pulse hammered.

A semi-truck emerged ahead, crawling up the incline like a lumbering beast, with no room to pass. My eyes darted to the oncoming headlights. A bus roared past, its blinding light grazing the edges of the Benz as I floored the gas pedal. I wrenched the wheel, nosing into the opposing lane. The truck became a blur on my right. I felt Colleen stiffen beside me, her breath caught on the precipice of terror.

Then I saw it. A rusty baby-blue Skoda chugging along like a dying animal. However, the genuine danger concealed itself behind us—the black oval grille, displaying the distinctive four-ring emblem and headlights of an Audi. My heart stopped.

"Looks like we have uninvited company behind us," I said through gritted teeth, swerving back into my lane just in time to avoid a collision. Colleen's nails dug into the armrest.

I slammed my foot down on the gas pedal, and the tires screeched against rain-slick asphalt as they struggled to find a grip, but I didn't let up. I punched the pedal again. The engine snarled as the car hurtled forward, the jolting momentum pressing us into our seats. In the rearview mirror, the hunter loomed closer. Outrunning them wasn't an option—we needed to lose them.

"Hold on!" I barked as I swung the car left onto a narrow village road.

The turn snapped Colleen's head sideways, and she scrambled to keep the map from sliding off her lap. The road snaked, lined with stone walls and shadows that seemed to reach out with clawed fingers. Around every curve, the menacing Audi headlights loomed closer like a predator stalking prey.

I braked hard, the tires fighting for traction as I took another sharp turn. My nerves crackled like live wires at the sight of red brake lights ahead. I veered to the right to dodge the SUV, then continued downhill. The Benz groaned as it grappled with the slick terrain while I navigated hairpin turns and blind corners as though playing an intense cat and mouse game.

Every turn threatened disaster. The car fishtailed. The headlights from oncoming traffic blinded me. The wipers screeched against the glass.

But as we reclaimed the main road, the rain eased and the Benz stabilized under steady acceleration.

“Have we lost them?” Colleen whispered, terror etched in every syllable.

I checked in the mirror. But those headlights had vanished into the dark. Relief washed over me like a clearing storm.

“For now,” I said, voice strained. But doubt lingered. They weren’t gone—they were waiting. Behind the shroud of darkness, they waited.

The road stretched ahead, lined with the promise of refuge. Hungarian inn. Goulash. My stomach growled, ravenous for safety as much as sustenance. But safety was tenuous. The chase wasn’t over—it had only begun.

***

Throughout the night, a symphony of thunder growled across the skies while flashes of lightning illuminated the windows in fleeting bursts. The relentless rhythm of rain drummed against the roof, a steady cadence that could have been intrusive. Yet inside the walls of our intimate refuge, none of it mattered. Cocooned in warmth with each other, time itself seemed to blur as passion overtook us, our bodies moving as one, reaching that shared crescendo that washed away every care in the world. For those precious hours, the storm outside was distant, irrelevant—a mere backdrop to our perfect tempest of love and connection.

By morning, reality crept back in. We had overlooked pulling the blinds, and sunlight flooded the room in golden streaks, casting its glow over everything it touched. The harsh storm was gone, replaced by the serenity of a new day. Had we slept in? The question lingered in the moment's stillness enveloping us. Nothing existed beyond the sunlight, the warmth of each other's presence, and the small Hungarian inn that had become our sanctuary for a brief spell.

I looked at my dead watch and jumped up to reach my smartphone. The time read 8:23 a.m. We were in no hurry as Vienna was only three hours away. I got dressed and went out to find breakfast while Colleen showered.

I first surveyed the parking lot. The black Audi was nowhere to be seen. I returned with a bounty of food and drinks from the lobby buffet.

Colleen, now dressed with her wet hair pulled back and her VPN-secured iPad in her lap, was eager to share her news. "I found a spectacular loft in the heart of Vienna's historic center. From the photos, it looks sophisticated with its marble floors and charming décor. From the reviews, it's 'secure and private.' Should I book it for three or four nights?"

"Assuming I can reach Professor Röhrlich in a few days, let's do four nights to be safe."

Professor Reinhard Röhrlich, a scholar at the University of Vienna, was a potential lifeline amid the chaos surrounding us. His reputation for dissecting the ideological clash between Communism and Capitalism had made him a prominent academic voice. More importantly, his connection to the answers I needed made him someone who could help us navigate the murkier waters we now found ourselves in. When I'd reached out to him under the pretense of writing my own book, his enthusiastic reply had been a minor triumph.

But as Colleen completed the booking and Vienna became our next destination, a bitter truth lingered just beneath the surface. The shadow of uncertainty followed us, unseen but not unfelt. Those black Audi headlights weren't gone. They were somewhere out there, waiting. And the most dangerous predators always knew when to let their prey believe, just for a moment, that they were safe.

9

Vienna

The elevator doors slid open, revealing an apartment entrance that oozed sophistication. The loft we'd rented on a quiet Vienna street was even better than it looked in the photos. Sleek, modern, and entirely unassuming from the outside—exactly what we needed. After setting our bags down, I immediately called Professor Röhrlich's office. No answer. I left a message and hung up. Waiting games were never my strongest suit.

Colleen, however, had other plans. "Let's see what Vienna offers," she said with a grin that hadn't surfaced in months.

I didn't hesitate. "Promise you'll let me play tour guide for dinner."

She shrugged, grabbed our backpack, and flashed me a playful smile. "Deal."

By midday, we'd wandered through Vienna's iconic Hundertwasserhaus, marveled at the Kunst Haus Wien Museum, and lost track of time exploring the sprawling Prater Park. Later, we collapsed side by side on the bed, with our shoes kicked off and the exhaustion that comes from walking miles. Yet we were feeling alive.

"This city . . ." Colleen whispered as she laced her fingers through mine.

"You'll love it even more tonight," I teased, leaning closer.

Her eyebrows rose. "What's happening tonight?"

"You'll see."

What began as an embrace intensified into primal instincts. The exhaustion melted in a way only intimacy allows.

By eight, we were on our way to my surprise. Typically, a reservation here required months of waiting, but a quick call to an old connection had worked its magic.

Inside, the two-star restaurant gleamed with understated opulence. Every table was a masterpiece illuminated by overhead lights that showcased the food. The steady hum of conversation from Vienna's elite filled the air.

"To retirement," I toasted, raising my water glass to Colleen's champagne glass.

Colleen smirked, already helping herself to a second pour. "Cheers to that."

The first dish, a delicate amuse-bouche, arrived—a single bite of spiced parsnip strudel crowned with crayfish and honey. It epitomized perfection.

But before I could savor it, the room was plunged into darkness.

For a moment, no one moved. Silence swept over the restaurant like a heavy fog. Then, murmurs of confusion rippled through the crowd. Was this an elaborate effect? A gimmick?

A chilling feeling gripped me. Something was wrong. My hands turned clammy. Around me, smartphone flashlights flickered to life.

Then came the smoke. Black smoke.

Thick, toxic, and billowing fast, it poured from the kitchen and filled the room. Chaos erupted. Diners screamed, tables toppled, and the clatter of broken glass cut through the smoky haze.

"Colleen!" I shouted, voice already hoarse.

Adrenaline kicked in. With my napkin pressed to my face, I dropped to my knees, trying to find clean air. I felt my way toward her and shouted her name again, the noise and smoke swallowing my words.

She wasn't there.

I recalled the layout of the restaurant. The entrance was the closest exit. As I crawled, someone tripped over me, sending my phone sliding across the floor. I lunged after it, securing the faint light it provided.

"Colleen!" I called again, louder this time, but still no answer.

The acrid smoke burned my throat, blurring my focus. I pressed forward, desperate to believe she'd made it outside.

Emerging into the crisp night air felt like a reprieve from suffocation. The park around the restaurant was unrecognizable in the chaos. Panicked guests spilled across the lawn, shouting into phones or clinging to one another in fear.

I stumbled over to the edge of the crowd, scanning for her face. Nothing. My frustration and fear mixed to create a growing nausea.

Finally, the wail of sirens pierced the night. Fire trucks arrived, spraying water into the building and flooding the area with beams of light. Police cordoned off the scene, herding the guests into small groups for questioning. I could see the devastation inside the restaurant through its large windows: shattered glass, overturned tables, and a battlefield of untouched gourmet food, but no Colleen.

When the fire captain addressed the crowd in German and English, he confirmed what I had been dreading. Two perpetrators, masked and armed, had infiltrated the kitchen through a service entrance, locking staff in a supply closet and igniting smoke bombs before vanishing.

I backed away into the park's shadows, my thoughts spiraling. This wasn't random. My gut screamed that this attack wasn't about any political statement; this was about us. But why *her*? Why not *me*? Had my call for a reservation triggered this?

I raced back to the loft, my thoughts a fractured storm of desperation and fear. The image of the burner phone in Colleen's backpack replayed in my mind. A lifeline I couldn't reach. No matter how many times I tried, her phone remained unanswered. Every ring felt hollow and miles away.

Minutes dragged into hours, each one a suffocating eternity. Time became viscous, stretching as the loft's walls closed in around me. Every breath felt heavier than the last. I scoured the TV channels, looking for any news that might offer a shred of hope. One report suggested ISIS terrorists. Images of the explosion were replayed—a chaotic aftermath, but no sign of her. No glimpse. No answers.

I stared at the screen, questions pounding in my head like hammers. *What happened to her? Where is she?*

Unable to sit still, I began pacing the room, my steps aimless but relentless. My restlessness grew into something primal. I circled like a caged animal desperate for escape. Then exhaustion crept in like a thief, stealing pieces of me until I collapsed on the couch, still dressed, adrenaline tangling with anguish. The shroud of helplessness was suffocating, and for hours, I couldn't make sense of anything. Eventually, sleep overtook me—not peacefully.

***

I woke with a jolt. The couch beneath me felt foreign, my back stiff and protesting as I tried to orient myself. The weight of the previous night slammed into me, clearing the haze from my mind in an instant. *Where is she?* My heart punched against my ribcage as I pushed myself upright. Every corner of the loft loomed in unbearable silence.

Then, I saw her.

She was sprawled on the bed, her body relaxed like she'd drifted to sleep without a care in the world. The sight didn't register at first. Then relief crashed through me, twisting into a pang of disbelief. A tight knot in my chest threatened to unravel me.

"Colleen?" My voice—trembling, frayed at the edges—barely escaped as I rushed to her side and shook her shoulder gently.

Her eyes fluttered open, blinking at me with a calmness that felt misplaced, her face peaceful.

"You're here," I choked out, the flood of emotions drowning every coherent thought. "You're *here*."

"Of course I am," she replied, stretching like she'd just woken from the calmest sleep. "You looked like you needed the rest—I didn't want to disturb you."

Her composure hit like a slap. Anger and impatience surged—untamed, undeniable. "Where the hell were you?" I snapped, my voice raw with urgency as I dropped onto the edge of the bed.

She shifted closer to me as she sat up, placing her hand on my leg—a gesture meant to calm me, but it only stoked the fire. "I'm okay," she said soothingly. "They weren't trying to hurt me."

Hurt her? My mind raced to fill in the blanks, failing at every turn. My brows knit in confusion. "What are you talking about?"

Her gaze didn't waver, though her next words sent ice through my veins. "The men from the restaurant—those who staged the attack—they're friends."

My body tightened. "Friends?" My voice cracked.

"Yes, ISIS friends," she replied with unsettling firmness, her eyes steady despite the weight of what she was revealing. "From my time working with the Global Relief Foundation in Syria. They contacted me to warn us."

An invisible floor beneath me crumbled away, leaving a void that sucked every sense of sanity from the room. "Warn us?" I echoed, dread wrapping tighter around my chest. "Warn us about what?"

Colleen's expression hardened, though her voice remained composed. "The Russians. They're tracking us. There's a bounty on our heads, Scott—on the dark web."

Her words cut through me like a blade. I couldn't breathe, couldn't think. My survival instincts screamed to take over, but the enormity of her words froze me in place.

She continued, her tone softening as if anything she added now could fix the wreckage growing between us. "The car . . . the one we're driving. It's compromised. There's a GPS tracker hidden inside. It seems it's a remnant of the previous owner, a corrupt Russian oligarch."

I stared at her, my pulse a deafening roar in my ears as my mind flashed back to the burly Russian who sold us the car. How much danger were we in? How could I defend her and us before catastrophe struck?

I had no answers, and for the first time, I realized the limits of my control were suffocating me.

Who was this woman, my wife of thirty-four years? The revelation about her extremist armed "friends," her mysterious past in Syria, and now the bounty on our heads—each piece of information cast a shadow over the woman I thought I knew. As Colleen spoke, her calm demeanor almost frightened me more than the words themselves. How could she remain so composed while revealing truths that turned our lives into a lethal pursuit?

I realized then that I didn't know her—not really. Not her deepest fears, not her darkest secrets, and not the full extent of her past at Global Relief Foundation. A part of her had always been inaccessible to me, a fortress that love, arguments, and late-night conversations could not breach. And now, I wondered if that hidden part of her had caused our separate lives.

Adding to my unease was her drinking, something I'd dismissed as the stress-induced habit of someone who'd seen too much of the world's harshest realities. Was it the memories she couldn't escape, or was it guilt? What truths were drowning at the bottom of those bottles she emptied in the night's silence? What was she anesthetizing herself against?

The image I had of Colleen was crumbling. The woman I had shared my life with, trusted with my dreams and fears, was a stranger cloaked in familiarity. And the terrifying part wasn't that she had been hiding something, but the realization that I didn't know who she was.

One thing was sure. I needed answers—and fast.

***

My body twitched when my phone rang. It could be only one person. I answered, "Hello."

"Hello, is this Mr. Barton?" he said with a strong German accent.

"Yes."

"I am Professor Reinhard Röhrlich." He went straight to his question. "I am intrigued to understand how a rare metal expert wants to know more about geopolitical dynamics." To give me some room to maneuver, he chuckled.

He had checked my social media profile.

"Well, thank you, Professor Röhrlich, for returning my call. I'm happy to explain more about my book in person." For fear someone was listening to our conversation, I wanted to get to the point. "Do you have any time to meet today or tomorrow?"

He scrutinized his calendar. "Today will not work, but I can make time tomorrow. How about fifteen hundred hours?"

"Excellent," I replied, trying to contain my excitement.

"Vienna University is . . . how do you say . . . a maze. It is not so easy to navigate. I will meet you at the main entrance. Top of the stairs. I look forward to hearing more about your book."

***

At three, I arrived at the Italian Renaissance–style building with a massive marble staircase leading to four arched pillars and a grand entrance. Beside the second pillar stood a dignified gentleman around my age with darker hair than mine. Of course, he was wearing a paisley blue-and-red bow tie with his gray suit to fit the professor's look. Professor Röhrlich welcomed me and we hurried through the pleasantries, then he asked me to follow him through the incredible 1800s architecture. He pointed out that the university was founded in 1365, making it the world's oldest German-speaking institution of higher education. As we emerged from the other side of the building, entering an arcade courtyard surrounded by four massive buildings, I understood the "maze" concept. Six minutes later, we were finally in his office, surrounded by bookshelves. To the right side of a grand desk piled high with more books and papers was a small seating area where we sat, facing two small windows that overlooked the massive courtyard.

I looked at my watch; we had already lost ten minutes. I leaned forward. "Thank you very much, Professor Röhrlich, for meeting me. Is it okay if I record our conversation?"

He nodded with a smile. "Yes. Please call me Reinhard."

"Okay, let me cut to the chase, Reinhard." I smiled as well. I wanted to eliminate the idea of writing a book by telling the truth, but I didn't want to endanger the professor. "My nonfiction book has been a passion since college, but I never had the time to pursue writing it until now. It's about political power, conspiracies, and global alliances. Specifically, the concept of creating a dominant power alliance."

"It is more than just a concept, Mr. Barton."

"Please call me Scott."

"As a matter of fact, Scott, after the French Revolution and Napoleonic Wars, Austria was the architect of establishing the Concert of Europe in 1814. Its aim was to maintain peace and stability on the continent by creating a balance of power and fostering cooperation among the major powers at the time: Austria, Prussia, Russia, Great Britain, and later France. Diplomats carefully redrew borders and influence to ensure a balance of power among nations, thus reducing incentives for territorial conquest or unilateral aggression. It lasted roughly for a hundred years until World War One broke out."

I knew I had to get this conversation back on track; otherwise, I'd be stuck there for the rest of the day. "Thank you for this historical context. It's helpful." Okay, I lied. "Have you heard of anything like this in more recent times?"

"What do you mean?" he asked, leaning closer to me with a confused look.

"There have been conspiracy theories that the Russians and Americans have such an agreement to block China and keep the rest of the world in check. Have you ever heard of such a thing?"

The professor's expression turned more solemn as he paused, then stood. "Let us go for a walk. It is a beautiful spring day."

It felt less like a question and more like a directive. It would also be more challenging for me to record the conversation.

We walked along the perimeter of the inner courtyard arcade, around two massive trees with newly blossomed leaves.

Professor Röhrlich said in a serious tone, "I have heard of the agreement you mentioned. In 1959, the President of the United States and the First Secretary of the Communist Party of the Soviet Union were reportedly said to have made such a secret agreement. There has been no proof. Some believe it continues today. But the balance of power differs from that of the Concert of Europe. This is not based on collaboration or cooperation but on conflict and chaos."

Finally, we're getting somewhere! "What do you mean?"

"First, let me be clear: they are arch-enemies, yet they allow each other to coexist by fueling wars, terrorism, and unrest in many parts of the world—even in their own countries—directly and indirectly."

"How so?"

"People believe the president knew about the 9/11 threat but did not stop it, then accused Saddam Hussein's regime of developing weapons of mass destruction and posing an imminent threat to the world. We know how that story ends." Professor Röhrlich stopped and looked directly at me. His eyes looked tired. "Their goal is not to advance their ideology but to profit from the madness as they play other nations like starving puppets. Utter madness." He stopped for a second to contemplate his words and then continued walking.

"If this is possible," I said with doubt, "how do they remain undetected?"

"No one in his or her right mind would consent to having his or her people die for these strategic games. Right?" He stopped again and looked at me as if I were the enemy. "Yet every war is between the US and Russia: the Korean War, the Vietnam War, and the Persian Gulf War. Since the twentieth century, over 187 million people have lost their lives because of war. Wars that were conveniently played outside their countries."

"How do they start these conflicts?" I asked as we began to walk again.

"Good question, Scott," he replied as if I were one of his star students. "Now we are getting into deeper conspiracy territory. Behind the scenes, they are supporting various terrorist groups with weapons, technology, training, and intelligence. But their most significant collaboration is through NGOs."

I stopped to clarify whether he had used the correct term. "Sorry, did you say NGOs?"

"Yes. This is hearsay, but they collectively fund nonprofit organizations through their intelligence agencies and run them as a cover to create their chaos."

I wasn't sure whether I was confused or shocked. "Together, you say?" I clarified again.

"All you need to do is follow the money."

Professor Röhrlich checked his watch and was alarmed at the late hour. "I am sorry, but I have another appointment outside the university. We will have to wrap this up. I can walk you back to the main entrance."

"Before I leave, is it possible for me to use your office phone? My cell phone isn't working here."

"Sure, I need to pick up my briefcase. Follow me."

***

From Röhrlich's office, I made two important calls. The first was to Research Professor Bruce Manning at UCLA. Bruce was an old friend from our days at the University of Toronto.

Although we had crossed paths in the mining industry, the instability of that world led him back to academia, where he focused on geological and tectonic research. I had last seen him in Singapore at the Rare Earth Industry Association Conference. Over drinks, we had exchanged contacts. Bruce was always youthful and energetic, born to mentor young minds. Unmarried, he led a well-groomed and disciplined life. Perhaps he was gay, but such matters had never come up.

As we spoke, I obscured the situation Colleen and I were in, careful not to deviate too much from the truth, and asked him to pass a letter to Leah, our daughter. Bruce confirmed his desire to help. Leah had been blocking our calls since our last contact in Los Cabos, where we had failed to convince her to join us. I promised Bruce I'd send a private letter to his Gmail account, which he could print out and hand-deliver to Leah. I also cautioned against using his university address to avoid drawing attention to himself.

My second call was to Mossad agent Daniel in Tel Aviv. His surprise at hearing my voice sent a chill down my spine, making me consider the possibility that he might have played a role in the Tel Aviv restaurant bombing. He was cryptic and hesitant, as if requiring authorization from someone else before planning our next meeting. Eventually, he warmed up and outlined our next steps with measured confidence.

First, we were to drive to Munich, Germany, to pick up an envelope addressed to "Karl Southgate" at the SmartCall store on 10 Wilhelmstraße. Inside the envelope, we'd find further instructions about a meeting in Zürich, Switzerland, the next day. The clandestine nature of this arrangement felt like scenes from a spy novel, but after the tragedy in Tel Aviv and the car bugging, we would heed such precautions.

10

Vienna

Back at the loft, I found Colleen lounging on the sofa, reading a paperback. It looked like a romance novel judging from the bare-chested hunk on the cover.

"Good book?" I teased.

She finished her page before glancing up. "It's better than the last one you got me." She grinned. "How did it go?"

I recounted my conversations with Professor Röhrlich, Professor Manning, and Daniel. I omitted any mention of NGOs, knowing it might set her off on one of her passionate speeches about their importance in developing nations, especially in conflict zones.

"While you were playing investigator at the university, I got the Mercedes debugged," she said proudly as she sat up. "They found two GPS trackers on the undercarriage. Two different makes."

I was confused. "What does this mean?"

"Good question. Two different surveillance groups could be following us. Actually, they are now following a garbage truck." She laughed.

"How in the hell did you find an expert in bug sweeping?" I asked, not wanting to know if she herself was an expert in spying and countersurveillance.

She stood and draped her arm over my shoulder as if to kiss my neck. As she leaned closer, she purred, "Darling, do you really want to know?" She was having fun at my expense. "If you must know, I searched online and found a company here in Vienna that specializes in bug sweeping. They even do a comprehensive TSCM aircraft bug sweep," she said, referring to the Technical Surveillance Countermeasures process. "Isn't Google amazing?" She laughed and kissed me on my cheek.

We needed to make an early start to our drive to Munich, so we went out for a quick dinner and then got ready for bed. Before drifting off to sleep, Colleen read her book and I opened the file named "1969–1974," which would contain the turbulent times of the famous Watergate scandal. I clicked on the audio file titled *Final Call, July 9, 1974*. I clicked the START arrow as I listened through my earbuds.

US President: Leonid, good evening. I trust the Black Sea still shines as brightly as when I left.

Russian General Secretary: It does, but the sea is

> *not why I called. [Pause] One week ago, we discussed matters of great importance. I wish for time to pass so that you could reflect on the realities of [unclear].*
> *US President: I've thought about it, yes. But I'm not sure I see the benefit of revisiting a conversation that, frankly, I found rather . . . discouraging.*
> *Russian General Secretary: Discouraging, perhaps. But necessary. Mr. President, you are no fool. You understand the world does not wait for a weakened leader to find his footing. You have enemies circling you in Washington—many of them of your own making.*

I heard a faint match-striking sound in the background. Perhaps Brezhnev was lighting a cigarette.

> *US President: Come on now, Leonid. Spare me the sanctimony. I'm no saint, and neither are you. You don't think I know how your operatives are watching and reporting every damned detail of what happens here? You probably know more about Watergate than my own party does.*
> *Russian General Secretary: I know only what is obvious: you are cornered. And a man in your po-*

sition does not just threaten himself; he threatens everything he touches. Including . . . FIST. [Pause] You must resign. Step away before you destroy yourself—and us.
US President: Resign? You're delusional! They'll have to drag me out of the White House kicking and [unclear]. Do you have any idea what I've endured to get here? And you expect me to walk away and let the hyenas win? Let them tear apart everything we've accomplished?
Russian General Secretary: Exactly my point, my friend. You have endured much, but there is no victory left for you. The hyenas, as you call them, have already set the stage for your fall. If you drag this out, you risk not just your own ruin, but the exposure of the alliances we have built.
US President: You think you can lecture me? Without me, FIST wouldn't be what it is today.

I could hear his voice change with anger.

US President: I made you stronger. I made both of us stronger on the global stage. Now you have the nerve to tell me to step away?
Russian General Secretary: Yes. If you wish to grow

old, Mr. President—if you want to preserve what little legacy you can salvage—you must remove FIST from your mind forever.

US President: So that's it. You're writing me off, just like that.

Russian General Secretary: This is not personal. It is practical. Power does not indulge sentiment. You know this. You always did. That is why I trusted you once, when we began this endeavor. But your time is over. You are no longer useful.

US President: No longer useful? You ungrateful son of a [unclear].

Russian General Secretary: Enough. I will not have this conversation devolve into petty anger. You need to decide, Mr. President, and time is very short.

US President: [sarcastic laughter] Short? You think I don't know what's going on here? You've always been a step ahead, haven't you? Watching, manipulating, waiting. My God, the leaks! The press frenzy—it was you, wasn't it? Feeding them enough to cut my legs out from under me!

Russian General Secretary: I didn't need to. You were always your own worst enemy.

US President: Damn you, Leonid. You think you can walk away from me? I have audiotape record-

ings.

Russian General Secretary: Are you threatening me?

US President: [voice quiet, almost defeated] And if I refuse to step down? If I fight to the bitter end?

Russian General Secretary: And that, Mr. President, is why you have failed. Power demands control, and you have lost control. Let this be the end before it becomes an even greater disaster. Step down or risk not growing old.

US President: [a long pause, his voice trembling] We're no longer allies, then? No longer . . . friends?

Russian General Secretary: [a soft chuckle, devoid of warmth] We were never friends. We were merely two men who understood the calculus of power. But now, only one of us still understands. Goodbye, Mr. President.

11

Munich, Germany

Colleen and I settled into our roles: I was the driver, and she was the navigator.

We left the loft at 8:00 a.m. and arrived in Munich by 1:00 p.m. The envelope at the SmartCall store contained a single address for the next leg of our journey: 29 Stüssistrasse, Apartment 4, at 14:30 the following day.

After collecting the envelope, we ate lunch and drove deep into Bavaria's Five Lakes Region, looking for a Gasthaus. This summer tourist destination area offered plenty of options in the off-season. Concerned about being tracked, we avoided booking hotels online. We found a charming Gasthaus along the shores of Wörthsee Lake and booked a room in person with cash.

The room was small but clean, with two pushed-together single beds, a modest bathroom, and a large window that overlooked the lake's calm waters. Approaching footsteps creaked on the wooden floor, acting as a basic alarm. The tantalizing aromas of roasted pork and stews wafted in from the restaurant and bar below, a comforting reminder that this was a fleeting pit stop before facing the unknown again.

That evening, Colleen and I composed a letter to Leah for Bruce to deliver.

Hi Leah,

We hope you're doing well and powering through finals. Your upcoming graduation is an incredible milestone, and we're so proud of you and excited for you.

There's important news we need to share. With help from Professor Bruce Manning, we've sent you this message. Since we last spoke in Los Cabos, we've been traveling in Europe, but unfortunately, we've encountered a serious situation.

For safety reasons, we had to disconnect from the digital world entirely to protect our identities. We don't want to alarm you, but our situation has placed us in danger, and it's possible you're being monitored as well—online and in person.

Here's what we need you to do: Please continue your daily routine as if nothing's wrong. Do not tell anyone about receiving this message. If you feel unsafe or threatened, go to the police immediately.

After reading this, please destroy the message. We'll contact you again once it's safe, likely when we're back in the States.

Stay safe, sweetheart. We love you more than anything.

Love,

Mom and Dad

XOXO

P.S. If you can use someone else's phone, text us (49 175 2543370) to confirm you're safe and well. DO NOT use your own phone. Be safe.

As we sent the Word document to Bruce via email, our thoughts remained heavy with worry for Leah, hoping this message wouldn't bring her further harm.

12

Zürich, Switzerland

The next day, we parked outside 29 Stüssistrasse before 2:30 p.m. Colleen stayed in the car to monitor street activity while I entered the building. It was a modest apartment complex filled with the sounds of daily life—children playing, a baby crying, a dog barking. The atmosphere felt disarmingly normal despite my tension.

I found myself unprepared for what I discovered when I knocked on the door marked Nr. 4.

A petite elderly woman in a floral dress opened the door. "Hallo!" she said warmly, wiping her hands on her apron. Her bright, dark eyes shone behind old-fashioned glasses; her silver hair was tied neatly back in a bun. The scent of baked cookies wafted from the kitchen.

I stammered, "I . . . Is . . . Daniel here?"

She beckoned for me to step inside as the kettle on the stove whistled. I followed her to the kitchen and explained I was there to see Daniel. She poured tea into a porcelain teapot and offered me almond chocolate chip cookies, fresh from the oven.

Moments later, the apartment door flew open. Daniel burst in, winded and apologizing profusely for being late. After a brief exchange between him and the woman, who turned out to be his mother, she disappeared into another room, leaving us alone at the small dining table.

Daniel wasted no time. His jerky, frantic movements revealed his anxiety as he pulled out documents from a worn leather satchel.

"I've spoken with the director of Mossad," he said, his tone low and serious. "They're prepared to offer you and your wife witness protection . . . on one condition: you provide the digital documents you possess on the FIST agreement between the US and Russia."

"Let's be clear," I said. "Neither the government of Russia nor the US sanctioned this agreement. It's a pact between their leaders—a rogue operation."

Daniel handed me a formal letter from the Mossad director that outlined the offer, which we had twenty-four hours to accept or reject. He explained the process in chilling detail: falsified deaths, new identities, and isolated lives far away from everything and everyone we had ever known, including our daughter, Leah.

"I'll need to discuss this with my wife," I said.

An awkward silence settled between us as I lifted my teacup. The faint clink of porcelain betrayed the tremor in my hand. My gaze drifted to the half-eaten cookie on the plate. Appetite had abandoned me long before the tea cooled.

He leaned back in his chair, studying me in that calculating way of his, as if weighing my resolve.

"That's fair," he replied finally, his voice measured but sharp enough to slice through my thoughts. Then his parting words struck like a hammer, the weight of them lingering long after he stood. "Whatever you decide, remember this—you're a traitor. If you're caught, your real death will be excruciating. Especially for your wife."

Because she's a woman? Or was there something else he wasn't telling me?

Daniel had arranged for us to stay at a Mossad safe house in the hills outside Zürich as we reflected on our decision. A van was waiting for us downstairs. I returned to Colleen, collected our luggage, and parked our car in a private garage. This was the last time we would ever see Daniel and our Mercedes.

***

As the van carried us along winding roads in darkness—black sacks over our heads—we clasped hands, our communication reduced to quiet squeezes and the occasional steadying touch.

Martha, a fit military woman in black, had barked that the blindfolds were "for your safety."

Time escaped us. Eventually, the van came to a halt and our blindfolds were ripped off. We squinted as the evening light filtered in. Before us was an enormous farmhouse, a picture of rural simplicity and charm; its exterior glowed in soft golden hues, framed by the sinking sun. Beyond the house stretched fertile green fields, patches of forest, and distant silhouettes of the snowcapped Alps.

Inside, the house was rustic yet inviting, a blend of practicality and warmth that made it feel like home. Exposed wood beams, a massive stone fireplace adorned with the Star of David, and a gigantic oak dining table gave the space its character. The sharp contrast between this idyllic setting and the clandestine nature of our predicament was unsettling.

The woman, Martha, ushered us up a wooden staircase, through a shadowy hallway, and into a private room. It felt cozy with a wrought iron bed, soft linens, a desk under the window, a snug couch, and a private bathroom. The view outside was postcard-perfect, but the past weeks weighed us down.

"Dinner's at eighteen hundred," Martha informed us bluntly before disappearing into the dim corridor.

Dinner was exceptional—a meal fit for a Swiss chalet. The dishes were local and comforting: rösti, a Swiss pan-fried potato specialty; a creamy veal sauté with onions and mushrooms; and a dessert spread that included cheeses, rustic bread, fruit, and bite-sized fruit tarts with whipped cream.

Despite our exhaustion, Colleen and I savored the quiet intimacy of the meal, careful to speak only of trivial matters. She warned in a whisper that the room might be bugged, and that warning lingered like an uninvited guest at the table. Later, as we snuggled on the couch with dessert, the profound weight of our pending decision settled in. Without speaking, we both understood that we'd save the deeper conversations for tomorrow—outside, beyond the reach of potential listening devices.

By nightfall the farmhouse had cooled down and our bodies were chilled by the mountain air, so we climbed into bed under a patchwork quilt and warmed each other up. Through the night, Colleen's quiet sobs pierced the silence, and though I reached for her to give her reassurance, I knew nothing I could do would ease her anguish at leaving our daughter.

***

Sunlight streamed through the window, illuminating the room with an almost mocking serenity. Breakfast arrived on time: a hearty omelet bursting with Gruyère cheese, wild mushrooms, and chives, alongside berries, yogurt, and hot coffee and tea.

By 9:30 a.m., we were in the farmhouse's cozy living room, waiting for our follow-up meeting with Milton Hartman, the Witness Protection Program director.

Dressed in jeans and a white shirt, his long gray beard lending an air of gravitas, Hartman exuded gruff confidence. Without preamble, he launched into a detailed explanation of the WPP. Beneath the farmhouse, he revealed, was a high-tech surveillance and counterintelligence hub staffed by over ninety personnel twenty-four hours a day.

"We're the best," he declared bluntly. "Your government might be big, but we're more agile and effective. Nobody tracks or eliminates threats like we do. Once you commit, you'll safely disappear without a trace."

Colleen's resolve faltered as Hartman outlined the harsh reality of the program. Contacting Leah would be impossible. They would declare us dead to the world—killed in the Tel Aviv restaurant bombing. Even the idea of relocating Leah to the WPP wasn't promising. Hartman explained how long the process would take and questioned whether she could endure the trauma.

Their offer—a modest middle-class life in anonymity and no contact with anyone from our past—was bleak.

"We aim for invisibility," Hartman explained. "No flashy cars, no yachts, no penthouses. You blend into the crowd. That's how you survive."

Though Hartman pitched the WPP as our salvation, I couldn't shake the feeling we were being handed a death sentence with a different name.

After the meeting, I requested some fresh air. Hartman approved, cautioning us that rainy weather was in the forecast. Martha, the woman in black fatigues, pointed out a meandering path through meadows, forests, and a bridge over a bubbling river.

Away from prying ears, Colleen and I finally spoke freely.

"We can't do this," she said, trembling. "We can't let Leah think we're dead. It's cruel. It would destroy her."

I nodded, considering. "There has to be another way. A middle ground. Maybe . . ." I hesitated, glancing over at her. "Maybe we accept our death in the bombing—start a new identity but skip their rules. No Mossad oversight. No government program dictating our lives."

She stopped walking, her yellow raincoat glistening with droplets. "You mean . . . leave our past behind? Start over somewhere on our terms?"

"Yes," I replied. "We control our destiny. Florida. California. Canada. Hell, we've stashed funds—enough to build something new. Leah inherits everything we leave behind. And she knows the truth, even if she can't say it out loud."

Colleen's expression softened, but I could see the unspoken questions in her eyes. How would we pull this off? Could we stay hidden without the support of Mossad intelligence? Most importantly, could we return to North America without passports and under constant threat?

***

Back at the farmhouse, lunch awaited us: a hearty vegetable soup served with Swiss Gruyère cubes, followed by Älplermagronen, a classic Swiss alpine macaroni dish paired with applesauce.

Seated at the table with Milton Hartman, I steered the conversation's tone.

"First," I began, "thank you for your government's generous hospitality and protection. We are grateful Israel has our backs, but"—Hartman raised an eyebrow, sensing where this was going—"we can't accept Mossad's terms as they stand."

Colleen looked down as I outlined an alternative plan.

"We'll give you only the classified communiqués we've got on FIST—tying the President of the United States and the First Secretary of the Communist Party of the Soviet Union to this rogue pact. But on one condition: you provide us with falsified death certificates stating that we died in the Tel Aviv bombing and smuggle us back to North America."

Hartman's piercing gaze scrutinized me. His bearded face gave little away, but I felt the weight of his analysis.

"Forget the witness protection program," I continued. "We'll vanish on our own terms. No WPP handlers. No Mossad oversight. In exchange, you get the evidence that FIST exists to leverage however you see fit."

Hartman leaned back, swiping a hand over his beard. "You're asking for a lot. But international diplomacy values information above all else. I'll admit we can conveniently manufacture your death." He paused. "If we do this, you're on your own. No more favors. No protection if something goes wrong."

Colleen and I nodded. "Understood."

As Hartman and I shook hands, I felt Colleen's fingers grip mine under the table. A tear rolled down her cheek, though her expression held firm. This choice was hard, but it granted us freedom and hope.

***

In the middle of the night, like the sound of a gunshot, my phone pinged, startling us awake.

Leah texted:

I'm OK. Be safe!

The next day, Colleen and I exchanged low, tense words amid a flurry of logistics. Hartman had vanished after we struck our deal because he needed to set the plans in motion. Martha appeared with a large DNA extraction kit. She pulled hair follicles from the backs of our necks, took oral swabs and fingernail clippings, and scraped skin from our feet and legs. She sealed each sample in a test tube, labeled it, and returned it to the kit box. They would use these DNA samples to fabricate evidence that we died in the bombing.

Colleen and I spent the rest of the day secluded in our room, planning our next steps: our new identities, our new home, and a bulletproof way to elude detection.

After two more days at this idyllic farm, it became more like a prison. Not being in control of our situation was frustrating. During our remaining time, Martha helped us transform our appearances with hair dyes, new haircuts, colored contact lenses, glasses, and a significant overhaul of our wardrobes.

Before dinner on the third evening, Martha knocked on our door with a steely look. She handed me a manila envelope.

"Here's a copy of the final documents required to return the remains of a deceased US citizen. Death certificates, police reports, and DNA documentation. It'll hold up to scrutiny," she said, her military precision clear in each word. "Your transport is being completed now. The plane leaves tomorrow afternoon. Hartman will brief you at dinner." She closed the door softly.

I glanced at the envelope to confirm its contents. The details were thorough: mortuary certificates, death certificates for Scott J. Barton and Colleen P. Barton issued by the Israeli Ministry of Interior, an affidavit from a funeral director, a US Embassy Report of the Death of Scott and Colleen Barton American

Citizens, DNA evidence from the crime scene, a transit permit from Tel Aviv to Washington, DC, and a pixel-blurred surveillance photo of us entering the restaurant before the bombing. It was real. Scott Barton and Colleen Barton were declared dead.

The meal was grander than its predecessors—a celebratory feast of sorts. But the dining room held a strange hush with only the two of us dining at the massive wood tables, as if others in the house were hiding.

Hartman joined us midway through the meal, resting his laptop on the table while nursing a glass of wine. He wasted no time diving straight into next-day plans. "At precisely zero nine hundred hours, you'll be transported to Zürich's private airfield. From there, a diplomatic envoy from Tel Aviv will depart for Washington, DC, with the remains of two American citizens." He looked up for a reaction.

Colleen and I stopped eating and waited for more clarification.

"We will smuggle you into the United States in two sealed caskets," Hartman explained. "You will board the plane in the cargo bay, and we will place you in the empty caskets just before landing. Martha will be with you throughout the journey to ensure the repatriation of your remains goes smoothly. If all goes well, we will release you en route to the crematorium to destroy any evidence of Mr. and Mrs. Barton. Upon your release in DC, the Israeli government will announce the discovery of the remains of two Americans in the Tel Aviv restaurant bombing. Your identities will be buried with the other bombing victims."

I faced Hartman while Colleen stared down at her plate, twisting her napkin in her lap. The only words that came to me were "Thank you."

Hartman closed his laptop with finality. "Martha will have the van pick you up just before lunch. That is, if you haven't changed your minds." He glared at us.

"We haven't," I replied evenly, though my internal doubts raged louder than ever. "Is it possible to stop at my Swiss bank on the way to the airport?" I had one million US dollars ready for pickup.

Hartman nodded.

In twenty-four hours, we would be in North America, and the Bartons, as the world knew them, would no longer exist.

13

Washington, DC

Martha bid us farewell as the black cargo van stopped in front of Washington Union Station at the intersection of Delaware Avenue and Columbus Circle. Two empty caskets, believed by all but a select few to contain our bodies, were in the back of the vehicle on their way to the crematorium. At this unremarkable yet bustling intersection, Mr. and Mrs. No-Name stood disguised, unrecognizable even to our own daughter if she walked past.

Colleen's transformation was astounding, brought on by both her intentional disguise and her unintentional loss of twenty pounds over the past month because of stress. She looked youthful and confident, sporting tight-fitting secondhand black jeans, an olive-green hoodie, and well-worn black running shoes. Chin-length auburn hair completed her new look. She even wore Ray-Bans to shield her gaze in the afternoon light. I would have struggled to recognize her myself if I hadn't known her my entire life.

My transformation was just as jarring. My hair was now ultra-short on the sides and styled in a casual crew cut on top. I wore clear black-rimmed glasses and a week-old scruffy beard that gave me a rugged appearance. Although I hadn't lost as much weight as Colleen, the leaner version of me, dressed in thrift-shop blue jeans, a black hoodie, and unbranded black running shoes, felt unfamiliar. The dependable backpack, slung over my shoulder, contained one million in US cash. We had filled our other military-style olive-green duffel bag with more unassuming secondhand clothes.

The roar of traffic paused, leaving a fleeting gap in the endless stream of vehicles.

I caught Colleen's eye and made a subtle nod. "Let's go," I said.

Without hesitation, we darted across the street and into the train station. Our destination: New York City.

Though not the NYC with the glittering skyline or the familiar warmth of our designer condo overlooking Central Park. That chapter was closed. Instead, we were bound for Brooklyn—cheap, practical, and devoid of ties to our previous lives. Colleen had worked her usual magic—she was undeniably skilled at this sort of thing. She managed to find a modest hotel near the Brooklyn train station that didn't question cash payments.

Onboard the train, we found two seats a few rows apart from others, privacy becoming our most precious luxury. From whispered conversations that masked nervous glances, our focus narrowed onto Leah. While building new identities was essential for our survival, nothing felt more urgent than reaching her before anyone else—authorities, lawyers, or the media—could deliver the devastating news of our "deaths."

"We can't leave her in the dark," Colleen murmured, her voice trembling but resolute.

I nodded. Our priority was clear: crafting a plan to reunite our family . . . before the window of opportunity slammed shut.

14

Brooklyn

When we arrived at Moynihan Train Hall at Penn Station in New York City, exhaustion had wrapped around us like a heavy blanket. The clock on my watch read 3:42 p.m. Hunger pangs consumed my stomach, but I couldn't give in. We wandered around Eighth Avenue until we found a drugstore, where we bought a thousand dollars' worth of prepaid credit cards and a fifty-dollar Amazon gift card. Then, we found an electronics store where we traded our laptops, iPads, and phones for brand-new ones, and purchased new SIM cards for our burner phones.

I hailed a cab and gave the driver directions to our hotel on Third Avenue and President Street in Brooklyn.

At any moment, we were expecting the media to report our untimely deaths in Tel Aviv. We needed to contact Leah to tell her we had survived. We also wanted her to fly to New York to see us. We assumed she would continue to be under surveillance until our trail went ice cold. So, no digital communication was possible. We'd already breached that by contacting her through Professor Bruce Manning after the bombing. Hopefully, he wouldn't connect the time I contacted him and the date of the restaurant bombing. Otherwise, he'd spoken to a ghost. Colleen suggested we send a letter via snail mail. I had a better idea.

As soon as we arrived at the hotel room, I booted up my new laptop, connected to the hotel's Wi-Fi, and set up a new address and VPN. I went straight to Amazon to open a new account. In the Amazon search bar, I typed *cat books*. I chose a hardcover book titled *My Book of Cats*. Unsurprisingly, pictures of cats and kittens adorned the cover. After a few clicks, I added Leah's address and the Amazon gift card information. Before clicking the PROCESS ORDER button, I selected the gift option to include a message with the book. This is where my unused poetic creativity shone.

While Toby is gone, we are here.
We need to be united, my dear.

3 questions will reveal the way:
The day Toby magically came to stay.
The trips to Cabos that you have made.
The lives Toby's had, from cradle to shade.

Combine #s in order; the answer ignited,
And in 12 days (Thu), we'll be united.

You guessed it. Toby was a cat. He was a gift for Leah's eighth birthday on the fifteenth of May. To our regret, she had never been to Los Cabos, so zero. The last clue was a number known only to the three of us. We always said Toby'd had just five lives, not nine, because he moved only five times with us before he passed away. Combining the numbers in order—15, 0, and 5—you have United Flight 1505 from LAX to EWR. I signed up for a three-month Prime trial to get next-day delivery. If everything went as planned, we would pick her up on Thursday afternoon at Newark Liberty International Airport in New Jersey from flight UA 1505.

In the box labeled FROM: I had misspelled *Us* as *Ua* in case Leah missed the "United" references. I didn't think she would.

As I pressed PROCESS ORDER and the confirmation appeared, I exclaimed, "The cat is out of the bag!"

I couldn't help but grin. We would reach Leah.

In just thirteen days, we would see our daughter again. This would give enough time for her to wrap up exams, for the authorities to notify her of our unfortunate deaths, and for our lawyers to probate our wills.

And Colleen and I could fade away—erased, untraceable, and reborn.

The hotel room was small, cheap, and forgettable—just what we needed after twenty hours of playing ghosts on a plane and train. The wallpaper peeled in places, but the bed was there, an oasis for two souls on the run.

Colleen had spoken little since we arrived, maybe contemplating our future. I could see weariness etching itself into her features as she emerged from a hot shower, with hair wet and a towel covering her body, and sat on the edge of the bed. Her shoulders slumped, the tension easing as she exhaled.

I sat beside her, wrapping my arms around her. "We're going to be fine."

The weight of our actions crushed us. We'd left everything behind, retaining a catalog of memories reserved only for each other: our home, our names, and our lives. Yet hope flickered beneath exhaustion and uncertainty. Possibility intertwined with fear, and we existed in a future we vowed to share.

"What now?" she murmured, her voice barely audible as the room's heating unit kicked in.

"Now," I replied quietly, tugging her toward the bed, "we rest. Tomorrow, we figure out who we're going to be from scratch."

She lay back beside me, and the world melted away as exhaustion overcame us both. The hum of traffic outside faded, replaced by the peculiar silence of two people on the brink of reinvention. Somewhere beyond this room, our old lives burned to ash. But here, in the cocoon of the nondescript hotel room, amid fraying sheets and four walls no one else would remember, we were about to begin again.

As my eyes closed, I felt the future waiting for us, unknown and uncertain—just as we wanted.

***

I woke up in an empty bed at the depressing hotel. Looking at the clock, I saw the time flash: 8:39 a.m. Maybe Colleen had gone out for breakfast or coffee—one of her slight gestures to combat the jet lag we still hadn't shaken. Rolling over, I let my eyes drift shut again, hoping the extra minutes of rest would help.

By 10:00 a.m., I grew concerned. Dragging myself out of bed, I wandered to the bathroom, catching my reflection in the mirror. The face staring back at me—altered, unfamiliar—shocked me and stopped me in my tracks.

Only at almost four did I hear a key scrape in the lock and the door groan open.

Colleen stepped inside, her face lit up with an enormous grin. "It's official," she announced, holding up a manila envelope like a trophy. "We are now Mr. John Miller and Mrs. Mary Miller."

"Where the hell were you?" I said after waiting for her for seven hours.

She hadn't realized the pain she had put me through with her disappearance. She sat beside me with an apologetic smile. "Sorry, my love, I lost track of time. But I have good news." She kissed me on my cheek and handed me the manila envelope as a makeup gift.

Inside was a collection of documents revealing our new names and detailed profiles of who we had become. I thumbed through them in disbelief.

> ***John M. Miller***
> ***Birth:*** *March 4, 1962, Rumney, New Hampshire. Currently 61 years old.*
> ***Career:*** *Carpenter turned entrepreneur. John worked as a general contractor for nearly two decades before founding Miller Landscaping alongside his wife. The business offered premium services in outdoor design, regularly catering to an affluent clientele across the Granite State. His entrepreneurial spirit led him to branch into real estate restoration projects, flipping older properties after upgrading them with his hands-on talent and attention to detail.*
> ***Backstory:*** *John is known for his rugged charm, entrepreneurial drive, and uncanny ability to spin elaborate, humorous backstories for the Civil War*

treasures he collects. His openness and knack for storytelling made him beloved in the Rumney community. He is a proud handyman, a terrible singer, and a karaoke enthusiast, with songs like "My Way," "A Wonderful World," and "Bohemian Rhapsody."

Mary A. (Wagner) Miller
Birth: *July 23, 1967, Somerville, Massachusetts. Currently 55 years old.*
Career: *Real estate professional turned business partner. After graduating from secretarial school and earning her real estate license, Mary spent years working with buyers and sellers to close prestigious deals. Later, she managed operations and client relationships for the couple's Miller Landscaping business, easily balancing her administrative skills with her warm, approachable demeanor. She also built a successful reputation in Rumney, juggling part-time jobs at Plymouth State University and the local village store to maintain her connection with the community.*
Backstory: *Mary's charm lies in her unyielding positivity, her natural empathy, and her uplifting spirit, which she carries into every role she undertakes. She is kind, nurturing, and always on the*

move—the "Energizer Bunny" with a love for antiques and a heart full of optimism. No stranger to the karaoke stage, her go-to songs are from Pearl Jam.

I stared at the documents in my hands, flipping through the flawless IDs, birth certificates, driver's licenses, passports, and other paperwork. Every detail, from the signatures to the raised seals and embossed textures, looked real enough to pass even the closest scrutiny. Beyond that, the backstories were rich narratives, crafted to slip seamlessly into any casual conversation.

"Seven hours," I muttered, shaking my head in disbelief as I skimmed over the familiar-yet-unfamiliar names. "How did you even pull this off?"

Colleen smirked and handed me a cup of tea, her green eyes gleaming with quiet satisfaction. "Let's just say . . . I know people, AI, and places."

Although she didn't elaborate, I knew what she meant. The new names and identities hadn't materialized out of thin air. Somewhere in the depths of the dark web, Colleen had found them: real people whose lives had come to an abrupt end.

Colleen pulled one last sheet of paper out of the envelope I was holding. She handed me an image of a news article from Plymouth, New Hampshire dated two days ago:

Husband, Wife Killed in Crash

Police said the driver, John Miller, 61, of Rumney, lost control of the Jeep Cherokee, veering left and crashing into the trees about 15 feet off the road. The crash also killed his wife, Mary Miller, 55.

Below the brief article was a photo of John and Mary in happier times. It was scary how closely we resembled them, especially after our makeover. Deep somewhere in the pit of my stomach, guilt twisted against necessity. Borrowing lives from the dead was inherently wrong. Yet in our world now, morality had become a luxury we could no longer afford. We weren't stealing who they were; we continued to be who we needed to be.

Colleen watched me as I wrestled with the weight of it. Her voice cut through the silence, soft yet firm. "No family, no connections. They were good people who won't be forgotten . . ." She leaned closer to touch my arm. "But we're doing this for Leah. For us. The world. And for now, these lives—they're our second chance."

I hesitated as I slid the documents back into the envelope. I didn't have the luxury of hesitation anymore, just as I didn't have the luxury of grief or sentimentality.

rs. Miller," I said, closing the envelope with final-
elt foreign in my mouth but resolute in purpose. "Let's finish what we started."

And with that, we each became someone else, bound not by the lives we'd led but by the futures we were fighting to save. But I wondered again, who was this woman I was living with?

***

Thursday afternoon, we melded into the airport's arrivals section—people surged, friends and family embraced, and frantic travelers seized luggage from the moving conveyor belts. The churning energy of it all was bafflingly calming for two fugitives like us, giving us a sense of anonymity in plain sight. But as we stood there, an unsettling thought crossed my mind: Were we being reckless by inviting Leah into our mess? Could she bring trouble with her?

We hoped that news of our "deaths" had closed our open files with both the Russians and the Americans. If the plan worked as intended, neither agency would have any reason to pursue us—or Leah—any further. Still, seeing her again meant taking on a risk we couldn't calculate.

Then we saw her—standing right by her flight's baggage carousel, scanning the crowd. Even in the surrounding frenzy, Leah stood out with her blonde hair, radiance, and self-assurance. She was as beautiful as her mother had been at her age. She wore a yellow blazer, a white blouse, and skinny jeans. Her appearance embodied that of a confident, modern young woman.

Colleen and I stood apart, far enough to avoid drawing attention, both of us still cautious and hyperaware of every shadow around us. Ever the actress, my wife enacted her part in the next phase of the plan with dramatic flair. She stopped a young man walking by and, before he could protest, thrust a piece of paper into his hand.

"Can you give this to the woman in the yellow jacket over there?" she asked, motioning toward Leah by the conveyor belt.

He looked confused, unsure whether to comply.

Colleen, never one to dwell on hesitation, blurted, "My car is being towed. I don't have time to explain!"

The man blinked, pocketed his curiosity, and turned in Leah's direction as Colleen vanished into the crowd before he could think twice.

Watching it unfold, I had to admire my wife's quick improvisation.

The man obeyed and walked over to Leah. "Excuse me," he said, pointing vaguely in the direction where Colleen had disappeared. "A woman asked me to give this to you." He handed her the small folded note.

Leah, looking perplexed, thanked him as he wandered off, his helpful deed completed. Spotting her luggage on the conveyor belt, she grabbed it and rushed away to examine the scrawled message.

> *Go to "Ride App Pick Up" and look for a white Toyota Corolla Hybrid with license plate LSH-5040. It's there to pick you up.*

A few minutes later, Colleen was vibrating with anticipation in the back seat of the car we'd rented from a peer-to-peer service. I was in the driver's seat, gripping the wheel and scanning the scene through the rearview mirror. The anxiety of waiting was palpable; every passing second felt like an eternity.

"There she is!" Colleen snapped, spotting Leah before I did.

I maneuvered the car forward like a typical aggressive New York driver, nudging out other vehicles to slide toward the curb.

Leah recognized the car, then her sharp eyes caught the license plate and she stepped forward with her bag.

With the remote, I opened the trunk and then watched her toss in the luggage and close the lid with precision.

When she opened the back door, Colleen couldn't contain herself. She pulled Leah inside and wrapped her in a fierce hug, whispering "It's okay, baby, it's us!" as if it were a prayer.

Meanwhile, I hit the gas and speedily merged into traffic, driving like everyone else in New York City: as if I were a getaway driver. Every few minutes, Colleen looked behind us to ensure no unusual vehicles were following.

Teary questions, choked-out answers, bursts of nervous laughter, and plenty of stolen glances filled the ride from the airport, as if none of us could believe we were actually reunited.

When we were safe in our modest hotel room, relief settling over us like a sudden warm blanket, I poured drinks: a scotch for Colleen, a glass of white wine for Leah, and club soda for me—someone needed a clear head.

"To Toby," I said, raising my glass to our beloved cat, who had been a central fixture of our family long before these chaotic days. The toast felt poignant, perhaps because it reminded us of the life we'd left behind.

Colleen and I tag-teamed the story of our escape from Los Cabos, Toronto, Tel Aviv, Limassol, Vienna, and Zürich to New York. We spun the harrowing tale with dramatic precision, leaving out any mention of the FIST pact and specific, unspeakable details that might frighten her—not even Colleen knew the entire truth, or at least I thought she didn't.

By midnight, Leah's exhaustion overwhelmed her, her sleepless flight and the emotional weight of the reunion bearing down on her. While I unfolded the sofa bed and transformed it into a makeshift sleeper, Colleen gathered sheets from the closet to make it comfortable.

We hugged Leah good night, holding her longer and tighter than we ever had in years past. "We love you," we told her, words that felt powerful because they had always gone unsaid. In the morning, we would sit her down and introduce her to Mr. and Mrs. Miller, telling her everything she needed to know about our new lives.

***

I slipped out before sunrise to grab pastries and gourmet coffee from a nearby bakery. When I returned, Colleen was sitting in bed, her legs crossed and a book in her hands, while Leah was still fast asleep on the sofa bed. In the tranquility, I noted how much time we had lost with our daughter—years of burying ourselves in our careers. Colleen had been flying around the globe chasing NGO stories of heartbreak and devastation, while I'd been chasing rare metals and the next big mining deal. Nannies and prep schools had shouldered much of the weight of raising Leah.

After Colleen stopped working, she had at least attempted to reconnect with Leah, to build that cherished mother–daughter bond. I'd stayed on autopilot, pursuing financial wealth and neglecting my role as a father. And now, here she was. Our twenty-five-year-old sleeping beauty had endured a litany of struggles, from depression, drug addiction, and toxic relationships to an unwanted pregnancy and abortion. Against all odds, she was weeks away from graduating with a master's degree from UCLA, having clawed her way from the bottom on her own, save for the checks we wrote. She deserved a better father, I thought sadly.

Around ten o'clock, Leah stirred awake, rubbing her eyes and sitting up.

"Good morning," I said, trying to sound nonchalant, though my heart swelled at the sight of her.

She greeted me half asleep, grabbed some clothes from her suitcase, and disappeared into the bathroom. Fifteen minutes later, she reemerged, now dressed in a black T-shirt and yesterday's jeans. Everything in her demeanor screamed discomfort.

Her eyes swept the room, and her brow furrowed. "Why are you in such a dump?"

I ignored the question, gesturing toward the coffee and pastries. "I got you some breakfast," I said casually. "Let's go for a walk. We're just blocks from Prospect Park. It'll allow us to explain part two of our story."

Leah shrugged, accepting the coffee and following us out the door.

The explosion of spring greenery in Prospect Park was a dramatic contrast against the city's grayscale monotony. The air was alive with the mingling sounds of chirping birds, rustling leaves, and the bubbling laughter of children. We followed a winding path into a secluded wooded section of the park, where sunlight filtered in through the canopy above us.

Colleen explained how she had crafted the Miller identities. Her storytelling was a seamless byproduct of practice and nerves of steel. She recounted the backstory with a poise and authenticity that might have fooled even me if I hadn't known better. When I had to explain my fabricated life, I stammered, while Colleen interjected now and then to correct details.

"So, how did you two meet?" Leah asked with a playful glint in her deep-blue eyes.

Colleen and I both stared at her, stunned.

"Good question," I replied, slightly amused and with the hope Colleen would rescue me.

"We haven't worked out that part of our new lives yet," Colleen admitted with a grin.

"Do you have kids?" Leah asked, quieter this time.

Colleen murmured, "Unfortunately, no children."

Leah's playful smile faded, replaced by a look of sadness that struck me to the core. "So, where does that leave me?" Her voice trembled despite her usual stoicism.

We stopped walking and sat on a nearby bench. Leah sat between us, her head lowered, and for a moment, it felt as though the weight of the entire world rested on her small shoulders.

"You will always be our daughter," Colleen said gently, taking Leah's arm.

I looked her in the eye as I spoke. "We'll need to be careful in how we interact with you, at least for now. The world believes we're dead, and as far as anyone else is concerned, you are our sole heir. You'll inherit all our assets. I'll help you navigate the legalities, but we'll live in two distinct worlds. Your mother and I will have to simplify our lives. No penthouses, no designer everything, no extravagant luxuries." I paused. "But we're still here, Leah. We're not disappearing."

Colleen leaned in, wrapping Leah in a warm embrace. "We love you," she whispered, her voice full of sincerity.

I joined the hug, pulling them both close. "We'll figure this out together," I promised.

Nodding, Leah sniffed back tears, the glint in her blue eyes returning as she stood up, brushed off her jeans, and walked over to a middle-aged black man sitting on a bench across from us.

What is she doing? I thought as she engaged in a quick conversation with the man.

Returning with a lit cigarette between her fingers, she took a long drag and slowly exhaled to calm her nerves. "Well," she said, attempting humor. "Is all this walking making anyone else hungry?"

Colleen smiled and linked her arm with Leah's as she took a deep inhale of Leah's cigarette. "How about a hot dog?" she asked. We stood and headed toward a nearby cart.

15

Manhattan

The following days were quiet but still active. Leah had taken on her new role as the executor of our estate, and although Colleen and I guided her in the background, helping her navigate the lingo, acronyms, and legalese, we marveled at the level of savvy and professionalism she displayed while managing the financial advisors, accountants, and attorneys with an expertise that belied her years, ensuring none of them took advantage of her naivety in such matters.

Meanwhile, Colleen began scouting for a more permanent place to call home. After much deliberation, Leah held onto our Manhattan condo for herself. Though excessive for one person, she deemed it a valuable long-term investment.

On Friday morning, I left our hotel to meet with Leah at the condo to walk her through the estate's portfolio, its market values, the intricacies of the investments, and the global network of accounts we'd established. We had designed our holdings' structure to minimize government taxation and interference. Now, transferring that wealth to Leah required minimizing losses to taxes and opportunistic intermediaries.

As my cab neared Manhattan Tower, I looked up at the massive 1,550-foot structure that seemed to disappear into the sky. The building held the distinction of being the world's tallest residential tower. Within its over one hundred floors was a world of luxurious living: a high-end department store on the main level, both indoor and outdoor pools on the fifteenth floor with a state-of-the-art fitness center and spa. The top floor boasted a three-star Michelin restaurant, ballroom, and cigar lounge. Convenience and opulence converged in the tower; leaving was unnecessary. Leah always called the apartment the Bird's Nest.

I arrived a bit earlier than planned, so I grabbed a coffee for Leah and a green tea for me from the coffee shop across the street. Since Leah had inherited my passcode and key fob, they still granted me access to the garage, the elevator, and the apartment, I made my way inside.

I pressed the elevator's Up button and was relieved when the doors sprang open. With the fob in hand, I selected the eighty-fourth floor. As the elevator climbed, my mind wandered to the countless times I'd ridden up that same shaft, burdened with to-do lists and pressing concerns. Tension gripped my body until the ding signaling my floor broke the spell. A wave of clarity swept over me: I had nothing left to conquer, prove, or react to. I stepped out onto the floor feeling free from the confines of the capitalist society that had once dictated the rhythm of my life.

When I entered the condo, destruction assaulted me. The scene before me looked as if either law enforcement or a thief had torn the place apart searching for evidence or treasure. The pungent smell of stale cigarette smoke mingled with the unmistakable odor of marijuana. It didn't take long to piece together the truth—Leah had thrown a party.

Party didn't seem an adequate term for the chaos. Red wine stained the carpets. Glasses and beer cans littered every visible surface. Men's and women's shoes lay tangled underfoot. The furniture and cushions were disheveled, and pizza boxes cluttered the kitchen counters. The condo resembled the aftermath of a frat house that had gone wild, not the elegant home it had been.

I felt my pulse quicken and forced myself to take several deep breaths before venturing farther into the apartment. Down the hallway toward the bedrooms, discarded clothing formed a trail—shirts, bras, pants. As I passed the guest bedrooms, I glimpsed sleeping bodies sprawled across and beside beds, in varying states of dress. Some were fully clothed, whereas others were nude or only in their underwear.

When I reached the master bedroom, the sight was similar. Five figures lay tangled in the sheets, Leah among them. Feeling overwhelmed, I returned to the kitchen to sip my tea and try to quiet the urge to scream at the top of my lungs, *Get out of my house! Now!*

But it wasn't my house anymore. Technically, Leah wasn't my daughter, and to the people in that condo, I was nothing more than an unwelcome intruder—a ghost.

I scribbled a note addressed to Leah, propped it against the coffeemaker alongside the cup of coffee I'd brought for her, and left. I waited for her call.

Later that day, Leah reached out to me with a sheepish apology for the scene I'd walked into. I accepted her apology, and we never spoke of the incident again. I didn't tell Colleen—not because I wanted to shield Leah from judgment but because it wouldn't have mattered.

Despite moments like this, Leah remained a young woman thrust into overwhelming responsibility. Repeatedly, she rose to the challenges with unyielding determination.

Over the course of the next week, Leah orchestrated the sale of our vacation home and arranged for the donation of my beloved car collection. She oversaw the auctioning of high-value artwork and several of Colleen's jewelry pieces.

With every step, Colleen and I saw a strength that had always been in Leah but that we had failed to recognize before because of her rebel attitude.

For the first time in years, I felt a sense of pride—not for the tasks she had completed, but for the person she was becoming.

Leah was our legacy. No matter the name we lived under now, she would carry forward all that we had built.

16

Manhattan

Having lost my network of influential friends in strategic positions around the world, it took me two weeks of constant calling and emailing under my guise as an author to secure even a single face-to-face meeting with someone at the NGO Branch of the United Nations Economic and Social Council, known as ECOSOC.

Meanwhile, Leah had flown back to Los Angeles to pack up her life and move into our Manhattan Tower apartment on West Fifty-Seventh Street on the infamous Billionaires' Row.

Standing in the lobby of the United Nations Secretariat Building on Manhattan's East Side, I adjusted my new dark-blue suit, trying to shake the sense of being an impostor. What did I know about NGOs beyond the pain they caused industries like mine? Over the years, I'd hated their anti-progress rhetoric, often rooted in selective truths twisted into public relations assaults. They were obstacles to innovation.

Taking a deep breath, I forced myself to remember why I was there. The purpose outweighed my biases. How far removed I felt from my conversation in Vienna with Professor Röhrlich, who'd hinted at shadowy rumors: Russian and American intelligence agencies supporting NGOs as tools for global manipulation behind the scenes. As incredible as it seemed, I needed answers.

My meeting was with Ming-Zhu Chang, an assistant director at the NGO Branch. After passing through layers of security and escorts, I entered a small meeting room on the twenty-fifth floor. The view was striking—expansive and vivid—looking down on East River, Long Island City, and the bustling boats below. For a moment, the dance of commerce and life playing out on the water mesmerized me. I didn't even notice when someone entered the room.

"You can get lost watching the city like that, can't you?" said a woman, breaking my trance.

Startled, I turned to find a tall, slender Asian woman in her early forties with a disarming smile.

She extended her hand. "Hi, I'm Ming-Zhu Chang."

"John Miller," I replied, shaking it firmly.

"Ah, the author," she remarked, glancing at her notepad. "Please have a seat."

As I settled into the chair, I loosened my tight tie. "Thank you for taking the time. I know you're extremely busy."

"We are all busy, Mr. Miller."

"Please call me John."

"All right, John," she said with a slight smile. "What can I assist you with today?"

I dove straight in, aware of the limited time. "ECOSOC works with nearly seven thousand NGOs globally. How does your organization ensure that none are corrupt or politically motivated to create instability, disruption, civil disobedience, or worse?"

She giggled. "You don't start with simple questions, do you?"

I stayed silent, awaiting her actual answer.

"While we can't entirely control what NGOs do, our accreditation process and compliance monitoring screen out organizations that deviate from United Nations values."

"Does this process include a detailed investigation of their funding sources?"

"Indeed. To qualify for consultative status, NGOs must disclose their sources of funding. A significant majority of their money must come independently of governments—from national affiliates, individual donors, or private groups. We also require regular activity reports."

It appeared as though she had taken her response straight from an ECOSOC brochure.

"So," I pressed, "has the UN ever uncovered cases where 'dark money'—undisclosed or covert funding—has flowed into NGOs, whether from governments or special interest groups, for ulterior motives?"

Her smile faltered, if only for a moment. "The UN's NGO Committee has, from time to time, recommended revoking consultative status for organizations that cannot meet our standards. The member states thoroughly review the complaints before they make it to the Economic and Social Council for a decision."

"No complaints connected to politically destabilizing activities or funding, right? Or what I called dark money?"

"Well... I've never encountered such a complaint. But I cannot speak to every case."

Her tone made it clear she was holding to official lines. Phrases like *never encountered* and *cannot speak to* were noncommittal safety nets. I sensed the stone wall wouldn't crumble.

I tried one last push. "There are rumors alleging that significant NGOs—funded by billions of dollars—are exacerbating conflicts around the world under the guise of humanitarian aid. Have you heard, perhaps unofficially, of any organization matching that description?"

"No," she answered abruptly, as though the question didn't need consideration.

The edge in my voice sharpened before I could stop it. "There are reports of millions slaughtered—women, children—and you're telling me you've never even heard a whisper?"

If my tone alarmed her, she didn't betray it. Instead, she remained calm as she replied, "Mr. Miller, I assure you that ECOSOC would vehemently oppose and condemn such atrocities. NGOs with consultative status are accountable to United Nations values and standards."

"Of course," I murmured, my frustration only partially masked. It was clear I would get nothing more from Ms. Chang. "I appreciate your thoughtful answers," I added, standing.

"Not at all," she replied, her expression briefly stunned by the abruptness of the meeting's conclusion. But she quickly recovered and gestured toward the door. "Let me show you out."

She leaned closer to me as we walked down the quiet hallway, away from the buzzing offices and probable listening devices. Her voice dropped to a faint whisper. "There's been one rumor. An NGO in Canada."

"Canada?" I stopped, confused. "What would Canada have to do with anything?"

The elevator pinged open as if on cue. Ming-Zhu Chang ushered me inside before I could ask more questions. "Goodbye, Mr. Miller," she said firmly but without breaking her composure.

The doors slid shut. I stood there in silence, holding on to one fragmented clue. It seemed I was about to embark on a wild Canadian goose chase, so to speak.

17

Brooklyn

Colleen and I moved into a newly renovated "Classic 6" apartment with modern design features. Though the mismatched furniture didn't suit our style, it felt like a temporary haven on a budget. In a historic Art Deco building along Brooklyn's Eastern Parkway, it bordered cultural gems like Prospect Park and the renowned Brooklyn Museum.

Using the privacy of my new office, I began researching Canadian NGOs. Narrowing my search to larger organizations, only two stood out: CARE and the Global Relief Foundation. The latter, GRF, was Colleen's former employer. My pulse quickened. I couldn't shake the gut feeling that GRF fit the profile of what I was looking for.

My research exposed nothing suspicious in their official annual reports and financial statements. However, a surprising link emerged after hours of cross-referencing keywords related to funding and ties to the US and Russia. A WikiLeaks document contained an encrypted spreadsheet linked to US government payments to agencies, associations, and NGOs. Buried among the rows was an unambiguous line: GRF | $525,654,771 | 2017.

The US government had funded GRF in 2017 with $525 million. If Russia had contributed the same, GRF coffers could surpass $1 billion annually.

A knock on the door startled me, and I snapped my laptop shut. My heart raced as Colleen walked in.

"Hey, lunch is ready. You've been in here all morning."

"Right," I muttered, following her into the kitchen, avoiding her probing gaze.

***

When Colleen graduated from law school at the top of her class three years after me, she was the high achiever everyone had expected her to be, with offers flooding in from the most prestigious law firms. She worked at one of the largest firms in the country, diving headlong into the competitive world of corporate law. Her brilliance shone, but over time the relentless hours and cutthroat environment took their toll. I watched her enthusiasm wane as the work drained her. The pursuit of wealth at all costs, devoid of a meaningful purpose, eroded the spark in her eyes.

After six years on this crushing professional treadmill, Colleen walked away. She prioritized something far more profound—our growing family. Leah's birth marked a turning point, a chance to redirect her life in a way that aligned with her values. Her decision to stay home for those early years brought calm and joy back into our lives. We fell into a lopsided rhythm as I was neck-deep in building Aurora Earth Ex. She poured her heart into motherhood. I threw myself into work, providing money but not providing in ways that mattered emotionally. I attributed any strain in our marriage to this imbalance, with me being absent and her feeling overwhelmed.

As Leah grew older and more independent, Colleen yearned for a purpose that extended beyond our home. Slowly, she transitioned into legal advisory work for nonprofits, a decision that brought her to the GRF. It seemed like the perfect marriage of her legal acumen and moral compass—an outlet where she could fight for humanitarian causes on a global stage. What I didn't realize then was that GRF didn't just give her purpose—it consumed her.

Colleen rocketed up the ranks. Within a few years, she became the head of GRF's legal department, and like with the law firm she had left behind, the job's demands followed her home. But this time, it wasn't late-night depositions or board member squabbles—it was geopolitical crises. For a decade, Colleen traveled relentlessly , dropping into hotspots fraught with conflict: Syria, the Balkans, sub-Saharan Africa. Wherever human suffering was at its most acute, she was there.

At first, she framed her assignments as "legal evaluations" or "policy-related discussions." But her missions became more secretive. I noticed that she was reserved upon her returns. Eventually, her absences extended into weeks at a time. When I asked about her travel plans or work, her voice would waver. The strain of the job had taken its toll, both psychologically and physically. She gained weight, drank in secret, and withdrew into herself, though she tried to appear strong around Leah. I often wondered if she was carrying more than the burden of her work. Was it guilt? Or something else completely? There seemed to be an inner demon working to destroy her slowly.

***

August 18, 2014. The summer day was ordinary, yet I will never forget it. Colleen arrived home unannounced that afternoon, pulling the suitcase she had taken on a rushed mission to Syria. Her pale face betrayed nothing more than exhaustion. Before I could even ask how her trip had gone, she said, "I quit." Her voice was flat, unceremonious. The weight of those two words hung in the air, striking me harder than any fight we'd ever had.

She left the room before I could press her for more details, but later that evening the TV filled in some blanks. News networks were ablaze with footage of an American reporter's brutal execution at the hands of ISIS, the masked executioner menacingly explaining that the young man's death was revenge for US airstrikes in Iraq. My stomach churned. Were the reporter's killers the men Colleen had met with weeks earlier in Syria, trying, as she had put it before, to "bridge the humanitarian divide"?

Later, I noticed her wiping tears when she thought no one was looking. She would never speak of that trip or why she had chosen that precise moment to quit GRF. But I couldn't escape the connection I'd made: Colleen had been doing something she could no longer square with her conscience—or her soul.

I wanted to believe that she finally stepped away because she'd reached her moral limits. But what if more was at stake? What if she'd realized that her work at GRF was what I suspected it to be—a weapon of influence, a tool wielded by puppet masters with agendas far darker than humanitarian aid?

For weeks after her resignation, Colleen retreated into herself. She avoided questions about Syria, the GRF, and anything else. And if I pushed, the wall she'd put up only grew higher. I'd chalked it up to burnout. But now, sitting in our Brooklyn apartment with damning evidence on my laptop, I wondered, *Did she already know?*

Flipping back through my mental timeline, a horrifying pattern emerged. Wherever Colleen went during her time with GRF, devastation often followed. Political uprisings gained momentum. Did her presence ignite civil wars? Was it her actions that left entire nations in a state of destabilization? Could it all be a coincidence? With my legal training, my natural inclination was to dismiss leaps in logic and demand solid evidence. But this was too much to ignore.

Then, the money emerged. The trail I found in that WikiLeaks document linked $525 million of US government funding to GRF annually. How could Colleen, with her sharp legal mind, not have seen it? Or had she been too deep in the GRF's operations to have a choice? The questions multiplied, as did the sickening realization that my wife's work may not have been misguided—it could have been complicit.

Now, I faced an impossible decision. Should I confront her and risk fracturing the fragile peace we'd built since her resignation? Or should I keep digging, unraveling the truth until I was sure?

For the first time in years, I felt fear. I feared not what I might uncover, but the woman I might discover my wife to be.

18

Brooklyn

I took a long, deliberate evening walk in Prospect Park, hoping the stillness of nature would untangle the web of thoughts spinning through my mind. The rustling of leaves and the occasional bark of a dog offered a brief respite from the relentless mental chase. Yet as much as I longed for the carefree hours of walking along the beach in Los Cabos, I recognized how alive I felt now, in the thick tangle of discovery.

For too many years, I'd mined the earth, searching for rare minerals deep beneath the surface. But tonight, and over the last few months, I'd been digging for something far rarer—the truth. In a world drowning in misinformation and falsehoods, truth gleams more valuable than gold or diamonds.

When I returned to the apartment, I found Colleen flipping pages of yet another romance novel to lull herself to sleep. She gave me a warm, knowing smile before disappearing into her fictional world. I could tell she was deliberately creating space for me, for my restless mind.

The walk had reinvigorated my focus. As I slid into bed under the comforting weight of blankets, the glow of my laptop screen cast shadows on the walls. I opened the file dated 1981 to 1988.

Two handwritten notes preserved echoes of communication between two of the world's most famous leaders. A translator had rendered the first note, a letter from the last leader of the Soviet Union, addressed to the US President.

> *June 10, 1988*
> *Dear Brother,*
> *I hope this note finds you well after the Moscow Summit. I wanted to thank you personally for your visit and the progress we've made, both publicly and privately. The theatrics of Tchaikovsky's timeless performances reflect much of our own shared stage—each move calculated, each scene carefully choreographed for the audience of the world. Yet you and I know that behind those gilded curtains, it is the unseen effort that connects everything together.*
> *Our commitment to public progress on arms reduction, exemplified through the INF Treaty and other agreements, has captured the imagination*

of millions. However, it is the creative structure of FIST that deserves our private applause. Together, we have turned conflict into a carefully managed instrument, stabilizing chaos to ensure the sustained strength of Washington and Moscow alike.

Your resolve to maintain a balance between our nations while ensuring the continued progress of FIST is commendable. It has not only kept the stage alive but has provided a foundation for enduring strength and influence. In these turbulent times, it is easy to underestimate signifying our collaborations—Afghanistan, Nicaragua, Angola, and many others stand as silent yet powerful examples of how calculated instability has fortified our positions.

Your leadership in navigating the complexities of FIST ensures its continued success. As we look forward, I believe this structure will outlast even our own time on this global stage, protecting both of our nations from the unforeseen tides of history. To partnerships, cooperation, and the unseen achievements of FIST.

Thank you for continuing to inspire confidence that our joint vision shall prevail.

Please give my regards to Nancy.
Sincerely, Misha

I leaned back, considering the chosen words. FIST had not been a benign handshake between states nor a diplomatic offshoot of goodwill. No, it hinted at something sinister. A high-stakes game played in the shadows, where calculated chaos was the glue holding two incredible superpowers together.

The President of the United States sent the second note, a reply, six months later, shortly before he left the presidency.

December 12, 1988
Dear Misha,
As my time in the Oval Office ends, I reflect on the incredible journey we've shared over these past years. The world knows of our treaties, summits, and photo opportunities, but it's the work behind the scenes—the sacrifices and the shared vision—that I hold most dear.
I wanted to express my gratitude for your private and strategic support during the recent election. Bush's decisive victory not only further secures many of the policies I've worked hard to advance but also ensures the continuity of our most critical achievement—FIST. Your subtle yet deliber-

ate global actions fully realized Bush's ability to lead the American people and his understanding of how strategy thrives in controlled instability. The results will resonate throughout history. A third consecutive term for our party will solidify not only the strength of the United States but also the equilibrium FIST provides globally. Your efforts in ensuring this balance do not go unnoticed, and I am deeply appreciative.

Your foresight regarding the necessity of balance secures what we've built, and I have full faith that you will continue to protect FIST's objectives from those who would misunderstand them. As you contend with the winds of reform and the challenges of glasnost and perestroika, I hope you'll remember that Washington remains your ally—perhaps in ways many will never fully appreciate.

I will privately encourage Bush, as we transition, to preserve the delicate but powerful equilibrium we've achieved. He will learn quickly and recognize, as you and I have, how essential FIST is to maintaining order amid chaos. The invisible threads we've woven must hold strong.

Thank you again, Misha, for the silent partnership that has not only secured our nations' futures but also crafted a legacy that will touch the course of

history. You've been an indispensable collaborator and, dare I say, a trusted friend.
May we both continue to guide this symphony of diplomacy invisibly, yet purposefully, for as long as we can. My regards to Raisa and your family.
Yours with enduring respect,
RR

Both notes revealed the chilling reality of FIST: a system engineered to manipulate political instability globally, mutually to benefit Washington and Moscow. A legacy of power built on conflict, not peace.

As midnight approached, the fatigue of the day finally caught up with me. I closed my laptop with the weight of the revelations bearing down on my chest.

In the dim light of the bedroom, I stared at the ceiling, pondering the two men who'd once helmed the global stage. Two leaders hailed by history as symbols of progress and diplomacy. Yet their true legacy, hidden in secret correspondence, had woven sinister threads of manipulation into the fabric of nations.

As sleep claimed me, I resolved to push further. Tomorrow, I would dig deeper into FIST.

For the first time, I feared that discovering the truth might come at an unthinkable cost.

19

Consumer Drive, Toronto

I flew into Canada alone, using my new identity as John Miller, and I went through customs with surprising ease. My supposed purpose was to meet Professor Yasinky, an American intellectual, political activist, and outspoken critic of US and Russian foreign policies. He now served as a visiting adjunct professor in the Department of Political Science at the University of Toronto.

While Yasinky's perspective on FIST might have offered unique insights, I doubted he could provide any resolution to the pressing issue at hand. In fact, his involvement could complicate matters further. Even Colleen eyed me with doubt when I floated his name as a pretext for my visit.

The real reason I was here, however, was to meet with the GRF, my wife's former employer. My goal was to uncover how they performed their magical alchemy on a global scale—transforming challenging circumstances into humanitarian success stories. I sought to understand whether they were masters of their own destiny or pawns in a larger geopolitical game.

Stuck in Toronto's endless congested traffic, I watched the minutes slip away, threatening the punctuality of my meeting. When I asked the driver about alternative routes, he shrugged in response. The thought of Colleen navigating this chaotic commute daily with far more patience than I possessed lingered in my mind.

After what felt like hours, we finally reached the front door of GRF's headquarters on Consumer Drive, a utilitarian three-story building that resembled a cement-and-brick relic from the 1960s, its facade punctuated by small windows. I realized I had never set foot inside despite Colleen's decade-plus of employment there.

In the lobby, I approached the security desk and introduced myself as John Miller, stating that I was there to meet the CEO, Cathy Dickson. I knew I had never encountered her before as Scott Barton, but I had to tread carefully. Other colleagues from Colleen's circle might recognize me, so maintaining a low profile was crucial.

My cover story painted me as an author working on a book about worldwide NGOs and their success in navigating global geopolitical tensions: a diplomatic "brag book" aimed at attracting donations. Initially, my interview request had been rejected until I hinted that refusal might imply secrecy, raising uncomfortable questions for the organization.

I was already late but was required to watch a three-minute safety video, pass through a metal detector, and place a bright-yellow guest badge on my coat before Dickson's assistant greeted me and took me to Dickson.

Upon entering her office, I found Dickson engrossed in a document, but then she glanced up and stood to greet me. After pleasantries and my apology for tardiness, she led me to a small table. Her assistant offered refreshments, and I chose water.

Cathy Dickson's face had a striking, disarmingly feminine quality. Though calm, her almond-shaped hazel eyes held the focused intensity of a soldier. She had the air of a fitness enthusiast: her movements sharp and deliberate, her posture dynamic even when still.

Yet her choice of attire told a different story, one that softened her edges and aimed to invite underestimation. Although she was already petite, her sleek dark-blue dress made her appear even more diminutive—a deceptive choice. The polished appearance concealed the strength hinted at by her toned arms. Her outfit and demeanor seemed crafted to create an image of a caring leader.

Despite her small stature and refined dress, Cathy still gave off the impression of controlled power.

She discussed Toronto's infamous traffic until her assistant returned with a glass of water and exited, closing the door behind her.

"Ms. Dickson, I appreciate you taking the time to meet with me," I began, pulling out my notebook for appearances.

"Please, call me Cathy."

"Only if you call me John," I replied, the assumed name feeling foreign on my tongue.

"So, John, how can I help you?"

I started with broad questions covering GRF's origin story, mission, vision, global projects, office locations, employees, and operational challenges. Cathy seemed to relish the opportunity to showcase her expertise, rattling off memorized figures and highlights from last year's annual report. She appeared pleased with her performance.

Shifting gears, I delved into her background, focusing on her experience in US military intelligence, including her roles in ISR—Intelligence, Surveillance, and Reconnaissance. For the first time in the discussion, her guard went up, her answers becoming measured and cautious.

Testing boundaries, I asked, "What level of security clearance did you hold?"

"This role doesn't require security clearance," she replied flatly.

"I imagine your intelligence expertise must be invaluable in navigating the political minefields GRF frequently faces."

She straightened in her chair, her tone becoming serious. "Effective diplomacy is crucial for achieving our humanitarian objectives. Understanding regimes with divergent interests, incompatible ideologies, and a desire for power and influence enables us to strategize and succeed."

"Would you say GRF's personnel in hostile regions act more like military operatives—building relationships, gathering intelligence, negotiating, and conducting measures short of violence?"

She smiled, pushing her hair off her face. "I hadn't considered our people as military operatives," she said. "They're deployed to save lives."

"Has GRF ever conducted covert operations with government backing—Canadian or otherwise?"

Her smile evaporated, and a measured edge crept into her voice. "I'm not sure what you're insinuating, Mr. Miller. We do occasionally receive project funding from governments when their mandates align with our objectives."

"Are these operatives volunteers, or are they recruited specifically for certain roles?"

"We have both. Most of our international personnel are highly trained professionals."

She was shifting into damage control. She must feel threatened, I realized, intrigued. Now I was getting somewhere.

"Would you know the breakdown of Canadian, American, or other nationalities among them?"

"We employ over two hundred people—a mix of nationalities, but I don't have specific data," she said hurriedly, glancing at the clock. "I see we're almost out of time—do you have any final questions?"

I leaned in, my tone serious. "Do you know how much financial support GRF receives from American and Russian sources?"

Her expression tightened. "I don't have those numbers readily available."

"Any rough estimates?"

"As you are aware, privacy laws prohibit us from disclosing donor-specific information."

"Fair enough. Can you please confirm the reports published on WikiLeaks suggesting the US government contributes over $500 million annually to GRF?"

The tension in the room was palpable, broken only by the rhythmic ticking of the wall clock. Cathy's eyes burned with fury as she fixed her unflinching gaze at me.

"Mr. Miller, I believe our conversation has ended." She rose quickly and sprang to the door. "I need to prepare for my next meeting. Have a good day."

Before I could respond, her diligent assistant escorted me toward the elevator.

I was now sure Colleen's work with GRF ran far more profoundly than I had ever imagined. I was more determined than ever to uncover the truth behind her role in this tangled web.

***

On my way to Toronto's airport, my smartphone rang. Only two people had this number: Colleen and Leah.

"Hey, what's—"

"Dad!" Leah's voice was trembling, tight with panic. "You need to come home. Now."

My chest tightened. "Leah, what happened? What's wrong?"

A pause lingered, during which I heard her attempt to steady her breathing. "It's Mom." Her voice broke, then her words came in shaky bursts. "There was an accident—a car . . . it hit her. She's in the ER right now. Dad, it's bad. She . . . she has a head injury . . . and broken bones. They're running tests."

"Leah . . ." I started, my voice caught somewhere between shock and the need to comfort her, but my throat felt dry. "What hospital? I'm on my way to the airport."

"Please . . . Please hurry, Dad. I'm scared." Her voice cracked on the last word as she hung up.

I felt a wave of nausea, a sickening realization that I might somehow bear responsibility for this disaster.

20

Brooklyn

The nurse in the emergency ward glanced at me with confusion. "I'm sorry, sir, but we don't have anyone under Colleen Barton."

Oh my God, I had just given the wrong name. What was I thinking? Panicking, I scrambled to collect my thoughts before blurting out, "Sorry, I'm not thinking straight. I'm here to see Mary Miller. My wife!"

The nurse frowned before turning back to her computer screen.

What a careless mistake! I had to be more alert, more careful.

"Yes," the nurse said, her expression now tinged with suspicion. "They moved her to the ICU. There's a young woman with her. She's in room B239. Go down the left corridor—four doors down on the right."

Each step brought me closer to her room, but my feet felt heavier with every stride, as though weighed down by the guilt

I carried. I knew I was responsible for this tragedy—however inadvertently—but accepting it seemed unbearable.

I froze outside room B239, struggling to steady myself. The problem ahead felt insurmountable, pressing against my chest like a thousand bricks. Unable to delay further, I forced myself inside.

I was greeted by a sight that made my stomach churn.

Leah sat beside Colleen, who lay motionless beneath hospital blankets on an adjustable bed, her body consumed by tubes and machinery. Her right leg hung in traction, secured by pulleys and weights. A cast encased her left arm. Her shoulder was immobilized by a brace. A breathing tube protruded from her mouth, mechanically aiding her fragile breaths. Beside her, monitors displayed vital signs: heart rate, fluctuating blood pressure, oxygen saturation levels, and intracranial pressure. The quiet beeping and humming of the machines cast an eerie and unrelenting rhythm over the scene.

Leah saw me and leaped up, embracing me. Swollen and red, her eyes streamed tears. I smelled a hint of marijuana on her clothes. I held on to her as tightly as I could, desperate to anchor her amid the storm.

"Oh my God, what happened?" I managed to ask, though my throat felt dry and constricted.

"She's in a coma with a skull fracture," Leah explained, her voice trembling. "She was crossing an intersection near Prospect Park when a vehicle hit her. It was a hit-and-run."

Rage bubbled inside me. "A hit-and-run?" I repeated. "The driver didn't stop?"

"No. The police are investigating—asking for witnesses, reviewing video footage—but they've got nothing so far."

I stood there in silence, suffocated by the crushing combination of guilt and simmering anger. Resolute, I left the room and sought the attending doctor, my need for answers consuming me.

The nurse intercepted me, her tone calm yet firm as she guided me back to Colleen's room. "I'll call the doctor and have him come to you."

Leah dashed to fetch tea and coffee for us as I stared at the medical equipment surrounding Colleen. The beeping monitors flashed numbers I didn't understand and the respirator's rhythmic whooshing filled the air—a haunting melody of survival.

Soon, the door opened and a dark-complexioned man in his late forties stepped in. A blue medical mask covered his mouth and nose. Pale green scrubs peeked out from beneath his crisp white lab coat, and a stethoscope dangled from his pocket.

"Mr. Miller?" His voice remained steady and gentle, yet it carried an undeniable weight.

I nodded, my eyes darting to the name on his badge—*Dr. Amir Choudhri*.

I didn't waste any time. "Doctor, is my wife going to be okay?"

The words hung in the air, heavy and raw, edged with desperation.

He paused for a moment, as though considering how best to begin. His eyes, the only part of his face visible above the mask, held a mix of empathy and seriousness. "Your wife is in critical condition," he said carefully. "The accident caused significant trauma. She suffered a severe head injury, and there's swelling in her brain. We've had to place her in a medically induced coma to reduce the pressure."

The words hit me like a physical blow, but after giving me time to absorb as much as I could, he continued. "There are also extensive fractures—several ribs, her pelvis, one leg, and an arm. One of the broken ribs punctured her lung, which caused it to collapse. She's on a ventilator now to help her breathe, and we've had to provide blood transfusions because of internal bleeding."

I felt my legs weaken, and I gripped the back of the nearest chair for support.

He pressed on, his voice deliberate but not insensitive. "Surgery will be required, but for now, we're focusing on stabilizing her condition. The next forty-eight hours will be critical as we monitor the swelling in her brain and assess the damage to her lung. After that, we'll have a better idea of the next steps."

I swallowed hard, my throat dry. "Doctor"—my voice cracked slightly—"will . . . will she make it?"

Dr. Choudhri lowered his gaze before meeting my eyes again, his face softening as he placed a hand on my shoulder. "I won't sugarcoat this—it's very serious. Her body has been through an extraordinary amount of trauma. Complications are possible, but . . . we're doing everything we can. Right now, we need to take it hour by hour, day by day. Her response in the coming days will give us a clearer picture."

I hesitated, the ache in my chest unbearable. "What are her chances?" My voice was a whisper. I wasn't sure if I could handle the answer.

Dr. Choudhri considered his words. "It's too early to give you a number or a guarantee. But what I can tell you is that we're committed to doing everything within our power. Don't lose hope, Mr. Miller. We're fighting for her."

Though my mind was racing with worst-case scenarios, the sincerity in his tone caught me off guard, making me clutch the shred of hope he offered. I nodded again, my throat tightening too much to respond.

***

For two weeks, Leah and I took turns by Colleen's side. We watched with cautious optimism as her condition improved: the swelling in her brain diminished and her lung healed. Doctors eased her out of the medically induced coma and removed the ventilator, but her neurological responses remained uncertain.

One evening as I sat beside her, exhausted, I rested my head on her bed, drifting between sleep and wakefulness. The rhythmic beeps of the monitors faded into the background until a physical sensation jolted me awake.

Colleen's hand squeezed mine.

I bolted upright, watching her eyes flutter open and close.

"You're going to be okay," I whispered softly, my forehead near hers. "You need to heal."

She strained toward my voice, her dry throat struggling to form words. Her first attempts were faint and unintelligible. I offered her water through a straw, and she sipped.

Weak but determined, her voice almost inaudible, she whispered with remarkable effort, "Super . . . cali . . . fragi . . . listic . . . expi . . ."

Her voice faded, and her head sank back onto the pillow—her last and only word: *Supercalifragilisticexpialidocious.*

***

On a cold, gray, rainy spring day, we gathered at the gravesite—just the two of us. Leah and I stood under the shelter of a white umbrella as Colleen's coffin was lowered into the earth. Leah threw a single white rose onto the casket, a gesture I repeated as we each said silent prayers.

The undertaker waited nearby in his black raincoat, signaling to the staff that the service was over. We headed toward our waiting car amid the falling rain.

A figure emerged from behind the trees—a woman wearing a full-length belted black coat, shielding herself from the rain with a matching umbrella. Instinctively, I shifted, positioning myself between the stranger and Leah.

As we approached, the woman stepped closer, revealing a sharp yet somber expression.

"I'm sorry for your loss," she said sincerely. "I worked with Colleen at GRF. We recently reconnected in Ottawa. I need to speak with you at your convenience. Here's my contact information."

She handed me a card and disappeared back among the trees. My pulse raced as I helped Leah into the car and slammed the door.

"Get us out of here," I instructed the driver, my voice urgent.

***

Grieving isn't something you plan for. It finds you at your weakest moment and clings to you, reshaping your soul in ways you didn't realize were possible. For me, the pain of losing

Colleen felt sharper than anything I expected. Losing my wife was not the only factor; I grasped for greater purpose, something to anchor me when every corner of our Brooklyn apartment reminded me of her absence.

Removing every item associated with Colleen felt like a desperate attempt to survive. I thought if I could box her memory away, I could somehow hide the pain, too. Her clothes, shoes, jewelry, books, toiletries—all packed and taped shut. Only two boxes contained her life as Mary Miller—only the beginning of a new life with me. These I left by the door for Leah to handle. I wasn't ready to bury them altogether, or perhaps I needed Leah to hold on to some piece of her memory when I couldn't.

That apartment became suffocating, and so I walked. Long stretches of Prospect Park became my daily outlet. The rain didn't stop me; neither did the chill in the air or the heat of the sun. I walked and walked, as though searching for pieces of myself scattered among the trees, pathways, and benches. Sometimes my mind wandered into the belief that I was now just a ghostly shadow, stuck somewhere between the living and the afterlife, searching for meaning, much like Colleen must have felt on her own journey.

Leah, though, was a different story. Leah handled the grief in her own way—or rather, didn't handle it at all. While I retreated into a foggy headspace, she propelled herself outward. Her sorrow was reckless, and louder than I could bear. Her pain was intense. It screamed through late-night raves, through drugs passed back and forth between strangers. I saw her trying to drown out the memories, the reality, with everything she could find to numb herself. Every night felt like a battle she waged against herself. In her wild spiral, I saw echoes of the person she had struggled to move past. I watched her slipping farther away from the promise of stability she had built over the last few years. She had toiled to escape that version of herself, the version that sought solace in darkness—but it reappeared, consuming her life.

I worried about her. I worried about both of us. We couldn't escape this all-consuming pain. We didn't discuss it. What was there to say? Words could not express it. Grieving is personal. It's alien in its intimacy, forcing you to face yourself while trying to shield others from the truth of your wounds. That's what Colleen had done to herself. I had failed to help her, and now, without her, I was failing Leah.

Who could I be for her when I didn't know who I was myself anymore? How could I shield her from her demons when mine were so overwhelming that I struggled to breathe some days? And yet, when morning light cracked through the apartment window, illuminating the boxes by the door, I realized they were only a minor piece of Colleen's presence. I knew the answer to the question that churned in my heart: Leah and I were all we had.

Pain takes time. It doesn't follow a set calendar or deadline. And building something new after such immense loss felt insurmountable. But the truth was, neither Leah nor I could move past this unless we took it one day at a time. Simple. Primal. One moment after the other.

We needed to find a purpose beyond surviving the grief. A purpose bigger than just the two of us, something meaningful enough to justify waking up each day. Maybe it wouldn't be big or dramatic; it didn't have to be—but it had to keep us grounded, together, alive.

And so, I reached out to Leah. No lectures. No criticisms. No demands for change. Instead, a simple truth: "We're in this together." A ghost of hope that maybe, amid all the pain and darkness, we could lean on each other until the grief lessened its hold.

Leah didn't respond right away, and that was okay. We didn't need more words right then. I would sit for hours with her in the oversized Bird's Nest condo that represented Colleen's past life.

Conversation does not fix grief; it's fixed by action, by patience, by holding each other and seeing whatever positive light remains, no matter how faint.

As we sat together in silence, her gaze distant and mine unfocused, I realized this was the beginning—raw and imperfect. We wouldn't heal overnight. We wouldn't find answers in days, weeks, or maybe even months. But we would try.

Together. One day at a time.

21

Lower Manhattan

The café was alive with the hum of chatter and clinking cups—typical of Lower Manhattan. I had arrived early, picking a table tucked away in a corner to escape the noise. As my green tea sat untouched, I sifted through the fragments of Colleen's life, searching for any connection to the woman who had approached me at the cemetery. Her sudden appearance and cryptic words left me uneasy yet curious. Who was she? Could I trust her? And even if I wanted to, what questions would peel back the truth?

When she entered, her arrival confirmed that I hadn't imagined her presence at the cemetery. Her stride was confident and deliberate, leaving no room for doubt that she was accustomed to authority. Her short haircut framed a face etched with experience, reflecting the vitality of someone who maintained a disciplined fitness regimen.

"Thanks for agreeing to meet," she said, sliding into the seat across from me.

I kept my response simple, offering my hand to shake. "I didn't catch your name before."

"You can call me Susan," she replied, her grip firm but not overpowering.

Once her order arrived—a double-shot, low-fat latte—Susan stirred the drink with precision, her demeanor calm but purposeful.

"I don't recall my wife ever mentioning your name during her time with GRF," I said cautiously, keeping any references to Colleen or even Mary as ambiguous as possible.

Susan didn't flinch. "Not surprising," she responded plainly. "Most of what we did together was strictly classified." She took a slow sip of her latte before she continued. "We didn't work on the same projects in Canada, but we collaborated extensively in the Middle East. Your wife was exceptional—a rare talent in an unusual place for an agent not aligned with either the Russians or Americans."

The word *agent* hit me like a sucker punch. "Agent?" I blurted out before I could contain myself.

Susan paused, then nodded. "Yes, agent. GRF was never really just an NGO. It's a front for special operatives working outside the traditional CIA and KGB frameworks. Our mission was to destabilize, bolster, or dismantle governments, regimes, and terrorist threats—all in the name of some vague idea of global peace. Both US and Russian leadership supported these operations."

My mind scrambled for footing. "How did Colleen—" I corrected myself with a more neutral approach: "How did she get involved with GRF?"

Susan's lips curled in what seemed to be both admiration and regret. "Canada's NGO scene was a perfect cover. Nobody suspects an innocuous lawyer in Toronto. But Colleen was too sharp; she saw through the facade instantly. She became a crucial asset, serving as a double agent for both Russia and America. Her strategic insights were uncanny, and her execution flawless."

I felt the foundation of my world crack beneath me, pieces falling away as I clung to the edges of what I thought I knew. Realization was creeping in, unwelcome and suffocating.

Careful not to betray the turmoil roaring inside me, I tested her words, my voice somehow steady despite the tremor rattling my soul. "Did you know her well? Were you with her in Tunisia in December 2010?"

Susan studied me, her gaze peeling away the thin mask I was trying to keep in place. With a small nod, she murmured, "Yes, just before Christmas. She was upset about missing your surprise twentieth-anniversary trip to Barbados."

It struck me like a knife in the center of my chest, twisting. Barbados. I had wondered why she'd pulled away during that time, why she'd seemed so distant, and now it sat before me. A truth so cruel I wanted to push it back into the shadows.

Susan hesitated, her eyes flicking toward the bustling street outside the café window. I could sense that the scene—the chaos surrounding us—lulled her back to a memory she didn't want to touch but couldn't avoid.

"We were there to tip the first domino," she began, her voice heavy, burdened by years of grief and guilt. "A single move meant to spark a wave of change so immense it would shake the Arab world to its core, reshape it forever."

My heart clenched as she paused, her gaze distant now, lost in the contours of past choices. When she spoke again, her tone was raw and purposeful.

"It all started in the dusty town of Sidi Bouzid, about an hour and a half by helicopter from Tunis, the capital. We needed a catalyst to incite the uprising—a symbol. We found it in the form of a poor young man, barely scraping by, hawking fruit in front of the municipal buildings every day. He was fiercely determined, but vulnerable. He was perfect."

I leaned forward despite myself, sensing the storm in her voice, the weight of what she was about to reveal.

"How old?" I asked, my throat tight.

Susan's eyes clouded. "He was just a boy," she admitted softly. "He was in his early twenties, full of dreams that would never come true. We chose him because he couldn't control his anger and wore his frustrations openly for the world to see. Vulnerability looks like courage when you're desperate. For a week, we pushed him, threatened him, harassed him."

I gripped my mug until my knuckles burned, frozen as the narrative unfolded.

"The few hours he tried to sleep he was trapped in relentless noise—we made sure of that." Her voice cracked, her shoulders sagging under the weight of her confession. "By the end of that week, he was broken, teetering on the edge. Survival wasn't an option for him. He needed to rebel. We gave him gasoline and planted the idea: disrupt the government, vandalize the building. He ran out of hope that Friday morning, December seventeenth."

Susan's breath shuddered. "The ultimate insult—the tipping point—was Colleen's idea; a calculated move. We had a female officer confiscate his fruit cart, his scale, and his livelihood. In front of everyone. You see, in a male-dominated tribal society, emasculation is like a death sentence."

Her hands trembled as she gripped the edge of the table. "When it happened, we watched from the shadows," she said, her voice faltering. "Cameras rolled as the officer humiliated him in front of the crowd. But he didn't follow the plan. He didn't take the gasoline to the walls of the building."

Her voice broke at last. The following words fell like stones, sinking my heart deeper into an abyss.

"He poured it over himself. Lit a match. I can still smell the burning flesh. I can still hear his hollow screaming." Her breath caught as tears slid down her cheeks, raw and unrestrained.

The world swirled around me—the memories of those days, the media frenzy, the viral footage of a man engulfed in flames. I had seen that moment repeatedly, like the rest of the world. But I hadn't really seen it. And now, I was witnessing it through Susan's eyes, and through the ghost of a woman I thought I had known—my wife.

The realization twisted my insides. Colleen was more than just mine. She had been part of something larger, something terrible and profound. A revolution that had toppled regimes in Tunisia, Egypt, and Libya. She had sparked unrest in Syria and Yemen, shifting the geopolitical landscape forever.

And I had been sitting in the safety of my world, busy lamenting a missed vacation in Barbados, too blind to see that she was risking her life for something I couldn't even grasp.

Tears burned at the edges of my eyes, blurring my vision. "Oh my God," I managed, the words barely audible, my voice cracking under the weight of my grief. "I didn't know."

Susan's gaze softened, though her own pain loomed in her expression. "She mentioned you often," she whispered. "I'm so sorry for your loss. Colleen . . . she was remarkable, a rare soul."

For the next twenty minutes, Susan unfolded a life I had never imagined for the wife I thought I had known but now realized I didn't. She painted the story of a brilliant strategist: fearless and relentless, privy to clandestine meetings with the presidents of America and Russia, a woman who believed in revolution but had grown disillusioned when the flames she sparked burned far beyond control. Colleen had carried the weight of failure, of ideals shattered by greed, terror, and manipulation, and Susan described how those burdens eroded her spirit.

As the story came to its final chapter, Susan's voice faltered. "She changed. We grew distant. She withdrew. There's another GRF agent who might fill the gaps—a woman whose name I can't be sure of. Katerina, maybe Kassie. But . . . I don't think anyone will really know the whole truth about her. Not even you."

I stood as Susan finished, my legs weak and my heart heavier than I had ever known. As I walked away, a crushing emptiness consumed me. The woman I loved was gone, and in her place stood a vibrant enigma I had failed to see. A warrior, a strategist, and a person haunted by the illusions she had fought for.

Unanswered questions followed me with every step, pressing down on me harder than they ever had before.

22

Brooklyn

I returned home to the Brooklyn apartment, the weight of the conversation clinging to me like fog. For the first time in months, I poured myself a glass of Colleen's favorite scotch. The amber liquid swirled in the glass as I stared out toward Prospect Park. For hours, Susan's words played on repeat in my mind.

Susan believed in the GRF's mission—a naïve belief that their manipulations served a noble cause. But Colleen had known better. The titanium USB drive I'd discovered on the beach was hers. She'd known I had it. But why was it left on the beach? Did she expect me to find it? It made little sense. What was her plan?

Without the password, it would have been impossible to unlock the secrets on the USB drive. Her giving me the password before she died proved her ownership, but it also identified her killer. It was her warning and evidence. She'd unloaded her nightmare on me.

Supercalifragilisticexpialidocious made perfect sense for Colleen's password as it had always been our family safe word. She'd put security and safety measures in place to protect the family, especially Leah, if someone impersonated a family member, such as in a scam or abduction attempt. It was ingenious, perplexing, and suited to a woman shrouded in secrecy.

When had our lives drifted apart beyond repair? Had I been so consumed by business deals, luxury cars, and my growing empire that I hadn't seen my wife and child slipping away into another reality?

Had Colleen set me up as an unwitting pawn? Could she have expected the danger of the information on that USB? Or worse, had she known people were targeting her—the rogue agent? Had she been murdered? And if so, who was responsible? The Russians? The Americans? Or both in a twisted collaboration?

Answers eluded me. But one thing was obvious: someone had helped Colleen create our new identities, someone who might hold the key to the truth. Was it this Katerina or Kassie who had helped her?

My mind couldn't hold the weight any longer. With another scotch in hand, I passed out on the couch.

***

Morning sunlight nudged me awake. As I stirred on the couch, my body felt like an uncooperative machine—aching joints, throbbing temples, and the fuzzy aftertaste of regret from pouring one scotch too many last night.

I dragged myself to the kitchen, then downed a glass of water, popped an acetaminophen, and promised myself the next step would be a return to my wellness routine. Life had already crumbled enough without me joining the wreckage.

After donning sweatpants, a T-shirt, and my running shoes, I set out for Prospect Park. Exercise could clear the haze and maybe sharpen my mind.

As I made my way out of the apartment's entrance, I noticed a parked white 2013 BMW 3 Series and remembered spotting the same model near the café where I had met Susan. Was I being followed? Was I becoming paranoid? The thought sent a shiver through me, but I turned toward the park and quickened my pace.

An hour later, sweat soaked my T-shirt and clarity had replaced the morning fog. Returning home, I noticed the BMW was gone, although the unease it brought lingered.

After a shower and breakfast, I sat in the office with Colleen's smartphone and iPad. This was my best shot at finding answers.

Hacking into the devices wasn't as difficult as I'd feared. I deciphered the passwords by using combinations of our birthdays. Her iPad yielded little—just a few scattered searches and a mundane browsing history. But her phone held something valuable: a Manhattan phone number called several times when we arrived in Brooklyn. I reverse tracked the number to an address near the Meatpacking District, close to High Line Park.

Was this the contact who helped her create new identities? Was this Katerina or Kassie? A person who held the key to unravel Colleen's hidden life?

Adjusting my chair, I leaned forward, staring at the address and holding the phone number like a piece of a puzzle I wasn't sure I could solve. Whatever answers lay ahead, I knew one thing—finding out the truth might change everything.

23

Brooklyn

Before going to sleep, I opened the file dated 1993 to 2000—the first Democrat president to hold two terms since FIST began. The document was called "BC-BY Phone Transcripts."

[White House, Washington, DC, and Novo-Ogaryovo Residence, Moscow Secure Line connected April 11, 1993, at 12:01 EST]
President of the US: Good evening, Boris. How are things in Moscow?
President of Russia: [chuckling] Ah, Bill, Moscow is as chaotic as ever. Spring here is a mix of slush and uncertainty, just like politics. And you, my friend? You have had some time to settle into that mighty chair in Washington. How is the beast treating you?

President of the US: [laughing softly] Eighty-two days in, and I'll admit—I'm still finding my footing. It's a hell of a role, Boris. I want to bring positive change, to build something that lasts, but it feels like balancing on a tightrope while juggling flaming torches.

President of Russia: [laughs deeply] You are learning. The world is a circus, and we are the reluctant ringmasters. But let me tell you, my American friend: optimism does not hold power. Strength does. Fear does. That is what anchors the elusive FIST—in diplomacy, in leadership. If you rely too heavily on ideals, the currents of chaos will swallow you whole.

President of the US: I hear you, but creating conflict to achieve peace . . . That's foreign to me. There has to be a way to move forward—stability, prosperity, maybe even a legacy worth protecting—without leaning on fear.

President of Russia: [voice firm, almost paternal] Stability and prosperity? Those are noble goals, but they do not come easily, Bill. They require sacrifices, and those sacrifices . . . well, they are often measured in lives. FIST is not just a blunt tool; it is a razor. Sharp, dangerous, precise.

President of the US: [pausing briefly before re-

sponding] You seem awfully comfortable with that reality, Boris.
President of Russia: Comfortable? No, my friend. I have learned to wield it, to bend it to my will. It is not about comfort; it is about survival, about shaping the fires of history to burn in your favor. Together, we can make it work for both of us. But remember—peace is rarely born from idealism. It is forged in conflict and, yes, sometimes with a hint of deception and lies.
President of the US: [hesitating, then muttering] If that's what it takes, I'll follow your lead.
President of Russia: That is the spirit! A steady hand and a measured lie can be the tools of leadership. The world is always watching us, but never trust that its eyes are friendly. Lead with strength and strategy. Deception is a tool to ensure survival.
President of the US: [pause] You give me a lot to think about. I understand the weight, but I'm not sure if I can fully embrace it the way you describe.
President of Russia: [chuckling warmly again] You are still young in this role. In time, you will learn—one way or another. For now, lean on me. The weight of history moves slower when shouldered together.

President of the US: Thank you, Boris. I'll keep that in mind.
[Secure Line disconnects at 12:06 EST]

***

[White House, Washington, DC, and Novo-Ogaryovo Residence, Moscow Secure Line connected November 28, 1999, at 12:02 EST]
President of the US: Evening, Boris. How's Moscow treating you?
President of Russia: It is cold as hell here, but that is Moscow for you. You called at a good time—I just sat down with my vodka.
President of the US: [chuckling] Trust you to have vodka ready at hand. Though I have to ask—are you spending these days reminiscing about all the chaos we've stirred up together?
President of Russia: [laughing heartily] Chaos? Bill, chaos is our legacy! If politics were an art form, we would be Picasso and Van Gogh—all over the canvas, creating masterpieces of organized disaster. Makes me wonder sometimes if we are

brilliant . . . or just lucky.

President of the US: Chaos as an art form—now that's a philosophy I can get behind. Look at Yemen. You made your move, I made mine—and suddenly, it's everyone else's problem. A diplomatic mess, yes, but beautifully executed chaos.

President of Russia: [mocking tone] Yemen, you say? That one was all yours. I sat back with my vodka thinking . . . How does he make it look so intentional?

President of the US: [laughs] Learned it from the best—watching you! Your handling of the Chechen war? A masterclass in lighting the fuse and waiting to see who gets burned first.

President of Russia: [feigning offense] Now, hold on! Kosovo was not exactly a picnic. You painted NATO as your weapon of choice, dropping bombs and calling it democracy-building? Impressive, even as it rattled the cage.

President of the US: Fair enough. But don't think Afghanistan escapes the list. Between the two of us, we've left future historians a pile of rubble to decipher.

President of Russia: [laughs] Here's to us—uninvited guests at the world's dinner table! We make a mess, but it is never boring.

President of the US: [joining in his laughter] That's one way to look at it. Boris, I'll admit—chaos aside, I've enjoyed working with you, even when we were at odds.

President of Russia: [voice softening slightly] Same here, Bill. I have laughed through it all, because there is not much point in crying. But truth be told, I will not be stirring the pot much longer.

President of the US: (concerned tone) What do you mean?

President of Russia: By year's end, I will step aside. Putin will take over. The man is sharp, cold, and calculating. I like vodka, games, and jokes—he likes order. A lot of order.

President of the US: Putin, huh? Well, wish me luck handling those reins. Something tells me I'll miss the warm camaraderie we've built over the years.

President of Russia: [chuckling] He will keep you on your toes—that much I can guarantee. But that is your concern now. Mine is sipping vodka and staying warm as I fade out of the spotlight.

President of the US: I'll miss you. Sure, we've left chaos around the globe, but we made it bearable—and dare I say, fun.

President of Russia: [laughing heartily again]

Fun? Absolutely, Bill! Do not let anyone accuse us of being boring leaders. We will go down in history as the ones who kept it . . . spicy!

President of the US: [laughing with him] Spicy, indeed. Good luck, Boris—and thanks for the memories, for better or worse.

President of Russia: Good luck to you, too, Bill—do not forget the vodka whenever the chaos gets overwhelming. And remember, history will call us troublemakers, but never dull ones.

[Secure Line disconnects at 12:08 EST]

24

New York

I arrived at 450 West Fifteenth Street, a warehouse converted into office spaces. Outside, the industrial charm mingled with the remnants of the Meatpacking District's gritty past, though now surrounded by boutique shops and gleaming glass facades. Dressed in black jeans, a sweatshirt, a black Ferrari cap, and dark sunglasses, I aimed to blend in as just another courier. My prop: a large white poly bubble mailer filled with old magazines.

In the lobby, I retrieved the phone number I'd found on Colleen's phone and dialed it. It rang three times.

"Hello?" answered a male voice briskly with a strong English accent.

"Hi. I've got a package for delivery, but the sender forgot to include your floor or office number," I said, adopting a hurried tone and genuinely hoping I hadn't miscalculated this gamble.

"I'll come down in a minute."

"Hey, I can't wait long. I'm in a no-parking zone—I need the office number."

After a pause, the man answered, "Fifth floor, Office 528."

I exhaled, relieved to be in the right building. The elevator ride to the fifth floor felt interminable, leaving enough time for my nerves to flare. What had I walked into? A simple transaction or a lion's den? My hope rested on something much less dangerous—an oversized kitten, perhaps.

The office door bearing the large number 528 had a button next to it with big red letters: *Press Button*. I pressed it, hearing a buzz from within. After a moment, the door eased open, revealing a tall, fit man in his forties with strikingly sharp features. He immediately reached out to grab the package, but I instinctively pulled it back, feigning compliance with company protocol.

"Sorry, I need a signature before I can release it." I patted my pockets with mock irritation, then aimed for a tone somewhere between apologetic and helpless. "Actually, I think I left my pen in the car. Do you have one?"

Annoyed at the delay, the man retreated into the room, leaving the door ajar. Sensing my opportunity, I darted in and closed the self-locking door behind me.

The interior was stark white, a small photo studio with professional lighting equipment and tripods arranged to one side. The room's minimal furniture grabbed my attention: two white leather-and-chrome Wassily chairs arranged against an oversized white French provincial desk. The desk was cluttered with several cameras, lenses of various sizes, papers, and electronic devices. However, one item stood out—a BMW key fob, identical to one used for a 2013 model.

A rush of panic surged through me, my fear paralyzing me in place.

The man returned with a pen, but his expression changed when he noticed me standing inside, the door shut behind me, my sunglasses now removed.

A smirk spread across his face, his pleasant English accent jolting me further. "Ah, Mr. Barton—or should I say John Miller? Welcome. I didn't know you'd started a new job."

Every nerve in my body screamed *Run!* but my mind refused to act.

"Please sit down. Can I get you anything?" he asked, his tone inviting. "Coffee, tea, or water?"

Finding my feet, I stumbled toward one of the Wassily chairs, though its stiff frame felt anything but inviting. "Water, please," I replied, my voice cautious.

Moments later, he returned with a glass of water for me and a steaming mug of coffee for himself. Relaxing into his chair, he folded his hands, studying me with curiosity and familiarity.

"So, you found my shop," he said, his tone softening, though sadness crept onto his face. "My condolences to you and your daughter. I loved your wife—I will miss her dearly." His voice gave way as he removed his glasses, wiping his eyes against his sleeve.

Watching his grief unfold disarmed me.

After regaining his composure, he spoke again. "How are you holding up?"

Annoyance replaced the lingering tension. Who was this guy? Why did he seem to know me, Colleen, and everything else in my life?

Unable to restrain my frustration, I let my words tumble out in one breath: "Sorry, but I'm lost. Who are you? How do you know my wife? And why were you following me?"

He gave a subtle smile, appearing unfazed and speaking calmly. "Fair questions. I assumed Colleen had mentioned me. I'm Frank Petrov. We go way back. I handled identity projects for her at GRF—mainly fabricating new credentials for her and others in the organization. Over time, we became close friends."

Sensing my skepticism, he blurted, "It was purely platonic, I assure you—I'm gay. Our friendship crossed no professional boundaries."

I leaned forward, tense despite his casual demeanor.

"I hadn't seen Colleen for years," he continued, "until she came looking for new identities for the two of you. She seemed frightened. Scared out of her wits, honestly. She made me promise to keep an eye on you if anything happened to her. I thought I'd reach out when the time was right . . ." He shrugged lightly. "But it seems you found me."

Relief washed over me, tempered by lingering unease. The lion had revealed itself as more of a house cat—one that seemed loyal to my wife even after her death.

The door buzzer startled both of us. Frank jumped from his chair, then glanced at his watch. "Was anyone with you?"

"No," I replied quickly, standing to stretch my stiff legs.

He gestured toward a doorway at the back of the room. "Wait in the back," he said firmly. "I'll see who it is."

Rolling with his urgency, I darted into the adjoining room. The contrast was striking—where the front office was stark and minimalist, this room was chaos incarnate. Black walls framed a mess of wires, computer screens, printers, and tables covered with papers, paint cans, plastics, guillotine paper cutters, and labeled boxes. Clearly, this was where Frank worked his magic, creating identities and credentials out of thin air.

Minutes later, he called out, "It's okay, you can come out now. Just a guy from the office next door dropping off a mis-delivered package. Seems couriers are as careless as ever."

Returning to the front room, I found him laughing at his own quip. "Are you up for a walk?"

I nodded; the fresh air would calm my nerves.

We ventured out onto the elevated High Line Park, walking above the bustling streets as the city pulsed below. As we walked, Frank uncovered pieces of my wife, the woman I never understood. His fondness for her was apparent, but his lack of interest in the details of GRF and its shadowy activities puzzled me.

He was a genius, a craftsman in forging identities and altering lives, but he appeared oblivious to the darker consequences of his work. I could see how Colleen valued him: charismatic, brilliant, and carefree. He was everything I wasn't.

As I was ready to part ways, Frank stopped mid-walk, his complexion paling.

"Oh, my God," he gasped, turning sharply toward me. "I nearly forgot! I have an envelope for you—from Colleen. It's back at my office."

My mind raced with possibilities as we returned to his office together. What secrets did this envelope from Colleen hold? Answers? Instructions? Or perhaps one more unanswered question in this labyrinth of her hidden life?

25

Brooklyn

I stared at the envelope in the quiet of my Prospect Park apartment, knowing its contents would shake my world. With a deep breath, I opened it and unfolded Colleen's letter, her handwriting a gentle reminder of her presence.

I'm so sorry you have to read this, my love. Please know that I love you deeply. XOXO.

Her words struck a chord of shared love and regret. She spoke of dreams that had pulled us apart and of our recent rediscovery of each other. The connection we had revived, a gift in those fleeting months.

What was once my dream job became a nightmare of destruction. Today, I raise my FIST against what has happened.

Cleverly, she had masked the identity of FIST, fearing that this message might fall into the wrong hands. The unexpected weight of her ambitious yet perilous reality burdened her confession. She went on to say that she was the keeper of the titanium USB. The secrets within it haunted her. To rid her of the devil and the secrets forever, she'd thrown the USB into the sea to release herself from her past. When she saw it plugged into my laptop the day we fled Mexico, she knew she was damned for eternity.

The agency's suspicions were a dark cloud over her, outlined painfully in her next words.

You already know the outcome of that ill-fated mission regarding the beheaded journalist in Syria, but you might not realize the danger you were in. While I was there, you were in Turkey, dealing with your mining deal near Eskişehir. They sent me a photo of you being held in Istanbul, negotiating visa issues. They made sure I knew your head could be next. Your freedom was the price for my silence.

Her admission was chilling. The letter exposed the leverage they used—our lives tangled in a web beyond our control.

Please understand that my silence has granted you freedom. Destroy whatever evidence you have. Please put down your fist and cherish the time with our daughter. She needs you now more than ever.

She was urging me to forsake retaliation and focus on Leah—our daughter, our light—a plea to step away from FIST's destructive path.

Finally, below her signature was the name *Katerina* and a German area code and phone number along with the message, *Call her if you ever get into trouble.*

With heavy resolve, I entered Katerina's number into my phone, then lit the letter on fire using the gas stove burner, watching it disintegrate into ash.

Seeking clarity, I walked through the park, grappling with decisions now laid bare.

***

An ache I couldn't ignore pulled me toward Leah, the one person who still made the world feel whole. I needed to see her. She mirrored Colleen's spirit—its strength and beauty clear in her gaze. We all struggled differently, yet Leah's presence comforted me.

That evening, I invited her over and prepared her favorite dinner: Caesar salad with my garlicky dressing and spicy sausage pasta. A bottle of Brunello di Montalcino 2018 sat ready, defying the brevity of life with its richness. So much for my heart health; life was now too short.

"For your mother," I said, raising my glass. "Our actions can carry her legacy forward."

Tears glistened in Leah's eyes as she responded, "To my mom, who I was just getting to know." Her words held an innocent longing.

"To my love of my life," I murmured.

With skill and empathy, Leah turned the conversation to me, drawing on her recent master's degree in psychology as she asked open-ended questions. We explored emotional terrains, her perspective guiding us to more profound truths.

Resolution settled within—I wouldn't hide from the truth. The wine offered a symphony of flavor, and I toasted once more, saying, "To a life well-lived rather than a life not lived. Cheers."

Through the night, I shared everything with Leah—from the harsh truths Susan had revealed, to the new identities Frank Petrov had given us, to Colleen's letter. I shared everything except the FIST information on the dreaded USB, now presumably buried in a landfill somewhere in Ontario. I feared that knowing the fact that the presidents of the US and Russia were behind all of this was a death warrant.

Dawn found Leah asleep on my couch, wrapped in a blanket. I settled into bed, tired but feeling the stirring of a new will to live—a fight to avenge Colleen's death.

***

Morning broke. Although wine remnants clouded my mind, revealing the truth had brought clarity—free of regret—and energy surged in my body.

As I brewed tea and coffee, I watched Leah doze on the couch.

"How do you feel?" I asked as she awoke, offering her a steaming cup of coffee.

She met my gaze, weariness giving way to understanding. "I'm exhausted but alive . . . What I mean is, I feel a sense of purpose for the first time in my life. It feels good."

Her words resonated with our shared determination, a newly formed kinship.

Embracing the day, Leah showered and chose fresh clothes from one of the boxes that still sat at the front door. She bundled her hair into a messy bun and put on sunglasses. Together, we ventured out. The sun hung high in the late-morning sky, warm and golden, as though unaware of the weight pressing down on us. The air carried the faint scent of lilacs and freshly cut grass, the gentle hum of Prospect Park wrapping around me like a balm trying to soothe an ache that felt unrelenting.

Leah walked beside me, both of us slow to shake off the hangover from the night before.

"I can't believe we slept in so late," she muttered, sipping from the coffee travel mug she'd insisted on bringing. "I feel like I got hit by a semi. How much Brunello did we even drink last night?"

"Enough," I said with a groan, running a hand over my face. "I can't drink like I used to." The sunlight felt merciless for a moment, but I let it wash over me. After the night we'd had, after the truths I'd shared, it felt like stepping into this beautiful day was an act of rebellion against the weight of it all.

Leah glanced at me from behind her sunglasses, her expression guarded but thoughtful. "Last night still feels . . . huge. I've been turning it over and over in my head. Mom's letter. Her other life. The secrets. Dad, you've been carrying so much, and I had no idea."

I didn't look at her right away, focusing my attention instead on the sprawling green expanse ahead of us. "It wasn't something I could just throw at you, Leah. I had to figure out how to make sense of it myself, and even now, I don't know that I've fully done that."

"I get it," she said softly, "but hearing it all . . ." She stopped in the middle of the path, forcing me to stop with her. "It's just—it's overwhelming, you know? I keep thinking there's no way we're actually talking about taking this on, about going after the people who did this. How are we even supposed to do that? Are we just supposed to become—I don't know—detectives, mercenaries, or whatever?"

I turned to her, my hands in my pockets. "Nothing like that. This isn't TV or the movies, Leah. Look, we might not know exactly where this will take us, or how we're going to get there, but I know this much: we can't let it end here. Your mother didn't deserve what happened. Nobody deserves this. And the people who did this think they're untouchable. That's the part I can't live with. This isn't about vengeance; it's about setting something right, even if it's just by exposing the truth."

Her jaw tightened, but her face was otherwise unreadable behind her sunglasses. "Okay, but what does exposing the truth even look like? Assuming we figure out how to do that, what's stopping these people from coming after us the same way they came after Mom?"

I exhaled slowly, considering her words. "That's a risk, yeah. But the difference is, they don't have the same advantage anymore. They built their power on secrecy. We know things they don't know. And we are in this whether or not we want to be." *Thanks to Colleen.*

Leah tilted her head toward the sky, the sunlight dancing over her cheekbones. "I get it, I do. But it's still . . . a lot to process. I don't know if I'm ready for this." She turned to me again, her tone shifting. "And, Dad, if we're in this together, you need to be in the right place. Literally."

I frowned. "What do you mean?"

"The apartment," she said, gesturing vaguely toward Eastern Parkway. "You don't need to live there anymore. You need to move back to the Bird's Nest. Your condo."

The mention of that place, our last real home, stirred a weight in my chest. Colleen's sanctuary. The mere thought of living there again, looking out over the view she'd always loved, felt like a stab. "Leah . . . I don't know."

She stepped toward me. "You do know," she said, her voice quiet but resolute. "Dad . . . It's where you belong." She rolled her eyes, but it came with the faintest hint of a smirk. "It's *our* condo, Dad. You know that. This way we can support each other, but it's got room for both of us to have space when we need it. And honestly . . . maybe I'll sleep better knowing you're not over here on your own, brooding or—God forbid—running off into danger." She nudged me lightly with her elbow. "Let me keep an eye on you, okay? Besides, I'm very responsible now. Master's degree in psychology and all."

I chuckled despite myself, shaking my head at her audacity. "I'm pretty sure the whole 'keeping an eye on' idea is supposed to work the other way around."

She shrugged, finally pulling off her sunglasses to meet my gaze, her expression softening. "All jokes aside, I mean it. I think it'd be good for us—for me. Everything you've shared over the last twenty-four hours . . . it's a lot to take in. And it opens doors to things that could get dangerous. Having you living there, in a space where I can be close to you and we can figure this whole thing out together—it feels right. Like we're not surviving individually but strategizing as a team."

I rubbed the back of my neck, scanning the path ahead of us as her words settled into me. The Bird's Nest. A haven threaded with memories and meaning. And Leah was right—the place was big enough for both of us to live our lives without tripping over each other, but close enough that we could make this fight ours together.

I let out a long breath, meeting her eyes again. "You really think it's something that'd work? Us living together again after all these years?"

She beamed. "I think it could be fun, Dad. And honestly? I don't think either of us is supposed to do this alone. It's a family thing—just us."

Her words tugged at something profound in my chest. I gave an almost imperceptible nod and smirked. "All right. You win."

Leah laughed and slipped her sunglasses back on, as if sealing the deal. "The wine haze must've worn off."

I chuckled as we resumed walking, the park opening up in front of us. Whatever lay ahead—the risks, the answers, the fight itself—we'd face it together.

Together. It was more than a word this time; it was a promise. A team. One day at a time.

And Colleen had left us one clue as to what we needed to do next: find Katerina, in Berlin, Germany.

26

Berlin

Our overnight flight from JFK to Berlin left us exhausted. After landing, we took a cab to our hotel, situated a couple of blocks from the Brandenburg Gate. Leah had crammed her belongings into a backpack, while I wheeled a carry-on suitcase and carried Colleen's emergency backpack.

Refreshed by a quick nap, showers, and brunch, we made plans to meet our elusive contact. I used the hotel phone to dial the Berlin number.

After a few rings, someone answered with a simple, "Hallo."

I didn't realize my nerves until I attempted to speak. "Hello. Is this Katerina?" I fumbled.

Her voice, calm yet cautious, replied in accented English. "Yes."

This was my chance before the line disconnected. "I'm Colleen's husband. Do you have any time to meet?"

A pause punctuated the atmosphere, and her next words indicated surprise and alarm. "Oh, are you okay?"

"Yes, thank you," I said, trying to keep my tone casual. "I'm in Berlin and thought it would be nice to meet."

Another pause followed. "Okay. Where are you staying?"

Her accent was elusive, perhaps Russian. We agreed to meet at a Bavarian restaurant a few blocks from our hotel at 7:00 p.m. Katerina said she'd wear a yellow scarf and sit outside if the weather allowed it. I hung up, realizing I hadn't mentioned Leah accompanying me—a minor detail overlooked.

Shortly before seven, Leah and I dressed in light jackets and braved the chill as the sun set behind the buildings. As we approached the restaurant, I spotted a woman with a yellow scarf at a corner table on the patio. Her surprise was obvious when she realized I wasn't alone.

"Sorry, I didn't mention my daughter, Leah, would be joining us. Is that okay?" I asked, looking for a third chair.

Katerina hugged Leah. "You are your mother's daughter. Pleased to meet you."

I pulled over an extra chair and greeted Katerina with a quick kiss on each cheek before sitting. With features reminiscent of Colleen's, Katerina could have been mistaken for her younger sister.

"It's a delight to meet you both," Katerina said, placing her napkin on her lap.

A waiter in lederhosen approached for drink orders, and we all opted for Berliner Pilsners. As we waited, Katerina asked about our trip and explored our knowledge of Berlin.

Once the beers arrived, she raised her glass, meeting my gaze. "Prost."

The evening unfolded with schnitzel, roasted potatoes, and conversation. Katerina recounted her shared history with Colleen during their time as operatives for the Global Relief Foundation. The stories painted a vivid tapestry of their enigmatic friendship forged in perilous situations—tales of unspoken missions, hard-earned victories, and near misses. Intrigue laced each anecdote, and a veil of cunning and danger shadowed it. Her words straddled the line between reality and myth, pushing away our jetlag and leaving us captivated by the tantalizing blend of raw truths and whispered mysteries.

As the sun set and the night grew colder, our table became the sole beacon of lingering conversation.

Katerina's voice softened with emotion. "I will miss my dear Colleen."

A sense of urgency gripped me. Leaning closer to her, I said, "We're here to learn more about GRF."

Dabbing her eyes, Katerina turned serious. "I thought so. But this isn't the time or place. I have a summer place near Schwielowsee. I'll pick you up tomorrow at 10:00 a.m. Bring your bags to stay overnight."

***

True to her word, Katerina arrived on time in a sleek black BMW M4 convertible, hair pulled back in a red scarf, sunglasses obscuring her eyes. The drive was a blur of speed and scenery, with the top down and wind in our hair.

When Katerina popped into a supermarket to get groceries for our stay, Leah turned around in the passenger seat to face me in the back seat and remarked, "I can see why Mom was friends with Katerina. She's led an extraordinary life." She proceeded to retell all the stories Katerina had told her during the drive, which I'd been unable to hear from where I sat.

Katerina returned, loaded the trunk, and we pressed on. The road narrowed, flanked by towering trees, until we emerged to glimpse Schwielowsee's shimmering waters.

"We're almost there," said Katerina with a smile.

A few sharp turns led us through a gate that opened with her remote, revealing a charming hillside house with a sunlit deck. The interior was an eclectic blend of Russian tapestries, varied furniture, and an impressive array of art. Books filled the shelves, representing a multitude of languages.

"Make yourselves at home. Choose a room down the hall while I put these away. Lunch will be in a few minutes," she said, disappearing into the kitchen.

Leah and I explored, choosing bedrooms with comforting views.

Returning, we found a feast laid out—meats, cheeses, and breads—accompanied by an offering of white wine.

Beyond, the lake stretched serenely.

"What a beautiful retreat you have," I commented.

"Thank you. It was my husband's family's summer place. It's become my sanctuary."

Over lunch, the conversation returned to the GRF's shadowy operations. Katerina described a complex scheme—a financial maze that laundered money through Canada's housing market, stretching across Russian and American interests in ways few could untangle. Each operational cell functioned independently, compartmentalized and unaware of the larger machinery it powered. Chaos concealed precision, a peculiar order that guarded moral ambiguity.

I noticed Leah squirming in her seat, her gaze drifting toward the window. The tension in the room was palpable, and she seemed unable to focus.

"Why don't you take a break—get some fresh air?" I coaxed.

She nodded, eager for the opportunity, and left without another word.

Now was the moment I'd hoped for: the chance to untangle the moral reckoning that had struck Colleen, shattering her sense of purpose. What had changed in her mind, in her heart, to make her question everything she'd been a part of? What had happened in Syria during the summer of 2014, leading up to the horrific execution of an American journalist, broadcast like a gruesome spectacle?

"Sorry to interrupt," I began cautiously. "Were you in Syria in 2014?"

Katerina's face froze and a shadow crossed her features, betraying the unease my question stirred. "I was there," she admitted quietly. "That mission didn't . . . it didn't go well."

"Can you tell me about it?"

Her face said no, but her words hesitated at the edge of agreement. "The plan," she began, her voice taking on an emotional weight, "was to push ISIS into plain view. Their territorial advances in Iraq and Syria were intolerable. Merciless. Terrorists who thrived on horror—using grotesque acts, like beheadings, as psychological warfare to instill fear within entire nations."

I could see her stiffen as memories resurfaced, raw and unrelenting.

"Our strategy," she continued, "had horrifying facets. The goal was to force ISIS into conducting public executions of 'military criminals.' It was calculated to heighten global perception of their barbarity, to manipulate how the world viewed terrorism through the most dreadful lens imaginable. To achieve this, the superiors wanted foreign hostages to be the linchpin. Western faces would humanize the atrocities. It was more than a strategy—it was exploiting lives to provoke outrage."

Her voice cracked on those last words, and my heart ached as Katerina's defenses crumbled.

"Colleen," she said, her hands trembling, "stood her ground. She refused to condone the use of innocent lives as bait for media manipulation. She argued passionately against the plan, insisting that it crossed every moral boundary. But . . . she was overruled."

Katerina paused, her face contorting as she fought back tears. "Colleen worked tirelessly to negotiate the release of the American journalist. She was close—so close—to securing his freedom. But instead . . . instead he became the tragic face of ISIS's horrors, condemned to death in front of cameras for the world to see."

Her voice was almost inaudible, as if the guilt had wrapped itself around her throat. "She never forgave herself. Knowing . . . knowing her efforts weren't enough. Knowing her compassion wasn't enough. She fought so hard, endured so much, and she still couldn't save him."

I placed a firm but gentle hand on Katerina's trembling shoulder, my own eyes stinging with emotion. "Katerina," I said softly, "thank you for sharing this. I can't imagine how it feels to carry something like this."

Her lips parted, but no words came at first. Then, through the tightness in her throat, she added, "But there's more. There's something else you need to know."

I nodded, bracing myself.

"They used you, Scott. They detained you in Turkey—pretending it was some routine visa issue—but it was a warning to Colleen. If she didn't comply, they told her subtly but unmistakably, the next beheaded American could be you." Her voice failed. "That was it for her, Scott. That was the moment she knew she couldn't continue. She couldn't serve people capable of such cruelty anymore. She wanted out."

We sat in silence as her words weighed down the room, suffocating in their burden. The pain of the past—hers, Colleen's, now mine—pressed into every corner, an inescapable shadow. We remained silent as no words could mend the damage.

That evening, the sun plunged, casting long shadows as we ate a quiet dinner of roasted vegetables and pork seasoned with rosemary and garlic. Glasses of robust red wine punctuated the solemnity of the moment.

Colleen's morality became clear as I carried the weight of the stories Katerina had shared. She had fought against the tide of manipulative cruelty, refusing to allow the innocent to be turned into pawns—even if it meant standing alone. Colleen's powerful sense of justice had compelled her to fight against cruelty and injustice, even when doing so meant challenging powerful forces alone. But when her efforts to save innocent lives failed, the immense sorrow and guilt of that loss became unbearable, crushing her spirit.

***

The following day, after breakfast, Katerina led us to Baumkronenpfad Beelitz-Heilstätten, a treetop walkway offering glimpses of World War II ruins below. The early hour gifted us solitude amid the expansive views.

Katerina knew nothing of FIST beyond Colleen's brief mentions. She spoke of Russian–American cooperation to contain China's geopolitical outreach, though the specifics of a balance-of-power strategy remained elusive.

Peering into the horizon from our treetop perch, I contemplated the historical echoes below—the lingering residue of the Potsdam Conference, where leaders plotted Europe's course after World War II. In its shadows, we gleaned pieces of the past, searching for clarity amid the remnants of war and the whispers of a legacy that seemed destined to shape our paths.

The Global Relief Foundation had to be destroyed. The question now was how?

27

Northern US

After a short return to New York to replenish our wardrobes, Leah and I loaded up her car for a road trip to Toronto, the headquarters of the Global Relief Foundation. As Leah packed up her last bag, I admired her new silver metallic Mercedes-AMG GT Coupe, with its 9-speed automatic V8 engine—an inheritance purchase. Technically, I suppose I was admiring *my* car, too. I had to give her credit; her passion for fast, elegant cars mirrored my own.

Sliding into the two-tone Nappa leather seat in black and red pepper, I inhaled the intoxicating new-car smell, savoring the moment until Leah jumped into the driver's seat, slammed the door, and shifted into drive. Without hesitation, she bolted out of the Bird's Nest underground parking garage onto the chaotic Manhattan street. We navigated west on West Fifty-Seventh Street, heading toward the Henry Hudson Parkway, and then north to the George Washington Bridge.

Driving through Manhattan's grid is not for the faint of heart. Even at seven in the morning, yellow cabs weaved, delivery trucks braked without warning, and aggressive cyclists darted unpredictably. But Leah was unfazed, weaving through the chaos with the confidence of a race car driver. Billie Eilish's *Lovely* played through the car's surround sound system, drowning out the city's noise as we exited Manhattan's frenetic maze.

Once we cleared New York City's congestion and were headed toward upstate New York, Leah finally released the beast under the hood—the 4.0-liter V8 bi-turbo engine with 577 horsepower. The car roared as she pressed the pedal, and the acceleration sent a thrill through me.

"So, what's the plan?" she asked, turning down the music.

"I was hoping you had it figured out," I replied playfully.

She smirked. "The simple solution? Cut off the money."

I couldn't disagree. "And how do we do that?"

"Well, we know the money sources—Russia and the US, right?"

"True. But it might be easier to work backward from GRF rather than the sources. How hard can that be?"

"If we're looking at major transactions, only six banks in Canada could handle billion-dollar movements without triggering alarms," she suggested.

"I doubt they'd make it that easy to track. Dozens of shell companies, spread among multiple banks, probably launder the funds."

Leah nodded. “Agreed.”

“Back when I was with Aurora EarthEx, we used foreign subsidiaries like Canary Financial Group or Frankfurt Bank for discreet international transactions. They’re notorious for turning a blind eye to following the money.”

Nods and conversation carried us for miles, the green hills outside our windows interrupted only by the occasional farm or highway billboard. A LEGOLAND sign on the outskirts of Goshen, NY, prompted our break. Pulling into a local diner for a quick meal, we found strong coffee and hearty, home-cooked food reminding us of better times.

***

The rhythmic hum of tires on asphalt filled the void between us, a steady background pulse to the stillness that hung in the Mercedes. Interstate 86 stretched ahead, its smooth pavement winding through forested hills and valleys. Outside, the early-afternoon light cast muted shadows across the road, the weather as indecisive as the silence between us.

I risked a glance at Leah. She sat rigid in the driver’s seat, both hands on the wheel, eyes fixed on the road ahead. Her jaw was set, and her lips were pressed into a hard line since leaving the diner. She uttered few words, lost in thought.

"You've been quiet," I said carefully, breaking the silence that had stretched thin and taut. "Something on your mind?"

It wasn't much, but it was a beginning—or so I thought. Leah didn't respond right away. Instead, she kept her face straight ahead, pretending the car in front of us held her attention.

"Just . . . thinking," she said finally, her voice flat. "A lot, actually. About . . . everything, I guess."

I wasn't sure what I'd expected—that she'd open up, pour out the years of emotions she'd locked away? That she'd forgive me before I finished the sentence? The sharp ache of guilt dug deeper with every passing mile.

"That's broad," I replied softly, trying not to sound defensive—or desperate. "I know your mother's death has been hard on you. Talk to me. Please."

Her silence lingered, dragging behind us like a ghost catching hold of the Mercedes. Then, without warning, she turned toward me, her voice colder, her words cutting with precision.

"You and Mom weren't there for me. Every damn time I needed you—every birthday, every bad day, everything that mattered—you weren't there. It wasn't boarding schools keeping me away—it was you."

It hurt to hear, but I didn't flinch. Truth wasn't something you dodged. "I know, Leah," I said, my throat thick. "I've wrestled with that guilt—not being there for you. Not being a parent you deserved."

"And have you figured out why?" she shot back, her tone sharp. "Why your 'careers' mattered more than your own kid? Or were you too blind to realize it?"

I wanted to respond, explain how hard those choices had been, how much I thought I was sacrificing for her security. But I froze, staring down the road ahead, the weight of her words sinking into cracks I hadn't wanted to explore.

"You're right," I admitted finally, my voice quiet. "I wasn't there for you, Leah. I'll never be able to make up for that. But I need you to know this . . . I thought—at the time—that I was making a better life for you. Sending you to the best schools. Back then, I thought money could buy happiness. I thought I was being a good dad."

"Oh, really? Then why didn't I feel happy?" Her voice wavered but stayed fierce. "I needed you . . . and Mom. Instead, you shipped me off, bought me presents, and paid for anything I wanted . . . like that was love."

"I know," I said, fighting the rising lump in my throat. "I see exactly how stupid I was. I failed you—both of us did. We made our careers the priority—and ignored what mattered most. Believe me when I tell you, Leah . . . I regret it every single day."

Something in her posture shifted—enough that I noticed. Her arms stayed on the steering wheel, but her jaw unclenched just enough to soften her voice when she trapped me with her next question.

"And now what?" she asked. "Do we pretend it never happened? Do we act like we're some perfect father–daughter duo? What?"

"No, Leah," I said sternly, still looking directly at her. "I can't undo anything, and I don't expect you to forgive me—not now, not right away. But I swear to you, I will be here from now on. No secrets, no excuses. You have my full attention—every part of me. That's a promise."

She took her eyes off the road to look at me, biting the inside of her lip as she weighed my words. Then she turned her head back toward the road, her voice softer now. "Okay," she said with a sigh. "We'll see."

I exhaled—I hadn't even realized I was holding my breath. A glimmer of hope. That was all I needed. "Fair enough," I said, placing my hand on her right shoulder.

Leah's face stiffened again; I witnessed profoundness, not anger. She turned her eyes back to me, her expression driven, focused. "And about Mom . . ." she said, her voice unwavering. "Whoever did this—whoever murdered her—they won't get away with it. No matter what it takes, or what we have to do, we're going to find them."

I nodded, my jaw tightening. The same fire burned within me. "You have my word, Leah. We'll find them. Together."

Her lips twitched almost imperceptibly. A hint of vulnerability breaking through the cracks. "Together," she whispered. Her voice was small, like it couldn't carry the weight of the word.

But it resonated enough in my chest.

I gave a small smile for the first time since we left the diner. "You're stuck with me now," I said lightly, trying—and failing—to sound casual. "Annoying dad jokes and all."

She laughed—the sound small and brief but real enough to settle the tension between us. "Don't push your luck."

As the car sped toward the horizon, the silence between us softened as promises replaced regrets. The road stretched long and unrelenting ahead, but I knew one thing for sure: whatever came next, we'd face it together.

***

As we waited to cross the Peace Bridge into Canada, I contemplated the daunting challenge ahead: accessing the GRF's financial database.

"We'll need someone on the inside or a really skilled hacker," I mused aloud.

Leah arched an eyebrow. "What about Igor Pikalov?" she asked before I could even clarify.

"Your computer geek friend from private school? What was his story? Immigrants from Ukraine? Russian?"

Leah rolled her deep-blue eyes. "Supposedly, his dad was an oligarch. Probably dirty money." She chuckled.

"I never figured out how they could afford Bayview Glen—forty grand a year in tuition!" I smirked. "Weren't you two pretty close friends?"

She shrugged. "As close as two stoner teenagers could be. I haven't talked to him since junior high."

I tapped the dashboard. "Do you think he could be our hacker?"

"He was always super smart. He was coding before anyone knew what it was."

"Do you know how to get in touch with him?"

"I can try. He's on my social network."

We reached the front of the line and Leah presented our US passports to the customs officer, who asked our purpose for visiting Canada.

"We're catching a Blue Jays game and the IndyCar race," she said with a poker face.

The officer spent an extra second sizing up the shiny new Mercedes, its driver, and the older passenger who could pass for her father or . . . something else entirely. "Enjoy your visit," he said, smiled, and handed the passports back.

The drive through southern Ontario brought us to St. Catharines for fuel and greasy cheeseburgers, which we consumed while leaning against our car in the gas station parking lot. This was Colleen's hometown. Her parents had emigrated from Northern Russia, instilling their country's culture into their three daughters. Memories of family lore and conflict resurfaced as Leah traced the outline of her burger on its wrapper.

"Do we have time to see Babka and Deda?" she asked between bites.

I hesitated, wiping ketchup from her chin with a napkin. Her childhood smile flashed back at me, and for a moment, I didn't want this memory to end.

"I don't think that's a good idea—remember, I'm supposed to be dead. Maybe you can drop by on the way back while I people-watch in Niagara Falls. What do you think?"

She nodded, catching my smile and tossing the trash from our meal. "I like that idea. Hey, you can drive. I don't know Toronto streets like you do."

As I settled into the driver's seat, she jumped in on the passenger side and checked her phone.

"Wow, Igor already replied—he'd love to meet up."

Surprised at her efficiency, I started the car.

28

Toronto

Two hours later, we arrived at our Airbnb, a sleek two-bedroom condo on Queen's Quay overlooking Lake Ontario. Its living area was open concept, with the south wall consisting of glass. It had a small gourmet kitchen and a bar-height counter with stools to divide the space. The view, rippling with warm evening light, kept Leah on the deck while I tackled settling in.

Dinner was at a French bistro nearby. I indulged in tartare de bœuf, steak frites, and glasses of Bordeaux. I left Leah to nibble at her healthier cocktail de crevettes and salade niçoise. More than once, I caught suspicious glances from patrons, likely wondering what an older man and a young woman so engrossed in private conversation could be plotting.

Our plan was simple: Leah would determine if Igor was up for the job as our hacker or if he could find us someone who was;

meanwhile, I'd scout GRF's Toronto headquarters to assess its layout, personnel, and security vulnerabilities.

We waved away dessert and, outside in the humid night, I felt humbled by the reconnection Leah and I had forged. Nine hours together in a car didn't leave space to avoid emotions. We resolved to avenge Colleen, full stop.

"Our Uber's here," Leah called, breaking my reverie.

Five minutes into our ride back to our Airbnb, her phone buzzed.

"Yes? . . . Now? . . . Sure. Where? . . . Okay, I'll be there."

The driver detoured to Bathurst and Queens at Leah's request.

"That was Igor," she explained to me. "He wants to meet now at Kult, a dance club. Some European DJ is playing." She glanced at her footwear. "I guess these will have to do."

The car slowed, and before I could reply, she leaped out, shouted "See you tomorrow!" and vanished into Toronto's nightlife.

***

Sunlight pierced through the open blinds and flooded the room like an unwelcome visitor. I shuffled to the bathroom, splashed water on my face, and wandered into the kitchen, hoping against hope that some remnants of tea lingered there. A glance at the front door revealed Leah's shoes, sparking a flicker of concern. What time had she come in? I questioned the wisdom of reconnecting her to an old acquaintance with a penchant for indulging in less-than-wholesome activities. Was her willpower stronger now? I could only hope.

Fortune smiled on me with enough supplies to make a cup of tea. I retreated to the balcony and watched the morning scene unfold: the walkers, the runners, the ferry boats moving through the water. It was already eight thirty. So much for an early start. I powered up my laptop, starting my delve into the murky waters of the Global Relief Foundation.

As the hours slipped by and the tea flowed, a pattern emerged while I searched the provincial land registry. Markland Properties had constructed the GRF building in 1974 and sold it fourteen years later to GBS Asset Management Inc. for $1.2 million. The owner's legal name then shifted every decade, hence now cloaked under the obscurity of Mount Royal Capital LLC. No trail, no details—this had the telltale signs of a shell company hiding in the shadows of tax havens like the British Virgin Islands, Cayman Islands, and beyond.

A voice interrupted my thoughts. Leah stood in the balcony doorway, with messy hair and casual attire. "Good morning," she said, though the watch on my wrist told me it was nearly noon.

"What time did you get in?" I asked more out of curiosity than accusation.

"All I know is it was late. I need a coffee."

She left and returned a few minutes later with a freshly brewed coffee. She found her place beside me and curled up in a lounge chair. "I'm getting too old for this."

"Really? You're only twenty-five."

"Almost twenty-six," she countered, gazing into the distance. Just as the silence settled in, she turned to me. "He's our hacker, for a price."

My interest was piqued. "Really?"

"He's a freelance digital security consultant," she explained, "offering his skills to companies across the globe, even in Russia, to expose their cybersecurity weaknesses."

My skepticism was hard to mask. "And his price?"

She smiled—a knowing, confident smile. "As a friend, he'd give us a family discount."

"When can he start?"

"I've already invited him for dinner tonight. What do you feel like cooking?"

I rose from my seat with renewed energy. "Okay. We need to go shopping."

***

Leah emerged from her room, enveloped in the warm embrace of a summer evening. The sun's golden glow streamed through the floor-to-ceiling windows, illuminating her long blonde hair cascading down her back. As she moved toward me in her white linen dress, her presence was ethereal.

A memory flickered—an echo of her mother from thirty years before. "Wow . . . you look stunning. Igor won't know what hit him. He'd better be ready for perfection!"

"Stop it. You're embarrassing me." She waved off my compliment, but the soft blush on her cheeks betrayed her pleasure.

I handed her a glass of rosé. "You'll knock him off his feet . . . with his shoes still on!" A mix of pride and protectiveness colored my tone.

She accepted the glass, my words dissolving in the air as she quieted me with a gentle look.

I lifted my glass. "To happiness."

Leah raised hers in return, her gaze steady and unwavering. "To the demise of GRF."

As I cleaned the kitchen, Leah answered the door. When I looked over, my mind raced, trying to connect the Igor of now with the pale, gangly young boy I remembered.

In his place stood a man whose presence filled the room and refused to be overlooked. His angular features were striking, and his glacial green eyes pierced the room with an intensity that felt razor-sharp. His white linen shirt hugged his tanned, muscular frame, while sleek black jeans gave him the polish of a *GQ* model rather than a tech savant buried in keyboards and code. The tattoos that danced across his forearms were vibrant and mysterious, telling stories I didn't know and didn't want to know. There was an air of confidence about him that bordered on arrogance, reinforced by his designer watch and large solitary diamond earring. There was something about him that set my instincts on edge.

"It's good to see you, Igor," I said, stepping forward.

His handshake was firm, almost challenging, and I reciprocated with a strength that belied my surprise.

"You look great," I commented, my voice betraying more wonder than intended.

"It's been a long time." His words were smooth; his smile was almost feline in nature.

"What can I get you—wine, beer, vodka?"

"Whatever you're having is fine." The hint of something more in his gaze tempered the casualness in his response.

As I poured, Leah slid seamlessly into conversation. Their chemistry was palpable, infused with a shared past and new possibilities.

With the ice broken, I shifted focus to the evening ahead. "I hope you're hungry. I've got steaks and prawns from the St. Lawrence Market—a classic surf and turf."

In the living room, with drinks in hand, I embarked on my subtle interrogation from the opposite armchair. "How are your parents?"

"They're fine, I suppose. They moved back to Crimea and have since split up. I keep in touch with my mom occasionally; with my father, not at all."

"I'm sorry to hear that."

"It's all right. When they left Canada, I finished school and went straight to U of T. From there, a scholarship took me to MIT for my PhD in Computer and Data Science. After a stint at BlackBerry, I turned to freelance IT security and forensic investigations. The financial independence suits me."

Leah had heard about his journey the previous night, but the familiar tale was no less impressive for its repetition.

I stood, deciding to leave them to their shared interests as I turned to the night's meal. "Leah just completed her master's in psychology at UCLA. She can fill you in while I start dinner. How do you like your meat?"

"Medium rare," Igor replied, a smirk playing on his lips.

From the kitchen, I could hear Leah delve into emotional, cognitive, and behavioral questions to investigate Igor's coping mechanisms and what made him tick.

As dusk settled and we made our way through our dinner of filet mignon medallions, tiger prawns, baked potatoes, and Ontario red wine, the conversation deepened. We unveiled glimpses of our past: Colleen's murder, the tangled web of GRF, and our resolve to dismantle the flow of illicit funds. Yet details of FIST and the undercurrent of global power went unsaid. Whenever

Leah spoke, Igor's attention zeroed in on her. She mesmerized him.

Post-dinner, Igor went onto the balcony, cigarette in hand. Leah followed, and through the windows, I watched their animated conversation; her laughter rang out like a melody.

Doubt crept in—had involving Igor been a mistake?

29

Beaches, Toronto

The next day, Leah thought it would be a good idea to see the city like a local commuter, so we took the longest streetcar journey along Queen Street, winding slowly toward Igor's place in the Beaches. The morning rush had subsided, yet many people still crowded the streetcar. Together, we rocked with the motion, our stop-and-go progress grating away at leisure.

The driver called Glen Manor Drive, and we disembarked with anticipation, making our way to Igor's address near the lake—his house, a duplex with a weathered beach charm, was nestled snugly near the boardwalk.

Leah bounded up the steps with the kind of energy youth grants and then rapped on the door. Igor greeted us with affection—Leah with an embrace, me with a fist bump.

Inside, stark whites contrasted with polished blacks, a study in monochrome minimalism. His living room window revealed

Lake Ontario and the beach boardwalk. As expected, Igor offered beverages before leading us into the depths of his lair.

Igor's dominion in the basement was a world apart—a striking shift from the monochrome precision of the house above. This was where Igor lived—truly lived—away from the pleasantries of daylight and human niceties. The walls and floors were both polished concrete. A long jet-black workstation dominated one side of the room, home to an arsenal of computers, each screen glowing with intricate data streams and cryptic codes. There were at least six high-resolution monitors arranged in a semicircle around his main chair. This sleek, ergonomic gaming chair resembled the cockpit of a spacecraft more than a piece of furniture. The monitors were alive, flashing between terminal windows, network maps, and unintelligible data streams.

Beneath the big desk, a fortress of computer towers—high-end, custom-built, adorned with glowing LEDs—hummed, their fans burning tirelessly to keep up with the load of Igor's digital world. Tangled cables ran between them in meticulous chaos, bundled and zip-tied in a way that only the owner would understand.

To the side, nestled in the corner, was a towering server rack. Its routers, switches, and NAS devices blinked in unison like a vault of secrets too complex for the untrained eye. It was the backbone of Igor's operation, a private fortress that connected this unassuming basement in Toronto to the farthest edges of cyberspace.

In the opposite corner of the room, a meeting table sat under a bright light. The table was spotless and glossy white, a stark contrast to the basement's industrial aesthetic. Two chic, high-design Aeron chairs flanked it, marking this as the space Igor reserved for face-to-face interactions—a rarity in his world.

The halo of screens cast shadows on the basement's surfaces, making the room seem suspended between light and dark.

Igor waved us toward the meeting table, and when we sat down, the glow of his workspace instantly fell thousands of miles away, though I still felt the room's silent energy humming beneath my skin. He pulled one of his gaming chairs over to join us and sank into its seat, balancing the casual air of a friend with the precision of a man about to deliver something monumental.

"I'll be honest," he began, his voice lower now, almost conspiratorial. "last night, I started probing the Global Relief Foundation's network." He leaned back, tilting his coffee mug to his lips, stalling as if deciding how much truth to reveal.

A knot of unease tightened in my chest. "Go on."

"What I found," Igor continued, sitting forward now, his hands resting on the table's edge, "wasn't . . . normal. They secured their network with something highly advanced, far beyond what you'd expect from a nonprofit organization. I identified a highly sophisticated intrusion detection system. It's called EINSTEIN—well, something almost identical to it."

Leah frowned, confused. "What's EINSTEIN?"

"It's a US government system," Igor said, his tone growing more serious with every word. "It's owned and operated by CISA, the Cybersecurity and Infrastructure Security Agency. It's a division of the Department of Homeland Security. EINSTEIN is used to monitor and defend federal networks from cyber threats. Essentially, this nonprofit's network has adopted the same advanced framework the United States government uses to safeguard its most critical systems. What I found inside GRF's infrastructure . . . is not something companies or foundations randomly implement."

The room felt smaller, the air heavier. Leah and I exchanged nervous glances.

Igor's eyes grew colder, sharper. "But that wasn't the part that stopped me."

"What do you mean?" I asked, feeling the pressure mount.

"When I searched more, something else emerged. It started with fragmented connections within the system's cryptographic framework. Then I saw details buried beneath layers of encoded data structures. My tools pinpointed traces . . . no, more than traces—entire protocols linked to GosSOPKA."

I froze.

Leah, a moment behind me, looked at Igor for an explanation. "What is GosSOPKA?" she asked, her voice careful, almost reluctant to disturb the deepening quiet.

Igor took a measured breath. "It's Russia's state-run cybersecurity system. Think of it as their digital eyes and ears. It's not only a defense; it's an offense. This is the system operated by Russian intelligence, including the SVR, their foreign intelligence service, to secure their most classified operations. The embedded traces of GosSOPKA within GRF's architecture suggest that they cooperated or directly interacted with Russian systems. Hacking into their chain is as dangerous as hacking the CIA—possibly worse because of how they handle their enemies."

Igor leaned back, setting down his now-empty coffee mug. He let the silence sink in for a moment, the gravity of his discovery seeping into the room like a slow poison.

My throat tightened as I processed his words.

"So, here's my question," he said finally, his piercing green eyes locking onto mine. "What *exactly* are you two dealing with? Because a nonprofit doesn't warrant this level of protection, let alone ties to US and Russian cyber intelligence. This charity's digital fortifications rival those of major banks." He looked at Leah and back at me. "So, I ask again, what aren't you telling me?"

30

Queen's Quay, Toronto

After yesterday's discovery that the GRF's network was untouchable, I sat on our balcony and searched every inch of the internet for any reference to or trace of the Global Relief Foundation's actions and reactions. I was looking to identify potential vulnerabilities—clues about threats or exposure. I found a couple of disgruntled employees commenting on Glassdoor, along with a job posting for a short-term assignment as the assistant to the president, a maternity leave announcement, and a notice about their upcoming fundraising gala. Nothing of value.

We needed another way to get to GRF and its dark, dirty secrets. I stared at my computer screen, then at the boats on the blue waters of Lake Ontario. I knew the answer was before me, but I couldn't see it.

Leah poked her head outside. "Good morning. Would you like a fresh cup of tea?"

"That would be nice."

She came back in a moment with my refill, then sat down beside me. Here we were on day four in Toronto, with no leads, sitting on the sunny deck, admiring the beautiful scenery. Except we had hired a hacker. I walked Leah through my latest findings, hoping she might see something I hadn't.

After scrolling through all my notes and screen grabs, she handed back my computer. "We need someone inside GRF to get behind their firewall," she said. "I need to apply for the assistant job. I have all the skills."

It was a brilliant idea. Why hadn't I thought of this? "Wouldn't they connect you to your mom?"

"She went by her maiden name at work, right? I don't think anyone in the office knew her well enough to connect the dots."

Once more, my daughter's brilliance shone.

This fortunate opportunity was a positive sign of good against evil. I felt re-energized. But this wasn't a done deal.

"Okay, how do we get you an interview? Remember, it's not what you know but who you know."

I began listing likely people and contacts who could help us get Leah added to the interview list. The most obvious people to approach were Colleen's past colleagues: Susan, who attended her funeral, and Katerina in Berlin. Hopefully, one of them would have sufficient influence and contacts to get Leah on the shortlist.

Taking no chances, I secured another burner phone to call Susan and Katerina. I started with Susan, who didn't answer, and left a brief message. Katerina was happy to hear my voice and said she would do what she could to help, tempering any expectations with the caveat that she had limited contacts in GRF's head office. We filled the rest of the conversation with talk about our travels and the transition since Colleen's passing. We both left the call in a depressed state, with Katerina promising to follow up with any news about getting Leah's name on the interview list.

Leah began working on her resume as well as her appearance to avoid being mistaken for Colleen's lookalike. She found the perfect makeover salon to create the transformation. After five hours of her face being cleansed, exfoliated, toned, threaded, waxed, and nourished, her eyelashes enhanced and tinted, and her hair colored, cut, and styled, she walked out a new person. The most dramatic change was her hair, which had been turned from blonde to a vivid red with some brown tones.

A few days later, I heard from Susan, who was delighted to help, as well as Katerina, who reached out to get a copy of Leah's resume. After Leah applied, a waiting game began.

31

Queen's Quay

I paced the condo as I thought about my actions, which had put Leah in the center of danger as she sat with Cathy Dickson, the head of the Global Relief Foundation. The organization that had destroyed her mother and my wife.

The support of Susan and Katerina had helped secure an interview with GRF. Now, it was up to Leah to convince the CEO that she was the perfect candidate to fill the short-term role as her assistant. I think I was more nervous than she was when she left the apartment, asking me to wish her luck.

To keep myself busy and focused, I opened one of the most recent files marked "2017–2021." A single document presented itself: an image of a neatly typed English letter devoid of letterhead.

Dear Friend,

Congratulations on reaching your first six months

as the President of the United States.

May I be so bold as to offer you my wisdom, gained from over 20 years of leadership experience?

You speak often of victories that are grand in scale and decisive in impact. Your vision favors boldness and displays of power. While this ambition is admirable, I urge you to consider one truth I have learned in my years at the helm: Chaos, which you so readily celebrate, is formidable only when controlled. Unchecked, it devours even its architects. Success, lasting success, belongs to those who master the storm without becoming consumed by it.

You are charismatic and instinctive, qualities that can rally a nation. However, you must temper instinct with strategy. Impulse without calculation is a liability, not a strength. Trust between leaders rests not on grand promises but on actions that consistently align with shared goals. If we continue to collaborate with FIST, I must see discipline from you, not recklessness.

As we champion the forward momentum of FIST and the philosophy behind it, I encourage you to pause and reflect on its significance. Elevating its impact requires an understanding of leverage and a commitment to precision rather than disruption. I have built my leadership on this principle and have navigated complexities with measured confidence. To achieve greatness, it is advisable to adopt this discipline.

You may see yourself as a voice on an unparalleled rise, but let me remind you: your actions ripple through history far more profoundly than your words ever could.

I will continue to watch your choices with keen interest. As we move forward, understand that you must earn trust. You cannot demand it. Should I sense threats to stability through impulsive action or mismanaging this moment, you will find that my patience has limits.

You once said that you admire my ability to operate in the shadows, out of the reach of scrutiny. I trust you understand the significance of such skills. With discipline, I use them, forging paths that chaos cannot breach. I urge you to employ a similar focus and restraint.

Actions—not proclamations—will determine the future. Remember this.

Yours faithfully,

V.P.

32

Consumer Drive

Leah clasped her hands in her lap. Even in contrast with the tired, nondescript office decor, her appearance seemed muted. She had made sure of that. Her hair, reddish brown enough to distract from the natural blonde underneath, hung loose in waves, lacking its usual polish. Her makeup, heavier than she usually wore, verged on the edge of noticeable: foundation that didn't quite match her natural skin tone, eyeliner extending too far. But no lipstick. These details weren't accidental. Nor was the plain navy sheath dress she had chosen, its boxy cut dulling the sharp lines of her athletic frame. Or the unassuming black ballet flats peeking out beneath the hem. Or the simple chain around her neck, its small pendant as forgettable as the cheap hoops that adorned her ears. She'd curated every inch of herself to blend in, avoid scrutiny, and erase the air of someone wealthy who commands attention upon entering a room.

Opposite her, Cathy Dickson scrutinized Leah's pared-down resume with the precision of someone who had spent years discovering lies. With her tailored suit and immaculately styled hair, the CEO of Global Relief Foundation projected the quiet authority of someone who didn't mince words, especially when there was no time to spare. Her expression was sharp but calm, her body language revealing neither skepticism nor encouragement. Finally, she looked across the table, leveling Leah with a measured gaze that invited only the truth—or a compelling enough version of it to impress her.

"Ms. Barton," Cathy Dickson began, her voice matter-of-fact yet laced with curiosity, "your resume is very impressive. Your background, degree, and experience—frankly, it all suggests that you're more than qualified for a bigger career opportunity. What puzzles me is this: Why would someone like you, who could launch a permanent career with many organizations, want to work on a short-term assignment here at Global Relief Foundation?"

The question hung in the air. Leah had expected it, of course—if the role were her cover, then her story would have to be airtight. She paused, adjusting her shoulders and smiling faintly as she leaned forward to convey both sincerity and engagement.

"Ms. Dickson, I appreciate the question, and I want to be completely transparent about my reasons for applying to this position. I have built my career on opportunities where I felt confident, capable, and in control of my next step. But life has a way of shifting priorities, and that's what's happened for me recently."

She hesitated, her gaze briefly dropping before meeting Cathy's again. Her tone softened. "I'm in Toronto temporarily to care for my grandmother, who has been the most important person in my life since I was a little girl. She recently became ill, and at her fragile age, it's been a challenge for her to remain in her home independently. My initial plan was to help her transition into a retirement facility so I could return home. But the process has been slower than I expected, especially with the waiting list for the care facility she needs. The reality is, I'll be here for at least a year, until she's safe and settled."

Leah's voice steadied, finding its rhythm as she adjusted focus. "I've been looking for meaningful work that provides financial support and aligns with what I care about. That's why Global Relief Foundation stands out to me. I'm deeply inspired by your work to support women and girls worldwide in dealing with critical issues. I've always seen tremendous value in helping others, and this role would give me the satisfaction of working toward a cause I believe in while I navigate this difficult period of my personal life."

She paused, checking Cathy's expression before she continued. "I don't need a long-term position right now—at this point, it's not about building my career in the traditional sense. It's about balancing my responsibility to my family with work that gives me purpose. GRF represents exactly that to me: the chance to help, to support a mission I admire, and to spend this time making an impact in a way that matters."

As she finished, her voice resonated with sincerity. Even she believed what she was saying. "I know my credentials might suggest I'm overqualified, but I believe the specifics of my experience—adapting, working with focus and precision, and approaching challenges with a problem-solving mindset—could allow me to offer real value, even in a short-term role. And honestly, I'd feel privileged to be a small part of the incredible work your team is doing."

With a serene smile, Leah allowed her answer to settle as she gently placed her unmanicured hands on the table and awaited Cathy's response. If there had been any nervousness earlier, it had dissolved into quiet confidence and, more importantly, she was certain this performance was Oscar-worthy.

In the shadows, agents Susan and Katerina performed their magic to ensure a smooth background check, including verification of education and working qualifications, references, and a clean criminal record. Everything, including Grandma's story, checked out with no security alarms going off.

It would all depend on Leah's performance.

33

Queen's Quay

"I got it! I start next week!" Leah screamed with delight, sprinting toward me and wrapping me in the biggest hug imaginable.

"Your very first job!" I said with a touch of irony, embracing her.

Happy tears flowed down her cheeks. "I knew it. Mom is working her magic." She pulled away with electrified energy. "We need to go shopping. I need new business clothes and shoes," she said excitedly, darting back to her bedroom to get dressed. "Oh! I need to tell Igor!"

Left in the living room, I stood in silence, a bittersweet knot forming in my chest. I wished Colleen were here to witness this milestone, to see how far Leah and I had come together. She would have been so proud—proud of Leah, proud of me. I closed my eyes and sent her a prayer: *We're going to need your help, Colleen, if this crazy plan is going to work.*

Last week felt like the calm before the storm. Leah had been spending time with Igor—going on long walks, sharing coffee talks, and enjoying cozy dinners via food delivery. As a father, I still grappled with whether Igor was good for her. I wanted to believe he was, but my optimism remained measured.

***

Monday arrived with a flurry of excitement. Leah's dresser and closet were brimming with fresh purchases. In keeping with the part she was playing, she'd gone for practical, budget-friendly staples. Simple, versatile pieces that paired perfectly with her freshly dyed reddish-brown hair.

"How do I look?" she asked, doing a graceful twirl.

Her polished look radiated confidence: a business pantsuit with her hair swept into a ponytail. She'd overdone the makeup to achieve a less sophisticated look, opting for bright lipstick.

Like a proud father seeing his child off on their first day of school, I couldn't help but smile, though the moment weighed on me. I had never been there to drop Leah off at school—my business schedule always took precedence in those years. This moment felt like a second chance.

"You look perfect," I reassured her.

Her first assignment was ambitious: to photograph every interior detail of the building's three floors, chart the security systems, identify cameras, motion sensors, and network devices, and assess the operational systems with precision. Her tasks would also include uncovering the depth of their cybersecurity measures—from firewalls and encryption to passwords and segmentations. Many of these protocol details would reveal themselves during her onboarding, aided by her covert use of her smartphone.

"Got to go. My Uber's almost here," Leah said, grabbing her tote bag as she leaned in to peck my cheek. "Love you."

Her words lingered in my mind, wrapping around me. "I love you back," I mumbled awkwardly. "Stay safe and . . . don't take any risks." I cringed at myself as the word *risks* tumbled out of my mouth.

Stupid fool. Why did you say that?

***

Thirty minutes later, my phone buzzed. Leah was calling me.

"Hello?" I answered, my heart quickening.

Traffic noise hummed in the background. Her voice was a mix of urgency and disappointment. "Hi, Dad. There's a problem."

My nerves tightened. "What's wrong?"

"I'm outside the GRF building. It's surrounded by a Faraday shield."

"A . . . what?" I asked, unfamiliar with the term.

"It's a barrier that blocks electromagnetic radiation—radio waves, signals. Essentially, cell phones don't function inside the building. Doesn't matter, though. They confiscate personal phones at the entrance and lock them until the end of the day."

The pieces clicked into place. That would explain the communication delays I noticed during her interview.

She continued, her tone a mix of concern and determination. "They'll issue me a company cell soon. I'll text you when it's set up, but know that they'll be monitoring everything. Every call. Every message."

I mustered encouragement, despite the heavy weight in my chest. "Understood. Stay sharp. And enjoy your first day."

She disconnected. My hands tightened around the phone. My only recourse was to prepare. *Buy a mini spy camera for Leah.*

34

Queen's Quay

In just two days, the apartment had transformed into something like a detective's lair. Every visible wall and window had become a canvas of taped-up images, information threads sprawling like a conspiracy's veins. The floor plan of GRF with cardinal directions and operational zones covered the wall above the sofa. Sticky notes annotated staff profiles, complete with roles, security levels, and unsettling fragments of personal data Leah had pieced together.

The wall beside the dining table was Igor's domain: a cryptic assembly of diagrams, acronyms, and IT jargon. He labored to decode GRF's cybersecurity infrastructure—a fortress of IPsec, SSL, TLS, DTLS, firewalls, and encryption layers that made my head swim. The jargon baffled Leah and me, but Igor devoured it.

The dining table was no longer used for meals. It had become a tactical base of stacked monitors, extra computer equipment, and a printer. The kitchen counter was "internal forensic"—an overflow of takeaway bags and disposable boxes from every kind of food delivery you could imagine.

Leah had already established a nightly routine. She was home from GRF by six and debriefed Igor and me, recounting every shred of intel in astonishing detail. The pen spy camera I'd got for her exceeded expectations, capturing full HD video and sharp photographs. We backed up everything to an external hard drive and printed key visuals in full color. What amazed me even more than the technology was Leah herself. The way she absorbed, memorized, and dissected every detail with no need for a single written note. It was like watching a born operative in action.

Each day, the intel grew more alarming. GRF's security design rivaled top-secret US military facilities. Every new guest to the building was required to watch the safety video, which was far more than a formality. While you watched, a hidden camera recorded biometric data, using a covert facial recognition system connected to GRF's internal database, which tied identities to access tiers. Computers snapped shut the second someone walked away, relying on live facial recognition.

Every discovery underscored the GRF's fortress-like nature. We unearthed protocols that ensured no data—no laptops or software—left the building. Every detail reinforced our understanding that this was not only a charity but also a secret vault of sorts.

***

On the third day, Leah returned with something extraordinary. We gathered in the living area of our condo for her debrief. She kicked off her heels, grabbed the glass of rosé I had poured for her, and downed half in one large sip before she dropped the bombshell. "You'll never guess what I discovered today."

"What?" I asked, leaning in.

"There's another level. A basement."

Igor shrugged it off. "Most buildings have basements."

Leah shook her head. "This isn't standard. Only employees with Level 4-B clearance are authorized to access it. I can access the three main floors with my 2-A clearance, but the basement is restricted."

"What's down there?" Igor asked, his curiosity now clearly piqued.

"My coworker said it's their communications center. Staffed 24/7."

I scrawled *Basement* on a yellow sticky note and stuck it to the wall. If the GRF building had felt like Fort Knox, this revelation strengthened that feeling.

35

Consumer Drive

The GRF employee lounge on the main floor was almost eerily quiet. Leah sat at a small table near the kitchenette, her hands wrapped around a steaming mug of coffee. She looked at the employee noticeboard, its neat rows of laminated updates presenting the latest company news. But the words were a blur—she wasn't registering any of it. The GRF basement occupied her thoughts. What was happening down there?

A soft rustling sound broke her reverie. She glanced up at the janitor, who moved with a steady efficiency around the coffee station as she worked in silence. She opened one of the low cabinets and pulled out a bulky box of paper towel rolls, lifting it onto the counter. The janitor popped one roll from the box and arranged it by the sink before turning to grab another stack of supplies.

Leah froze, her hands tightening on her mug as her gaze lingered on the industrial box. Its sheer size was almost comical on the counter. It could conceal someone's face—or more. A spark of an idea ignited in her thoughts. The idea transformed into a plan. Daring. Risky. Possible.

She couldn't get into the basement on her own. No badge. No clearance. No way in. However, the janitor could move freely and unnoticed. And the tools of her trade? They were ordinary, unexceptional, and totally unthreatening. Leah glanced briefly at the oversized box again, her pulse quickening. A box like that could be her cover, her excuse, and her way down.

The janitor, now moving toward the storage closet, smiled at Leah. "Forgot something," she muttered before stepping out of sight.

Seizing the moment, Leah sprang from her chair. Her heart hammered, adrenaline urging her forward. She reached for the extra apron hanging on the janitor's cart, slipped it off the hook, and secured it under her arm. Without a second thought, she scurried back to her desk, her mind racing.

She would wait for the right moment. Timing would be everything.

***

Hours later, Leah stood outside the elevator on the far side of the GRF lobby. She adjusted the oversized janitor's apron draped over her front, giving her a semblance of authenticity. The large cardboard box in her arms added another layer to her disguise, one that doubled as concealment for the small pen camera clipped to its upper corner. The spy camera was positioned perfectly, ready to capture everything ahead of her.

Leah's knees trembled under the weight of her plan, but she willed herself steady. Every fiber of her being screamed *Caution!* but she couldn't stop now. She stared at her reflection in the brushed steel doors of the elevator. Head down. Eyes inconspicuous. She looked every bit the part of a casual employee on a mundane errand. It would have to be convincing enough.

The elevator chimed, its quiet hum blending with the distant murmur of conversations around her. Leah's pulse raced as she waited. Her face remained obscured by the box as she hovered near the buttons. She couldn't press the down button to the basement herself. She needed patience. And luck.

Minutes dragged. Two employees passed by, neither heading for the basement. Leah swayed from foot to foot, her grip on the box tightening. She told herself to breathe. Someone would come. And then luck turned.

A tall man dressed goth-like in all black approached the elevator. Leah's heart leaped as he reached out and pressed the Down button. The soft chime echoed, and the elevator doors slid open.

"Hold the door, please?" Leah said, her voice light, threaded with polite urgency.

The man glanced her way but kindly caught the door as she shuffled in behind him.

Clutching the box with both hands, Leah stepped into the elevator, her heart thudding with anticipation. She took her place in the corner, tweaking the box. The camera inside had a perfect view of the control panel as he swiped his security card and pressed the button for the basement level. Leah's pulse quickened further. This was what she needed. The soft hum of the elevator vibrated through the floor beneath her feet, each second heavier than the last.

The ding of the elevator landing broke the silence and Leah's stomach lurched. The doors slid open slowly, revealing an expanse that even her overactive imagination couldn't have prepared her for.

The basement was vast. A sprawling, windowless cavern filled with the quiet hum of machinery and faint, engineered white noise. Sterile fluorescent lighting gave everything a clinical glow. Enormous screens lined one wall, with some displaying grids of surveillance footage and others showing live satellite imagery. The maps flickered, zooming in and out with timestamps marking different time zones. Rows of desks, each grouped into clusters of three or six, stretched in every direction. Occupying each chair was a person hunched over computer monitors. Most wore sleek headsets as they worked.

The rhythmic tapping of keys drowned out the soft murmurs of conversation. Leah adjusted her box, ensuring the camera captured every inch of the scene. She had expected something secretive—but this? This was industrial. Organized. Far more massive than she had imagined.

The goth man stepped out without a word, striding toward one of the desk clusters near the back. Leah remained frozen. Every instinct urged her to depart. She couldn't risk further exposure. Forcing her trembling hand to move, she darted her finger to the control panel and pressed the button for the first floor.

She caught one last fleeting glimpse of the expanse before the reflective elevator doors closed. Her own face stared back at her—a mask of determination concealing the adrenaline roaring in her veins. The trip back up felt torturous, every second drawing her farther from the scene she'd just captured. But not from the questions it had burned into her mind.

When the doors opened again, Leah clutched the box and stepped out with her head low, her pace brisk. Hopeful the pen camera had captured whatever secrets the GRF basement held.

***

Later that evening, I watched Leah's footage play on the computer monitor on the dining room table. She stood by the kitchen, her face expressionless yet her intensity palpable. Igor, sitting closest to the screen, leaned forward, concentrating. I sat beside him, silent but gripped by what we were seeing.

The footage unfolded like a glimpse into another world. Igor paused on a vivid image of the basement—rows of pod-like desk formations, the quiet activity of hundreds of people administering data or watching live feeds. For a long moment, none of us spoke.

"There are over one hundred thirty pods," Igor said finally, his voice low and tense. "If each pod represents an operational team or campaign . . ."

I finished his thought. "That means one hundred and thirty initiatives running simultaneously."

Igor's expression darkened further, the wheels in his mind spinning. "And if they're operating two shifts around the clock . . ."

"Two hundred and sixty," I whispered with disbelief. "They're operating everywhere. Everywhere."

The realization hit us all with a crushing weight. This encompassed more than intelligence work. This was managing and controlling on a scale we hadn't dared to imagine.

No one said it aloud, but the unspoken question hung in the air.

What else were they capable of?

36

Consumer Drive

Leah adjusted the hem of her terracotta wrap dress, gripping her coffee tightly as she stepped into Cathy Dickson's office. She did her best to present herself professionally, and her boss greeted her warmly.

"Good morning. How has your first week gone so far?" Cathy asked, motioning Leah to a small table instead of the imposing desk behind her.

Leah fidgeted as she sat. "Honestly, it's been a whirlwind. It's all acronyms, systems, and information overload. But I'm enjoying it." She placed her coffee unsteadily on the table, noticing the slight clamminess in her hands.

"I apologize for not being here to greet you when you started. I was in New York all week, but you knew that." Cathy's tone was efficient and her expression was neutral as she straightened her posture. "First, welcome again. I hope your time with us will be rewarding."

Leah glanced behind Cathy, her curiosity getting the better of her. The space revealed nothing about this enigmatic woman—no photos, no personal items—just a sterile office devoid of warmth or personality. If Cathy orchestrated the lives of agents, spies, and killers, she'd left no trace of herself in the process.

"I have two urgent requests," Cathy said.

The word *urgent* snapped Leah's focus back to the conversation.

Cathy leaned forward slightly. "First, are you available to work this weekend? An important report needs to be completed by Monday. I've been without admin support for weeks, and I'm behind on submitting a critical report to the board."

Leah blinked, surprised at the workload already piling up. "Yes, absolutely. What do you need me to do?"

"I'm preparing the annual donor report for the board. The materials are highly sensitive, so I'll need to temporarily change your security clearance to Level 4-A to access the data." Cathy paused, her tone firm. "I'll speak to security as soon as possible."

Leah's interest was piqued. "And the second request?"

"Yes, about that. Our annual fundraising gala is in two months. You'll be handling the final coordination. We've already chosen the venue, catering, and theme, but we still need to complete the invitations, agenda, and smaller logistical details. Unfortunately, we're behind schedule."

Leah tried to mask her unease, though her grip tightened on the chair's arms. "That sounds . . . fun. I'll take care of it."

"There should be a cloud folder labeled 'Gala Event' with the materials you'll need. We'll talk more next week," Cathy said briskly as she stood, signaling the meeting's end. "After your clearance is upgraded, you can access last year's donor report as a template."

"Of course," Leah said, following suit. She returned to her desk, her nerves jumping between excitement and trepidation. Logging onto her laptop, she began hunting for the gala event's folder.

37

Spadina Avenue, Toronto

Friday night called for a break from the routine and a small celebration of Leah's achievements at GRF. Leah, Igor, and I escaped to a hole-in-the-wall Chinese restaurant on Spadina Avenue, north of Dundas Street, with disposable plastic tablecloths covering the tables. Despite its simplicity, Igor swore the food was exceptional, and the clientele was Asian, which I took to be a good sign.

We snagged a small table in the quiet back corner. There wasn't much time to waste on small talk, not with Igor's plan looming. Leah's surprise clearance upgrade to 4-A was a gift we hadn't expected and couldn't squander.

Igor leaned in, explaining slowly as if he were teaching a class. "Think of data exchange as packets moving through a locked network. Each packet is both encrypted and protected to ensure its authenticity. Once it reaches its destination, the system verifies that it came from a trusted source."

His plan was anything but ordinary.

"The goal," Igor continued, "is to inject a script inside GRF's system using Leah's clearance. Their firewall inspects everything at the perimeter, blocking unauthorized transmissions. Leah's access, however, gives us the perfect way in—without triggering alarms."

A waiter dropped a steaming teapot in the center of the table, briefly interrupting as he placed porcelain teacups in front of each of us.

I raised an eyebrow. "Won't they notice an external server pulling their data?"

Igor smirked. "Good question, Professor."

I was unsure whether he was mocking me or trying to be endearing.

"As a matter of fact, the server is invisible to GRF's system. We're only duplicating the data packets, not intercepting them directly. To their eyes, everything will look normal while the duplicate flows to our external server."

Leah leaned in, her voice tinged with curiosity. "And once we have the data?"

"We'll have access to GRF's global network. It'll expose everything."

Concern was visible on Leah's face. "And your server? How do we guarantee it doesn't lead back to us?"

"It's untraceable," he reassured her. "The duplicate bounces around international servers before it lands in a server farm outside Moscow. No one will know where it originates."

The food began arriving: spring rolls and fried squid with chili, and more to follow. Despite the intensity of the conversation, hunger won out, and we began picking at the dishes.

"We'll act Sunday evening," Igor said between bites. "Leah will finish the donor report over the weekend. I'll show up at six to drop off a box of 'your stuff' for your workspace—photos, certificates, real plants, and silly ornaments. It's an innocent cover story, giving me the excuse to enter the building."

"How will you get past security?" I asked.

"A bit of charm, a quick chat about Leah needing some personality in her office, and the promise I would carry her heavy box from the car to her office. I'll be in and out in five minutes without leaving a fingerprint."

Leah nodded but worried aloud, "The facial recognition system on my computer—how do we get around that?"

Igor chuckled. "The camera does live input, right? Built-in or mounted?"

"Mounted above my monitor."

"Perfect. We'll simply shift it slightly. You'll sit next to me and mimic my keyboard movements so you appear to be the one working. If the camera settings remain the same, the system won't pick up on the difference in real time."

The table now overflowed with BBQ pork, fried noodles, Szechuan shrimp, beef in black bean sauce, and rice.

For now, the plan seemed solid.

I poured the tea, lifting my cup to make a toast. “To Igor’s audacious plan.”

As the green tea warmed my hands, I couldn’t help but feel the weight of what we were attempting: infiltrating GRF’s network and laying bare their operations. If this worked, Leah wouldn’t only be writing reports—she’d be the key to uncovering a global syndicate of chaos.

By the night’s end, all that remained were empty plates and the resolve to act.

38

Queen's Quay

The command center had transformed the apartment's walnut dining table. My Saturday morning tea sat forgotten at the edge of the table, cooling next to a collection of notebook pages scrawled with ideas and leads about the Global Relief Foundation.

Igor had shown up unannounced after Leah had left for work and now sat partially reclined on the sofa, scrolling on his phone, his legs crossed in a casual sprawl. He didn't seem to notice—or care—that his wet boots were still on. "What are you doing, Professor?" he asked, bemused.

The reflection of the stormy sky across his pale face warped his features, making his sharp cheekbones look even more angular.

I fumbled with the search bar on my laptop. "Searching online for anything incriminating about the GRF," I replied, jabbing the Enter key like it owed me something.

Igor raised an eyebrow, the corner of his mouth twitching upward. "Google?" he asked, dragging the word out as though he were speaking to a frustrated child. "You're using Google?"

"It's a starting point," I insisted.

He shook his head with an exasperated smile. "It's an ending point if you're serious about surveillance," he countered, jumping up and moving closer to me at the table. "Professor, please. If you want real dirt—not the sanitized information GRF wants the world to see—you must venture into . . . how do I say . . . less polite neighborhoods of the internet."

"The dark web," I said flatly, having heard him use the term enough to pick up the unspoken meaning behind his words.

"Exactly." He slapped his hand on the table for effect.

"Well, then," I murmured, straightening in my chair, "if you're going to lecture me about what I'm doing wrong, you need to show me how to do it right." I looked up at him with a smile.

***

By lunchtime, the dining table had become unrecognizable. A workhorse had replaced my modest laptop. Igor called it "a beast."

The gaming PC stood under the table at the far end, facing the windows. It housed one of the most advanced processors on the market, a Nvidia RTX 4090 GPU, with 64GB of RAM and a futuristic liquid cooling system.

But that wasn't all.

"This is just the hardware," Igor said, his fingers almost dancing across the keyboard as he fine-tuned the operating system like a maestro conducting an orchestra. "The armor is coming next."

He started with layered security: a bulletproof VPN hosted in Panama, where no data retention laws existed. Next came a firewall, anti-malware software, and encryption protocols that, by the time he was done, rendered the machine invisible. To ensure that no one could breach the system without my knowledge, Igor installed an advanced alert system that would ping me if anyone or anything so much as glanced in my direction.

"To browse the dark web, you'll need The Onion Router," he said, bringing up the TOR browser on the screen.

Behind him, dark storm clouds and flashes of lightning cast patterns over the room's floor, creating a strange interplay between the room's serenity and the shadowy, hidden world I was preparing to enter.

He made adjustments to the browser, disabling plugins and configuring settings to block ads, trackers, and even the tiniest chance of an IP address leak. "This is not child's play," he said. "You're stepping into a place where the predators have dangerous weapons—but so do you. Now you need virtual cash. The dark web doesn't take credit cards, Professor," Igor explained with a grin as he guided me through setting up a cryptocurrency wallet.

By the time my first Bitcoin transaction went through, he looked like a proud father watching a toddler take their first steps.

I sighed, leaning back and crossing my arms. "So, tell me—now that I have this . . . armor and bank account, what am I actually looking for?"

Igor spent the afternoon introducing me to software tools that seemed to be straight out of a spy film: web scrapers, keyloggers, forensic crawlers . . . Each one came with its own risks and rewards.

He clicked through menus at a dizzying speed as he explained, "This web scraper helps find information GRF may try to erase—deleted webpages, archived files . . . dirty laundry everywhere." Another click. "Stalkerware. Only for good stalking, yes?" Another click. "Remote Access Trojans let you monitor from kilometers away." Another click. "Packet sniffers, very sexy. These tools give you data trails."

"And they're legal?" I raised an eyebrow.

"Like a gun." Igor shrugged. "It's how you use them that decides legality." He paused, his face turning serious. "But the dark web is not to be trusted. Everyone there lies, everyone hunts. Keep anonymity, or you will become the prey."

***

Leah didn't step through the door until 8:00 p.m., sopping wet from the relentless rainstorm that had loomed overhead all day. She looked exhausted but determined, her hands clutching a water-streaked tote bag stuffed with notes. Whatever the donor file revealed had piqued her curiosity to the fullest extent.

"You're soaked," I said, handing her a glass of rosé as she collapsed onto the sofa, kicking off her shoes with the precision of someone who'd reached their physical and mental limit.

"I'm also fed," she groaned, gesturing in protest when I offered her leftovers. "Pizza at the office around five. Didn't even want it, but Cathy ordered it, so . . ." She shrugged and took a generous sip of wine.

Igor, ever eager to bolster Leah's morale, had already gone home, sad that he couldn't bid her goodnight in person.

I moved a stack of papers off my armchair to sit across from her. As soon as she exhaled, I knew she would unload.

"That was the craziest day," she said. Leaning forward, wineglass held precariously in one hand, she latched onto the corner of the coffee table. "The donor report is an absolute maze. There's no structure, no meaningful patterns, just consistent sums donated by companies I've never even heard of. Crystal Holding, Bear Investments, K2 Limited—they're all big contributors, but under strange circumstances. Like Crystal Holding, which donates 100,000 euros every month on the fifth. K2 Limited pushes 160,000 US dollars every two months, always on the thirtieth—but then there are one-off donations over a million dollars, totally random, in all sorts of currencies."

She paused to take another sip, her eyes darting between thought fragments. "It's like they're intentionally chaotic. And their accounting . . . It barely exists!"

I got up and grabbed a bag of potato chips from the kitchen and returned, ripping the seal open as I sat back down. "Do you think it's deliberate? The randomness?" I didn't wait for her response. "These sound like shell companies, Leah. Fake corporations designed to funnel money through layers of distractions. A mechanism to avoid detection by authorities."

"Exactly," she said, reaching without hesitation for a handful of chips. The immediate ease in her rapport made her feel less like a spy-in-training and more like an investigator making a historic breakthrough.

I slid the chips closer to her and stood to grab a notebook from the dining table. Leaning across, I dropped it beside her. "You need to write down the names of every one of these donors while they're fresh in your memory. I'll dig into the companies first thing tomorrow." Now that I had my new internet weapon.

Before she could respond, her phone buzzed. It was Igor. Recognizing the look on her face, I left the room to give them space, allowing her to work out the details.

Still, my mind wouldn't quit. How did a nonprofit rake in billions of dollars without legitimate donors—and with no one asking questions? The dissonance sank into my chest as I sprawled across the bed, unable to sleep or settle. Flipping on the TV, I welcomed the comfortable, ridiculous escape of *Ocean's Eleven*.

At some point, Leah tapped at my door. "I'm going to sleep," she said. "Tomorrow's a big day. Night."

Pretending I was drowsy, I replied, "Yup. Big day. Jays and Yankees doubleheader, right?"

She smirked. "You're funny. Good night, Dad."

39

Toronto

Alone in the command center with my green tea beside me, I spent the day peeling back layers of deception in the glow of my laptop. The target of my relentless search: GRF, a charity organization that boasted its mission was to help girls and women worldwide.

On my screen, the GRF homepage gleamed with a curated sheen of integrity. Images showcased humanitarian awards, success stories, and declarations of empowerment. But my gaze froze on one photo: a polished corporate snapshot of Cathy Dickson, GRF's CEO, standing proud at an award ceremony. She looked regal, magnetic, as she accepted the prestigious Mother Teresa Medal "for promoting peace, equality, and social justice" at the United Nations in New York.

But I didn't stop at her confident pose or radiant smile. My eyes locked onto the background.

There stood Ming-Zhu Chang, the woman I had met at the UN, hovering like a shadow behind Cathy. Expressionless, her face gave nothing away, a mask as unreadable as stone. I couldn't help but wonder—what was running through her mind at that exact moment?

The caption sang Cathy's praises: a newly appointed CEO with under six months on the job, a leader who had "redefined" humanitarian work with passion and integrity. The news releases followed the same laudatory script, her name commanding respect in charities, boardrooms, and the global philanthropic circuit.

But I had seen past all that. Beneath the polished LinkedIn profile, the glowing media blurbs, and the endless humanitarian accolades, something else lurked. Something jagged. Something darker.

With my new digital arsenal—tools and techniques culled from VPN rabbit holes, darknet whispers, and amateur investigators on YouTube—I cast a more sinister light on Cathy Dickson's perfect narrative. Armed with database scrapers, military and government records, black-market travel logs, OSINT tools, and facial recognition apps, I turned over every digital stone. I scoured visa registries, tracked down archived images, and pieced together fragments of her story, which were hidden across the internet.

Hours slid by unnoticed. My body ached from the tension in my shoulders, my eyes burned from the pale blue screen, and hunger gnawed at me. After lunch, I had assembled the unfinished puzzle of Cathy Dickson.

Born in 1982, she entered the world as Cathy Bronsky, the daughter of poor Slavic immigrants in Cleveland. Her father spent his years as a school janitor while her mother worked in the kitchen of a small Russian bakery. Cleveland was a city of transition for many like them, its neighborhoods shaped by Cold War refugees and the quiet yet bustling presence of immigrants trying to build modest futures.

Cathy's own beginnings felt unremarkable, almost idyllic in their simplicity. A bright child, she graduated with honors from Cleveland Heights High School. Her yearbook photo—her crooked half-smile, her disheveled hair—spoke poetically of her, the caption beneath reading: *President of the Russian Club. Visionary. Future Leader.*

It looked innocent. It was not the case.

After high school, the trail grew faint. Here, the story thickened after the US Army recruited Cathy. Her Slavic background and fluency in Russian gave her an unmatched edge. She had skills the military would have prized. But what officially remained of her early Army career didn't add up. Roles were vague or omitted entirely. It seemed someone had scrubbed entire chapters from the records, making them too neat.

And then she vanished.

It happened around the time she joined the 75th Ranger Regiment. For most soldiers, making it through its grueling assessment and selection program was an accomplishment that bordered on the impossible. The 75th Regiment wasn't any infantry. They were an elite Tier 2 light infantry raid force, capable of deploying anywhere in eighteen hours for high-value targets or missions carved straight out of war-zone nightmares.

For a woman to have survived this ordeal in the mid-2000s was mythical. Then something even more startling emerged from the fog of her records: silent confirmation of a brief stint with Delta Force.

Delta Force, 1st Special Forces Operational Detachment-Delta. The Unit. A name whispered more often in conspiracies than conversations. Delta Force didn't exist, or at least not on paper. But those who knew about it would describe a force trained in counterterrorism, hostage rescue, assassinations, black-ops missions, and top-priority intelligence work.

I traced this connection back to a deleted old military forum, archived by the web scraper, that most would dismiss as useless. But buried in this forgotten thread was a grainy reposted photo—Delta operatives posed in fatigues, their faces obscured by scarves and shadows. Yet one operative stood out in the same way a single bright flame burns in darkness. Cathy Bronsky. Or rather, Cathy Dickson.

Her face remained partially uncovered, and something in her posture—solid, confident, commanding—confirmed that she belonged there, an elite within an elite. The image had reportedly surfaced for a brief window on an official Army domain, only to be hastily removed by higher-ups. Now, the original site showed a 404 error, but the internet had cached this fragment.

The military wasn't sloppy, not with Delta Force. If they erased a name, a face, or a photo, it wasn't careless bureaucracy. So, was this deliberate?

She reemerged at thirty-seven as if stepping into a different life, trading her black-ops stealth for tailored business suits and conference podiums. Her first step into public philanthropy was the Middle East Children's Foundation of America. For five years, she built a reputation as a protector of children from war-torn countries before stepping into the top chair at GRF.

But my search revealed the cracks beneath this polished career climb. Beyond being skilled at creating an image, Cathy Dickson was a master tactician at weaponizing perception. Her entire public life as a woman of warmth, intelligence, and compassion hid a grittier truth she had stitched together from shadows.

One lead struck me like a hammer. Facial recognition software matched Cathy to photos on Russia's VKontakte social media platform. They were casual snapshots: a younger Cathy in shadowed Moscow clubs, at wild parties, and always lingering close to a man who once used the handle @armychuvak, which translated into English as "army dude."

The gaps in her timeline screamed danger. During those years, Cathy vanished—no tax returns, no driver's license renewals, no digital footprint in America. Yet here she was, alive and thriving in Moscow. Her presence felt deliberate. Calculated. I knew this wasn't downtime or personal exploration; it was reconnaissance.

As I leaned back in my chair, Cathy's photo glared at me from GRF's website. I studied her calm face, her gentle confidence. What kind of person could slip in and out of extremes—from black ops to global philanthropy? From surgical strikes overseas to promoting equality and peace?

A master manipulator. Someone for whom the razor-thin line between moral good and sinister intent was another battlefield.

Cathy wasn't just GRF's CEO. She was its architect and the mastermind behind FIST, a sinister network hidden beneath the charity's altruistic facade. What appeared to be a beacon of hope and humanitarianism was, in truth, a cover for something dark, calculated, and far more insidious than anyone realized.

And if she knew I was this close to uncovering her truth? She could and would make me disappear.

***

It was 6:04 in the evening when Igor and I rolled silently into the parking lot of the Global Relief Foundation. A storm having passed, the summer humidity made every breath feel heavy. The lot, vast and deserted, amplified the tension in the car as Igor and I stared up at GRF's three-story building.

Igor had spouted idle chatter the entire drive here. I realized his endless stream of small talk, silly jokes, and tangents was a way to keep his nerves in check. I let him have his process, right until I pulled the car off to the far side of the lot, wanting to avoid it being a glaring target in the otherwise barren space.

"This is it," I said, breaking the silence.

"Leah texted a thumbs-up from her work phone. Green light," Igor said, jumping into action. "Open the trunk."

He got out and went to the rear of the car, where he hoisted a cardboard box into his arms. It looked far too big, but with two bushy plants sticking out, it carried just the right air of innocent intentions. "Wish me luck."

His movements seemed rehearsed as he strode toward the building. I checked the dashboard clock: 6:07 p.m. We'd estimated he had only fifteen minutes before any lapse in protocol would raise questions at the security desk.

I turned on the radio, scanning for the Jays–Yankees game to distract myself from spiraling into worry. Too much could go wrong. We were amateurs. Did we believe we could outwit governments, technicians, operatives—all watching GRF's network like hawks?

The radio promised relief: bottom of the eighth, Jays trailing the Yankees 1–2. Guerrero was at the plate with one ball, one strike, and one out.

Vlad smashed the next pitch, sending the crowd into a frenzy.

6:18 p.m. Still no Igor.

I turned off the game, unable to sit still. My patience was evaporating with each passing second. "Colleen," I muttered under my breath, "get them out of there."

As if pried loose by divine request, the building's front door swung open. Leah appeared first, with Igor just inches behind her, carrying an empty box. They froze in the doorway as if the guard had caught them.

My pulse quickened, panic creeping in.

They sauntered toward the car as the humid air pressed in tight. I had already started the engine, which was cooling the interior.

Sliding into the backseat, both shared an exhilarated, nervous laugh.

"What the hell happened back there?" I asked, seizing the wheel.

Igor smirked, catching his breath. "The guard wanted to make sure we knew the Jays came from behind to beat the Yankees in the ninth."

I groaned but chuckled despite myself, shifting the car into gear and tearing out of the parking lot with more speed than necessary.

Leah shot me a look, already buckling her seatbelt. "I'm going to need something stronger than wine tonight," she said deadpan.

Igor recounted their risky entry as we coasted through the city against the game's traffic. The guard had been enraptured by the game and had let Igor bypass every security protocol—no safety video, biometrics scan, or sign-in registry. A quick drop-off and a box in hand had been enough to dull any suspicion. Leah had escorted Igor straight to her desk, and he'd embedded the well-rehearsed script into GRF's network within ten minutes. The code was now in place, mirroring every data packet from GRF through a maze of servers to a secure location outside Moscow.

No alarms. No alerts. No mistakes.

Now, all we had to do was wait and see what GRF's shadowy empire would reveal.

40

Consumer Drive

Monday morning. Leah swept her desk clean, meticulously erasing any trace of Sunday's infiltration. Her hands quivered as she stowed files and straightened loose ends. The weight of it all pressed down as she marked the eighth endless day in that godforsaken place.

Her company cell phone buzzed against the desk, splintering her thoughts and pulling her back into the present. She grabbed it and answered, stitching together false cheer with practiced ease.

"Hello, Leah speaking! . . . Oh, she's stepped away from her desk. I'll make sure she gets your message as soon as possible... Have a wonderful day!"

She disconnected and stared at the phone. Urgency hummed in the air like static. Something about the call didn't feel right. Leah's uneasiness mounted as she checked Cathy's calendar.

She did not have another meeting scheduled for at least an hour. So where was she?

Leah hurried down the floor, past cubicles and shadowy figures hunched over laptops. The kitchen loomed ahead. The coffee machine—a perfect excuse for Cathy to be cornered into meaningless pleasantries. But the space was empty. Silent.

Leah's instincts kicked in. Her legs carried her to the elevator, her movements quickening. Down to security, she decided. They had eyes everywhere. They might know. She jabbed the button. The hum of machinery stilled her breath.

The elevator stopped at the second floor and the door slid open, revealing an older woman, short and plump, with cropped white hair, oversized black glasses, and a face lined with practiced kindness. She stepped in, cradling a stack of files, and greeted Leah with a warm "Good morning."

But as her gaze locked on Leah's face, her eyes widened as if confronted by something impossible. Her complexion paled and her expression shifted from cordial warmth to raw fear. The files slipped from her rigid hands, spreadsheets tumbling to the elevator floor.

Leah froze, her chest tightening. Something was wrong. Very wrong. Without waiting to think, she bolted the moment the doors hissed open.

Behind her, the older woman scrambled to gather the papers, her movements frantic, as the elevator swallowed her from sight.

***

Meanwhile, in the cavernous dark basement, bathed in harsh bluish-white light from hundreds of computer monitors, Cathy Dickson stood in command before her audience. The massive screens behind her flickered with live satellite feeds; surveillance footage painted the room in shadows of maps and figures. Over three hundred agents watched her, hanging on her words.

Her voice was amplified by a microphone: steady, commanding, cold. It cut through the silent space like a gleaming scalpel.

"The work we do here matters—more than the world will ever know. Every action we take impacts lives, communities, and global stability. But our success hinges on one thing: confidentiality."

She paused, her gaze piercing the room as though she could see into every agent's soul, see their every fear, every tremor of uncertainty.

"One careless word," she continued, her voice hardening, "one breach of trust, and it all unravels. Our missions are compromised. Thousands of agents exposed. Lives lost. The consequences of failure are unimaginable."

Her words seized the silence, as if the room held its breath.

"The enemy is relentless," Cathy pressed on. "They scour for vulnerabilities, waiting for that single crack to exploit. We cannot afford to give them one. You must honor your pledge, your discipline, your silence. Our mission depends on it."

Her hand tightened on the microphone. Her voice softened, heavy with purpose.

"Remember: we are not just battling chaos. We are protecting peace. Global stability hangs in the balance. Hold the line. Guard this mission, this vision, with every fiber of your being."

Dead silence greeted her last words. Then, almost reluctantly, the agents rose to clap. The echo of applause reverberated, hollow, fading almost as quickly as it started. Cathy's gaze never wavered—fixed, unyielding, ready for anything.

And somewhere above, Leah ran, tearing at the walls, ripping through the very foundation of the FIST mission that Cathy fought to preserve.

41

Queen's Quay

Summer had taken over Toronto in full force. Most days, the heat made sitting on the condo deck overlooking Lake Ontario impossible. Below, the boardwalk never stopped buzzing with life—people jogging, biking, and strolling in search of even the faintest breeze off the lake. But I overlooked it. While Leah went to GRF every morning with her brave face glued on, pretending nothing was amiss as she hunted for secrets buried in GRF's cloud files, I stayed back, locked in a silent war with the internet. My battleground? A list of eighteen shell companies Leah had identified. Every name was a door I had to pry open, one thin layer at a time, knowing something—or someone—might be waiting on the other side.

And then I found her.

Using every trick in the book—online resources, public records, forums, obscure database leaks like the Panama Papers and Paradise Papers—I started seeing the outlines of a puzzle piece that had no business existing. Several of these companies were not merely connected, they were all controlled by one person: Evelyn Charles.

Her name alone was a mystery. George Town, Cayman Islands, where her listed address sat, wasn't only her home. It was an economic black hole, a paradise of murky finances where over forty of the world's fifty largest banks had set up shop. This tiny place managed 75 percent of the globe's hedge funds, boasted more limited liability companies than people, and wouldn't dare tax a dime of personal or corporate income. Add in privacy laws enforced like religion, and you had fertile ground for tax evasion, money laundering, and corporate crime. A place where the GRF could thrive unchecked.

Leaning back in my chair, I stared at Evelyn Charles's name at the top of my notes, the first real person I'd found behind the dozens of empty companies. If she were as connected to GRF as I suspected, finding her could add gasoline to our fire and burn GRF's financial network to ashes. Yet the deeper I dug into her world, the more I realized how my world felt . . . off.

Goosebumps skittered up my arms like an invisible touch, like someone was watching me.

***

By early evening, Igor had already arrived at our apartment, just like every day. On the surface, it was for Leah's nightly debrief—at least, that's what he claimed. But anyone paying attention could see the real reason. He hated missing a moment of her presence, his every move orbiting around her in a subdued manner, whether standing by the window when she walked through the door or sitting a little closer to her on the couch than he needed to. Igor radiated nervous energy when Leah wasn't in the room. It might've been almost endearing if I hadn't been so focused on digital breadcrumbs and theories about GRF.

But tonight, he seemed altered. Instead of sprawling on the couch, Igor paced the living room, his hands jammed deep in the pockets of his Bermuda shorts. His eyes flicked toward the boardwalk outside, then back to the floor, as though he were expecting an unwelcome visitor at any moment.

"What's up with you?" I finally asked, not bothering to disguise the edge in my voice.

He finally met my gaze. "She's in danger," he said, blurting the words like they'd been simmering too long in his gut.

My chest tightened and I set my tea down. "What are you talking about?"

"I've been monitoring the mirrored data from the Moscow server," Igor said, his voice low. "They've noticed her digging in files she shouldn't even have access to. GRF's cybersecurity—it's better than I thought."

I felt sick. "Do you think they've traced anything back to her?"

He didn't answer, only stared at the floor like he wasn't sure where to start. Minutes passed as we debated the best strategy to keep Leah safe, ways to stay ahead of GRF and identify its weaknesses. But then Igor pivoted—his voice quieter, almost bitter.

"You think I'm paranoid," he said. It was not a question. "You think this is all some game I'm playing. Russian roulette. Big Brother. Cloak-and-dagger bullshit."

I shifted, caught off guard. "I don't think—"

"Do you remember the 2016 election?"

His words hung in the air long enough for my breath to catch. One heartbeat, then another, before I forced my question. "What are you telling me? You worked on it?"

He nodded almost imperceptibly. "Professor, I wrote code. It wasn't my idea; it wasn't even my project. But I helped open doors. The doors Russia walked through. Voter databases, back-end systems, planting backdoors—things I barely understood. I was just a kid."

I stared at him, doing the math in my head. Sixteen. Essentially a child. But that didn't erase the weight of what he'd done. It explained so much—his paranoia, his insistence on always being two steps ahead of everyone else. But it also planted a seed of doubt. If Igor had betrayed one democracy, who was to say he didn't have his own agenda now? Did Leah know this?

Any chance I had to press him evaporated when Leah walked into the apartment, cutting off the conversation like a guillotine.

Her exhaustion showed; she kicked off her shoes and collapsed onto the sofa beside Igor, barely acknowledging the tension in the room. "I wish I had just one boring day at GRF," she muttered, sarcasm scraping the edge of her tone. "Cathy's impossible. Passive-aggressive emails all morning, no clear instructions, and then—oh, the best part—she forgot to restore my security access after the weekend. Total chaos."

She paused, sipping chilled French rosé from the wineglass I handed her. "But it gave me access to certain files I wouldn't normally see," she admitted with a faint grin.

Igor stiffened beside her, leaning in ever so slightly. "What files?"

Leah waved it off, trying to sound casual, but the tension in her shoulders gave her away. She recounted how Cathy had called her into a meeting that afternoon, playing her usual manipulative mind games. The way she phrased her comments wasn't outright accusatory—but it didn't scream "You're in the clear" either.

"I feel someone's watching me," Leah said. Her voice was light, but her words hit me like a punch to the gut.

Igor stayed quiet, holding himself back. But his jaw tightened, and his gaze locked onto her movements, as though she might vanish. Whatever he wanted to say, he kept it to himself for now.

I revealed my discovery about the shell companies—the money trail and, above all, Evelyn Charles. Leah listened, her exhaustion yielding to curiosity, but Igor stayed silent, his green eyes unreadable.

I decided right then and there: I'd go after Charles myself. Leah would soon leave GRF, and Igor already had too much work with the Moscow server and his consultancy. If anyone was going to confront the woman holding GRF's financial keys, it had to be me. I knew Igor would welcome the idea of seeing less of me so he could spend more time with Leah.

And something told me Evelyn Charles would not roll out the welcome mat.

42

George Town, Grand Cayman

After a flight of less than four hours, I touched down on the beautiful island of Grand Cayman in time for lunch. Hurricane season was the hottest period, and tourism was stagnant. I'd dressed the part, opting for Caribbean casual business attire: a plain off-white Guayabera shirt, beige linen pants, and tan loafers. With my Italian tanned leather briefcase slung over my shoulder, aviator sunglasses, and a classic Panama hat made from Toquilla palm with a black grosgrain band, I could pass for a local banker. Except, of course, for my pale skin. The only thing missing from the picture of my constructed image was a Cuban cigar.

My cover was solid: I was John Miller, blending into a sea of eight thousand other John Millers on LinkedIn. Officially, I was in town to investigate opening a limited liability company and bank account on behalf of my high-net-worth client, Leah Barton. Orphaned by the dramatic and very public deaths of her parents, she had inherited millions she wanted to transfer from Zürich to a more "convenient" financial community closer to home. The move would allow her to fund lucrative real estate investments while "legally" avoiding capital gains and exorbitant tax liabilities.

But the offshore finance hustle wasn't my focus. I was here for one person: Evelyn Charles.

In George Town, the line between paradise and shadows blurred with every step. Tourists strolled along in sandals and sunglasses, soaking up the turquoise waters and tropical breeze, but the island whispered its secrets beneath the surface. Cayman wasn't solely about luxury vacations; it was where trillions of dollars were hidden under layers of secrecy and shielded from prying eyes.

***

For two days straight, I chased half-truths and dead ends, searching for Evelyn Charles. Her surname was as common as palm trees in the Caribbean, present everywhere but impossible to trace. Frosted-glass office buildings, private banking institutions, and unmarked doors in busy plazas finally led me to her workplace: Republic Bank. At first glance, the bank looked unremarkable, but I knew better. This was one of those institutions that excelled in moving billions discreetly, a vital cog in the machine of offshore financial secrecy.

She wasn't in a pristine corner office on the second floor but on the main floor behind a desk in a cubicle where the actual work took place. Walking through the bank, I examined the nameplates on the cubicles. They didn't include full names; only first names and last initials were included, and this was likely an initial security measure. That's when I spotted it: *Evelyn C.* My heart quickened, and I felt my throat tighten.

Before I could approach, a pleasant young woman intercepted me with a polite smile.

"Can I help you?" she asked.

Composing myself, I blurted, "Yes, uh . . . Can I exchange US dollars for Cayman dollars here?"

She seemed amused. "You'd get a better rate at a kiosk on the street."

I nodded an awkward thank-you, but my focus shifted back to the cubicle. A moment later, Evelyn Charles emerged, shaking hands with a client who was leaving her office. Her face was tired, weathered, and worn out, like someone who had borne too many burdens for too long.

***

Around 1:00 p.m., I spotted Evelyn Charles leaving the bank with a lunch bag. She crossed the street and headed to a small park with several wooden picnic tables under the shade of sparse palm trees. Selecting the farthest table, she sat down, opened her bag, and removed a food container.

She moved at a slow, deliberate pace for someone who didn't have the luxury of rest. She melded into the daily grind of hard-working Black Caymanians, unremarkable at first glance, but I noticed the telltale signs of her grit.

She was heavyset, with broad shoulders and a deep tawny-brown complexion that glowed in the Caribbean sun. Her navy-blue blazer, though professional, was snug enough to strain at her shoulders, and her sensible black flats showed wear from overuse. Her cropped hair was neat and practical, with dangling silver hoop earrings as the only nod to her style. Evelyn Charles was a woman who carried more than her fair share of burdens, both in stature and in spirit.

I crept toward her, careful not to alarm her.

"Excuse me," I whispered, standing a polite distance away. "Are you Evelyn Charles?"

She froze, narrowing her almond-shaped eyes. Her lined face scanned me for any danger.

"Who wants to know?" Her tone was sharp, guarded.

"John Miller," I said, keeping my voice steady and nonthreatening. "I don't mean to bother you during lunch, but I was hoping you might help me. May I sit down?"

She seemed uncomfortable as she glanced around. The park was mostly empty, except for a bicyclist passing by. She let out a resigned sigh and stared toward the bench. “You’ve got five minutes Mr. . . . did you say Miller?”

Up close, Evelyn’s guarded demeanor didn’t ease, but I could see that the tension in her jaw and shoulders was subtle. Wary but not hardened beyond reason. This wasn’t a woman with untouchable confidence. No, Evelyn’s strength was born of necessity, the kind that could weather storms but splinter if pushed too hard.

“What do you want?” she asked, her voice lilting with the Caribbean’s soft, rhythmic cadence.

“A friend recommended you and your bank for setting up a limited liability company,” I began cautiously.

Evelyn scrutinized me. “Who’s your friend?”

I leaned forward, lowering my voice. “You’re listed as the CEO of several companies that work with the Global Relief Foundation. It’s a charity that focuses on helping women and girls in developing nations.”

Her expression remained impassive, but I could tell she was assessing my words. After a moment, she sighed and stared toward the clear blue waters visible beyond the street and buildings.

“All I do is fill in forms and sign documents,” she said bluntly. “I’m not sure what help you’re looking for.”

I tilted my head. "People like you keep the wheels turning. Nothing works without the foundations you build—the companies, the banking systems. Without you and the money, GRF doesn't function."

She let out a bitter, exhausted laugh. "You think I want to do this? I'm living the dream! A single mother with two kids to feed, Mr. Miller—bills to pay. Brenda is ten and full of adventure and optimism. Jared is fifteen, already dreaming of attending university to make a better life. To escape this island. But university costs money. If I don't keep this job, what do I tell him? That my morals are more important than his future?"

Her voice faltered, betraying the raw emotion beneath.

"So, this is just a job?" I coaxed.

"What else would it be?" she whispered. "You think I do this by choice? I push the papers through and don't ask questions. If I did, I'd lose my job—or worse."

She checked the time on her phone and glanced back toward the bank. "My lunch break is over."

As Evelyn gathered her belongings, preparing to end the conversation and return to her job, I leaned forward, urgency weaving its way into my voice.

"Ms. Charles," I began carefully, "I know you're busy, and I can see the weight you carry. But before you go, I'd like to tell you something personal—if you'd allow me."

She paused, her grip tightening around her lunch bag. Her eyes, still skeptical, met mine. There was no hostile energy, just guarded curiosity. She didn't speak but didn't turn away either, granting me a sliver of space to continue.

"Years ago, I lost my way—not in business, but as a parent. My daughter grew up without me. It wasn't supposed to be like that. My wife and I had plans, dreams for her, yet our own ambitions took us away from her when she needed us most. And now, the woman she's become . . . she's smart, strong, but she carries scars the world doesn't see. Scars caused by my absence."

I hesitated, letting my voice soften as the vulnerability seeped through. "I can't undo the past, but I can try to make things right with her before it's too late. She doesn't need my excuses—what she needs is me. And Brenda and Jared need you."

I noticed the sharp edges of Evelyn's expression dissolving. She wasn't warm, but her guarded posture softened enough for me to press forward.

"I don't have all the answers, Evelyn, but one thing I do know is that our children are the legacy we leave behind. The world won't remember us, but our children will. I understand the power of education and the doors it can open, not just for Brenda and Jared but for your peace of mind. No strings. No expectations of favors from you. All I want is the chance to speak again—this time without the rush, in a quieter setting."

I reached into my jacket pocket and handed her my card. "I promise to help you make your children's dreams a reality if you meet with me again. No strings attached. It's a gift for the future—your kids' future and the world's."

Evelyn held my simple card that had my name and mobile number, staring at it for a moment. She didn't look at me right away, but the tension in her face loosened as she glanced toward the distant blue Caribbean. The mention of her children had sparked something in her. It was subtle, but unmistakable.

"Caribbean Café. On Edward and Dr. Roys. Be there tomorrow at 8:00 a.m.—and don't waste my time." Without another word, she tucked my card into her bag and headed back to the bank, the slight sway in her walk a sign she'd found reason to believe in the possibility of something better.

Evelyn didn't give me a second glance, but I knew she wasn't walking away forever. For now, that was enough.

***

I reached the Caribbean Café at 8:00 a.m. The morning air was still fresh and crisp, with the hum of distant waves and the occasional chirp of island birds providing a natural soundtrack. Evelyn was already sitting at a table beneath the shading palms with her coffee. She looked composed, dressed in her professional white blouse, yet her posture betrayed a sense of wariness—her guard was up, as though she'd anticipated the weight of this meeting from the moment she agreed to it.

"I see you're not on island time," she greeted me, wrapping her hands around her cup as if it grounded her. "I don't have long before work starts."

Appreciating her directness, I nodded. "Thank you for meeting me, Evelyn. I know time is important to you, especially with all the responsibilities you carry. But I wouldn't have asked for another meeting if it weren't about something urgent."

Her sharp eyes drilled into me, sizing me up again. She didn't speak, allowing the silence to push me further.

I tilted forward, keeping my voice steady. "I want to assure you again: I'm not here to put your job or your family at risk. That isn't my intention—not now, not ever. I'm looking for your help. Your knowledge. What you know might be the key to stopping something devastating—something that's killing people, children, families across the world. You told me last time that you push the paperwork, but I believe you've seen more than you know. Enough to fill in gaps I can't fill on my own."

Evelyn clutched her arms across her chest. "You think I'm the answer to all of this? I work a job, Mr. Miller. One that pays the bills and keeps the lights on. What you're asking—it's above my security level and way beyond anything I want to get involved in."

I nodded, acknowledging her concerns. "I understand. And I'm not trying to drag you into danger, Evelyn—truly, I'm not. But sometimes people like you, the ones who work behind the curtain, see the things others don't. Not because you want to, but because you're close enough to the machine that it becomes impossible to ignore. And sometimes those very truths—however small—can be the difference between stopping something terrible or standing by helplessly as it destroys everything."

For the first time, Evelyn sighed, tension flickering in her jaw. I could tell that she was at least listening, though she wasn't convinced yet.

"Everything I do is for my kids," she replied, her tone softening ever so slightly. "Jared and Brenda. They deserve better than this life—better than me signing shady paperwork for companies that don't care about anything but hiding money in offshore accounts. I don't care about the scandals or the crimes. What I care about is keeping the roof over my kids' heads and giving them a chance to do more, to be better."

Her mention of her children opened a crack in the wall. "Do you have a picture of Jared and Brenda?"

She hesitated, her guarded demeanor wavering as she reached into her purse. "Why?" she asked suspiciously.

"I want to see them," I said honestly. "You've spoken about them twice now. I can tell they're your world—and I want to understand what you're fighting for."

After a moment's pause, she pulled out a worn photograph and handed it to me across the table. I took it with care, studying it as if the details mattered—which they did.

It was a photo from a family wedding. Jared, tall and awkward but with bright eyes, stood in an oversized suit. Brenda, younger with braided black hair and a red dress, leaned against her brother in a pose that showed sibling affection. Their smiles radiated pride, and their untouched innocence shone.

"They're beautiful kids," I said, genuinely moved. I handed the photo back, careful not to smudge its surface. "You've done an incredible job raising them, Evelyn. And I understand why you fight every day to keep their future secure."

Her lips tightened, yet her eyes reflected gratitude as she returned the photo to her purse. "Thank you. But that doesn't change what you're asking."

"It might," I suggested carefully. "Because if I can't stop what's happening, no kid has a bright future, including Jared and Brenda. What I'm fighting to stop, Evelyn, might seem far away from here, but that's the thing about global corruption—it touches everyone, even on islands like this. And if we don't stand up to it, then people like Jared and Brenda pay the price. You know it's true; you've seen pieces of it in the clients you work with."

Evelyn's gaze remained on her coffee, but her hardened edges softened. "You want me to give you names, don't you?"

"No," I said, quickly cutting her assumption off. "Not names, not specifics, not anything that would put you in harm's way. Just patterns, connections—the threads that tie shady companies together. Things you've noticed, even if they seem insignificant. That's all I need."

She remained silent, absorbing my words as though weighing the cost of helping against the risk of exposing more than she felt safe doing.

After a long pause, she sighed. "All right," she mumbled. "But you listen carefully—I don't do this lightly."

Over the course of the next thirty minutes, Evelyn unraveled pieces of her knowledge—setting up shell companies, filing incorporation documents, and establishing the banking infrastructure necessary to facilitate money laundering. Transactions arrived, mainly in American currency, shrouded in anonymity.

When I mentioned potential Russian clients, she shook her head. "Not me," she said. "All my instructions come from the US."

Probing further, I identified several shell companies associated with her name. "Do they have the same client behind them?"

Her lips parted as if to confirm, then she hesitated before retreating. "It's all above my pay grade," she murmured. "I just push the paperwork." Her voice never rose above a whisper, but the details were enough to pull back the veil farther than I had dared hope.

As her story concluded, Evelyn grabbed her purse and prepared to leave for work. Before she could stand, I reached into my jacket and slid a large envelope across the table.

She froze, staring at it. "What's this?"

"It's for Jared and Brenda," I said. "No strings attached. This isn't shady money—it's clean, earned legitimately, and it's yours to use for their future. I meant what I said: I want to help. And I trust you'll put it to good use."

Evelyn reached for the envelope, her movements tentative, hesitant. She tucked it into her purse without a word, then stood, her gaze hard but not unkind. As she turned to leave, she reversed course to give me a parting gift.

"All the companies you listed," she said, her voice barely above a whisper, "had the same area code: 202."

I stayed seated for a moment, watching her retreat and marveling at how a single photo, a single mother's pride, had opened the door to possibilities that had once seemed hopeless.

I didn't need to look up the area code. It was Washington, DC—the seat of American power, including the White House.

43

Queen's Quay

The moment Igor discovered Leah's dad was in the Cayman Islands, everything changed. He had seized the opportunity to step into Leah's life in a way she couldn't ignore, using his charm as his weapon of choice.

She pushed through the door of her apartment after a draining long day at work, only to be met with the most unexpected, rich, savory scent filling the air. There was an initial sense of panic about having her apartment broken into until she saw him.

"Surprise!" Igor greeted her, stepping out of her kitchen before she could even process what was happening. He stood there with a grin that was both mischievous and inviting. Her gaze fell on the dining table, set like something out of a magazine, with candles flickering warmly and wineglasses catching the soft light. At the center of it all was a golden puff pastry that

Igor declared was salmon coulibiac—a Russian dish so rich it whispered indulgence.

"I thought you could use a brief escape," he said smoothly, leading her toward the table before she could object.

She wanted to question how he had even gotten into her apartment, but the exhaustion of her day mixed with the tempting aroma made it a moot point.

Dinner was nothing short of enchanting. Each bite of flaky pastry, salmon, and the bright tang of dill lemon sauce melted her layers of tension. The wine helped, of course, but Igor's presence, even his jokes, was what began to dissolve her defenses. By the time they moved to the balcony with the last of their wine in hand, she felt lighter than she had in weeks.

Lake Ontario stretched out before them, its serene waters reflecting hues of orange and pink as the sun lowered itself beneath the horizon. Igor leaned back in his chair, giving her space to vent as she unloaded the burdens of her day. Ms. Dickson, the militant and demanding boss, had once again driven her to the brink. Words spilled from her about the frustration she had endured, including unrealistic requests, thankless tasks, and micromanagement that left her feeling drained.

Igor listened without interruption, nodding at the right moments, offering soft reassurances when necessary. As she spoke, she began to feel the tension she hadn't realized had collected in her neck and shoulders, her body betraying what her words couldn't convey.

"You carry too much stress," he said softly, moving behind her lounge chair.

Before she could respond, his hands were on her shoulders. Her breath hitched at first, but soon she melted under his skilled hands, firm yet gentle, and leaned into the comfort he offered.

"You don't have to deal with it all on your own," he murmured as his fingers worked their magic. His voice was low, steady, laced with a promise of support.

She looked up at him, her own eyes soft, almost vulnerable. Without a word, she turned to face him, and then, as if drawn by some invisible force, she nestled into his embrace.

When their lips met, it felt natural, unhurried, even inevitable. The kiss left her breathless, more from the intensity of the emotions it stirred than anything else. She didn't resist as he guided her inside and led her to her bedroom.

The night was theirs. Tender touches gave way to passion, whispers turned to quiet laughter, and the barriers she had kept up crumbled in the safety of his presence. For the first time in too long, Leah let herself feel something other than exhaustion or frustration.

Igor didn't leave that night. Nor did he leave the next day. By the end of the week, he had integrated himself into her life. Where loneliness and grief had lingered, Igor brought her company. Where tension from the mission had persisted, Igor brought her comfort. Where boredom had crept in, Igor brought her excitement.

Leah had no way of knowing exactly what Igor was doing, though she sensed he played his role perfectly.

44

Queen's Quay

I hated traveling. It hadn't always been this way, but airports felt like battlegrounds of chaos and fatigue these days, and the return to Toronto felt more like a retreat than relief. I sensed the difference the moment I arrived at the Queen's Quay condo unannounced, lugging my carry-on and wearing my travel weariness.

The air felt lighter, more fragrant, and the mood of the space was happier. It no longer resembled the war room of a detective buried in conspiracies. The clutter of images and notes once scrawled on the walls—all gone. What I found instead was a lived-in home. Igor's coat was draped across a dining room chair, a half-empty bowl of popcorn sat on the coffee table, and the faint smell of spices lingered in the air.

"Hello?" I called out.

The condo was silent.

I walked toward Leah's bedroom but hesitated when my eye caught that the door was ajar enough for me to peek inside. I confirmed my suspicions when I saw more of Igor's belongings near Leah's neatly hung clothes. I looked around the apartment. Several empty wine bottles stood on the kitchen counter, and the sink was full of dirty dishes. The ashtray on the balcony overflowed with cigarette butts. Was he living here? The thought disturbed me.

An hour passed in the quiet solitude of my room until the front door creaked open. I heard their voices—soft laughter, easy chatter—before a sudden pause. They must have seen my suitcase beside the entrance closet.

"Dad? Are you home?" Leah called out, her voice cautious.

When I stepped out of my room, Leah's face flushed with joy. She dropped her purse and closed the distance between us, pulling me into a hug.

"I missed you," she said earnestly.

The embrace lasted a moment too long as I absorbed her warmth, her presence.

Igor's voice broke in, a stark reminder that I wasn't the only one she cared about anymore. "Welcome home, Professor," he said, his tone neutral but firm.

We all sat in the living room. Leah and Igor were together on the sofa, and I was in the oversized chair. There was a shared energy between them, a comfort that told me everything I hadn't dared to ask. They were a couple. My daughter was with Igor.

And though I couldn't immediately pin my feelings about it, I knew this realization would take some getting used to.

Igor was the first to speak, leaning forward with unmistakable curiosity. "So, how did it go, Professor? Did you find the woman—Evelyn?"

Before I could answer, Leah's nurturing instincts kicked in. "Did you eat? Are you hungry? Do you need something to drink?"

I waved her off. "I'm fine. Sit down."

And as the hours of the night pressed on, I told them everything.

***

I woke to the sound of voices drifting from the kitchen, an inaudible murmur punctuated by laughter and the clink of spoons against bowls.

When I walked out, the sight startled me. Leah and Igor sat at the table, eating cereal in animated conversation about whether the Blue Jays had a shot at making the playoffs. They both wore running gear, their runners at the front door. Were they headed out for a jog, or had they just returned?

"Good morning," I said, trying to mask my bewilderment. "No work today?"

"Today is my grandmother's funeral," Leah replied. She grinned at me, amused at my confusion. "We need to catch you up," she said, barely pausing as she shoveled another spoonful of cereal into her mouth. "Get a bowl and join us," she added with a mischievous grin.

I sat down with them, and Leah wasted no time filling me in.

She explained that tensions were rising within GRF. They'd tightened security measures, restricted her access, and slowed the flow of information to a trickle. Finally, she'd resigned. Given her role as Cathy Dickson's executive assistant, she'd crafted a plausible excuse: the sudden passing of her "grandma," which required her to move back to her "old home."

"Cathy didn't even flinch," Leah said, shaking her head. "She didn't ask about my fake grandma, barely even reacted. All she wanted was for me to help find a replacement."

"What did you say?" I asked.

"I agreed to a two-week transition period, but to be honest, I think they'll be glad to be rid of me. I don't think they trust me anymore."

Though the job still crushed her, relief was visible on her face as she spoke. Leah didn't like to leave responsibilities unfinished, even when self-preservation demanded it.

Igor, having polished off two bowls of cereal, took his turn to speak. With a serious expression, he confirmed Leah's suspicions. Through the server's email communications and intel, he could see that GRF's security continued to monitor her activities.

"They know something's off," Igor said, his tone grave. "Getting her out of there is the right call—it's getting dangerous."

Then, leaning forward, he proclaimed freshly uncovered information from the shadowy GRF-mirrored server in Moscow. Through meticulous digging, Igor had identified new patterns and connections that deepened the dark picture of GRF's operations. When he finished speaking, my revelation about the Washington, DC, area code felt like a mere footnote in comparison.

It was clear: we had enough evidence to bring GRF down, to expose their corrupt web for the world to see.

The next step seemed obvious to me.

"We send the data to a trusted journalist," I proposed. "Someone with the reach and credibility to make this go public."

All eyes turned to me as I explained my pick: Adam Cohen, the renowned political columnist for the *New York Star*. A hard-hitting journalist with a bestselling book on corruption and a popular political podcast. His reputation was impeccable. We'd met at a charity fundraiser, and though we exchanged little more than business cards, I never forgot the respect he commanded in the room.

Igor leaned back in his chair with a serious expression. "Okay, Professor. How do we get the data to him without putting ourselves in danger?"

I suggested sending a USB memory stick incognito. Simple and effective.

But Igor shook his head. "If we copy this data over the internet, they'll track it. The only safe way is a direct extraction from the server in Moscow—no internet, no traceable lines."

It was a sobering realization.

We had to pivot and start a new plan. While Leah wrapped up her final two weeks at GRF, Igor would undertake the journey to Moscow to retrieve a physical copy of the incriminating data. Yet my gut told me I shouldn't place so much trust in Igor's ability to secure the server's contents and transport them from Russia to North America. He had no real stake in this dangerous game—no personal investment to ensure its success. I needed to be there with him.

This wasn't only about verifying the server's contents, however. For me, it was also a rare chance to see beyond Igor's veneer of charm, to learn who he truly was. I had to determine if he deserved my daughter's trust, her affection, and potentially, her future.

What started as a phase in our investigation had evolved into something much more significant. This was personal now—for Leah, for me, for all of us. And the stakes had never been higher.

***

For most people, entering Russia would have been a labyrinthine endeavor requiring weeks or months of meticulous planning. The visa application process gave a false impression of simplicity. A current passport photo wasn't enough; you needed precise formatting and clarity. An invitation letter from within Russia was essential, along with detailed information about travel arrangements, places to visit, and every country visited in the past decade. Paper trails that painted a picture of your existence.

Igor took the reins. He didn't just guide me through the process—he obliterated the hurdles. With surgical precision, he penned the Russian visa application. He directed me where to sign, calculating my compliance with the ease of someone who demanded trust without question.

Six hundred dollars left my hands for an expedited submission at the Russian Consulate General in Toronto. A drop in the ocean compared to the urgency of our mission. And somehow, against all odds, Igor delivered.

I don't know how he managed it, but fifty hours after the conversation about Moscow servers, we held visas in hand and boarded a plane. Life didn't give people miracles; Igor created them.

The day before we left, I'd asked Leah for a ride to the drugstore to pick up my cardio meds. It was my only chance for a conversation with her without Igor hovering nearby, providing his sarcastic commentary or unnerving insights. I didn't harbor ill will toward him, but ever since he'd stepped into her life, I'd wrestled with an unrelenting need to understand the dynamics between them, what he meant to her, and if he was the man who could stand the test of time.

I knew Leah well enough to know there was no point drilling her with questions. That would put her defenses up faster than a bullet train. Instead, I kept things casual as we sat inside the Mercedes waiting for the garage door to open.

"So . . . how's it going?" I asked, forcing all desperation from my tone and hoping to tiptoe into the conversation.

She didn't look at me as she pulled the car out of the garage and onto the street. Without missing a beat, she replied, "I'll be happy when I'm finished reporting to Cathy Dickson. She's a bitch."

Her response surprised me. Her words had bite, but the weariness in her voice—a frustration she rarely let show—lingered longer than intended.

"I know," I said carefully, trying to sidestep her stress for now. "Just a couple more weeks. Your mother would be so proud of what you've done so far—an actual spy."

"Yeah," she said with a light laugh as she pressed on the gas, taking a sharp left up Freeland Street. "Like daughter, like mother!"

The laughter was fleeting, replaced by the tension in her grip on the wheel. I glanced sideways at her, wanting to say more but unsure whether the timing was right. My thoughts felt tangled; there was too much to unravel in the few minutes it would take to get to the drugstore.

"How are you doing . . . Professor?" She flashed me a dry smile that didn't reach her eyes.

I realized instantly she was baiting me. Igor had been sitting in the shadows of this conversation from the moment we'd gotten in the car, and now, she was cutting straight to it.

I cleared my throat, keeping my tone even. "We haven't had an opportunity to talk about Igor since he moved in."

Leah's posture hardened and her grip tightened on the steering wheel as we turned east onto Lake Shore Boulevard. "What's to talk about?" she asked, her response clipped.

It was a loaded question, even if she wanted to pass it off as dismissive.

I tried to phrase my next words thoughtfully, but they sounded flat, heavier than I intended. "I don't know . . . How are things going? Do you see a future with him?"

Leah didn't respond. Instead, she fixed her gaze on the road ahead, her jaw tense, with the slightest flicker of emotion visible in her profile.

"What I see in him," she began, but then cut herself off, as though unsure how much she was willing to share. She exhaled a heavy breath. "Igor . . . he's different, you know? He's smart—brilliant, really. There's more to him than people notice at first."

I nodded, unsure how much prodding I could get away with. "Okay. But what does . . . different mean? Is this serious?"

Her tone intensified, the defensive edge creeping back into her voice. "What's your idea of serious, Dad? A man who spends every waking moment looking to save the world?"

I faltered, realizing I'd hit a sore spot. "No, I didn't mean it like that," I mumbled, my words tripping over themselves.

Leah glanced at me, looking irritated, before focusing back on the road. "Look, I don't know where this is going. Igor's . . . important to me, but I don't want to overthink it right now. I'd rather let time tell me what's real and what's not."

"But you're hoping he's the guy," I hazarded cautiously.

Her lips pressed into a thin line, and I could see walls rise around her. "Maybe I am," she admitted, her voice barely above a whisper. "But you don't have to interrogate me."

"I'm just—"

"You're just making everything awkward," she snapped, her frustration bubbling over. "You pick now, in the middle of traffic, to grill me about my relationships?"

I held my tongue, realizing I'd stirred the pot too hard. The air in the car grew heavy as we pulled up to a red light, quiet except for the faint ticking of the turn signal.

We drove the rest of the way in silence, the tension lingering like a storm cloud overhead. Beside me, Leah stared straight ahead, her expression unreadable. I wanted to say something—to bridge the distance between us—but the words stuck in my throat.

When we pulled into the drugstore's parking lot, Leah let out a sharp sigh, her grip slackening on the wheel. "You grab your meds. I'll find a parking spot," she muttered, her voice distant.

I nodded and unbuckled my seatbelt. As I stepped out, I glanced at her through the window. She had fixed her gaze on the dashboard, avoiding eye contact with me.

Leah was guarded, I reminded myself, protective of her feelings, fiercely independent. She was growing into her own person, and I'd better accept that—even if it meant accepting Igor, for better or worse. That day, I was playing dad.

The drive back was quiet. The silence between us was an unspoken reminder: some questions, especially about matters of the heart, were better left to time itself.

45

Moscow

Igor seemed at ease to me, as if Moscow were his natural habitat. The fluidity with which he spoke Russian to the cab driver further cemented this impression; his voice carried a confident tone of command as he instructed the driver to take us to our hotel. I sat back, absorbing the language I didn't understand, trying to process how the geeky boy from Toronto had become so . . . Russian. However, my thoughts kept circling back to the trip getting here.

The journey had been grueling, with nearly twenty-four hours of travel from Toronto, including a five-hour layover in Dubai. Ever thoughtful, Leah had ensured our trip was as comfortable as possible by booking first class on Emirates. The experience was a throwback to my corporate days: ensconced in luxury, shielded from the mortal struggle of economy class. Back then, it hadn't been about enjoying luxury so much as expecting it, even demanding it. Now, with hindsight and humility, I allowed myself to savor the secluded pod of soft leather, the ambient lighting, and the unequaled comfort. But even the serene and understated opulence of Emirates couldn't quite prepare me for Igor, unleashed in the fancy airport lounge at our stopover.

It had started harmlessly enough—on the flight from Toronto, Igor had had several glasses of the Dalmore King Alexander III, a very expensive single malt scotch. In the lounge at Dubai, he had focused on consuming more of the free-flowing expensive liquor.

"Your daughter is a genius," he proclaimed, feeling no pain as he ordered another double on ice.

I hesitated, unsure of where this spontaneous appraisal was heading. "She's brilliant, no doubt about that," I offered, trying to steer the conversation toward safer ground.

But Igor wasn't being steered—oh no, he was speeding up. He raised his almost empty crystal glass as he waved toward the server. "She is beautiful, radiant, like this scotch," he declared.

I looked around to see if anyone was listening to our conversation and willed the bartender to water down his drinks.

"Did I tell you about the night we met at Kult?"

I showed my confusion and shook my head.

In a louder voice, he said, "The dance club!"

I nodded.

"It was like . . . love at first sight. I knew I was smitten from that moment on. We danced all night long. We connected immediately."

By the time we reached hour three of the layover, Igor was deep into his single malt odyssey, his words blurring at the edges. The accolades poured out of him like an uneven waterfall. She was *stunning*, with kindness unmatched by humanity. She was the *sun*, illuminating the lives of those lucky enough to orbit close to her flame. She was *brilliant*, a generational talent, unmatched by any woman Igor had ever met.

The volume of his speech reached a crescendo, drawing curious glances from others. I felt my ears burning with embarrassment, yet I also couldn't help but crack a reluctant smile. Igor, for all his singular lack of tact, meant every word. His devotion to Leah was both touching and cringeworthy, wrapped up in an incoherent stream of metaphors that I silently prayed wouldn't delve deeper into more personal territory.

"Scott . . . John, whatever your name, I tell you the truth. Truth! If the famous Russian poets lived today, they would write about Leah. All the love in my heart . . ." His voice trailed off, thankfully.

At that exact moment, it was as if divine intervention had occurred; the announcement to board the flight to Moscow had saved us both. I'd sprung to my feet, eager to put distance between myself and Igor's effusive, alcohol-fueled declarations.

Igor, far less graceful, had stumbled from his seat but managed a grin as he grabbed his carry-on.

"Ah, Scott! What a good drink," he had declared, half-swaying and utterly content.

"Let's get you on the flight," I had said, trying to suppress a smile.

As our cab now rolled down Tverskaya Street, Igor seemed transformed, the hungover version of his former self. Reserved. Poised. Sober—a word I wouldn't have bet on during the chaotic charm of our layover. Yet still, the echoes of his drunken words stuck with me. Beneath the scotch-fueled exaggeration lay something layered and real: Igor didn't just admire Leah's intellect and beauty—he revered her. And while his methods were questionable, I found myself willing to grant him a pardon for his stumble through the scotch-colored lens of affection.

We passed a grand cathedral, the ornate facade shining in the evening light, and my thoughts returned to the task ahead. Igor may have been a funny, likable drunk, but the echoes of his strange poetry only deepened my discomfort about this trip. He had secrets layered within his devotion, just as Moscow had hidden stories waiting around each corner.

As we neared our destination, the city revealed itself in splashes of history and grandeur. The golden steeple of the red-brick Historical Museum caught the last of the day's sun, basking in a soft, golden light. Finally, we stopped in front of the Four Seasons Hotel, its elegant appearance mirroring the city's blend of past and present. We checked into our two-bedroom suite with little fanfare. I felt drained, yet alert.

With an enthusiasm I couldn't match, Igor declared he was heading out for food.

I declined. My body craved sleep, not sustenance.

I scarcely heard the door close behind him. When he returned—just before midnight—I pretended to be asleep.

Kids, I thought, already lapsing into unconsciousness.

***

The next morning, I woke early as sunlight spilled through the hotel room windows. My body clock was still adjusting, and finding a decent cup of tea was at the top of my list of priorities. Moscow beckoned, so I left the quiet of the suite, my curiosity pulling me toward the mysteries of Red Square.

The air outside was invigorating—a crisp breeze hinting at the heat that would soon dominate the late-summer day. The square unfolded like a scene from a historical painting, its cobblestones worn smooth by centuries of footsteps. Tourists clustered in small groups, cameras in hand, their presence blending with the palpable gravitas of the surrounding architecture.

St. Basil's Cathedral stood as the pièce de résistance, its famed onion-shaped domes bursting with color and geometric whimsy. Each turret was a unique masterpiece, spun from a palette fit for a dream. The Kremlin's red-brick walls loomed on its right. The golden stars atop its towers shimmered in the sunlight, a reminder of Russian power and influence.

Nearby, Lenin's mausoleum stood in austere contrast, stoic and silent against the kaleidoscope of history around it. I paused, letting the moment's weight anchor me: this place, these monuments, represented both triumph and tragedy. It was overwhelming in its entirety.

After soaking in the atmosphere and snapping some mental photos, I returned to the hotel armed with a fresh cup of coffee. I found Igor lounging in the suite's living room, clad only in his underwear, his athletic frame angled toward the TV. He was watching Russia Today, the English news channel, and sipping something I assumed he had gotten while I was away.

"Good morning," I said, holding out the coffee. "It's a beautiful day out there."

Igor reached for the cup, flashing a calm smile. "Thanks. Professor, I never thought you and I would be sharing a hotel room in Moscow."

He laughed, and while I chuckled politely, it felt . . . odd. A subtle distance had settled between us, which I couldn't dispel.

The news anchor's voice caught my attention. "One person is dead, and six remain missing after a luxury superyacht sank off the Sicilian coast. Among the missing are a British tech magnate and his daughter."

The grim broadcast filled the room. I moved on. "So, what's the plan today?"

Standing, Igor stretched. That's when I noticed the tattoo. A striking design on his upper shoulder. It was circular, with a skull at its center, caught in the middle of bright-red crosshairs. *ЧВК Вагнер* in Cyrillic letters encircled it.

I tried not to stare, but he caught my hesitation. Sensing my unease, Igor turned and headed toward his bedroom.

"After breakfast, I'm going to rent a car," he said. "The server farm is about an hour southeast. We'll need to get there before noon."

While Igor arranged the car rental, I found myself glued to my laptop, researching the tattoo hovering in my mind. The letters *ЧВК Вагнер* translated clearly enough: Wagner Group. Shivers went down my spine.

Known for shadowy operations, the Wagner Group was a Russian state-funded private military company. Its soldiers were mercenaries, men who fought in unmarked uniforms under questionable allegiances. Why would Igor have the Wagner Group emblem permanently etched into his skin?

A bitter sense of dread gripped me. Was this man sleeping with my daughter who he claimed to be?

The laptop hummed as I dug deeper into Igor's past. I typed his full name, *Igor Pikalov*, into the search engine. My heart raced as I skimmed the results. It was as though Igor Pikalov had vanished after June 2017. No recent photos. No social media presence.

Blyat!

Leaning closer, I scrutinized his teenage Facebook profile picture. In the photo, he must have been fifteen or sixteen, scrawny and awkward, with a mop of dark hair. I zoomed in on his face—brown eyes and a faint mole on the right cheek, near his mouth.

The man renting a car downstairs was not the Igor Pikalov that Leah had grown up with.

***

The Lada Vesta Sports sedan lurched as Igor shifted into third gear, the rhythm of the road punctuated by the engine's sound. We left Moscow behind, heading south along the Garden Ring, and eventually merged onto the M5 highway, Volgogradsky Prospekt. I found the car's interior stifling despite the air vents, though the tension inside weighed more than the summer heat.

I couldn't stop analyzing Igor as he drove, my mind a battlefield of doubts and accusations.

"So, when did your parents move back to Russia?" I asked, feigning casual conversation.

Eyes fixed on the road, Igor let out a small sigh. "I was around seventeen or eighteen," he replied. "Just finished high school. That was . . . 2017."

"That's pretty young to be left alone, don't you think?"

He shook his head, his tone firm. "Most kids my age were already living on campus, going to college. Not that strange."

I continued digging to unearth something, anything. "How often do you see your parents now?"

Without looking at me, Igor's voice rose. "Professor, what's with all the questions? I told you already—I'm not close to my parents. We don't talk much." The edge in his words warned me to stop.

Before I could say more, he turned up the car's radio, drowning the conversation in a pounding rock beat. The message was obvious: my interrogation was over.

But the questions burned in my mind, unanswered. Who the hell was driving this car—and, more importantly, who had I allowed into my daughter's life?

46

Lyubertsy, Moscow

We turned off the M5 highway at Lyubertsy, a suburb southeast of Moscow. The contrast with the Russian capital's grandeur was stark and oppressive. Entering the town felt like stepping into a different era, a place lingering in the shadows of Soviet industrial ambition. Rows of drab, imposing apartment blocks dominated the skyline—relics of Khrushchev's and Brezhnev's housing initiatives. Rusting playgrounds stood abandoned on patches of overgrown weeds, the courtyards quiet and empty, as though children hadn't played there in decades.

Igor eased the car to a stop in front of an unremarkable two-story structure. The discolored concrete building was featureless and windowless, with no signs to show a trace of identity or purpose. Its anonymity was its first layer of defense, merging into the surrounding industrial sprawl.

"Here we are," Igor said, his calm tone projecting the confidence of someone who had been there many times before.

I scrambled to reach into my backpack and pulled out a portable twenty-four-terabyte hard drive, giving it an absent inspection. The device looked like an oversized smartphone tangled with cords and connectors. Its sleek exterior belied its significance. "We're good to go," I replied.

I followed Igor into the building. Inside the modest lobby, the atmosphere was subdued, almost too quiet. Behind a simple counter stood a blonde woman, dressed with precision but leaning toward gaudy—her heavy eye makeup and bright lipstick struck an odd contrast against the sterile, utilitarian surroundings. Though she was composed, her greeting in Russian was robotic and curt. A pair of cameras hung from the ceiling, monitoring the area without apparent urgency. In a surprising lapse of security, no guards were visible.

She requested photo identification, then scanned our passports to capture digital copies. Igor, calm and collected, explained the presence of the hard drive in my bag. Her expression turned brusque. Pointing at my backpack, she declared that only the hard drive was allowed inside. "The bag will remain with me," she assured us, her tone leaving no room for negotiation.

After asking Igor a series of questions, she handed us each a security pass and gestured toward the single heavy metal door at the edge of the room. Igor tapped the pass against the reader, releasing the electronic lock with a dull beep. As the door creaked open, the frigid air from within hit us—a deliberate chill meant to preserve the equipment housed here.

The corridor was dimly lit, its bare concrete walls dampened by shadows. Fluorescent lights flickered above, casting a sterile and almost sinister glow. We walked in silence; the sound of our footsteps was amplified against the unforgiving floors and walls. At last, we stopped at a door labeled with a simple *E*.

Igor swiped the keycard again, and the lock clicked open. The room beyond was institutional in every sense, its walls painted a gleaming white. A single fluorescent light hummed overhead, reflecting off the polished surfaces. A technician was perched at a desk, his shoulders sharp in the creases of his white lab coat. In front of him, a bank of monitors streamed endless lines of data and cryptic code, blinking in constant motion. He turned to face us, his expression stern and unfriendly.

Igor instantly produced his ID once more, handing it over without hesitation. The technician eyed him, tapping on his keyboard before gesturing toward a small biometric scanner near the corner of his desk. Igor placed his hand on the scanner's surface, and with a soft beep, the system granted him access.

The technician rose and led us through another door. This one was glass and reinforced, the faint hiss of its airtight mechanism filling the air as it unlocked. What lay beyond was both overwhelming and mesmerizing.

Row upon row of server cabinets stretched into the distance. Tall and uniform, they stood like soldiers in precise formation, each housing endless amounts of data. The cabinets shimmered black, their sleek surfaces reflecting the sterile white light overhead. A low, omnipresent hum—the ceaseless activity of countless processors working in unison—filled the air. The air felt charged, brimming with the invisible information pulse flowing through countless cables and circuits.

At the far end of the room was another glass door, cordoning off a private bank of servers. To access it, another layer of security came into play. Igor placed his hand on the scanner, and the technician followed with an eye scan, Igor's gaze lingering in the machine's lens. Only then did the door unlock, revealing a bank of private servers. Small LED lights blinked in perfect coordination, as though whispering among themselves, communicating in a language only they understood.

In what felt like a cathedral of modern technology, I stood awestruck and unsettled by the immensity of it all. This was a fortress of secrets. A repository of unimaginable wealth and power.

With silent efficiency, the technician connected the portable hard drive to the server. Within seconds, his expression turned into annoyance. He held up the AC adapter's plug and frowned. The cord's rating was 120 volts—the North American standard, not the 220 volts used here. He glared at us, unimpressed. "Do you have a plug adapter?" he asked impatiently.

Both Igor and I shrugged with feigned helplessness.

With a hissed curse under his breath, the technician stormed out, slamming the door behind him. The sound echoed like a gunshot, leaving a vacuum of silence in his wake.

Igor didn't waste a second. From his pocket, he fished out a small adapter and plugged it into the drive. His fingers moved with the precision of a surgeon, swift and deliberate, as the screen flickered to life. Lines of data cascaded across the monitor, pouring onto the hard drive like an unrelenting river.

"Eight and a half minutes," he muttered, barely above a whisper, but the weight of those words hit me like a ticking time bomb.

The room felt heavy, the air dense, as he finally glanced up, locking eyes with me. His gaze burned with a fierce determination, but his voice was eerily calm, calculated. "He's going to come back," he said flatly, his tone sending a chill down my spine. "Professor, go help him. Stall him."

No time to question—only to act. Without another word, I turned and left, my steps quickening as I moved deeper into the labyrinthine corridors. My gut churned with the realization: I was now part of a plan I hadn't fully grasped until this very moment. The aim was somber, clear—steal the data, then obliterate all traces of it.

The seconds dragged like hours, every footstep I took echoing in my ears over the deafening thrum of my own racing heartbeat. I turned corner after corner, the dimly lit hallway stretching farther than it should. My sense of direction had failed me; I was lost.

I came to a steel door, its dark surface gleaming under the flickering fluorescent lights. My fingers fumbled as I pulled out my pass card and swiped it against the reader. A red light flashed, taunting me. Access denied. Desperation clawing at me, I back-tracked to a door I'd passed earlier. Just as I neared it, a deafening alarm erupted around me. Red lights began strobing along the corridor, casting the hallway with a sinister, pulsing glow. My breath hitched. Was it a fire? Or something worse?

Panic tightened its grip as I tried the handle of the nearest door. This one gave way, revealing a room bathed in the eerie flickering glow of monitors streaming data. The alarm's shrill wail burrowed into my skull, my head pounding in protest as I darted to another door. The first one I tried didn't budge, but the second, mercifully, clicked open when I swiped my card.

I burst into another corridor—a maze of red flashes, blaring sirens, and chaos. I tried to inhale, but the air was thick and acrid, a chemical smoke swirling around me. The stench clawed at my throat, sharp and familiar. Tel Aviv. The bombing. The memory slammed into me like a freight train, leaving me gasping.

"Evakuiruyus!" a panicked voice blared in Russian over the loudspeakers, the command repeated in a gut-wrenching rhythm. *Evacuate*, my strained mind translated. The word whipped my legs into action. I ran. My strides were frantic, aimless, until my eyes latched onto a pair of steel double doors at the end of the hall, beneath a glaring red sign reading Выход. Later, I'd learn it meant Exit.

I barreled into the push bar, throwing my weight into it. The doors crashed open with a metallic groan, and the sunlight that greeted me blinded me, prompting me to shield my eyes. I staggered onto the pavement, gulping down the fresh air like a drowning man breaking the water's surface. My lungs burned as they filled.

"Professor! Get in the car!" Igor's voice cut through the haze like a blade.

I turned to see him leaning out of the driver's side window of the rented car, his expression sharp, his tone commanding. Chaos churned all around us. Black smoke billowed from the building's roof, and people poured out of various exits, their faces panicked, the fire alarm's screech relentless.

"Now!" he shouted, urgency dripping from the word.

My feet obeyed before my brain did, carrying me to the car. I threw open the passenger door and hastily shoved my backpack aside as I tumbled into the seat. Before I could even pull the door closed, Igor's foot slammed on the gas. The tires screeched, and the car lurched forward, tearing away from the curb in a sharp turn that had me grabbing at the seatbelt.

As I fumbled with the strap and glanced down, something caught my eye. A hard drive nestled in my backpack, the very one Igor had plugged in over ten minutes earlier. My stomach twisted. He'd recovered my backpack and stuffed the remote hard drive into it.

Igor drove like a man possessed, whipping the car through turns with the precision of a professional racer. The fire alarms and muffled chaos of the building faded behind us, replaced by the pounding thrum of my heartbeat. My breath came in ragged bursts as I leaned back against the seat, staring at the road ahead but seeing only the smoke, the flashing lights, the wreckage we'd left in our wake.

"What the hell happened?" I finally forced the words out, my voice shaking.

Igor's jaw tightened, his knuckles white against the steering wheel. He didn't look at me as he spoke, his tone cutting through the tension like a razor. "The private server bank is gone," he said. "Burned."

He didn't elaborate, and I didn't need him to. The deliberate fire had consumed everything, erasing not just the evidence of what we'd done but the data we had taken. We had the prize—the rest was ash.

And yet, as the car sped forward, a chilling thought gnawed at the edge of my mind. This was far from over. This felt less like escaping and more like the opening move in a long, sinister game.

Whatever happened next, there would be no turning back. The terabytes of data in my backpack held the power to destroy GRF and even FIST, but our task was just beginning.

Now, we had to focus on the next critical step: escaping the bear's den.

47

Moscow

With music blaring from the radio, Igor wasted no time driving the Lada back to the hotel. He dropped me off, saying, "I'll meet you in the room," before speeding off to the car rental.

I called Leah to give her a cryptic update, mindful that Russian authorities might be listening. Her voice betrayed how much she missed us. I ached to tell her all I had discovered about the man who went by Igor Pikalov, but that conversation would have to wait until we were face to face.

Hours seemed to pass before Igor finally returned to the hotel room. He swaggered in with a triumphant mood, possibly heightened by alcohol. "Professor, we need to celebrate with a fine Russian meal," he announced enthusiastically. "We deserve it!"

He was right; we deserved it. Yet the idea of dining with him left me uncertain. "What did you have in mind?"

"Thanks to the concierge, we've got reservations at a pop-up restaurant, Pink Rabbit, a couple blocks away."

"What time?"

"Seven. I booked early so you can get up for a city tour before our afternoon flight."

"Okay. That gives me a couple of hours to hit the gym." My body was stiff from the day's stress.

***

The restaurant, set in a modern building with its eight floors of glass and steel, stood out against the city's historic backdrop. We entered the elevator and chose the top floor, where a temporary sign indicated the Pink Rabbit to be. Igor looked like a man on the prowl, clad entirely in Hugo Boss: fitted white shirt, black pants, and black silk-and-linen blazer.

We stepped into a vibrant, festive atmosphere as the elevator doors opened. Floor-to-ceiling windows around the room presented breathtaking views of Red Square, the Kremlin, and beyond. Topped with crisp white tablecloths, the tables glowed with gold cutlery, lively pink flower arrangements, and bright-pink furry chairs. The staff, all dressed in white, sought to make a good impression.

We plopped down at a cozy round table with glasses of champagne. Igor, acting like the host, ordered the five-course prix fixe meal with sturgeon caviar. Beside us sat a table of four young and attractive models. Igor wasted no time flirting, sending several bottles of champagne their way. I wondered who was paying the bill.

Each course arrived with new arranged plates, cutlery, and wineglasses. The portions were modest but artfully presented, delivering a feast for the eyes long before the palate.

Igor convinced me to try the chef's signature dessert, a masterful finale known as the Candy Dostoevsky Cigar. Our server arrived with a large plate under a glass dome of swirling smoke and placed it in front of me. As they lifted the dome, I was enveloped by a waft of smoke. Igor urged me to take a deep breath.

I closed my eyes and inhaled deeply, the smoke searing my lungs sharply as I absorbed a warm, nutty sweetness touched with undertones of caramelized sugar. An aroma of subtle spice—cinnamon or cloves—and the smoky essence of brandy-soaked applewood filled my senses. The scent honored the literary genius with its robust, sophisticated fragrance.

As my eyes opened, my lungs suddenly felt leaden, each breath becoming a struggle.

Igor fixed me with a concerned gaze. "Are you okay? Try the Armagnac with it."

With the smoke clearing, I saw before me a white ashtray holding a lifelike cigar crafted from dark chocolate and filled with cigar-smoke ice cream, garnished with a powdered black sugar-spice mix that resembled cigar ash.

I sipped the Armagnac, but I felt dizzy and my need for fresh air became urgent. I excused myself and headed for the elevator, feeling increasingly disoriented and on the edge of nausea. Before the sickness got to me, I needed to escape outside.

***

I woke up feeling like a freight train had hit me. My body ached, and the pounding in my head was relentless. Somehow, I'd found my way back into my hotel bed. I glanced at my phone and realized it was 11:00 a.m. Panic flickered in my mind—my flight back to Toronto demanded my presence at the airport in under two hours.

I'd experienced bouts of vomiting throughout the night; my stomach was now empty but still churning. The dizziness had finally eased, but my throat felt raw and sore, each breath labored as if I'd smoked an entire pack of cigarettes in one sitting.

Trying to find my footing, I searched the hotel room for water. My eyes landed on the bar in the sitting room, where a single unopened water bottle rested. Without a second thought, I grabbed the bottle, scrambled to find a bottle opener, then popped the cap and drained it in one desperate gulp. The cold liquid did little to soothe my throat, but the rush of hydration jolted my senses, reminding me I needed to pull myself together and get out of this country.

A sudden pang of concern swept over me—where was Igor? Had he overslept, too? His door was ajar, so I carefully peered inside. His bed was untouched. My breathing became shallow, my chest tightening with a mix of pain and burgeoning panic as I scanned the space. Nothing. No trace of him. His suitcase and his toiletries were gone.

The realization hit me like a cold slap. Racing to the coffee table, I grabbed my black backpack and tore into it, hands trembling. Relief flooded through me as I pulled out the portable hard drive—terabytes of incriminating GRF data, safe and sound.

I exhaled deeply, gathering what little focus I had left. There was no time to dwell. I hurried to dress, pack, and get to Moscow International Airport. Maybe Igor had found somewhere else to crash last night after his determined antics to charm the models at the restaurant. I convinced myself he'd be at the airport when I arrived. Though his disappearance sent shivers crawling up my spine, my priority remained clear: getting out of Russia with the hard drive.

48

Toronto

The flight home felt heavier without Igor's presence. I'd texted and called him multiple times before boarding, but each attempt was met with silence. It was as if he had vanished.

I slept almost the entire fourteen-hour stretch from Dubai, my body desperate to recover from whatever illness had taken hold of me in Moscow. Although my condition had improved slightly, I was still not back to normal. My mind felt muddled, my limbs were weak, and fatigue weighed me down like bricks.

Landing in Toronto late on Friday morning, the familiar feel of the city calmed me. I arrived exhausted at the rented condo on Queen's Quay. Leah wasn't home, but she was still wrapping up her last days at GRF. I dropped my bag by the door, sank onto the couch, and turned on the TV. The static distractions bridged the gap as I waited for her to return, lulling me into a deep, dreamless sleep.

***

I stirred on the couch as a familiar voice pulled me to consciousness. Leah's smiling face hovered above me, her presence lightening the weight on my chest. I embraced her as though it might be the last time I'd ever hold her, but then I quickly warned her to stay away.

"You don't want whatever Moscow gave me," I muttered through a weary laugh.

She disappeared into the kitchen, returning moments later with water for me and rosé for herself, a reward for another long week behind her. She settled into the oversized chair opposite me with an expression of concern written across her face.

"Tell me what happened," she whispered.

For the next hour, I unpacked everything as if I were reliving it: The tangled web of our impostor, Igor. The server farm. The fire. The portable hard drive. The strange illness that followed the dinner at Pink Rabbit. Igor's mysterious disappearance.

As I told my story, Leah's reactions were as raw as the events. She crossed the room to wrap her arms around me, as though trying to contain the ache we both shared. Tears streamed down her face as she listened, her emotions mirroring my own.

When I finally finished, she reached out, pressing her palm to my forehead, her voice soft with concern. "We need to get you to a doctor."

I didn't have the heart to argue. Instead, I rose slowly from the couch and retrieved my black backpack, pulling out the portable hard drive. "It was all worth it for this," I said, holding it up as though it were the grail itself. "The evidence to dismantle GRF."

Leah took the hard drive from my hand. Her expression was a mix of determination and hope as she carried it to the laptop perched on the dining room table. She connected the drive and powered up the laptop, and the large monitor flickered to life.

We both leaned in as she opened the only file on the drive.

The screen displayed: *This folder is EMPTY.*

Time seemed to stop. My breath hitched as I stared in disbelief, the moment's weight crashing down on me like a tidal wave.

Leah looked at me wide-eyed, her lips trembling. "Is this some kind of joke?" she whispered, desperation creeping into her voice.

I didn't have an answer. The realization clawed at me, threatening to strangle the hope I'd been clinging to all along. Everything—absolutely everything—might have been for nothing.

49

Toronto

The days following the discovery of the empty hard drive blurred together, a haze of disappointment and lingering illness. My chronic cough persisted, each bout sending fiery pain through my lungs, reminding me I was far from recovered.

Whoever the fake Igor was, he'd orchestrated an elaborate ruse. Feeding us updates, he'd left us in the dark, uncertain whether the GRF data had ever existed on that mirrored server. The burning question remained: Who was this man? My mission was to find out. Borrowing Leah's car, I drove to the Beaches to see whether he was still occupying his residence. The duplex we'd visited over a month before still stood unassuming, with a FOR RENT sign staked in the front yard. I called the rental agency with an impulsive urge to view it.

The agent promised to meet me in two hours. With time to kill, I planted myself on a bench along the boardwalk, my gaze trailing across Lake Ontario's placid blue expanse. My thoughts betrayed an unexpected darkness: What would I do if I confronted Igor face to face? Would rage boil over into action? Could I—if it came to it—kill another man? It wasn't a question I shied away from. At that moment, I felt I could.

Two hours later, I stood inside the duplex. Empty of furniture, the space seemed larger. The agent explained that a TV documentary had recently used the property as a set, but he revealed little else about it. Downstairs, the basement—a dim concrete void with light barely seeping through narrow windows—offered no trace of Igor's computer tech haven. No clues. Nothing.

Defeated, I exited the duplex alongside the realtor, who continued his enthusiastic sales pitch about why the place should be mine. I humored him, offering a vague promise to think about it. But my cough must've scared him because he suddenly handed me his business card and drove off in an old Volvo sedan.

As I stood catching my breath, something caught my eye. It was garbage day, and so black bins lined the street. All except in front of the duplex I'd visited. Curious, I wandered to the side of the building, noticing three containers neatly tucked against its wall: one black, one blue, and one green. I peered inside the black garbage bin first. Empty. The blue recycling bin, however, held something unusual—a scattered mess of papers and file folders.

I tipped the bin over, desperate to fish out what I could. Maybe, just maybe, there was something valuable among the refuse. Like a scavenger, I grabbed every scrap of paper and bolted back to the car, my heart pounding from both exertion and panic.

"Excuse me, sir," a voice called out from behind me.

Panic surged. I ran harder, only stopping once I was safe inside the car, papers tossed haphazardly onto the passenger seat.

Through the window, I saw her—a tall, athletic woman walking a dog. She eyed my car with caution as she grasped a handful of paper. I rolled down the window, breathless and wary.

"You dropped these," she said politely as she handed them to me.

I thanked her, choking as a violent coughing fit overtook me. The sound startled her, and she whirled away, retreating down the sidewalk with her dog in tow.

I slumped forward over the steering wheel, wheezing. The effort to breathe was overwhelming. I needed a doctor. Desperately. But first, I needed answers. I needed to uncover the identity of the fake Igor Pikalov. I shifted Leah's Mercedes into gear and headed for Queen's Quay.

Once back at the condo, I sat cross-legged on the living room floor, the salvaged papers strewn out before me like I was a child sorting Halloween candy. This wasn't candy, though—it was hundreds of documents and records, each one an invasive breach of privacy. Credit card statements. Medical reports. Prescriptions. Bank account statements. Tax records. Travel itineraries. Parking tickets.

I organized the papers into five distinct piles: Colleen/Mary, Leah, Me (Scott/John), Cathy Dickson, and GRF. To my horror, the papers contained photos of us: surveillance grabs from cameras positioned on streets, in buildings, and in public spaces. They had violated every corner of our lives, reducing our privacy to scraps tossed thoughtlessly into a recycling bin. My rage boiled as I stared at the piles.

The GRF pile was the most intriguing. It contained blueprints of the headquarters, bank data, detailed security protocols, lists of employee records, and IP addresses. Technical jargon covered several documents. But one name jumped out: Mount Royal Capital LLC.

The name stirred a memory. Katerina, back in Germany, had mentioned a complex financial structure using shell companies to launder money through Canada's lucrative housing market. Could this be the thread we needed to tie it back to Grand Cayman? The implications were monumental.

Then came the Cathy Dickson pile—only five documents, but loaded with meaning:

1. A Land Registry property document for a four-million-dollar building on Ellis Avenue, west of High Park. Unsurprisingly, it was owned by Mount Royal Capital LLC. Most likely her residence.

2. Flight records outlining her recent travel. Six months of jet-setting trips to New York (four), Frankfurt (five), and Hong Kong (one).

3. Her gym membership activity. She'd been in attendance 163 times in the past year.

4. A list of food deliveries to the Ellis address. Italian cuisine dominated the menu.

5. Her entertainment preferences—movies and shows devoured on Netflix and Prime. Murder and romance documentaries appeared to be her favorites.

But disturbingly absent was any solid information about Igor Pikalov himself. Only three receipts provided even a whisper of his existence.

One receipt dated back to the time he had entered our lives—a purchase from a store called Spy Gadgets. The itemized receipt listed two "Sound LD-03" devices: high-tech mini microphones with real-time Wi-Fi audio transmission.

Another receipt was for a month of drop-in passes at the Fitness Club near Queen's Quay.

The last receipt, for two steak dinners at the CN Tower's 360 Restaurant, felt like a stab to the chest. The date aligned with the week I had been in Grand Cayman. My stomach tightened in anger.

Igor had been watching, listening, planning, and deceiving. My gut had warned me I couldn't trust him, but I hadn't listened.

50

Toronto

Leah's fingers entwined with mine as we sat facing the oncologist. His words hit me like a punch, robbing me of breath.

"I'm sorry," he said, "but you have stage 2 lung cancer. Several malignant tumors are present in both lungs, concentrated notably at the segmental bronchi bifurcations."

"I don't smoke," I protested, disbelief coloring my voice.

"That is surprising," the doctor noted. "Such concentrations are common in chronic smokers. There is a natural radioisotope found in tobacco linked to lung cancer—polonium-210."

"I've heard of polonium-210," Leah interjected, concern written on her face. "Isn't it a poison?"

"Over twenty years ago, a Russian KGB spy died from radiation poisoning caused by polonium-210," the doctor said with a smirk in an attempt to lighten the mood.

"Could I have inhaled the poison?" I inquired, trying to steady my frayed nerves.

"Are you a spy, Mr. Miller?" the doctor quipped, but then quickly sobered. "It's theoretically possible, but someone would require access and expertise, polonium being more toxic than hydrogen cyanide."

Igor's voice echoed in my memory: *Take a deep breath.*

"We'll start with a combination of chemotherapy and radiation to shrink the tumors," the doctor continued, "making them more responsive to treatment. Surgery is a last resort."

All I could think about at that precise moment was my hair. Since becoming Mr. John Miller, I'd had a buzz cut, so no one would notice the difference if I lost my hair.

Leah's tears glistened in a silent cascade as I tunneled through thoughts of her safety, GRF's downfall, and what I must achieve before my time was up.

She squeezed my hand as we walked to the car. My head swam from the weight of everything crashing down on me: Igor, the GRF conspiracy, and now the ticking time bomb in my chest. But the shock of the cancer diagnosis had crystallized something inside me—a strange calm, a sharp focus. If my time was limited, I would spend it protecting Leah and finishing what we started. But first, we needed to find Igor's listening devices.

***

Back at the condo, Leah was on the brink. She wanted to talk about the diagnosis, plan my treatment, and grieve, but I couldn't allow that. Not yet. I told her I needed to move forward; it was the only way I could think clearly. I needed action.

Ignoring her worried gaze, I began tearing through the apartment, searching for the evidence that had lit a fire in my gut. Somewhere within this space, Igor's two listening devices had to be hidden.

Alarmed by my erratic behavior, Leah finally snapped. "What the hell are you doing?" she cried out, her voice edged with panic.

I stopped abruptly and turned to her, placing a finger to my lips—a signal for silence. Then, I gestured toward the balcony. Puzzled, she followed me without a word, her concern unspoken yet palpable.

Once we'd stepped outside and I'd slid the door shut, Leah's frustration boiled over. "What the hell is going on?" she demanded, her voice trembling with impatience.

I inhaled sharply, steadying my words. "Igor planted two bugs—listening devices—in the condo. When I visited his place, I found files about us, along with a receipt for them. I'll check the living room; you take your bedroom."

Her face twisted in disgust. "Seriously?" She stormed off to her room without waiting for further explanation.

The search didn't take long. It turned out the apartment wasn't a fortress of secrets but a battleground for subtle espionage. I found one device hidden in the lampshade beside the sofa and the other beneath the kitchen's breakfast bar counter. Leah's search came up empty. Her bedroom was clean. Without hesitation, she scooped up both bugs, wrapped them in a small bag, and tossed them into the first garbage can she found on the boardwalk outside our building.

I turned my focus back to the pile of GRF papers that had haunted me since the first time I rifled through them. Leah begrudgingly joined me, her exhaustion apparent but her urgency matching mine. Somehow, this wasn't only a mission about justice anymore; it had morphed into one about survival.

My instincts led me to Mount Royal Capital—the heart of GRF's financial secrets. Firing up my digital toolbox, I took to the dark corners of the internet, tracing any mention of or movement linked to the company. What emerged was a sprawling network of shell corporations masking transactions through obscure accounts hidden in offshore tax havens. The patterns were transparent to someone who knew what to look for. Faceless entities funneled hundreds of millions of dollars to purchase luxury condos, vacant properties, and ghost developments across Toronto and Vancouver.

It was money laundering. Exactly what Katerina had hinted at. Mount Royal Capital wasn't simply GRF's financial crutch, it was their spine, the very framework that held everything together.

The operation's methods weren't unfamiliar. Traditional financial institutions, money services, shell companies, hawala systems. They were all in play. But the evolution of their tactics revealed something troubling. Cryptocurrency had emerged as their next frontier. Two names surfaced repeatedly: WTF! Market (a notorious darknet marketplace facilitating illicit transactions) and the Russian cryptocurrency exchange Garantech (a central node in financial crime, enabling money laundering for criminal syndicates, ransomware groups, and other shadowy entities).

This wasn't only financial fraud but calculated deceit that secretly fueled the GRF mission. But the insistence on laundering the money puzzled me. The funds were coming from clean sources—two prominent nations funneling contributions to GRF. To prevent tracing the legitimate money back to them, they needed to conceal it. A charitable organization like GRF couldn't legally hold millions in dormant accounts; it would raise suspicion, especially in years when covert global disruptions were minimal. Hiding an influx of funds in plain sight was more than necessary—it was brilliant, albeit deeply unethical.

Fueled by a sense of renewed purpose, I refused to stop until the pieces clicked together. Sleep was a forgotten concept, my energy reserved for connecting disjointed dots in the machinery of deception. The longer I worked, the less my anger burned toward GRF, FIST, and even Igor himself. What consumed me now was anger at time—its fragility, its fleeting nature. Everything I cared about felt perched on the brink of collapse, yet time continued to stretch and compress as though mocking me.

But this anger couldn't persist. Anger was poison, and I was already battling enough. If there was one certainty left, it was that I would fight. Not just for answers, but for survival, justice, and everything else this mission seemed to demand from me.

And I knew I wouldn't be fighting alone. Leah and I brought different strengths to the battle ahead. Where I focused on strategy and dismantling the machinery of chaos, she focused on the human cost of innocent lives swallowed by that chaos. She saw the faces behind the mayhem. Together, we were greater than the sum of our abilities.

Tomorrow marked her last day at GRF. It wasn't an ending; it marked a turning point. A new beginning. And together, we would face a far greater fight, armed not just with resolve, but with each other's strengths.

51

Toronto

I received Leah's text. She was on her way. I parked as close as I could to the front door of GRF's office, watching the entrance like I was waiting for a signal.

It wasn't long before I saw her struggling to open the door, clutching a box overflowing with personal items and plants. A security guard stepped out to hold the door, allowing her to say her goodbyes.

As soon as she saw me, her face lit up and the biggest smile spread across her lips. She hurried toward the car, her excitement palpable.

There was something about that smile; it reflected more than relief from leaving GRF. There was something deeper to it.

When the GRF office disappeared in the rearview mirror, Leah turned to me, clearly ready to share something urgent. "How are you feeling?" she said, leading with a surprising question.

"Good," I replied, distracted, eager to hear what was on her mind. "How was your last day?"

She pulled a pink envelope from her purse with a flourish as I merged onto the Don Valley Parkway South.

"I got two farewell cards," she said, her voice filled with excitement. "The first was from my team. And this one," she paused, staring at me, "this one's from a secret admirer."

I frowned, confused by her tone.

Without waiting for my response, she opened the card and read aloud. "You are in danger. Please meet me tomorrow at The Pier Café on the south side of the Queen's Quay Terminal along the waterfront trail at 10:00 a.m. Come alone."

The café was a ten-minute walk from our condo. Did this person know where we lived? I could not let Leah go by herself.

***

The next morning, I insisted she arrive early—not too early, which might draw suspicion, but early enough to ensure she ordered her own coffee. Who knew what games people played?

It was a late-summer morning with crisp air meeting the warmth of the rising sun. I sat at the water's edge, between a tour boat and a party boat, blending into the flow of runners, dog walkers, and curious tourists. From my vantage point, I could see Leah seated outside, separated from the other tables.

Her phone sat on the table, broadcasting what was happening through the AirPods in my ears.

Seven minutes before ten, a short and plump woman with cropped white hair and oversized black glasses approached Leah.

"Oh my God, it's the woman from the elevator," Leah whispered.

"Hello," the stranger said breathlessly. She sat across from Leah, staring at her face as if she'd seen a ghost. "You look so much like your mother. It's uncanny. Sorry for staring at you so much."

Leah hesitated, clearly struggling to understand what this woman wanted. "I— Sorry," she stammered, and I could sense her curiosity edging toward caution. "Do I know you?"

The woman offered a soft smile. "I'm Dorothy Steele. At GRF, I work in the finance department. I . . . I knew your mother when she worked there. I saw you once in the elevator before you left. Honestly, I thought I was seeing her ghost."

Leah looked stunned as she tried to process the woman's words. A waiter interrupted to take Dorothy's coffee order, giving Leah a moment to pull herself together.

She lowered her head slightly, overwhelmed by the flattery and the weight of Dorothy's words. "Thank you," she mumbled. She paused, her tone shifting to alarm. "Did anyone else know I was her daughter?"

"No," Dorothy replied quickly, shaking her head. "Your mother kept her maiden name. She was careful, but . . ." Her voice trailed off before steadying. "She was a wonderful person. I never thought her death was an accident. Is that why you took the part-time role at GRF?"

Dorothy's coffee arrived at that moment, and she sipped it, her expression growing more cautious.

Leah glanced at me for support, her eyes briefly locking with mine. I nodded in encouragement from the waterfront edge.

"I . . . have my suspicions too," Leah admitted quietly.

Dorothy scanned the environment before leaning closer to Leah. "GRF is not what it seems," she whispered, her tone weighted with urgency. "We talk about helping women and girls in need, but we are more of a threat than a solution. People—not just employees—associated with GRF . . . they seem to vanish. Many ex-employees mysteriously die."

Dorothy tensed, her face taut, as though she feared her words had crossed a dangerous threshold. She took another sip of her coffee, her hands trembling. When she spoke again, her words were slower, more deliberate. "I worked with your mother on several real estate deals back then. When we noticed irregularities and asked questions, they told us it was all necessary. Preserving the GRF's assets was supposedly the key to saving thousands of women and girls. Like fools, we believed them."

A couple sat down at a table nearby, the sound of their chairs scraping against the cement patio interrupting the conversation.

Dorothy's face shifted, nervous again. She leaned in even closer. "I need you to know there's a much darker, sinister side to GRF. Your mother . . ." Her voice shook. "Colleen would want me to keep you safe. But—" She abruptly stood, placing ten dollars on the table.

Leah grabbed Dorothy's arm. "How can I reach you?" she pleaded desperately. "I need to know more."

Dorothy dug into her purse and then slipped a white card into Leah's hand without meeting her eyes. "Here's my private number. If I can help, I will," she said, her voice thick with emotion. Her eyes glistened as tears threatened to fall. "I owe your mother."

And with that, Dorothy vanished into the crowd, leaving Leah shaken and clutching the card like a lifeline.

Catching my breath, I typed *Dorothy Steele* into the LinkedIn app. She had no profile photo and only forty-eight connections, one of which was my late wife, Colleen. She'd graduated from McMaster University with a Bachelor of Commerce. Simultaneously, she and Colleen had started working at GRF. In her thirty years at GRF, she had earned two promotions, reaching her current position as controller. She was younger than Colleen by a couple of years, but if looks counted, she appeared much older. I switched to Facebook and found nothing that matched her name and location.

I hoped for all our sakes that Dorothy was the fuse to the destruction of the Global Relief Foundation.

52

Toronto

The first four weeks of chemo and radiation tested me in ways I never thought possible. My body felt like it was undergoing a daily battle, a war fought on both physical and emotional fronts. Some days left me breathless, the exhaustion weighing me down like lead, as though my body was resisting everything I was asking of it. But I learned something surprising through it, something life-changing: I'd stopped thinking of the experience as suffering and started seeing it as a transformation.

Yes, my appetite was minimal, my weight dropping so that my head seemed oversized on my thin frame. Yes, my crew cut turned into a bowling ball, and nausea came and went like an unwelcome guest. But despite it all, I'd never felt closer to understanding my resilience. It wasn't the end; it was an awakening. My illness didn't define me; it revealed me.

I would look in the mirror and see someone fighting tooth and nail for his life, his family, and the truth to destroy GRF.

I saw someone who refused to let the battle dictate his spirit. Every hour that I endured, every moment that I pushed forward despite the weakness clawing at me, strengthened my will. Survival was not the only factor. It was about regaining the strength to fight back harder and win on all fronts.

It was not just about me. Leah's unyielding support reminded me daily that this battle impacted more than just my life—it impacted hers and those of countless others affected by GRF's evil actions.

While I worked to reclaim my health, Leah was digging deeper into GRF's operations, stepping far beyond her comfort zone. She began holding a series of clandestine meetings with Dorothy Steele in Toronto parks, coffeehouses, and hotel lobbies, always careful not to be followed. Leah had the intensity of an investigative journalist, untangling the convoluted web of records and corporate structures that Dorothy shared with her. Together, they sifted through the noise, separating distractions from the cold, hard evidence beneath.

Over several weeks of painstaking work, Leah and Dorothy built a damning picture of Mount Royal Capital LLC, a so-called real estate investment firm responsible for acquiring high-value, distressed properties, most notably in Toronto. MRC was more than dabbling in the real estate game—they were thriving. The shell company had amassed an impressive and shadowy portfolio of properties, including the building that housed GRF's global headquarters. Their transactions stank of corruption: enormous sums of cash, crypto transfers, and wires from offshore accounts in places like the Cayman Islands, Cyprus, and Estonia.

For thirty years, Dorothy had carried the weight of deceit, a lifetime woven with lies, half-truths, and orchestrated cover-ups. Now, the dam had broken. Words spilled from her lips in a torrent, a desperate purging of her soul from the stain of fraudulent acts and the burden of complicity in illicit accounting schemes. Each confession seemed to strip away a layer of her guilt, as if her very conscience demanded absolution from the shadows that had consumed her for decades.

She exposed how the real estate investments siphoned off donor money, generating profits of 20 to 30 percent or more. She provided Leah with stunning evidence: internal financial records, bank statements, wire transfer slips, Bitcoin trades, and even land registry titles. Every thread seemed to lead back to Mount Royal Capital—a Cayman Islands–registered shell company at the center of it all. Two major financial players, Toronto Bank and the Republic of Moscow Bank, frequently handled the transactions; both had been repeatedly flagged for weak anti-money-laundering safeguards. Poor customer due diligence? Check. Inadequate transaction monitoring? Check. A willingness to turn a blind eye to suspicious activities? Absolutely.

Dorothy admitted that while the transactions were technically legal—carefully structured to avoid regulatory scrutiny and capital gains taxes—the entire operation reeked of criminality. The layering of funds through multiple offshore accounts masked their true origins. She suspected that this was about more than real estate profits. "Wherever this money comes from," she told Leah during one of their late-night meetings, "it's dirty. It's money flowing from corrupt or criminal organizations, funneled through MRC and GRF to sanitize it."

Dorothy also noted an alarming trend: an increasing reliance on cryptocurrency. Unlike traditional banking systems that could leave a paper trail, these transactions moved in seconds, encrypted and impossible to trace. Leah unearthed emails between GRF's CEO and CFO alluding to "layering" funds—evidence that the organization was scheming to avoid suspicion.

But that was only part of the story. As Leah and I knew, Dorothy suspected the corruption extended far beyond hidden real estate gains or illicit money. But she was unaware of the deeper operations beneath the GRF's polished exterior. Under the GRF building, hundreds of agents controlled by the GRF were working as part of an extensive espionage network. This network disseminated disinformation and propaganda, orchestrated political and social warfare, destabilized governments, and created or removed obstacles in pursuit of global chaos intended to benefit specific powers.

Systematically, Leah had organized Dorothy's mountain of evidence and the cryptic trail I had discovered on the digital net, distilling it all into a coherent, devastating exposé. Once completed, even the most novice of investigative journalists could follow GRF's trail of deceit and fraud. Our hope was monumental but straightforward: to deliver this exposé to a seasoned reporter who could publish it in a paper like the *New York Star*. It would lay bare GRF's misuse of donations, implicate them in laundering criminal funds, and expose their profiteering—all while pretending to act in the name of helping women and girls.

The plan was perilous, yet retreat was impossible. If GRF's true story came to light, we wouldn't only be taking down a corrupt operation, we'd also be pulling the rug out from under a sinister organization that had been hiding in plain sight for decades.

And for the first time in weeks, despite the pain and fatigue gnawing at me, I felt something close to hope flickering in my chest. It was not over yet.

My fingers tightened around the edge of the dossier Leah had put together. "Let's do it," I said resolutely. "Every front, every battle—we're winning this, no matter what it takes."

Leah smiled. The kind of smile that gave me strength, the kind that said she believed in me, in us, and in what we were about to accomplish.

53

New York

I was ready. Or at least as ready as anyone could be when preparing to hand over evidence that had the potential to topple one of the most powerful charity organizations in the world. It needed to be given to someone with a name big enough to make the world listen and tenacious enough not to back down when things got dangerous. Leah and I planned the meeting with care: Adam Cohen, the political columnist for the *New York Star*, was the kind of journalist born to take down giants. Hard-nosed, relentless, and almost immune to intimidation, he had made a career exposing corruption, power abuse, and financial malfeasance.

Though I'd met Adam years ago at a fundraiser as Scott Barton, I was changed enough physically to feel certain he wouldn't connect Scott to John Miller. Still, the risk was heavy, so Leah and I agreed I would handle this meeting alone. She deserved to stay as far from this storm as possible. If anyone was going to take the fall, it would be me.

Sitting alone in a dark Irish pub across the street from the *New York Star*'s offices in the Port Authority Bus Terminal, its walls smelling of stale beer mixed with decades-old wood, I felt a nervous twist in my stomach. A glass of water sat in front of me. I'd passed on the beer, knowing that chemo and alcohol would never mix. Beside me on the banquette bench was a manila envelope, ten inches by fourteen, packed with over one hundred pages of evidence. This was more than a dossier—it was an encyclopedia of GRF's criminality: internal documents, transaction records, wire transfers, cryptocurrency trades, links, and incriminating emails. Dorothy had risked everything to provide firsthand accounts, bolstered by years of documentation. The envelope was our weapon; the truth inside could decimate GRF's facade.

When Adam walked in, he had no trouble spotting me, given all the empty tables except for mine. He looked older than I remembered, with thinning hair and deepening wrinkles etched into his face, but those piercing eyes still burned fiercely. They were the eyes that saw through people, through lies, through pretenses.

"Hi, I'm Adam Cohen," he said, offering a smile and an extended hand. His handshake was a firm gesture of confidence and curiosity.

"John. Thanks for coming," I said, my voice steady though I'd purposely omitted my surname. The fewer details I gave, the better. "Please have a seat."

The waiter, looking as worn-down as the pub itself, ambled over, clearly hoping that someone might order something more substantial than water. Adam looked like he frequented this place. Without hesitation, he ordered a Guinness stout before giving his full attention to me.

I didn't wait for his beer to arrive. As soon as the waiter walked away, I dove in. I weighed my words to reveal the unbelievable truth. As I spoke, I saw his expression shift from polite interest to razor-sharp focus.

When his Guinness finally came, he paused for the first sip before responding. "If even half of what you're telling me can be verified," he said with a dry, wry smile, "this could be the scandal of the year."

At that moment, I knew he was hooked. I placed the manila envelope in front of him as he wiped foam off his upper lip. He opened the envelope with the care and precision of someone who understood the weight of the moment. His brows furrowed in concentration as he flipped through the documents, his expression shifting between intrigue and incredulity.

"This is solid," Adam murmured, mostly to himself, though his eyes were now locked on me with an unsettling confidence. "I think I can work with this."

Excitement coursed through me, though dread tempered it. There was no turning back from this moment—not for me, not for Adam.

"Will the insider be available for follow-ups?" he asked, carefully replacing the pages in the envelope.

"As long as their identity remains anonymous," I said firmly, leaning closer as a group of chatty businesspeople loudly rearranged tables near the center of the room. I lowered my voice, aware of every sound around us. "You need to understand. We don't know exactly where the millions in donations come from, but we've found ties to Russia, the US, and what very well may be criminal enterprises." My words were slow, deliberate, pacing the gravity of what I was sharing. "Follow the money, Adam. Billions allocated to the GRF's charitable projects—helping girls and women—are completely unaccounted for. And this isn't just financial malpractice. GRF is highly sophisticated, their security operations rivaling the American NSA or the Russian Spetsnaz GRU."

Adam leaned back, his face unreadable, though I could sense his mind racing behind his expression.

My voice hardened as the reality of our situation began hitting me all at once. "These people won't hesitate to kill anyone who tries to expose them. Do you understand me?"

For a moment, the intensity in his gaze faltered—not from fear, I believed, but from the weight of what he'd just agreed to shoulder.

I could only hope that he would wield his words like weapons, destroying GRF from the inside out with the power of his pen.

***

Back at the Bird's Nest, I felt the light breeze that carried in the sounds of Manhattan through the open window. Home sat on the infamous Billionaires' Row, but its splendor felt muted by the situation. My room, the guest bedroom, overlooked the Hudson River toward Union City in New Jersey, giving me the perfect vantage point for reflection. Leah had insisted I take the larger master suite, but the memories tied to Colleen made it impossible for me to set foot in that room. Some distance, however small, felt necessary, even healing.

I glanced at my watch, knowing Leah should arrive soon. She'd left Toronto in the morning to drive back in her sleek Mercedes Coupe. My flight had brought me to New York the day before because I could not tolerate a long drive in my current condition.

Standing by the floor-to-ceiling window, I gazed out at the multitude of buildings, their silhouettes against the late-afternoon sun. I whispered a quiet prayer under my breath.

"Colleen, if you're listening, give Adam Cohen the strength to carry this story to the world. We both know that exposing the GRF is only the beginning. But it's a start. And sometimes that's enough."

The city hummed below me, restless and alive, as I clung to the hope that our gamble would strike where it mattered most.

54

New York

I leaned over the bathroom sink, staring into the mirror. The man looking back at me was unfamiliar, but not in the way I'd grown used to. The hollows in my cheeks had filled out again, and a hint of color had returned to my skin. It wasn't much, but it was something. Maybe I was on the road to healing.

"Morning." Leah's voice quietly cut through the solitude, making me jump as I wandered groggily into the kitchen. A steaming mug of tea was already in her outstretched hand, and she gestured toward a plate of fresh muffins on the counter.

I broke off a muffin's top—always the best part—and took a confident bite. The buttery sweetness and the plump raisins hit my tongue. These days, eating wasn't the chore it had been for so long. For the first time in what felt like forever, my appetite seemed to meet me halfway, like a long-slumbering instinct waking up again.

"You look good," Leah said, her tone light but deliberate. She wasn't one for unnecessary compliments, which meant this wasn't coming from nowhere.

"Good?" I raised an eyebrow at her as I swallowed another bite.

"You look stronger," she said, setting her cup of coffee down to pick at her plate. Her eyes swept over me as though inspecting for signs of further improvement.

She wasn't wrong. I hadn't felt invincible in years. Not since the heart attack and the poisoning. But today, I felt . . . steady. The clarity was fleeting, though, because no matter how much focus I tried to pour into my recovery, my thoughts always circled back to Adam Cohen.

It had been two weeks. Two long, silent weeks since I'd handed him that manila envelope in the dark corner of that Irish pub. Two weeks since I had thrown him headfirst into the pit of everything we'd been unearthing for months. And he'd remained silent for those two weeks. Each passing day felt heavier than the last, stretching out the painful stalemate of waiting.

Leah, as always, channeled her energy into "fixing" me, which conveniently doubled as her distraction. Morning walks through Central Park had become a ritual, she insisted I at least try some yoga poses, and healthy smoothies had overtaken the morning routine. Her latest concoction was a kale-colored drink loaded with organic fruit, turmeric, and ginger. Even though the taste bordered on medicinal, I drank it because she insisted it was good for inflammation and I knew it made her feel she was helping.

"Do you think we've given him enough?" The question escaped my lips before I realized I'd spoken it aloud.

Leah glanced up from her smartphone, pausing from scrolling through her social media feed. Her tone was steady, almost clinical. "It's more than enough. It's irrefutable. The only problem is getting it out there."

I watched as she renewed her focus on her screen. "Maybe I should check in," I muttered, already reaching for my phone. Before she could answer, I'd opened my secure ProtonMail account and typed two quick sentences. My clipped, emotionless message bought me enough distance from the vulnerability of asking for information.

The reply came within an hour. Adam apologized for not reaching out sooner.

We need to talk in person tomorrow, he wrote. *Same place, same time.*

The message was obscure, but I grasped its meaning.

***

The next afternoon, I was back at the same banquette in that tired, dark Irish pub. The room hummed with a late-afternoon Friday crowd—businesspeople enjoying their post-work rituals.

I ordered an iced tea this time, knowing I couldn't risk clouding my mind. I'd barely slept the night prior, my mind running on endless loops of outcomes. Scenarios had played out with maddening clarity, only to crumble apart under the weight of the unknown.

Finally, Adam burst through the door, looking disheveled and rushed. Gone was the calm professionalism of our first encounter. "Sorry, I'm late," he said breathlessly. He waved a waiter over to our table. "I'll have a Guinness. Large."

The usual pleasantries were absent. He sat down, running both hands through his hair, and exhaled deeply before leaning forward. "There's been a problem," he said, his voice dropping slightly.

He rubbed the pads of his thumbs together in a jittery rhythm. His eyes darted around the room, never landing on one spot for too long. "Look," he started, his voice low. "My management . . . they're not on board with running the story. Apparently, my digging into GRF, its banks, and those shell companies stirred up more trouble than I expected. And now, my boss—he's scared. Really scared. I've never seen him like this before."

I stared at him, trying to comprehend, as his words sank like lead weights, one after the other. He looked terrible—haunted, like someone who hadn't slept in days and carried the weight of the world on his shoulders.

When his drink arrived, he grabbed it like a lifeline, tipping it back with a forceful gulp and clinking the glass hard against the table when he set it down.

"So . . . we're nowhere?" The question fell out of my mouth before I could stop it, unbidden but sharp with disappointment and bitterness.

Adam flinched at my tone. He stared into his drink, the silence stretching between us like a chasm.

I flagged the waiter and ordered a scotch on ice, the sting of all this pressure and frustration twisting tighter in my chest. Would this story even see the light of day? Had everything we worked for, everything we fought for, crumbled before we even got the chance to fight?

I couldn't take the ambiguity anymore. My voice was sharper than it should've been when I finally asked, "So what are you telling me, Adam? Are you backing out? Is your paper pulling the plug?"

Adam sighed, slumping in his chair. His exhaustion radiated from him now, an almost palpable weight. "I don't know yet," he said, his tone a mix of fear and frustration. His fingers wrapped around his glass as he brought it to his lips again, his eyes narrowing at the dark stout inside. After another long sip, he added, "All I know is I've never seen my boss spook like this before. Ever. It's usually the lawyers that kill a story, not him."

His words hung there, heavy and suffocating. My stomach churned, equal parts anger and despair. It wasn't just his boss who was scared. He, too, was scared. His every movement, every hesitation, screamed it.

"Well, they can't bury this," I said, my voice steely and low. "It's too important."

Adam didn't meet my eyes. He kept staring down at his drink, his shoulders sagging farther under the weight of it all.

And in that moment, I knew—this fight was far from over, but the battlefield wasn't where I had expected it to be. It wasn't merely GRF or its tangled web of lies we were up against. It was fear. The fear that silenced even the loudest voices. And that chill, that darkness, was the enemy now.

When my drink arrived, I took a long sip, the burn from the alcohol pushing against the tension already rising in my chest. I welcomed the immediate effect.

***

I was still unraveling the conversation by the time I reached the Bird's Nest, trying and failing to map out our next move. I was uncoordinated, and I fumbled in my pockets for my condo key fob. Coming up short, I knocked, embarrassed.

Leah inched the door open, her face a blend of mild irritation and surprise. "Forgot your key?"

"Can't seem to find it," I muttered as I brushed past her and headed straight to the bathroom. I needed a minute to compose myself.

She said nothing. I felt her watching me, but I knew better than to expect an interrogation right away.

When I emerged from the bathroom, key fob now in hand, I waved it haphazardly. "Found it," I said with an apologetic grin.

Leah crossed her arms but softened. "You smell like alcohol."

I leaned heavily against the couch. "Okay, I had a few. My first in a long time. They hit me harder than I expected."

Her stance relaxed, though her eyes betrayed concern. "You know you're not at a hundred percent." She headed to the kitchen and came back with a glass of water and an acetaminophen. "You need to be careful."

Nodding in faint agreement, I downed the pill and water. "Thanks," I mumbled.

Leah sat beside me, patient but expectant. I could feel her waiting for me to share what was weighing on me.

But the words wouldn't come. Not yet.

55

New York

When the email came through my ProtonMail account, I already felt a sinking feeling in my gut before I opened it. The subject line was unassuming—*Update on GRF.* But the words inside gutted me.

The story was dead.

Leah was in the kitchen making her morning smoothies. Today's blend included bananas, chia seeds, and unidentified greens. She heard my sharp exhale and turned her head.

"It's not happening," I muttered. I didn't even look up from my smartphone.

Her silence spoke volumes. She didn't need to ask. When I finally looked up, I saw the understanding in her eyes. After months of collecting evidence, coaxing Dorothy for more proof, and watching our lives spiral out of control because of one decision to take on GRF, it had all crumbled a second time. No story would be published. No one would hear the proof. And GRF . . . well, they'd continue their deadly game, unscathed.

"What happened?" Leah eventually whispered.

There wasn't much to read. Adam's editor had caved, suffocated by unseen forces—the bankers, the corporations, and strings GRF pulled from the shadows... or was it much higher?

"It's over," I said, my voice breaking before I could stop it.

Leah touched my shoulder and squeezed it.

Neither of us spoke for a long time as we drank our healthy smoothies.

My thoughts spiraled into the dark. This was the second time we had hit a dead end. But we had lost too much to stop now. First, a calculated hit-and-run stole Colleen's life. Then my health deteriorated after chasing GRF's wrongdoing. And now, that corrupt organization had forever intertwined Leah's life with it because of what it had done to our family.

I clenched my fists, my eyes burning as a tidal wave of anger and defeat crashed over me. How much more could I lose to this monster doing the devil's work?

There had to be another way; maybe another reporter or publication would take on our fight. Leah and I began exploring potential new options.

Our fight wasn't over yet—or was it, and we didn't know it?

***

The news of Adam Cohen's death hit me like a hammer to the chest—abrupt, merciless, leaving me breathless and disoriented.

Leah was the messenger. She shook me awake, her tear-streaked face and quivering frame betraying a desperation to find a steady footing, if only long enough to speak the words aloud.

"Dad . . . he's dead."

Panic seized me. Who? What had happened? The knot in my stomach tightened before my lips could form a question.

"What are you talking about?" I rasped, my voice above a whisper, though part of me already knew.

Leah's hands trembled in the low morning light. "It's on the news," she managed. "Adam is dead. He never showed up for work. They're calling it suicide."

The words hung in the air like a specter.

I stopped breathing, my body heavy as lead, frozen, but my heartbeat raced, pounding in my ears as the world sharpened cruelly around me.

Images of Colleen surged like a tidal wave—scenes I couldn't control, echoes of grief and outrage threatening to drown me whole. This wasn't suicide. I didn't believe it. Adam wasn't that kind of man. He was a fighter. A journalist who crossed lines and risked everything for the truth.

But disbelief wouldn't change reality. I forced myself to speak, though the words felt clumsy on my tongue. "Are you sure?" I asked—a stupid question. Of course she was sure.

Leah didn't speak. Instead, she crumpled as I motioned for her to sit beside me. I pulled her into my arms.

Words had failed. Whatever hope we'd had seemed to slip farther from reach.

"It . . . it happened last night," Leah said, her voice faltering as though she wasn't ready to commit to the story's full weight. "Dad . . . there's no way this was a suicide."

She didn't need to convince me. Whether spoken or unspoken, her anguish mirrored my own.

Details came creeping in, unwelcome yet unavoidable. Adam, they said, had overdosed on opioids in his apartment. That silent killer—yet another footnote etched into the ledgers of an American epidemic. Stressful job. Possible addiction. Filler talking points. The story painted him as another tragic name in a nation too broken to fix itself. No one probed the vital questions: had someone forced the drugs on him, or had he chosen them?

Later, I leaned against the kitchen counter, staring at my phone. The TV blared in the background as Leah's trembling recount was echoed in the reporters' voices. Adam Cohen died by suicide. That was the narrative now—a guttural punctuation to a man's fearless pursuit of justice.

The GRF story had died with him. Tainted as it was by scandal, fear, and doubt, no credible journalist would ever touch it again. GRF, for now, would remain a fortress of secrecy.

Grief confronted me, familiar but unwelcome. No tears came; that wasn't how my mind processed despair anymore. The death was more than tragic—it enraged and smothered me. Anger burned its way through my chest, thick and caustic, demanding action. Somebody had orchestrated this. Somebody thought they could scare the entire world into submission by killing a journalist, burying the truth, and walking away free.

But they didn't know Adam's editor. And as it turned out, neither did I.

56

New York

Two days of grim news had drained my stamina for my morning ritual of skimming headlines. Still, I opened my laptop and pulled up the *New York Star* homepage. A photo of a younger Adam Cohen stared back at me. Above it, the bold headline slashed across the screen: **SINISTER OPERATIONS HIDDEN BEHIND A GLOBAL CHARITY ORGANIZATION**

My breath hitched. My hand trembled as I clicked the link.

The screen flickered as the article loaded.

The webpage displayed an almost theatrical layout: On the right was an obituary framed as a tribute to Adam's life's work. On the left, an exposé blazed across three columns—the breadth of Adam's final article.

But this was more than an exposé; it was his magnum opus—a manifesto of unapologetic truth. Adam had dismantled GRF's crafted image to reveal the rotten foundation beneath. Each detail painted the organization's corruption: illegal shell companies, laundered money disguised in charity programs, tax evasion, deceitful claims about empowering women, and grotesque exploitation masquerading as goodwill. Names, dates, and transactions were precise, surgical, and devastating.

This was a weapon, not a story.

Typically, such revelations were behind paywalls. Not this time. Adam's editor, seething with grief and rage, unleashed the piece to the public—no charge, no restrictions. This wasn't journalism anymore; it was a rebellion against suppression.

We publish this not merely to honor Adam Cohen's work but to remind the world of the stakes, the editorial read. *Adam Cohen's voice cannot speak again, but his truth will not be silenced. We must resist suppression, or we lose ourselves.*

By midday, Adam's article had ignited an inferno. It was everywhere—global media, independent outlets, local podcasts and blogs. The suspicious details of Adam's suicide fueled public fury. Social media erupted, their timelines dominated by #JusticeForCohen and #GRFExposed. Activists dissected GRF's scandals in real time, spreading unchecked outrage that no PR strategy could contain.

Leah and I watched the fallout consume the news, shifting between channels as they all cycled through the same story. GRF's damage control appeared amateur under the spotlight. Clips of Cathy Dickson's rebuttals, riddled with hubris, became viral memes that deepened the public's contempt.

Cathy, battle-worn yet unyielding, no longer fought with charm or empathy. Those tactics had shattered. What remained were primal survival instincts—honed long ago in the military—ready to face the incoming storm. Yet she could not dominate this battlefield. Disaster loomed over her like an impatient shadow.

***

Gray skies rolled overhead as rain drizzled onto East Forty-Ninth Street. I stood outside Adam Cohen's old apartment building, fingers tingling with unease. The building was two blocks north of the UN headquarters. A fact that somehow made his death feel heavier, colder.

Adam had taken his final breath on the third floor.

Between a Japanese restaurant and a cluttered smoke shop, the building's narrow entrance disappeared into the scenery. Heavy surveillance covered the two shops, with external cameras looming over each one. Across the street sat a shuttered Thai restaurant, its grimy windows half-covered in old newspapers.

The Japanese restaurant wasn't open yet, so I entered the disheveled smoke shop first. Inside was a chaotic labyrinth stuffed with everything from snacks and lottery tickets to camera equipment and ancient computers.

Behind the counter sat a hulking Middle Eastern man with a large bald head. His nicotine-stained smile revealed yellow teeth. "Can I help you?" His accent, colored but crisp, filled the space.

"Yes, I hope so. I'm a reporter—the man who died recently in the apartment above you was a colleague of mine. I'm doing a follow-up story."

His expression blanked, as if I'd spoken in an unknown tongue.

Gesturing toward the exterior security camera, I asked, "Do you keep its recordings?"

He spat into a crusty bucket on the counter—saliva and tobacco staining the liquid inside—as a sheepish grin crept across his face. Leaning forward, he whispered, "The camera? It doesn't work. Hasn't been for years. Don't tell anyone, okay?"

I swallowed disappointment hard, then thanked him.

As I turned to leave, his voice rang across the cluttered shop: "The Jap next door has one!"

I became excited and said nothing else.

Even though it was five minutes before the Japanese restaurant opened, it was buzzing inside and I walked in anyway. A chime signaled my arrival and an older Japanese woman warmly welcomed me. She bowed and motioned toward a table of arranged bowls and chopsticks.

Her warmth evaporated when I asked for the owner. Suspicion filled the pause before she replied, "Who wants to know?"

I softened my posture. "John. I was friends with Adam Cohen, who lived upstairs. He passed last week. Investigative work—trying to retrace his last steps. Does your outside camera work?"

My words shifted her demeanor again, sympathy lighting her expression. "One moment," she said, disappearing into the back. She returned with her husband, a thin, short chef.

After several innocent questions, he led me to his small office, a nook off the kitchen, where he granted me access to the security feed. He explained the system held only two weeks of video and only recorded when the restaurant was closed, from ten at night to eleven the next morning. Hours of motion-triggered, time-stamped footage rolled through the cloud server. I calculated I needed to go back four days to the footage taken after 10:00 p.m. on the day Adam died.

The camera's field of view barely encompassed the apartment entrance, which was dimly lit. Over the first hour, trickles of movement followed: an elderly man entered at 22:13; two women entered at 22:21 and 22:44; and a young black man left at 22:56. Then came 23:06—a man in dark clothing jimmied the lock on the building's door. The figure paused, glanced sideways, and slipped inside.

I froze the blurry frame as recognition stabbed through my stomach.

It looked like Igor.

Twenty-three minutes later, Igor reemerged, disappearing into the night.

I clipped the recording, saved it, emailed it to myself, and deleted the recording from 18:38 to 23:29 to remove traces of my actions.

I mumbled a thank-you to the chef as I slipped into a coughing fit, feeling like I was suffocating as my lungs burned. I fled, trembling, as death continued to follow me.

***

The story—GRF's collapse—dominated headlines for days. TV crews swarmed GRF's Toronto headquarters, hungry for more of Cathy Dickson's razor-edged sound bites. Public venom crowned her with a new title: "The Warlord of Lies."

Leah sat cross-legged on the rug in the family room, her eyes reflecting satisfaction. "This is bigger than I could've hoped," she murmured.

Her words grazed the silence hanging around us.

Adam's work—his legacy of relentless precision—had struck its target with unnerving force. His editor's defiance had amplified the message. And now, the world couldn't turn away.

The United Nations ECOSOC revoked GRF's NGO status, condemning its betrayal of UN values and denouncing its operations. Political pressure seeped into the Canadian federal and provincial governments, compelling them to act against corporate players linked to the GRF's corruption. The fallout was immeasurable.

And then came the breaking news: the Ontario Provincial Police had obtained a search warrant for GRF's head office.

From our couch, Leah and I watched live raid footage unfold like a cinematic finale. Officers carried out boxes of laptops, records, and other evidence by the dozens, stacking the spoils of years of organized manipulation onto crowded streets. Vans awaited deliveries under the grim supervision of uniformed officers.

Through the chaos, a reporter stammered, "The Ontario Provincial Police uncovered GRF's command center in the basement." Her voice was laced with disbelief. "This was much more than a money play. There was something more sinister going on in this organization. Back to you, Robert."

Leah leaned into me as both of us released deep, exhausted sighs, the kind that usually arrive in victory.

This day, this reckoning, belonged to Adam.

And to Colleen.

This was their day, and ours.

***

Throughout the whirlwind of chaos that enveloped GRF's head office, Cathy Dickson vanished as if swallowed by the shadows she had long commanded. The enigmatic leader behind GRF's facade disappeared without so much as a ripple, leaving city police and federal financial crimes investigators grasping at air. Her mugshot, plastered across "Most Wanted" lists alongside the most infamous fugitives, was a futile plea to the public to uncover her whereabouts. Yet deep down, I knew the truth—she was untouchable, hidden within the vast and impenetrable networks of American or Russian elite military operations, where ghosts like her thrived.

What troubled me more was the inevitability that another Cathy Dickson had already risen—a new puppet master in FIST's relentless pursuit to sustain its global foothold. GRF's dismantling was nothing more than a speed bump along the vast highway of their clandestine agendas. They concealed their dirty dealings within many shells, so GRF had always been expendable. The collapse of their so-called charity wouldn't halt the empire's machinery; if anything, it might only speed up the creation of a successor organization, sleeker and savvier, ready to resume operations without missing a beat.

Our victory felt hollow. FIST was too mighty, too entrenched, too big to fail. This wasn't the end. This was a reshuffling of pieces in their endless game of global domination. And somewhere in the wings, Cathy Dickson was preparing to make her next move.

57

New York

Another morning, another ritual: scrolling through my news feed with a grim sense of anticipation. The collapse of GRF hadn't swept the headlines clear. It had only scattered fresh carcasses for the media vultures to circle. The latest story to grip public attention centered on Adam Cohen, the journalist who first exposed GRF. Headlines blazed with urgency, proclaiming that Adam's death, once dismissed as suicide, was murder.

The investigative storm began with articles dissecting his death, laying bare the inconsistencies in the original case. The public wasn't buying the official narrative anymore, and the relentless outcry had forced both the NYPD and the FBI to reopen the investigation. In glaring detail, the article I was reading charted the case's newfound direction, including speculation about motives, potential suspects, and a troubling mention of a person of interest.

Adam's face appeared in stark grayscale beside the headline. The image was a profile headshot from the *New York Star* newspaper. My stomach twisted as I read on, my pulse quickening with every word.

By the third paragraph, the dread in my chest had turned to ice. The article claimed the police were hunting for a middle-aged white male with a scruffy appearance—someone connected to Adam that night. Someone who'd claimed to be his friend. But worse, they believed this man had tampered with surveillance footage near the scene on the night Adam died. Whoever he might be, investigators were pursuing him as a person of interest in this murder case.

Fear rippled through me as though an icy hand had gripped the base of my spine. I sat there, paralyzed, rereading the words that screamed louder with every pass. They were looking for me. I could feel it in my bones. My fingers clenched around the iPad as my stomach churned with the thought of a knock on my door, of handcuffs snapping shut around my wrists.

My thoughts spiraled until I forced myself to blink, to exhale, to scroll.

But the next story I stumbled upon only deepened the sense of unease crawling over my skin.

On the screen before me, an image surfaced that brought me to another grim halt—an older-model white BMW 3 Series being lifted from the murky depths of the Hudson River. The battered car hung suspended in the air, its windshield blown out like a hollow eye socket.

My stomach knotted.

The accompanying article identified the car's owner as Frank Petrov, a New York fashion photographer. Yet the driver's identity and whereabouts remained unknown. Police divers combed the cold abyss for drowned bodies, their movements a desperate search for answers beneath the surface. Authorities could not explain how or why the driver had careered off the abandoned Pier 98 and plummeted into the Hudson.

I felt it in my chest before the realization even formed. Panic spread like wildfire through my lungs, my breath locking tight. As air eluded me, pain flared sharp and hot, forcing my body into a violent coughing fit. The thought struck hard: Was this another marker—a shadow of Igor's handiwork? Had he been there, tying off yet another loose thread?

I dialed Frank's cell number with trembling fingers.

"Hi, sorry I missed your call. Please leave a message, and I'll get back to you as soon as possible."

The voicemail greeted me like a taunting ghost. I didn't bother leaving a message; I knew I would never hear Frank's voice again.

Was Igor sweeping up the trail? Purging the mess left behind, and anyone who linked back to me? Closing gaps, cutting threads, burying whatever dangerous secrets still lingered?

My mind fired into survival mode. Instinctively, I began rattling off names in my head. *Katerina. Susan. Dorothy. Leah. Me.* Who among them might be next? Who was unguarded and vulnerable?

A chill slithered down my spine as one name leaped to the forefront: Dorothy. She was the weakest link, the one most precariously perched and least prepared for what might come.

I found the black backpack in the corner and clawed through its contents. My hands landed on the burner phone buried deep within. My pulse hammered as I fired it up, pulling Dorothy's number from a saved file on my iPad.

I called. No answer. The silence on the line stretched long, feeding the gnawing pit of tension in my gut. I hung up.

Susan and Katerina surfaced next in the mental whirlwind. I hesitated longer this time. Both their phones were under surveillance—high-grade, sophisticated monitoring. Still, I had to say something. The shadow of Colleen loomed large in my mind, pulling words from my chest like threads spun from grief.

"I've been thinking about Colleen a lot," I began when I reached each of them, my voice low and even. A faint quake sputtered across my cryptic words. "Crazy that nothing ever came of it, right? Sometimes it feels like when things like that happen, they don't just stop—they ripple out, affecting more people than we realize. I hope those kinds of shadows aren't still lurking. It feels like unresolved pasts leave no one safe."

Dead silence.

The pause on the other end of each line was deafening before they hung up without a word. Their silence spoke volumes—a tacit acknowledgment of my warning wrapped in the contours of their fear.

And then, Leah. My only family. The one I had to protect at all costs, even if it meant burying my own fears beneath hers. She was the reason I had to stay alive and out of jail. She was my tether. My purpose.

The danger pressed closer, compounding with each moment. I wasn't sure how long I could keep the shadows at bay. Igor was moving—and he was ruthless.

I couldn't shake the gnawing certainty that before long, my own name would bleed from the shadows into the next headline.

58

Manhattan

Leah harbored a deep disdain for lawyers. She had grown up watching them demand her father's attention, often at her expense. Their phone calls, punctuated by urgency, seemed to always pull her father away from family dinners, school performances, games, and significant moments in her life. The lawyers were the gatekeepers of his energy and time, siphoning them into business deals, lawsuits against competitors, and battles with untrustworthy partners.

As her cab inched its way down Park Avenue, Leah stared out of the backseat window at the endless crowd flowing along the sidewalks. Her thoughts churned with contempt. Every time her father had answered a lawyer's call, turbulence followed. The dynamics of their family would shift and the house would grow tense, heavy with his impatience and occasional temper—qualities that had replaced the loving disposition of the man who had once tucked her in at night.

Now, her own life seemed shadowed by the same tension as she approached the sleek legal offices on Park Avenue housing the firm that had presided over her parents' wills. To Leah, they were opportunistic bloodsuckers, raking in millions in fees to move ownership titles from one name to another.

The message summoning her had been abrupt, brusque: "We urgently need to speak to you. Can you meet me at my office tomorrow at 10:30 a.m.?" No introductions. No pleasantries. None required.

As she stepped into the towering office building's immaculate lobby, a middle-aged receptionist welcomed her. The woman had perfectly coiffed hair and wore a tailored, crisp suit. After greeting Leah and taking her coat, she offered to get her a cup of coffee. Leah accepted, hoping the caffeine might pull her out of the fog caused by yet another late night in a city that never sleeps.

The receptionist then led Leah to Mr. Richardson's office, taking her through a maze of hallways to a spacious triangular room in the southeast corner. Its floor-to-ceiling windows framed dazzling views of the East River and the United Nations building, and a massive antique desk was its centerpiece, where the glass walls met. Behind her, shelves of leather-bound legal books lined the base of the space, creating an almost theatrical display of knowledge and authority.

Leah stepped into the office's seating area, which was arranged with clinical precision. Two oversized black leather chairs flanked a low round glass coffee table, and an accompanying sofa looked stylish but tortuously uncomfortable.

Mr. Richardson, a trim man in his late fifties with a groomed salt-and-pepper beard, rose from his desk as Leah entered. Quickly, he closed his laptop and gestured toward the chairs. "Welcome, Ms. Barton. Thank you for coming in on such short notice."

Before Leah could respond, the receptionist returned with two steaming cups of coffee on delicate white china saucers. After placing them on the coffee table, she slipped away, shutting the door behind her. Leah chose a chair and settled herself, her black slacks and cream cashmere turtleneck fusing with the office's monochrome palette.

Mr. Richardson sat across from her, his demeanor shifting almost immediately.

Leah took a sip of her coffee, hoping it would chase some of the fatigue from her mind. "What's up?" she asked, setting her cup down.

Tension lined Mr. Richardson's face, and his voice carried the clipped urgency of someone in possession of troubling information. "I wanted to inform you about a situation the IRS has brought to our attention," he began, leaning forward.

Leah froze, alarm flashing through her. "The IRS?"

"Yes, the Internal Revenue Service is conducting a criminal investigation involving your late father, Scott Barton." Sliding a file across the table, he continued, his tone unwavering. "It appears your father had a private account in Switzerland that contained funds tied to questionable activities. Specifically, there was a mining transaction in Turkey in August 2014 worth billions of dollars. When your father was CEO of Aurora EarthEx, he allegedly received significant kickbacks from the deal—millions of dollars—which he then concealed in Switzerland." He paused as if giving her time to absorb the revelation.

Leah's hands gripped her coffee cup as her head throbbed. The tranquil air of calculated professionalism in Richardson's voice only made her nausea worse. He didn't speak with empathy but rather with the detached satisfaction of someone recounting news destined to increase his firm's billable hours. She avoided eye contact and allowed herself another sip of coffee, though it didn't ease the tension that had filled her chest.

"But wait," Richardson added, a thin smile breaking through his otherwise professional demeanor. "The story becomes even more unusual. According to the IRS, your father's Swiss bank account didn't stay in his name. After his passing, the account ownership was transferred to a man named John Miller of Rumney, New Hampshire."

Leah's stomach churned. She placed her coffee cup down and pushed herself up from the chair. "Excuse me," she said, her words clipped and urgent. "I need the restroom."

Richardson jumped to his feet and escorted her to the nearest washroom. She shut herself inside, her nausea overwhelming her as she braced herself against the sink.

When she returned to Richardson's office, her face was flushed and her clothes damp with perspiration. She needed an escape but forced herself back into her chair.

"Would you like a glass of water?" he asked, genuine concern creeping into his voice.

"No," she said firmly. "Just finish what you were about to say."

"Right," he said, gathering his thoughts. "While John Miller is a fairly common name, this specific individual died in a car accident several months before inheriting your father's account. He and his wife passed away together in Rumney, New Hampshire. The IRS believes this is a case of identity theft involving the financial assets of your late father."

Leah exhaled, attempting to process the layers of complexity. "So, someone's trying to steal his money? . . . I mean, my money!"

"It seems that way. The good news is that we're prepared to assist you in securing these assets and resolving the matter. Of course, we'll need your authorization to establish a retainer agreement."

"Of course," Leah replied, masking her frustration with sarcasm.

Later, in the backseat of another cab with the window rolled down, Leah started connecting the dots. Her father's refusal to ask for financial help wasn't about pride or struggling with money; it was about shielding her. The hidden Swiss bank account was proof that he had more than enough to cover his mounting expenses. It was a buffer that ensured his independence while keeping any ties between them invisible. He deliberately shielded her from the transactions, preventing any trails from implicating her. It all made sense now. The secret protected his dignity and safeguarded her.

Whatever the IRS had discovered, Leah knew she'd have to carry this knowledge in silence, trusting her father's judgment and respecting his decision to keep her at arm's length from the enemies he faced.

59

New York

As the clock ticked closer to midnight on a stormy fall evening, I found myself lost in a sea of unanswered questions while I sat in the living room listening to jazz music. Somewhere out there, perhaps in an echoing marble room without prying eyes, perhaps on the other end of a secure satellite connection, the two presidents were likely holding court, crafting the next chapter of their empire. They were more than two heads of state—they were architects of a sophisticated political terrorism and killing machine that grew stronger every year.

With FIST's secret dealings entangled across borders and hidden within layers of insulation, I couldn't afford false optimism. The GRF wasn't needed anymore. The two men would already have set their sights on its successor: a new shape, a new name, a cleaner public face. The phoenix of their operation was already flapping its wings, ready to rise in another form.

But the essence of FIST—its shadowy partnerships, intelligence tentacles, and militarized precision—would remain unchanged.

What would their next incarnation look like? Both presidents, seasoned in the art of international manipulation, would have already planted a seed of destruction. Together, they had a calculus rooted not in altruism but in opportunism: how best to preserve FIST while shaping it into something no whistleblower could unravel?

Across the darkened living room where New York's lights danced in the background, Leah's voice startled me. "You're thinking again." She looked up from her Kindle; her lips held a soft smirk.

She knew me too well.

I struggled to hear the jazz music over the thunderous storm of speculation in my mind.

"They're already rebuilding," I said after a pause. "Somewhere, somehow. GRF was just a mask. They'll have another one ready before the ash settles."

"And you think you can stop them?" Her tone wasn't cynical, just laced with subtle skepticism and a trace of hope.

Stop them? No, that sounded naïve, even as I let the idea drift through my head. But expecting their new incarnation? Getting ahead of their moves? That could change the game. That might slow the phoenix before it rose.

If I were them, I'd stick to what works: build something sleek, global, and impenetrable. GRF had thrived in the charity sector because it had camouflaged greed beneath virtue, and philanthropy had become its currency of trust. But this time, they might pivot. The charity sector now smelled of controversy, thanks to Adam's exposé. GRF's collapse had rendered the old model obsolete, forcing FIST to innovate.

Technology. Convenience concealed humanity's weakness. My gut told me their next move would emerge there—smart tech, AI solutions, blockchain systems. The ideal face for FIST's rebirth would offer dazzling innovation, claiming to connect communities while embedding deep within global infrastructures. They could market their creation with promises of societal change while funneling funds and influence toward their true agenda.

Where would it appear? Silicon Valley was too visible, too scrutinized. This felt like it would be something subtler, perhaps incubated in regions where oversight weakened and ambition thrived. Brazil? Estonia? Dubai? Switzerland? Eastern Europe? These were fertile grounds for FIST's brand of exploitation: a sophisticated talent pool in crypto technology, a strong financial infrastructure, and an undercurrent of a dark market. These were places FIST could hide in plain sight while building its phoenix anew.

But location wasn't the trick. The trick was in the mask. FIST didn't choose a place; they chose a narrative, a story that cast them as saviors rather than operators. If we could untangle the threads of their past operations, if we could map their partnerships across GRF, Toronto Bank, Republic of Moscow Bank, and Mount Royal Capital, then perhaps we could expose the lie before it took root.

To get ahead, we needed a strategy that mirrored their thinking, but with an angle that exposed their layers. We couldn't do this alone. We'd need allies with expertise in tech, finance, and investigative reconnaissance. Activists with influence, whistleblowers who'd grown disillusioned, and a digital army to trace the breadcrumbs they hadn't swept away.

Leah interrupted my thoughts again, her voice sharper this time. "If you're serious about this, we need something tangible. They didn't vanish; they evolved. You know their pattern—you can think like them. Where's the first clue? How do we find them before they get too big to stop?"

She was right. GRF had provided institutional blueprints for FIST's operations with its shell companies, paper trails, and fake partnerships. Identifying their next move required building profiles of key players who'd gone dark in GRF's aftermath. Cathy Dickson wasn't the only one who'd vanished; dozens of talented mid-level operatives in Canada had scattered, but to where? Where did Susan, Dorothy, and Katerina go?

And Igor—where was he? His blurry image stuck in my mind like a jagged shard embedded too far to remove. He had ties far stronger than convenience; his loyalties might be the thread that unraveled their plans. If I could find him, maybe he'd lead me straight to their phoenix nest.

After a short coughing fit, I turned to face Leah across the room. "We trace everything connected to GRF's fallout—all the people, all the bank accounts, all the shell companies, all the crypto signatures. You know they're rebuilding under the radar. All we need is one loose end . . . one mistake they don't expect. That's where we find them."

Rain began hammering the windowpanes, yet the storm in my mind eclipsed the noise. FIST wasn't too big to fail—not if we could catch them while the phoenix was still vulnerable, learning to fly.

60

New York

The cemetery was silent except for the faint rustle of wind threading through fall's leaves in the trees and on the wet ground. The late-afternoon sky hung low and gray, blanketing the world in a suffocating gloom. I stood there, shoulders slumped, frail from the sickness that had stolen more time than I could count. Cancer had taken years from me, but not enough to stop me from being there.

Leah stood at my side, steady and unyielding. She looked so much like her mother: tall, sharp, and sure, her eyes carrying wisdom I once doubted she'd ever grow into. She said nothing as we moved down the gravel path that wound through neat rows of headstones, each one a silent monument to a life that once was. Names and dates etched into stone tried to summarize entire human existences, but all they did was point at the finality of it all.

The path felt heavier and slower beneath our feet today. The chill and dampness in the air seemed to seep deeper into my bones as we walked, as though the earth itself wanted to grind us to a halt. And yet, we pressed on.

At last, we reached Colleen's grave. Her headstone displayed her real name. The one known by her loved ones and the enemies who took her life. ***Colleen***. No surname, just Colleen.

The gravestone itself was simple. Polished black granite with a modest gleam, unadorned save for the name, the years she lived, and a single line chiseled into its surface:

Peace is the ultimate goal.

Leah kneeled on the damp grass. She held a single white lily, stark and vivid against the weightless gray hanging over us. She placed it at the base of the stone and rested her palm on the cold granite, as if she could somehow reach through time and touch the woman who had left us behind.

I swallowed hard, but my throat was dry and unyielding. When I spoke, my voice was coarse and gravelly. "She'd hate this," I rasped. "The prayers. The grieving. Wasting time in a place like this."

Leah turned her head toward me, the corners of her lips softening in a faint smile. It was a look of understanding, not joy. She rose from her crouch, brushing away the debris from her knees. "Maybe," she whispered, her voice measured. "But she's the reason we're here together. And the reason we're still fighting."

A long, weary sigh escaped me, carrying the weight of too many unanswered questions. A lifetime of battles had left me feeling hollow—not triumphant, not even defeated, just . . . empty. I didn't know what victory looked like anymore. Regardless, we'd failed to find it. Not yet.

Sure, we'd fought. Against presidents. Against systems. Against the hidden hands pulling the strings to uphold their "balance of power." But in the end, we'd failed to topple empires. We hadn't exposed the conspiracies buried under layers of secrecy, bureaucracy, and misdirection. What had we accomplished?

Persistence. That's all. Survival. Endurance. And in the middle of it all, I'd found Leah. My daughter. And myself.

That, at least, was something.

We both had the same reason to fight—not each other, but Colleen's murderers.

And like that, we'd picked up where Colleen left off.

The battles that followed weren't easy. Figuring out what Colleen had truly been fighting against—or for—was maddening and uncertain work. The "balance of power" was an illusion; it was simply two of the world's most potent leaders fueling chaos to keep their dominance—a self-perpetuating system driven by wealth, power, secrets, and fear.

We weren't heroes. We weren't revolutionaries. Like gnats, we buzzed around something too big to kill. But we kept going—for Colleen, for ourselves, for the world.

And somewhere in the middle of the chaos, we'd found each other again. It lacked a fairy-tale ending, no grand moments of forgiveness. We worked together because we had to, and it evolved into something more. Slowly, we constructed something real. And for me, after living in my head, being real was enough.

Now, standing at Colleen's grave, I felt all the years pressing down on me. I reached out with one unsteady hand, letting my fingers brush against the smooth top of the cold granite.

Peace is the ultimate goal.

I didn't know whether she ever found it. But she maintained her belief until the end. Peace for the world. Peace for her family. Peace for herself.

"She's at peace," Leah said suddenly, her voice cutting through the silence. "Wherever she is."

I took my time to nod. The words lingered in the air, heavy yet grounding. I let them settle as we turned and started walking back toward the car, the gravestones fading into the mist behind us.

"We didn't win," I muttered.

"No," Leah replied with a faint sense of resolve. "But we didn't lose either. And maybe for now . . . that's enough."

The longer we walked, the more I thought about Colleen's words. Peace had always felt like a destination, a goal you could someday cross off a list. But now? Maybe peace wasn't something you earned and kept. Perhaps it was a constant fight—against the world, against yourself.

We weren't there yet. But we were closer. And that, I thought, would have to be enough—for now.

Author's Note

Balance of Evil is my first novel, a political thriller, crafted for entertainment. The names, characters, places, and incidents portrayed within the story are products of my imagination or have been used fictitiously. Any resemblance to actual businesses, events, locations, or persons, living or deceased, is entirely coincidental.

First and foremost, I want to express my gratitude to you, the reader, for reaching this message. Your support means the world to me. If you've enjoyed the book, I have one more favor to ask: please consider leaving a review on Amazon and/or Goodreads. Reviews are vital for the survival of authors in today's competitive book market, whether you assign a star rating (the more stars, the better!) or share your thoughts and feedback.

Next, I would like to extend my heartfelt thanks to my beta readers and subject-matter experts, whose invaluable feedback helped refine this novel. I'm also deeply grateful to my copy editor, proofreader, and design team, who played critical roles in elevating *Balance of Evil* into the book you see today. Without the insights and commitment of these extraordinary individuals, this work would not have been possible.

Many of the locations depicted in the book are actual cities, towns, and streets; however, the buildings featured may not be accurate representations. To clarify, the charity organizations Global Relief Foundation (GRF), Middle East Children's Foundation of America, and the Mother Teresa Medal are purely fictional.

My love for food has inspired me to include authentic culinary dishes throughout the story, including the unique *Candy Dostoevsky Cigar*—though minus any poison! As for the Ilana Goor Museum in Port Jaffa, it's an actual venue, and based on my research and the images I've seen, it's definitely on my bucket list if I ever visit Tel Aviv. The book features real vehicle models, and yes, I've put them all on my Christmas wish list. Google research revealed the existence of a Wagner Group tattoo design. And EINSTEIN and GosSOPKA also exist.

The companies Aurora EarthEx Co., Mount Royal Capital LLC, Crystal Holding, Bear Investments, and K2 Limited are fictional, as are the financial institutions Republic Bank, Toronto Bank, the Republic of Moscow Bank, as well as the WFT! Market and Garantech cryptocurrency exchanges. While imaginary, these elements reflect real-world practices, as anonymous shell companies often help conceal wealth and evade taxes. Sadly, money laundering remains a pervasive issue globally.

The United Nations Office on Drugs and Crime reports that money laundering annually amounts to about 2 to 5 percent of global GDP—or $800 billion to $2 trillion in current US dollars. TRM Labs' Crypto Crime Report similarly shows that illicit crypto activities range from $59 billion to $75 billion annually, with growth expected because of advancements in technology such as AI.

Finally, I urge vigilance as we face an era marked by increasing political polarization. Around the world, we are witnessing the erosion of democratic values in favor of authoritarian populism, often built on fear, arrogance, protectionism, and divisiveness (*Us* vs. *Them* mentality). Reduced tolerance of diversity, inclusion, and free trade accompanies this troubling shift. Disinformation, misinformation, conspiracies, and a loss of political trust are becoming all too common.

Globalization, digital technologies, and generative artificial intelligence will continue to reshape our socioeconomic realities in both positive and negative ways. As history shows, progress doesn't follow a straight path. We have fought hard for freedom; don't take it for granted. Keep fighting for it.

Thank you for reading, and let's work together to make the world a better place.

Introduction to the Sequel: LIES

As the last pages of *Balance of Evil* close, the dust settles but shadows remain—looming threats, unanswered questions, and secrets still buried deep. Where will Scott and Leah go next? What does Igor's disappearance mean? How does Colleen's past intertwine deeply with FIST and the GRF? The conspiracy has only just unraveled, and the stakes have never been higher.

But some truths stay hidden. And some lies demand to be revealed.

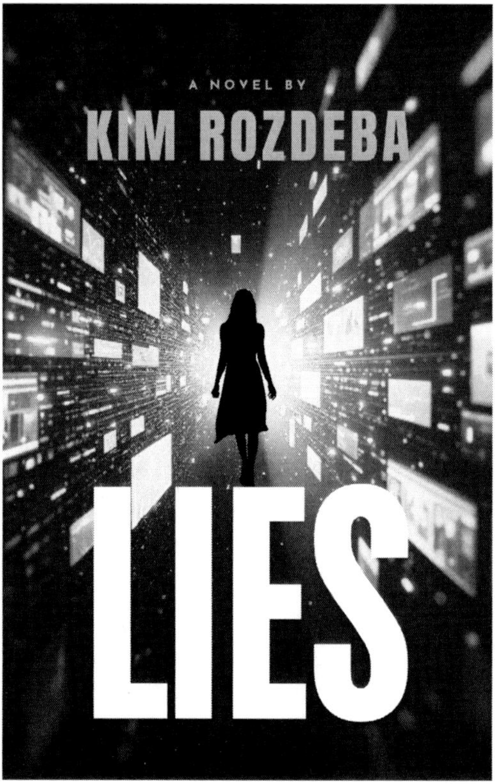
A NOVEL BY
KIM ROZDEBA
LIES

Sneak Peek: Chapter 1 of LIES

New York

Leah pulled her metallic silver Mercedes-AMG GT Coupe up to the curb in front of the Memorial Cancer Center. Midtown Manhattan buzzed with impatient energy, its rhythm dictated by the cacophony of horns honking and pedestrians dodging traffic.

She smiled at her father as he stepped into the car, his nasal cannula discreetly connected to a shoulder bag. Scott's short-cropped hair, now more white than gray, betrayed his battles with illness, making him look weathered but resilient at sixty-three. Leah watched him settle into the passenger seat before guiding the car into a precise U-turn.

"How did it go?" she asked casually, though her eyes flicked briefly toward him, gauging the tension in his furrowed brow.

Scott stared out the window. His hands rested in his lap, but his fingers twisted, a silent giveaway to his unease. "Okay," he said, his voice tight. Then, after glancing at the side mirror, he added, "Yeah . . . okay."

Leah remained unconvinced. She pressed on the accelerator, pushing them west on East Twentieth Street while the setting afternoon sun stretched long shadows across Stuyvesant Town's brick facades. "Are you sure?" she prodded, flicking her gaze between the road and her father.

Scott exhaled deeply but couldn't keep his sarcastic edge in check. "Oh, you know, my lungs are miraculously healing from surgery, no cancer cells have appeared post-treatment, and everything is just rainbows. Sure, I'm great."

Leah wasn't buying it. "Why are you staring at the mirror like that?"

His jaw tightened, the veins in his neck rigid like cables. "There's a car."

"A car?"

He reached over to the dashboard and adjusted the ventilation, masking the faint wheeze of his breathing tube. "It was parked down the street from where you picked me up. A white Tesla. Four cars back. It's following us."

Leah's grip on the steering wheel tightened. The city's chaos blurred into her peripheral view. She glanced once in the mirror, catching only a fleeting glimpse of a sleek white Tesla. Its presence was precise—a deliberate hunter stalking its prey amid the congestion. She exhaled, adjusting her posture. Her pulse quickened as she flicked her wrist, shifting gears.

"Park Avenue. North." Scott barked. "Now!"

Leah slammed the accelerator, and the Coupe shot forward, roaring like an unleashed beast. The car fishtailed before catching traction, then it swiveled onto Park Avenue. Around them, cars jerked in response, some nosing forward and others screeching to abrupt stops.

"Driver's ed definitely didn't prepare me for this!" Leah muttered, her voice dry and tinged with deadpan humor.

"Less sarcasm, more focus!" Scott snapped, his eyes glued to the side mirror as the Tesla pursued them, like a hornet quietly chasing.

The avenue ahead stretched like a tightrope: endless rows of cars, zipping bicycles, and pedestrians challenging the existence of crosswalks. Leah darted left, squeezing past a utility truck, its startled driver gesturing intensely.

"East Thirty-fourth Street—make a sharp turn!" Scott ordered.

Leah cranked the wheel hard, just missing a school bus as it groaned to a halt to let passengers disembark. She swerved left to avoid an impatient cyclist, horns erupting behind her like an angry symphony.

"We can't shake them," she said, glancing in her mirrors before weaving through a thicket of delivery trucks clogging the avenue. The Tesla stayed locked in pursuit; its presence loomed at the edge of her vision.

"Sixth Avenue. North!"

Leah hesitated for less than a second before swinging onto Sixth, the car's tires squealing in protest. The avenue was a labyrinth of yellow cabs, delivery vans, and jaywalking pedestrians—ordinary Manhattan afternoon chaos, amplified by rush-hour gridlock.

Pedestrians leaped back onto sidewalks as Leah sliced through and sounded her horn, the car's exhaust echoing like a panther's growl. The Tesla lingered like a shadow, silently, unnervingly stalking them through the pandemonium.

"Times Square. Use the crowds."

Leah's stomach spasmed. "What? Times Square during rush hour?"

"It's the diversion we need. Do it!"

She gritted her teeth and slammed into a lower gear, cutting westward onto Forty-fifth Street. Color exploded around them like confetti—neon billboards and tourist buses reflecting the chaos of Midtown's beating heart. The street was constricted, swarming with pedestrians and crawling with cars.

A cabbie flung open his door on her right, narrowly missing her passenger side as she sped through. The Mercedes, sleek and furious, carved through clogged traffic like a scalpel—its motion purposeful, deadly.

Finally, for a fleeting moment, the congestion swallowed the Tesla.

"They're gone," Leah whispered tentatively, her breath shaky. Relief teased at the edge of her panic, threatening to pull her into its embrace.

"Keep moving—don't stop!"

She nodded, wiping her hand across her forehead before gripping the wheel tighter. Her muscles loosened, but the tension in the moments crawling forward refused to ease.

As they approached Eighth Avenue, dread surged back in a tidal wave.

The avenue was gridlocked. Cars stretched in hopeless queues, their brake lights glowing like bloodied halos against the city's gloomy fall palette. Ahead, a fender-bender sprawled across the intersection, strangling the flow of traffic to a standstill.

Leah slammed on the brakes. "Dammit."

Scott glanced toward her, his face grim, his breathing shallow, labored.

Behind them, the white Tesla reappeared, its predatory precision calm against the surrounding chaos.

It pulled to an unsettling stop two cars behind them.

Leah's chest burned as she looked into the rearview mirror, catching sight of the driver's door swinging open, slow and deliberate. "Dad," she whispered. "Get my gun." She pointed toward the glove compartment.

Scott flipped open the glove box without hesitation. Inside, a semi-automatic pistol glinted, nestled beneath a pack of tissues.

He pushed the weapon toward her, his expression stoic but questioning. “When did you get a gun?” His voice was low, with a hint of horror cracking through his composure.

Leah gripped the gun as Scott unbuckled his seatbelt. She could sense his resolve tightening like a spring under pressure.

“Stay low,” he ordered, his voice steady as he opened the door to confront whatever was coming.

Leah watched her father step out, his oxygen tubes hissing amid the roar of idling engines. He stood taller than he had in months, his body steady despite the frailty gnawing at its edges, as he surveyed the battlefield of snarled traffic around him.

From the Tesla emerged a young, athletic man—calm, calculated, his face concealed beneath sunglasses and a baseball cap. With his shoulders squared, his tattooed arms flexed as he walked toward the Mercedes.

Leah tightened her grip on the gun.

Then the stranger raised his hands, palms open, as if stepping into friendship. “Professor! It’s me, Igor.”

“Who?” Scott asked, the confusion in his tone cutting through the din of horns and sirens enveloping the sea of vehicles.

But everything about Igor—from his broad grin to his lean posture—spoke to his control of the moment. He pivoted, bypassing Scott and making his way toward the driver’s side window of the Mercedes.

Leah cracked the window open as Igor approached, her trembling fingers clutching the gun just out of sight.

He handed her a white business card, lingering a moment as his piercing gaze locked with hers—silent, but brimming with intent.

As the horns ahead dimmed and the wreck cleared, Igor jogged back to the Tesla, his movements smooth and practiced.

Leah stared at the card, her mind reeling.

Igor. The hacker. Her ex-boyfriend. The man responsible for her father's cancer. The murderer.

Traffic lurched forward, easing from its strangled halt, but Leah couldn't move. Her breath caught as the card shook in her unsteady hands.

***

Want more? Find out about the release of *LIES* before anyone else!

Sign up now to stay updated on the release date for the anticipated sequel, ***LIES***. Visit **rozdeba.com/lies** to register your email today!

Manufactured by Amazon.ca
Acheson, AB

33810063R00234